'Stories which inhabit the land between surfaces of realism and the larger unknowable darknesses.' — *Dominion*

'I'm an admirer of Owen Marshall's literature, with my favourite stories, chapters, etc.' — Janet Frame

'Owen Marshall has established himself as one of the masters of the short story.' — *Livres Hebdo*, Paris

'I find myself exclaiming over and again with delight at the precision, the beauty, the near perfection of his writing.' — Dame Fiona Kidman

'Owen Marshall is, quite simply, the most able and the most successful short story writer currently writing in New Zealand.' — Michael King

'It is the genius of the man that takes us beyond his deceptively simple, almost opaque exterior to his real life, the life of the writer in the room two inches behind the eyes.' — Kate De Goldi

'New Zealand's best prose writer.' — Sir Vincent O'Sullivan

Owen Marshall is an award-winning novelist, short-story writer, poet and anthologist, who has written or edited over 35 books, including the bestselling novel *The Larnachs*. Awards include the New Zealand Literary Fund Scholarship in Letters, the American Express Short Story Award, fellowships and residencies at the universities of Otago, Canterbury and Massey, the Montana New Zealand Book Awards Deutz Medal for Fiction, and the Katherine Mansfield Memorial Fellowship in Menton, France. In 2000 he became an Officer of the New Zealand Order of Merit (ONZM), in 2012 was made a Companion (CNZM), and in 2013 he received the Prime Minister's Award for Literary Achievement in Fiction.

Three of his works have been adapted for film: 'The Philosopher'; 'The Rule Of Jenny Pen'; and 'Coming Home In The Dark', which premiered at the 2021 Sundance Film Festival.

Marshall graduated with an MA (Hons) in history from the University of Canterbury, which in 2002 awarded him the honorary degree of Doctor of Letters, and in 2005 appointed him an adjunct professor.

New Stories

Owen Marshall

PENGUIN BOOKS

For Jackie, Andrea and Belinda

Contents

Fortuna's Whim

No matter what your talent, or how hard you work, there's an element of chance in everything that happens. I'm thinking of this because I've come across the journal I kept during my first trip overseas. The Big OE, as they say. I was looking for a later notebook concerning a conference in San Francisco. I needed an address from it but saw first the Big OE journal. Inside the cover was a jewellery sales docket from Capri, on the back of which was written: *I pledge 2,000 euros to deckhand David if he sings. Roger Ettick*. I haven't thought of Mr Ettick for a long time.

A lot of students go overseas after they graduate; most to gain a wider experience of the world, a few to escape their student loan perhaps. In my case it was largely because no irresistible job offer came my way. That's not uncommon when your degree is in classics — ancient history and some reading ability in dead languages are not prized currency, especially here in Aotearoa. I could have carried on with tutoring at the university, but that paid bugger all. Also, classics is all about Europe, isn't it, and I wanted to visit the places I knew a lot about but had never seen. An enthusiasm for Pergamon or Ephesus seems especially inexplicable to other people if you've never been there.

I scraped up enough money for a one-way ticket to Paris and trusted to luck that I would earn enough in Europe to be able to return home. I believe in life as a challenge, not a threat. Paris was great. Old Paris I mean, for the modern suburbs are totally without mystique. After a month or so, I had to move on, though, because money was short. It wasn't that I couldn't get work but that everything was so expensive, especially accommodation. I had a closet room in Saint-Denis, nearly ten ks from the inner city, and a job cleaning taxis for the LeCompte company.

One of the drivers for LeCompte was from Valence, and he arranged a job for me there with his brother, who had a business delivering goods from the railway hub. I was able to save money at Valence, which had an interesting and lengthy history, being an important centre in Roman times. From there, I went briefly to Marseilles, which I didn't like, then to Nice, which I did like very much. Again, a very interesting history, but more importantly I met Celine and Manon in a backpackers there, sisters from La Rochelle who were heading for Turkey. Celine and I hit it off pretty well, very well, and I was keen to go east with them, but Manon said she wasn't going to trip around there with the pair of us entwined. The sisters were close, and so that was it.

Nice wasn't the same once they left, and a couple of weeks later I crossed into Italy and got a vineyard job on the terraces above Vernazza. The Cinque Terre is very touristy, and many locals can speak English. I like working outdoors, and in the evenings I could walk down the track with others to a small café in the village where prices were lower: Trattoria Testa di Pesce. Quieter at that time as well, with most of the tourists gone. Seafood, pasta and coffee — not wine, for we could get that cheaper at our work. White wine is what's made there, and damn good too.

After an early harvest, several of us got laid off, so Mick and I decided to go to Genoa and find work. Mick was from Birmingham and said he was a guitarist and front man in a band there. I never heard him play, or sing, and I didn't like him all that much, but you link up, then split up, with all sorts of people when you're on the road. It's less than a hundred ks from the Cinque Terre to Genoa, but it was a tiresome bus journey that took well over two hours. Almost dark when we arrived there, so we bought a take-away and found a little terrace in the old part of the city, where we spent the night, sitting, talking, sleeping, and not cold at all. I can't remember anyone coming past us, but twice during the night there was a ferocious cat fight behind the pale-yellow wall we leant on.

Genoa has been inhabited continuously for thousands of years and was one of the great maritime republics, especially in the fourteenth and fifteen centuries. I wanted to see something of the old town for a day or two before looking for work, but Mick was more interested in the modern scene and making some money, and meeting women. We had a drink together in the morning, swapped phone numbers, agreed to check in if either of us found good work prospects, and then went our own way. The main thing I recall of him now is his choking laugh on indrawn breath. Maybe when he settled back in Birmingham, he established a rock band called 'The Sphincters' or 'Doppelgänger Daze'.

Yes, I saw the Cattedrale di San Lorenzo and the underground museum, and late in the afternoon received a text from Mick to say he'd been down to the lesser marina and been offered a job that he didn't want. The yacht *Vagabonda*, he said. I still owe him for that tip.

It was a hassle to get to the marina, but the sun stayed up for ages at that time of year. I'd never had anything to do with boats. Lots of people overseas found that odd. Just because we live on islands in New Zealand doesn't mean we're all sailors, but I suppose people knew about our yachting success. I was expecting a boat with sails but was to learn that the yachts of rich people in Europe are usually not sail driven at all but are like big launches. After a lot of traipsing around and many abortive queries in English, I found the berth of the *Vagabonda*, which was blue and white, impressive, but only one of many such pleasure craft in the marina. I couldn't see anyone on board, but the simple gangway was down, and I went to the top of it and called out, 'Hello, anybody here? Hello.' No answer, just the water slopping on the hull and, strangely enough, a small drone that hovered low before heading off over the boats towards the city. I called again, and a man came on deck from the enclosed section, approaching until his face was closer to mine than I was accustomed to from a stranger.

'So, what business?' he said calmly.

'A friend of mine met someone this morning who said there might be a job going.'

'Where do you come from?'

'From New Zealand.'

'All Blacks,' he said.

'Yes.'

'You're on your own?'

'Yes.'

'Come and sit down,' he said, and he led the way to a wooden table with deckchairs. The table had a shiny brass tube at its centre to anchor it.

That was my first meeting with Tullio Altamura, who was the skipper and who was proud of having been born in Polignano a Mare. Tall for an Italian, dark, lean and an experienced captain on tourist and private craft, which accounted for his good English. I was to learn also that he was called skipper, or captain, to his face, and Arab behind his back.

Tullio told me that the deckhand they'd signed up in Valencia had abruptly left the night before, and they were due to leave Genoa in a day's time. He asked me what experience I had with boats. I was tempted to lie but told the truth. He asked me what jobs I'd had since coming to Europe, and as I answered he lifted my backpack from the deck to assess its weight. There were only three crew, he said: himself, the cook and the person I wanted to be, who from his description was a sort of general rousie. It sounded fine to me, I told him, as long as I didn't have to sign up for much more than a month.

'You seem all right,' Tullio said after a pause for another close scrutiny of my face, 'but I can't be definite until Mr Ettick returns. There's only Luka and me on board. All the others are in the city. You can wait if you like or come back in an hour or so. If you wait you could go below and ask Luka for a drink.'

I sat on the deck and watched the sun going down and people begin drifting back along the marina to their vessels, loud in conversation, vigorous in gesture and with a walk of assurance. Tullio was busy elsewhere on the boat and there was no sign of any Luka. It was dusk when Mr Ettick and his party returned to the yacht, eight of them all together, and as an uninvited stranger I didn't want to be found sitting in a deckchair. I took my pack and stood on the deck a few paces down from the gangway. The people looked at me as they boarded but kept on talking amongst themselves. The four women retreated inside, while the men made for the deckchairs. Tullio appeared almost at once and said something to one of the men, who walked over with him. A well-built man in yellow summer trousers and with his greying hair combed back over his head and a splendid watch on his left wrist.

'Mr Ettick, this is David who wants to take Raul's place,' Tullio said.

'Is he okay?' Mr Ettick asked.

'I've talked with him,' said Tullio. His manner to his employer was respectful, but not as an inferior.

'Where are you from?' Mr Ettick asked me.

'New Zealand.'

'Hiking about, eh?' he said, after a glance at the backpack, and before I could reply he turned to Tullio. 'If you're happy, that's fine by me. I just hope he doesn't bugger off suddenly like the last one. Ask Mr Brownlee to get him to sign up and whatever.' He turned back to me. 'We can have a talk tomorrow. I'm with guests now. David is it?'

'Yes,' I said, 'and thank you very much.'

When Mr Ettick walked back to his friends, Tullio told me that Mr Brownlee was one of the guests, but also Mr Ettick's lawyer. 'The one with the striped shirt and smoking,' he said, 'but we won't bother him until tomorrow. I'll show you where you'll sleep and let you meet Luka. He does the cooking, and you'll be odd jobbing for him a good deal.' It didn't take long to see all of my accommodation: a coffin next to both the engine room and the galley. Luka Pelosi was small and furtive, maybe because he had a bad stutter. Pelosi meant hairy, and that was ironic because Luka was so bald his head shone. He was preparing tomatoes and onions for the next day, and Tullio said that would be one of my jobs when settled in.

I found there were other jobs as well, lots of them, ranging from cleaning the heads to handling the mooring ropes and securing the gangway, from washing the dishes to taking the guests' best laundry ashore when in port, and later retrieving it. There're lots of jobs on a luxury launch, even a relatively modest one like the *Vagabonda*. One of the things that did surprise me was how much direct contact I had with the Etticks and their guests, and I think that was because Luka was embarrassed by his stutter. I usually brought out the meals and supplied the drinks, as well as running the errands in port and answering queries at any time. Luka always accompanied me, however, when we were provisioning, because he had Italian, Greek and some English, despite the stutter.

Tullio's explanation of my duties wasn't exhaustive. Basically, I was expected to do everything asked of me by anybody on board. A process of learning by experience, and that included gaining some understanding of the people I served. I'll leave a description of Roger Ettick till last, despite his formal suzerainty. Mrs Ettick, Raquel, was a pleasant, staid woman who was easily satisfied, but always oppressed by the heat. She found it slightly difficult, I think, to adjust socially to her husband's achievement of wealth comparatively late in life. The Hapazes were better matched: Bernard, outgoing, cultivated and the majority shareholder in a printing company; Virginia, convivial, knowledgeable and with an enthusiasm for ruins. The sharing of that interest with me was minimal, however, because of our respective status on the yacht. Of the guests, the Hapazes were my favourites. The Wrights were the least interesting. Noel Wright was easy to overlook, deficient in originality, a prattler with no apparent talents and present, I think, only because he had considerable family money to invest. His wife, Susan, laughed a lot and often changed her clothes several times a day. I found myself wondering how rich people meet up and become friends. The Etticks, Hapazes and Wrights were very different folk.

Dylan Brownlee was also an Ettick guest, but as Tullio had mentioned, with the additional affiliation of being Mr Ettick's lawyer. A heavy, precise man, who often stayed on board when we were in port and used his computer to continue his work. He allowed himself five cigarettes a day and took conspicuous pleasure in each of them. No doubt he had clients additional to Roger Ettick. I never felt his Christian name suited him. It had lyrical connotations that were quite out of place. He was a watchful man and had considerable presence. Dominique, his wife, was younger, the most attractive woman on the yacht, and generally everywhere else as well, but never flaunted it. The awareness, however, gave her a calm assurance, and she had a slow smile that persisted, even when the occasion for it had passed. She didn't especially dress to enhance her appearance. There was no need for that: somehow your eyes tended to rest on her.

All of these people became outwardly familiar to me, but some allowed more connection than others. We were gathered together, especially when the *Vagabonda* was at sea, and, despite my humble role, interaction was inevitable. When in port, there was release, and occasionally couples or foursomes took trips and stayed away for a night or two. Other times they all went, leaving Tullio, Luka and me on the yacht. These were the best times because I was able to make my own limited expeditions to sites, galleries and museums. There was little opportunity for such visits when the guests were on board, but I was an employee first, of course, and tourist a far second.

I didn't grumble. We moored in interesting places, all of which I would have been happy to visit on an itinerary of my own — after Genoa there was Livorno, Civitavecchia, Cagliari in Sardinia, and then Capri. No, the thing that marred the trip for me was that Roger Ettick enjoyed mocking me in front of the others. I'm not sure of the reason for his dislike — perhaps my education, perhaps my youth, perhaps to emphasise that he was head honcho. Maybe it wasn't dislike, just that he didn't think I mattered.

He would keep me standing behind the deckchairs when they ate on deck. He would ask me for information he knew I wouldn't know and would cut abruptly away during my response to resume the closed conversation of the table. He often pointed out my ignorance of things maritime, disparaged my accent, which he called Ocker, and mocked my few clothes. 'What a surprise,' he'd say, 'our David is wearing his jeans and his blue T-shirt.'

A couple of times he asked me to do the haka for them. My school has a haka that I remember well, but I knew he wanted to make fun of it, and me, so I didn't perform any haka on the *Vagabonda*. He was a bit of a prick was Roger Ettick, despite the entrepreneurial skills he must have had. No wonder the last deckhand had jumped ship at Genoa. I could see that some of the others were uncomfortable with Mr Ettick's little games. Dylan Brownlee and the Hapazes, in particular, often refused to join in, even supported me, but it was a difficult situation for any of the guests, so I treated the jibes as jokes, which minimised Roger Ettick's pleasure.

One afternoon in the harbour of Cagliari when the others were ashore, Dylan Brownlee talked to me briefly about it. He was working on the deck, at the table with computer, papers, a spreading straw hat above his small-featured face.

'Wait a moment, David,' he said when I had brought him a coffee. 'I want to say something about Mr Ettick.' He lit a cigarette in his usual deliberate, indulgent way, leaned back from the computer, gazed over the bobbing and glistening harbour for a moment as if surprised to find himself there, and then looked up at me. 'Mr Ettick has you on sometimes, doesn't he. It's just his way, and don't worry about it. He thinks it's an entertainment for his friends. I hope you don't take it to heart.'

'It's okay,' I said. 'I don't let it bother me.'

'He's been looking forward to this trip for a long time. He wants everyone to be cheerful, so he tries to be funny. Goes a bit far at times without realising it. You're enjoying the voyage, though?'

'I am, yes.'

'You're seeing a lot of places special to you and getting paid a bit as well.'

'I wish I had more time to get about when we're in port,' I said, 'but you can't have it both ways, I guess.'

'That's right. Here I am, too, in Cagliari and working on the computer instead of being with my wife and the others enjoying the sights and local wine. Anyway, I just wanted to say that about Mr Ettick so you don't take anything too seriously. And thanks for the coffee.'

Tullio noticed what went on as well. He said to let it wash over me and that people like Mr Ettick felt built up by putting other people down. He'd met plenty like that in his job. He told me that Roger Ettick wasn't anybody all that special and that the *Vagabonda* was a chartered vessel, not a private yacht. Tullio had known a lot of rich men, many with a lot more money than Mr Ettick and better manners. He said to simply do my job and smile. Tullio's status on the boat was unique: he was an employee, like Luka and me, but also the captain whose word was law on so much. He mixed with the Etticks and guests as an equal but often chose his own company and rarely accompanied them when ashore. He seemed often to have his own friends and objectives in the places we visited.

Capri was our destination after Sardinia. One of the reasons I was glad to get there was that for the first time on the voyage I was seasick. Normally, we had good knowledge of the weather and stayed in port if things were likely to get nasty, but that time we were caught out and it was rough stuff. In the end, I was dry retching and the muscles of my stomach ached. Most of the others suffered too, including Mr Ettick, and there was satisfaction in that, but Tullio and Luka of course were unperturbed. However, the more important reason for my pleasure on reaching Capri was its place in antiquity. What a history. Capri has been inhabited since the Neolithic and a resort since the time of the Roman Republic. Augustus developed the island with temples, villas and gardens, and later Tiberius did the same. I visited the ruins of his Villa Jovis. Capri has it all really, not just the history, but the climate and natural beauty as well. No wonder it's drawn so many rich and notable people over the centuries.

The morning after we arrived, when Mr Ettick was on the deck alone, I asked him if I could have a word. He wasn't having any breakfast except coffee. Still feeling seedy, I guessed, and wished I had left any request until later.

'Okay, what is it?' he said.

'I wondered how long we were likely to be here.'

'Sick of the place already, David?' and he laughed. 'Give Capri a chance, surely.'

'No, it's just that I'd like a whole day off if that's all right with you. I'm keen to go up to Anacapri and visit historical sites there, other places too. So much to see here that I've read about.'

'Always the scholar, eh. Hoping to discover a bag of gold coins, or Caesar's skull, make yourself famous.' I could have said something about Caesar's skull but kept quiet and smiled. 'Look, we plan to be here for four or five days,' he said. 'You get your work done and if Tullio's happy, then you can run off for a few hours. Not a whole day, though, there's still meals, and you can't expect Luka to do everything while you're gazing at pottery and bones.'

'Thank you,' I said.

'I could do with more water,' he said. 'My stomach still isn't right.'

Tullio was more helpful. He arranged it so that I was given a full afternoon off, which would follow a morning doing jobs for him in the town. The chores didn't exist, and that day was one of the best for me during the entire voyage. The Villa Damecuta, Blue Grotto, chairlift to Monte Solaro, Munthe's Villa San Michele and so much more. I met Bernard and Virginia Hapaz in Anacapri, and we talked there for some time.

Conversation was easier, more equal, away from the *Vagabonda*, and it was in the afternoon, so no problem if they mentioned it to Mr Ettick. They even invited me to have drinks with them, but that may have created awkwardness when we were back to an on-board relationship. We talked history, and they were interested in where I'd been in Europe and what places I still wished to see. Greece was wonderful, Virginia said, I'd enjoy it there.

I wonder where the Hapazes are now and how the way the voyage ended has affected them. A pleasant, intelligent couple, whom I observed rather than got to know.

I saw two others from the yacht as well that afternoon, not in Anacapri but down again in the main town. I was having a coffee by a small dribbling fountain after a shorter-than-I-wished visit to the Ignazio Cerio museum, and I saw Roger Ettick and Dominique Brownlee walking on the other side of the small square. On the way to join some of the others, I supposed. Dominique at ease in a loose, pink dress; Mr Ettick turned towards her, talking to ensure her attention. Off the yacht, he seemed smaller, less significant.

That evening, Mr Ettick, Tullio and the other guests had their meal on the deck as usual, even though we were moored quite close to a larger craft on which a party was taking place: music, loud talk and laughter, people moving about, some looking over to the *Vagabonda* and its comparatively staid group around the dinner table. The juxtaposition only made Mr Ettick more determined to maintain an independent presence, and he put his back to the party-goers and talked more loudly. Noel Wright prattled away as usual too, but no one took much notice of him. Presumably he never realised how little he was listened to. Mr Ettick told me to get champagne — Bollinger, which was Dominique Brownlee's favourite. Drinking Bollinger was Roger Ettick's way of giving the finger to the party-goers, I supposed. Also, he kept me busy in attendance more than usual, perhaps to emphasise to the party-boat that he had minions.

After the meal, when darkness had fallen and only those craft in the marina that were lit up could be discerned, and scales of light glittered and slid on the restless water, Mr Ettick and the others continued to talk and drink. Mr Ettick worked to hold attention, but at times some of his guests were surreptitious observers of their more flamboyant neighbours. Only Dylan Brownlee seemed disengaged with what was happening on either vessel and sat quietly, looking towards the steady lights of Capri, and with a napkin over his champagne glass to show he wished for no more.

As an entertainment, Mr Ettick asked me again to perform a haka, and again I said that I didn't know one — untrue — but to keep the refusal light-hearted I said I'd sing our national anthem if he'd make it worthwhile.

'How much is the going rate?' he said. 'I don't think I've ever heard the New Zealand anthem. Has it got kiwis in it?' I told him there were no kiwi, but that god was in it and that raised the price. 'One thousand euros. Is that enough?' he said.

'Two thousand, and it's a deal,' I said. The others enjoyed the joke, and I wanted to keep on Roger Ettick's good side, for I hoped that when I signed off from the *Vagabonda* there might be a bonus. I knew too that, essentially, I was being demeaned, exhibited like a dog walking on its hind legs.

'Done,' he said, raising his voice and hands in emphasis, and the Wrights laughed a lot. A good deal of champagne had gone down.

'In writing,' Mr Brownlee said, finally showing interest and playing his expected part as legal eagle.

'Done!' Mr Ettick said, even louder, and he wrote quickly on the back of a sales docket lying on the table, then flourished it.

I sang badly, was mockingly applauded, resumed my subordinate role and moved back again from the group. In case I was needed, I waited on the warm deck by the cabin door, watching the jostling throng not far away on the party-boat, rather than my companions, who were talking of destinations still to come and when it would be best to leave Capri. In the end, though, they were outlasted by the party-boat people, who were more numerous, younger and had obviously drunk greater amounts, even if not of the quality of Mr Ettick's Bollinger.

Raquel Ettick, Susan Wright and the Hapazes retired to their cabins first, later Noel Wright and then Dominique, so that only Tullio, Mr Ettick and Dylan Brownlee were left. Mr Ettick continued to talk with authority; Tullio contributed amiably, but with a certain detachment; and Mr Brownlee concentrated on his last permissible cigarette of the day and looked to the party-goers on the adjacent yacht. It was almost midnight when the three men went inside, and I was left to tidy up and take stuff to the galley. I picked up the docket with Mr Ettick's promise of two thousand euros. I knew it wouldn't be redeemed, but it could serve as a memento of my time on *Vagabonda*.

When Luka and I finished in the galley, we sat on deck again. With the lights off, he and I could relax in deckchairs, observe the party-boat without being noticed ourselves, eat potato chips and nuts at Roger Ettick's expense, share what remained in a bottle of champagne. There was more wind than usual, and the marina vessels bobbed at their moorings as if impatient to be on their way. I could see many lights of various colours, some in a dance, those of the town further off fixed in location, but shimmering nevertheless, and growing fewer up the mountain side.

Luka's English wasn't great, but his stutter was less severe when he relaxed, and I was surprised by how much he knew about the places I'd visited on Capri that day. Luka was a very ordinary guy, but I wasn't in a position to feel superior to anybody. It was late when we went below. The party was still going on not far away, but less frenetic, less noisy, although I did hear a splash and cheering, so I assumed someone had taken a plunge. I heard someone go out onto our deck again too and wondered if Dylan Brownlee wished to have a secret smoke before morning. Before sleep, I had a quick look at some of the day's photos on my phone. I made a file of them when back home and still look at them from time to time. Mixed emotions.

Despite being late to kip, Luka and I had to be up earlier than the others so that all was prepared for them. Things were very quiet on the party-boat, which was unsurprising. Tullio appeared in the entrance of the cramped galley where I was helping Luka and asked us if we had seen Mr Ettick. Neither of us had since the night before.

'Mrs Ettick doesn't know where he is,' he said. 'He wasn't there when she woke this morning and doesn't think he's been in the bed at all. He never goes ashore by himself this early, so I'm not sure what's going on.'

Tullio and I went on deck to check again. We looked over to the party-boat. Its lights were off, and the only movement was the rocking of the yacht itself. Tullio stood on the gangway and looked along our line of the marina.

'He never said anything to me about going anywhere early, but who knows with him. Don't say anything to the others, but David, you go and walk along the docks in case he's walking there somewhere.'

Tullio didn't seem worried, so I wasn't much concerned either. Mr Ettick always pleased himself without much concern for others. I left the *Vagabonda* and walked along the nearer extensions of the marina. There was little activity at that time in the morning and no sign of my employer. There were crafts of all sorts and sizes, from one-man sailing yachts to private launches that looked as if they could cross oceans with ease. The *Vagabonda* was just an ordinary member of the assembly.

When I returned, everyone was on deck with their attention centred on a distressed Mrs Ettick. Tullio looked at me as I came aboard, and I shook my head.

'His phone's still here,' he said quietly. 'All his stuff's still in the cabin.' It was awkward for me as the deckhand to offer emotional support to Mrs Ettick, but I went over and said I hoped her husband would soon turn up. She gazed at me for a moment, nodded and turned to Virginia Hapaz for comfort. Tullio and Mr Brownlee talked together, and then Mr Brownlee told the others that they'd waited long enough, and it was best the police were called.

'They've got the resources to find out where Roger is,' he reassured Mrs Ettick.

'Why would he go away?' she said. 'Why would he? Something's happened, I know.'

'I'll get in touch with them,' said Tullio. 'Luka and David will get coffee and something to eat for you all before they arrive.'

Only one policeman turned up, but surprisingly promptly. In Italy, I found government employees in general dislike to be hurried. The more you push, the more uncooperative they become. Wearing an open-necked shirt and minimal insignia, unlike so many Italian police, the policeman looked younger even than me, but his dark moustache proved his adulthood. He quickly established that Tullio was the man to deal with, and they talked together in their own language, and the policeman made notes and used his large-issue mobile. He then went quickly through the boat. The only other person he spoke to was Mrs Ettick, but not to much effect, for his English wasn't great and she didn't speak Italian. When the policeman left, Tullio said we all had to go to police headquarters at eleven o'clock if Mr Ettick hadn't returned.

He didn't turn up, so as a party we caught taxis to the police station and gave our statements, showed our passports and had our photographs taken. There Tullio was our manager, just as he was on the boat.

We had lunch at the Verginiello restaurant in Capri, the first time all of us had been together for a meal off the *Vagabonda*, and afterwards went back to the yacht as the police wished. We weren't there much more than an hour before a different officer arrived, older, more formal in uniform, and he told Tullio that Mr Ettick's body had been found in the water beneath a projection of the marina only a hundred metres from our own boat.

It was terrible for his wife, of course, and a shock to us all. She didn't want to stay on the yacht any more, and all of the guests decided they would go with her to a hotel for support. She kept saying she wanted to fly home straight away and take the body too, but the police said she couldn't do that. Tullio encouraged her to contact her family and have someone fly to Naples, and Mr Brownlee said he'd help with that.

All the guests gathered up their belongings and went off into the town, Tullio with them to make sure they got settled. I never had the chance to say something to Mrs Ettick, and felt bad about that, but the whole thing became a muddle — emotion and a sense of disbelief overwhelming normal behaviour.

Luka and I were left on the boat with not much to do until Tullio returned. We tidied the cabins, not sure when they'd be used again and later sat together in the deckchairs usually occupied by others. The breeze had died and the *Vagabonda* had only a slight roll, affectionately nudging the empty tyres on the dockside. Luka wore a sunhat to protect his bald scalp from the fierce sun. It had been Dylan Brownlee's and offered to him when Mr Brownlee bought a new banded one in Cagliari. The sunhat sat well down on Luka's head and emphasised his small size. We talked about what had happened to Roger Ettick and how it might have come about. Whether he'd fallen off the *Vagabonda* and the body had drifted away, or if he'd gone ashore and something had happened there. I wondered whether the people on the party-boat might have seen something, maybe even Mr Ettick had gone over there, although that wasn't likely. I hadn't thought to mention the party to the police, but Luka said they knew. Mr Ettick wasn't a likable man, not to me anyway, but it was an awful thing to happen, and I told Luka I supposed he must have had too much expensive bubbly and with the yacht pitching a bit had done a header overboard. Luka gave his small grimace smile.

'With a help, you think so?' he said, the first two words sounding like 'wither'.

'Who would that be then?' I thought it was his form of humour.

'How long you been on board?' said Luka.

'What do you mean?'

'Talk to captain,' he said.

I could do that not long after when Tullio came back. The voyage of the *Vagabonda* was over, of course, at least as far as Mr Ettick's charter went. Tullio said we would have only one more day in Capri and then — unless the police disagreed — we would sail to Naples, where Mrs Ettick, the Brownlees, Hapazes and Wrights could catch flights for a sad dispersal. He told me I'd have to finish in Naples, too, and that he and Luka would wait there to see what the charter company wanted them to do next.

It was strange that night, just the three of us on board and little service required. Tullio squashed into the galley for a while, and the three of us talked as Luka made frittata. Tullio and Luka argued in a friendly way about the ingredients, and there was mention of the bottles of Bollinger that remained. The decision was it would be disrespectful to drink champagne on the evening after Mr Ettick's death. We took the meal to the deck and ate there together. None of us pretended to be overwhelmed with grief, but it was a subdued night. A man we'd been living alongside, a man who had been employing us, had died, unexpectedly and unpleasantly. Fortuna had struck. Of all the old gods, Fortuna is the most unpredictable — the goddess of chance.

Mr Brownlee boarded the yacht late next morning to pay us and talk about leaving Capri the next day. He said the police had given permission, and we could sail in the afternoon unless any new information about Mr Ettick's death prevented that. Afterwards, he talked to each of us individually at the table and paid us in cash. There was a receipt to be signed and an agreement concerning the abrupt ending of the voyage. I was paid more than I expected, and I suspect the others were too.

'I'm sorry, David,' he said. 'A tragic way for things to end and no explanation whatsoever, but I hope you go on to happier times in your travels. Put it behind you as best you can.'

The four of us sat together and had coffee and crêpes, Mr Brownlee wearing his new banded sunhat and Luka wearing the former one. We must have seemed an oddly assorted foursome: Dylan Brownlee still very much the precise, English lawyer, despite his holiday clothes; Luka wrinkled, reduced, uneasy in speech and posture; Tullio Altamura from Polignano a Mare, tall and dark, with the serene gaze of a skipper. And me in jeans and T-shirt, with long hair bleached by the sun and a bulge beneath the shirt because of the canvas pouch in which I carried my passport and credit card. I was almost paranoid about them. I haven't a photo of us there that day, but the image is sharp in memory. Even the sun's glitter on the brass stanchion of the wooden table. One of my tasks was to burnish that.

Tullio asked Mr Brownlee if there would be legal and business complications because of the nature of Mr Ettick's death, and the answer was yes.

'It'll keep me busy a while, but he was an orderly man, and we'll get through it. I've been his adviser for some years, and this is a nasty way to have it finish. The best thing is that it's a close family, so Raquel will have support. One of the daughters is flying out. Anyway, there're still things to be sorted here, but I'd appreciate it if you made sure all's set to leave tomorrow afternoon. We're keen to get across to Naples as soon as we can. I'll keep in touch with you.'

He took up his leather satchel and went off without looking back. We watched him walking away down the marina, wearing light-weight, floppy trousers as usual and his new sunhat. I never saw him in shorts.

'It can't be easy to have a beautiful wife,' said Tullio.

'Sempre pericolo,' stuttered Luka.

'What's that?' I asked.

'Nothing at all,' said Tullio. 'Seabird words.'

Dominique Brownlee was a good-looking woman all right, but I didn't see that as any disadvantage at all for a husband. It was only thinking about it later, when I was by myself in the afternoon, having coffee again in the same small square in the town, that I recalled seeing Dominique and Roger Ettick walking there together, and how intent he seemed on her.

There was no objection from the police to our brief trip from Capri to Naples the next day. Mrs Ettick kept to her cabin, the other women often in attendance, and little conversation among any of us. We were thinking ahead, already with an acceptance of separation. The weather remained superb, but we seemed different people.

After I left the *Vagabonda*, I decided to go on to Salerno, where I found work gardening and mowing lawns in municipal parks for several weeks before moving on to Brindisi, and then across to Greece. I never saw any police, or newspaper, reports about Mr Ettick's death, never met any of those people again. There's still the journal though, still the docket with Roger Ettick's unredeemed pledge of two thousand euros, and still the deckhand memories of the voyage, although no full understanding of the outcome. I remember now, thinking of that time, how the engine would throb and whine beside me if we were voyaging at night, and the pitch and roll of the boat that took time to become accustomed to. Some other deckhand will have that coffin bunk now and serve another set of rich people easing their way from one Mediterranean port to another, but just maybe Tullio Altamura from Polignano a Mare is still at the helm.

Fading Light

Ethan told people he'd retired, which wasn't the full story. He'd applied for voluntary redundancy at the invitation of the university, technically not the same as being made redundant, though it may have come to that if he hadn't volunteered. He'd never know now. People in the Language faculty said they admired him for his decision. He was an associate professor, so his going saved the jobs of others more junior. That had been a consideration, but also it ensured at least a dignified exit with agreed financial compensation. Although he didn't say so, he thought the teaching of German would cease at the university within a few years: not enough people chose it to maintain the student-to-staff ratio that the number crunchers deemed necessary. The vice-chancellor had privately hinted as much. The German language is still sullied by its association with the Nazis, he said. It wasn't fair, but there it was. Neither, Ethan knew, was it fair to lay all blame for staff cuts on the university administrators, for money is a harsh ruler.

He'd been quite touched by the farewell his colleagues organised for him, its warmth surely arising from more than just relief that their own positions were made more secure by the loss of his own. The harbour venue was impressive, the meal and wines of some quality, and he and Tania received a large and splendidly coloured glass bowl from the Venetian island of Murano. They had once visited there, but as long-distance travellers had been unable to take home such a valuable and delicate memento. All the language people were there, even Chad Meyers, who had never forgiven Ethan's review of *Swabian German Today*. Chad and a couple of others left after the meal, but most stayed until late, with an increasing number of foreign languages being spoken indiscriminately.

There were, however, serious decisions to be made. He had been teaching in universities for over thirty years, but still needed an occupation rather than recreation, not so much for financial reasons, but to provide something meaningful in life. An objective greater than self-gratification. His language skills would have secured alternative teaching opportunities, offers from translation agencies and international firms, even a government department position perhaps, but Ethan wanted a more fundamental reset. A change of direction, he told Tania.

'Need I be concerned?' she'd replied and smiled. Equanimity was the trait of her personality he most admired — that and her honesty. Her childhood had been ideal and her subsequent life overall a happy one. Good health, two daughters, a career of her own and, as far as he knew, a marriage she didn't regret. Tania was a paediatrician and so had never been overawed by Ethan's academic profession. It's generally acknowledged that medical qualifications have no superiors.

An overseas trip was an obvious choice following Ethan's severance, but Tania, who was seven years younger, was too busy to go, and he had no wish to travel without her, not even to Europe where his language skills were best employed.

'Indulge yourself,' Tania said. 'Do something just because you want to.'

'Indulgence is selfish though, isn't it?'

'You've earned it,' she said, 'provided it's not leaving me for some blonde German tennis player.'

'I could do charity work,' Ethan said, 'or help with refugee social adjustment.'

'That would be good, but later. Right now, you should do something selfish for once and have the feeling of it. You don't want to get stuffy, do you?'

He was slightly offended by that. 'You think I'm stuffy?'

'I didn't say that. I said you don't want to become stuffy.'

'So, what does stuffy mean anyway?'

'To me it means holding back rather than giving new things a go.'

'So, it's break-out time at fifty-seven, you reckon,' said Ethan. 'Fantasies to the fore.'

'I wouldn't say fantasies. More the aspirations that practicality's denied.'

They were having layered fruit pancakes at Saffron on the waterfront. Outdoors, where two sparrows hopped about the table and a seagull perched not far away. The bollards had coloured streamers around them, somewhat tattered, so whatever party they celebrated must have been days ago. It was a Thursday, and Tania had just the hour to spare. In the past, it had been difficult to meet like this on weekdays, but Ethan could now be with her whenever she was able to get away from her rooms, or the hospital. They had studied and worked hard for many years, but Ethan knew they had been lucky too, born in the right country and with many opportunities. The television confronted him each evening with the plight of so many other people in the world.

'I thought I might try politics,' Ethan said.

'Wow,' Tania said, with such emphasis that the table sparrows took fright. 'So, I might end up as the prime minister's wife.'

'Hardly. Only the city council. There're some pretty important local issues just now: roading, the central-business area, airport extension, the proposed alteration to the recreation zoning of Tomely Reserve. That one's a biggie for me.'

'Well, why not? These things matter, and you worry about them, I know, so now you can maybe do something about it. I didn't realise you wanted to be involved so directly.'

'I'm only thinking about it now because elections are coming up. I don't know anything about the rules, selection, party affiliation, any of that stuff, and I might just work to elect someone with similar views who's more likely as a candidate.'

'Why not go for it? Good on you, I say, but what happens if I don't agree with you?' Tania smiled as she said it. 'I might have to stand against you.'

'You're too busy,' he said.

'Absolutely right, and I have to leave now, so you're going to have to save the city for both of us. You can run your policies past me tonight.' Ethan was left in the sun with his coffee, almost surprised by his own statement of intent and realising that, having made it, he should act on it. He was experienced enough to know that it was one thing to evaluate and criticise from the sideline and another to achieve improvement when wielding influence. So much was about personal relationships rather than policy.

Over the next few days, they talked more about it when Tania had any leisure to do so. She was supportive for personal reasons, rather than an enthusiasm for local government. She did suggest he talk with Trent Grebber, who was a friend and had served two terms on the city council. Ethan had been thinking of Trent but thanked her for a useful suggestion. Trent had also been on the hospital board and the community arts trust. He ran a successful construction firm and had a social conscience as well as a considerable opinion of himself that was tempered by self-awareness.

'He'll be able to tell you all the pros and cons,' Tania said. 'Why don't I ask them for dinner soon. It's our turn, isn't it? You can show off your new-found cooking skills.'

The Grebbers came on a Sunday evening: he with an attractive blue linen shirt, snowy head and the sheen of accomplishment; Marie svelte, intelligent and adept at conversation. Ethan always felt he had to be at his best to match the Grebbers, although they provoked no competition and were genuine in friendship. They all sat together on the deck and drank Pegasus sauvignon semillon, ate cheese, crackers and grapes.

Trent said he envied Ethan such an early retirement, and Ethan said he had thought of writing a biography of the German scholar Ulrich Ammon — which was true, but not his priority. Trent, Marie and Tania all had interesting things to say about their professions and the windows they provided on the world. Nothing of significance had occurred for Ethan since he'd left the university, but he was able to ask the sorts of questions that showed he was still astute.

Not until they had gone inside and had the meal of ravioli and salad that Ethan had helped prepare, did he ask Trent for advice about possible involvement in local politics. His friend's response was unequivocal and unexpected.

'Keep well away,' Trent said firmly. 'It's a damn dispiriting business. Constant demands and criticism, never any gratitude from the public, and little Hitlers contesting for influence.' Ethan knew that Trent may well have been disillusioned, especially after being defeated following two terms on the council, but the vehemence of his opinion was surprising. 'You wouldn't believe how much of it is about factions, ambition and affiliation with the big parties,' Trent said. 'And a bloody stack of reading if you want to be at all prepared. Crushingly dull stuff. I thought I could do something worthwhile, but it's just a circus really.'

Despite feeling strongly, Trent didn't rave on about his local-body experience. His social skills were too well developed for him to become a bore, or hog the conversation, and he moved on from mention of his time on the hospital board to ask Tania for her opinion on the new birthing unit.

Ethan didn't ask him any more about local politics. Not that evening, and not at any meeting afterwards. He decided to give standing for council a miss.

'There's no hurry,' said Tania when he told her. 'You don't have to feel guilty about taking it easy for a while. You should write that Ammon book you've been talking about or go through all those articles and essays you've done and select the best for a collection.'

'Publishers aren't much interested in academic stuff, especially here. Maybe I could find one in Germany for Ulrich Ammon. Bios are easier to find a home for than collections of academic articles and essays. I've got connections in a couple of places and should put out feelers, I guess.'

Before he got around to that, Tania came up with the idea that if he wanted to do something in the meantime he could deliver meals. The hospital ran Meals on Wheels for the benefit of those who had difficulty providing their own. Mainly the old or disabled.

'You could do that,' Tania said. 'It's a community thing, but you wouldn't have any of the hassle of local body stuff that Trent went on about. You just say how many days a week you can deliver, and you get a round allocated, places closest to where you live usually, I think. There's no payment of course, not even for petrol, so you're earning Brownie points. You could combine it with something else. You don't have to commit yourself for any set period.'

'How long does it take each day?'

'It varies I think, but not much more than an hour, I'd say. I can easily find out for you if you're interested.'

She found out everything he needed to know, and more, so Ethan signed up for Tuesday, Wednesday and Thursday. He had squash on Mondays, and Friday was best left free so that long weekends away were possible. There were eleven people on his round, which took him into some streets and byways quite new to him, despite not being far from his own home. At eleven-thirty in the morning, he would pick up the meals at the stop behind the hospital kitchen. Each meal was in a plastic container and labelled with a name, for they weren't interchangeable — several of the recipients had individual dietary requirements, allergies or aversions.

Like all activities, it took some time to work out the most efficient means of accomplishment. What order to make the delivery, where best to park, what form of contact was to be expected and which avoided. Ethan also got to know other drivers who did rounds on the same days. They had time to talk as they waited for the trolleys to be wheeled out from the kitchen. It was in that way he discovered a friend from secondary school days, whom he hadn't seen since: Noel Percival, who had excelled at mathematics when young and since become a partner in a leading real-estate company.

'You need to give a little bit back, don't you?' he told Ethan. He also advised him to use a vehicle with a separate boot because the smell of the food lingered, even from lidded containers.

Meals on Wheels made Ethan more aware of his good fortune in life, but also of the precarious nature of that good fortune, especially with the passing of the years. Not all the people he visited were poor, but most of them were old and all of them were facing difficulties. For some he was a welcome if brief visitor in a lonely life; for some a source of apprehension no matter how often he called without introducing harm; for some just an unseen genie who left food on a small table by the door, rang the bell and went away.

Several of the people on Ethan's round became passing acquaintances, Mrs Sanderson a friend. Because of that he usually visited her last, despite that not being the most logical order. Mrs Sanderson was elderly, large and almost blind. She was also talented, brave and a woman of achievement.

'I can't see you very well,' she said at their first meeting in the doorway, 'so I'll imagine you,' and she smiled and put both hands out for the food trays.

Mrs Sanderson's house was quite modern and in a good suburb. Her daughter Evonne dropped in most days and a gardener regularly, although Mrs Sanderson rarely went outside by herself. 'I know the house intimately,' she told Ethan after a much later delivery, 'but things can change outside and move around. Just an empty drink bottle, and you're flat on your face. Crossing the road is like Everest. You lose confidence.'

Ethan developed the habit of carrying her meal in and placing the main in the microwave, putting out the one plate and cutlery. Sometimes they would talk a while before he left and she had her meal. She said she didn't like to eat in front of people in case she dribbled or something. Being nearly blind made you more aware of scrutiny, not less, she said, and she hadn't expected that. 'You don't spend a lot of time looking at yourself in the mirror when you're eighty-three,' she told him.

Like Ethan, Mrs Sanderson had been an academic. Economics, which had a limited overlap with German language and culture, but the university context meant they had plenty in common, even though their institutions varied. They shared the experience of a specific milieu.

Usually when Ethan approached the door, he could hear music. Sibelius often and less so Vaughan Williams or Grieg.

'You have good taste,' Ethan had volunteered. 'Sibelius is a great.'

'Sound has become more important as a compensation for fading sight. I can listen to books too. They record them.'

'I'm into music myself much more now that I've got the time,' said Ethan.

'I have something going most of the day and not just high-brow stuff. Even country music, soul music, jazz. The only thing I can't stand is rap, and that's because of my age, I suspect. Evonne tells me that I listen too much. Sometimes I don't hear the phone, and that's important to me now. Who knows how long I can stay here on my own?'

Ethan wondered that too. Her husband had died seven years before, and she had lived alone since, the world more recently dimming around her. Once, as Ethan and she sat talking after his delivery, she referred to her husband in an unexpected way.

'Your voice reminds me of my George,' she said. 'Do you think that's silly?'

'Not at all,' Ethan said.

'And because I can't see your face clearly, it comes to look like his. I hope that doesn't sound weird.' A few times she called him George too, but Ethan knew she was unaware of doing so and never made mention of it.

George had also been an academic, also in economics. Ethan asked her what that was like, being married to someone who worked in the same field. Would it be constricting and competitive, or supportive and a bond?

'Oh, we worked in different areas of study, really,' she told him. 'George focused on natural resources and the environment — prices, markets and changing technologies. My interest was public economics — the role of government decision making, tax systems and so on. You'll know yourself that there's a wide diversity of study within the general tags like history, chemistry, or whatever. There was nothing competitive between George and me, just encouragement, though we did squabble over desserts sometimes. He was a devil for the sweet stuff that made me put on weight.'

Mrs Sanderson was the most interesting of the people on Ethan's round, and he talked of her to his wife more often than he did of the others. She was interested when Ethan first told her about being called George.

'Sad,' she said. 'That's so sad. I think I'd lose any of the other senses rather than sight. I imagine she's had consultations with the best people?'

'I guess so. There doesn't seem to be any shortage of money.'

'What did her husband do?'

'He was an academic as well and in economics too but a different focus.'

'I don't think I'd like that,' she said. 'Both the same subject, I mean.

Wouldn't your talk tend to be turning to that all the time?'

'She says not. They were a close couple, I think. We talk mostly about university teaching and music. Her daughter's been there several times. She followed me out to the car once and said her mother enjoyed the chats with me. Mrs Sanderson doesn't like to go outside much, even with Evonne, but she's switched on intellectually and she has her music.'

'Awful to be old, a widow and then to have your life diminished again by losing your sight.'

'And it's getting worse.'

Ethan developed something of a routine. He'd work on the Ammon biography in the early morning, deliver the Meals on Wheels on the days applicable, and in the afternoons do household and section stuff, catch up with friends or play squash. It was flexible, and things apart from the meals run were easily swapped around, especially to suit Tania. He wanted his own freedom to benefit her as well. After a while, he knew where things were in the supermarket and learnt the difference between a cucumber, a luffa and a zucchini. He could even match fabrics to the correct cycle when using the washing machine. Tania said she'd always wanted a house-husband.

It was over a year before things had to change for Mrs Sanderson. By then there had been several alterations to Ethan's round. Mr Grater, who had the three-legged dog, had died; Mrs McGregor had been taken into care; and Bobby Southgate had wandered off and never been found. New people had been added to Ethan's list as replacements, including Mrs Hapeta, who used to sing on television. Mrs Sanderson was always interested, not because she was a gossip, or took satisfaction in the vicissitudes of others, but because she was largely housebound and almost blind.

Her sight became so bad that, even within the familiar confines of her home, she couldn't cope, and Evonne decided to have her mother live with her, at least until another place could be found. There was no need of Meals on Wheels there, for Evonne was a caring daughter. When Ethan made his last call, he stayed longer than usual because he knew he might well not see Mrs Sanderson again. He was pleased, though, that she was going to live with Evonne, for he'd noticed she was losing confidence. He put her food trays on the top of the microwave and saw she already had a cloth on the table, plates and utensils as well, salt and pepper — the salt-shaker much bigger to make identification easier.

Mrs Sanderson was sitting in her usual armchair in the lounge, with a square of sunlight around her from the glass slides. She no longer answered the door; instead Ethan would knock and enter — the expected arrival at the expected time. He could see her from the kitchen, face turned in his direction and her blue eyes tracked him as he walked through, but he knew he was a moving blur and that it was sound she relied on.

'Thank you,' she said. 'Can you sit a while? I'm going to Evonne's tomorrow, you know.'

'Yes, I know. She'll take good care of you.' In the year or so that he'd been coming to the house, Mrs Sanderson had put on more weight, quite understandable because she moved about so little, but she was always neat and well dressed. Evonne had been dropping by even more often in recent months, and there was a woman, too, who came in the mornings.

'I can feel the sun on my face, and it's like a big pulsating glow even when I close my eyes. Nothing has any boundaries now. It's a world in flux.'

'I'm a bit surprised you haven't any music on,' Ethan said.

'Evonne and an agent are coming around after lunch. I'm thinking of things I need to do and say, and things I want to keep. When you've been in your own place for over thirty years, how do you move into someone else's? It's a form of dispossession in a way. I know it has to happen, and I'm lucky to have Evonne, but it's another step down. I suppose it's what you must expect when you're eighty-four and blind.'

'You'll be safe with her, though, and you'll get to know your way around her place.'

'She and Rob are moving out of the big bedroom so that I can have some of my stuff there. My armchair as well. I said it wasn't necessary, but she's insistent.'

'You're lucky to have such a daughter,' Ethan said.

'Oh, I am, I am, and Rob and the boys too, but I'll miss my home — and our talks of course,' Mrs Sanderson said.

'You'll have a family around you. Things going on. You'll be able to get out more.'

'I'm lucky, I know, but it won't be the same. You never think when you're at your best in life that you'll end up in one room in a place not your own, but yes, you're quite right, Evonne and Rob are very kind. I'll be fine, and you'll have one less delivery to make.'

'I'll miss that delivery,' Ethan said. 'It's my favourite.'

Meals on Wheels wasn't the same for Ethan after Mrs Sanderson shifted to her daughter's. He decided he'd stop the volunteer deliveries and spend more time on the Ammon biography. Kassel University Press had been impressed by his outline and qualifications and commissioned him to complete the book. He told Tania that when Mrs Sanderson had settled in at her daughter's home, he'd call around and see how she was doing, but weeks went by, and it was Evonne who got in touch.

'I just thought you'd like to know,' she said when she rang, 'Mum's had a fall and she's not so good.'

A windy Wednesday morning, and Ethan was in his study, not writing, but trying to get a new printer set up. It wasn't going well, and he was glad to leave it and drive to Evonne's place. He felt some guilt too because he hadn't been to see Mrs Sanderson in her new home. On arrival, what he noticed particularly wasn't the house itself, or the ample section, but the signs of adolescent children. The homes of his friends and acquaintances, his own also, no longer bore such evidence: a trampoline; a basketball hoop above the garage door; a blue hoodie on the barbecue chair; and a Honda 125 motorbike with the front wheel off.

Evonne answered the door. Before taking him to see her mother, she stood with Ethan in the kitchen to talk privately. He could sense she was unhappy, and for a moment they were both silent, looking from the window to the garden, where the wind flounced the shrubs and flowers and billowed the shrouds of the trampoline.

'Mum hasn't been happy here at all,' she said. 'I thought it was for the best, but she hasn't settled. It was the wrong move, perhaps, but the experts said she couldn't go on living alone.'

'You took the best advice. That's all you can do, surely. How is she now?'

'She had a tumble in the bathroom. I only left her a few minutes, and she fell into the bath and smacked her head. Nothing broken, the doctor said, but it's left her confused and sad. She's gone downhill ever since she moved in, ever since she left her own home.'

'Maybe I shouldn't disturb her,' said Ethan.

'I think she'd like to see you. It might take her mind off things. She doesn't have many people call. Most of her friends have passed on, or just like her they've got something the matter and don't get around much.'

He accompanied Evonne down the hall into what Mrs Sanderson, before her shift, had called the big bedroom. An attractive room, with large windows, but of course the light was of little significance for her. She was sitting in the armchair he recognised from her own home, and she had headphones on. He'd never seen her wear them before. Her face was bruised, and her shoulders were drawn in, rather as a perching bird hunches its wings sometimes.

'It's Dr Norrish, Mum,' Evonne said, and when her mother didn't respond she went closer and gently took off the headphones. 'Dr Norrish's here,' she said.

Mrs Sanderson looked in the direction of her daughter's voice and smiled.

'Who's here?' she asked.

'I've come to see how you are,' said Ethan with assumed brightness of tone. He was sad to see how much she'd altered.

'So good to hear your voice again,' she said.

'I'll leave you two to talk,' said Evonne. 'I'll be in the kitchen.'

There was a padded stool at the end of the bed, which Ethan moved so he could sit by Mrs Sanderson. 'What have you been listening to?' he asked.

'Guess,' she said.

'Sibelius.'

'The *Karelia Suite*,' she said. 'I use headphones often now so that I'm not subjecting others in the house to my own choices. Everyone's different, aren't they, George.'

Ethan took no notice of the name for he knew the source.

'I'm sorry you've had a fall,' he said.

'My own fault. I forgot for a moment I wasn't in my own bathroom. My balance isn't good now. I must look a real sight. Evonne told me there's quite a lot of bruising, and I can feel where it is.'

'It'll go away,' said Ethan. 'And it's good nothing serious happened.'

'I'm okay. The family here look after me, and I don't have to lift a finger. I even go walking with one of them most days unless it's wet. It's windy now, isn't it? I can hear it.'

'A southerly,' said Ethan. 'I think there's a change coming.'

'We've sold my place,' said Mrs Sanderson after a pause. 'It's the sort of home that needs a family in it, really. Evonne and Rob did think of shifting into it themselves but decided against that.'

Ethan could tell from her voice that the topic wasn't a happy one. She was in a home where she was loved and well cared for, but it was a foreign place with features unfamiliar to her. He told her about giving up his round of Meals on Wheels and finding a German publisher for his book. That interested her because she too had experience with publishers and editors of journals. Ethan encouraged her to talk of that, and she said she still had copies of journals in which her work had appeared. They were in boxes in Evonne's garage, she said, but Evonne could sort one out for him. Mostly on the social impact of economic policies, she said, and they sat and talked of academic work and its publication. It perked Mrs Sanderson up a bit, and she became more attentive, her bruised face raised somewhat, an occasional smile.

As they talked, Ethan heard a young man's voice from the kitchen, the words coming quickly, and Evonne's laughter following. 'That's Sam,' said Mrs Sanderson. 'He's a lovely boy. I wish I could see him properly now, but I remember how he looked before. A lovely boy.'

'And there's another grandson, isn't there?'

'There's Ruben too. He's flatting now but comes home sometimes. He's the musical one, so we can talk about that. He not only plays but sings too. A lovely boy — a man now. I always thought he was your favourite, though you took care not to show it.'

Ethan made no reply to her confusion, just smiled, although she could have no awareness of it.

Mrs Sanderson continued to talk generously of her grandsons for a while but quite suddenly became preoccupied with her left slipper and seemed to lose track of things.

'Well, I'd better head away. It's lunchtime already,' Ethan said. 'I've got a squash game this afternoon, then I'm picking Tania up.' The comment made her more aware again.

'All I can do for exercise is walk and stretch,' she said, 'and both are boring when you can't see anything.'

'The squash is mainly exercise for me. I'm not great at it, but it's a catch-up with friends.'

'It's just family for me now,' Mrs Sanderson said. She softly fingered the bruises on her face and then tapped her top front teeth with her fingernail.

'Did you bang your teeth too?'

'I did, but they seem okay. Evonne had a look at them.'

Ethan got up from the stool. 'I'll come again sometime soon,' he said, 'and I'll say goodbye to Evonne on the way out. You look after yourself.' He wished he hadn't said the last bit — a silly thing to say.

Mrs Sanderson was pressing her fingers to her face again, and through the window behind her he could see the agitated trees.

'Don't be long, George,' she said, and she put a hand out towards him. 'I miss you, haven't heard your voice for ages. I don't know why they keep us apart now.'

Double Whammy

They say the only thing more stressful than moving house is divorce. I can think of worse, but I must say I feel sorry for Ryan Neckermann, who got divorced and moved house simultaneously. A double whammy, and Ryan's not a guy who copes well with change. He works at the city museum, where things stay in their appointed places and the range of visitors is both limited and predictable. I work there too, also appreciating the reassurance of guidelines, protocols and best practice, although not wedded to them as he is.

Maybe that's why Rachel wanted out. She's a bit of free spirit is Rachel, and it's a wonder they married in the first place, being such different personalities, though some believe that opposites attract. There's a son called Bernard. Very cute as a kid, but who the hell these days calls their child Bernard? I reckon Ryan must have come across it in his files. Bernard's at Canterbury uni now, in a hall. Both parents adore their son and stayed together for his sake, I imagine, but it was different when he left, especially on Rachel's side. It got too tough. They told me that, separately and in confidence. I'm a friend in the way that colleagues tend to become friends because you spend so much of your life with them, and with their wives and children, unless there's active dislike. Proximity is usually the foundation of friendship. It's a mundane observation but true. Ryan's head of catalogues and records. I'm head of installations. Being employed by the same institution gives you a lot in common, and Rachel and Carrie get on fine too, so as couples we saw a good deal of each other.

No surprise then when they told us they were splitting up, but it altered so much, of course. These things don't happen overnight, and there's a good deal of damage — emotional and otherwise — no matter the good intentions of those involved. A lot of pain, a lot of confusion, even though they tried not to load it on us. I remember when Carrie was driving me to work not long after their decision, she said there was also a lesson for us in it — about the need to work at marriage and not take things for granted.

'People change,' she said, 'and what works at one life stage mightn't at another. Relationships evolve and you can influence that.'

'Not always enough perhaps,' I said.

'You try, though, don't you? And both of you need to try.'

'Yeah. Do you think Rachel hung in there enough?'

'Just because she's the one pushing more for the split doesn't mean she hasn't made as much effort. She made more concessions.'

'What sort of concessions?' I asked because Rachel talked more intimately with her; as Ryan did with me, although he's a stoic in some ways.

'She wants to open up her life,' Carrie said. She had pulled into my museum parking space, but I didn't get out. I realised that what we were talking about was quite important, for us as well as our friends. 'She feels constrained,' she continued. 'Says that Ryan doesn't want to grow any more.'

'Grow?'

'Try new things, travel, new people, make an effort to deepen their relationship. She's keen to get into community work.'

'Do you think she's found someone else?'

'You think that would be exciting?'

'No. Just wondered. It often happens, doesn't it?' As a husband, I have to be aware and careful in such conversations.

'I don't think that's it. Not the way she talks, not the sort of impatience that she expresses to me.'

'Well, all I know is that it's really sad,' I said. 'Sad for both of them, even though they try not to show it. They're different now, aren't they? Years together and now for what?'

'Let's try to keep both of them as friends when they've separated,' Carrie said. 'So often one fades away.'

'Ryan will still be working with me. He hasn't said any different. Just the changes to his home life. We'll see plenty of each other.'

'Has he said where he'll live?'

'He's putting it off, I think. Sometimes he feels he'd like to patch things up. Other times he knows it's best over. Your emotions must be all over the damn place when splitting up.'

'I'm glad it's not you and me,' Carrie said before she drove away.

Amen to that, I thought.

Ryan and Rachel did separate and began divorce proceedings but without apparent urgency. Ryan seemed to accept that he was the one who should move out, despite not being as keen on splitting. I think it had a good deal to do with Bernard's room. Rachel wanted to keep it as it was — filled with reminders of his life with them and always ready for his visits. There's a Lego castle on the windowsill, and on the chest of drawers two chrome trophies for table tennis, no bigger than egg cups. A plastic skeleton on a hook, also the pencil marks on the door frame as a record of his growth. He's become a tall guy, has Bernard.

Ryan went into a couple of rooms at the Globus Backpackers. A temporary measure, he said, until he sorted out a more permanent place. Most of his stuff was left in the garage of their home. It gave him an excuse to return there from time to time, I think. Rachel didn't seem to mind. Their separation wasn't one of screaming and dish smashing; rather the gradual and painful dissolution of once-close ties.

A relationship break-up is a common enough thing, but each happens in its own way. Ryan didn't start drinking heavily or obviously neglecting his appearance, but he became oddly distant and passive at the museum. He did his job conscientiously enough but was no longer vitally concerned as to outcomes. At planning meetings, he would give his opinion quite cogently but accept decisions with equanimity. Whether the new wing was to have a children's space or whether a digital-imaging department was required were questions of purely professional concern and dead to him outside his work. He spent more time in his office but only because it filled in some of the hours previously spent with family.

Carrie and I invited him around for meals, and a few times he accepted. Rachel came more often but not on the same occasions. She would ask me how he was getting on at work, for she remained concerned about him. Ryan didn't talk much about her. Not because he didn't care but because it made him sad to sit with us and so be reminded of the failure of his own marriage. To see us comfortable with each other and with two teenage daughters casually content within the family. He told me as much after one evening visit, as he and I stood at his car before he left.

'I really appreciate you guys sticking with me,' he said, 'but whenever I visit I'm reminded of better times. The four of us together and our kids too. I'd go back to that if I could. I've no idea how Rachel and I got to where we are, while you and Carrie are just the same, just fine.'

'We have our moments like everybody. Things might still work out for you and Rachel.' What can you offer except platitudes at such a time?

'She thinks I'm dull. That's it, I reckon. I'm dull to be married to, and it's taken her all these years to work that out. She wants to move on. What the hell does that mean? I don't get it.'

'People change,' I said.

'She seems to think life should be a perpetual carnival.'

'Is that right?' Not a helpful reply, but I had no better response.

'You know, it's good of you both to have me round like this, and I don't want you to take it the wrong way, but it's a downer when I come.' He turned to look at me directly. As there was only the dim light from the street, our expressions hard to read, I think he was encouraged to continue. 'I see you with your kids: that ordinary family stuff you take for granted until it's lost. I'm adrift sometimes, sitting with you and Carrie and wishing it was still the same for me and Rachel.'

'Bernard leaving home might have made the difference. Empty nest and all that.'

'He's doing damn well.' Ryan was relieved to segue from painful disclosure. 'Damn well. Much better motivated than I was at that age. We're proud of him. He understands how things are. He came round to the Globus just this Thursday and we went to that Chinese place by the library.'

'Right. That's good. I've been there.'

'He'll fly through. He's always been the same: so focused on doing well. And he could go either way, arts or science, whereas I was a complete drongo at maths.'

'So was I,' I said.

'Well, better be on my way. Thanks again to Carrie. See you tomorrow.' Ryan assumed the briskness of departure and gave a brief wave as he drove away. Back to the Globus and his two rooms that stank of bewilderment and isolation.

In general, my advice would be not to meddle in the marriages of your friends, but I did so in this case, nevertheless. I saw that Ryan was hurting a good deal, and I wanted to make some effort to mitigate that.

'I need to say something to her,' I told Carrie. 'Even if it doesn't make any difference at all, I'd feel better having said something about how he really is.'

'You think she doesn't know a lot better than you how he is?' she said. 'We've talked with her here. You've heard her. I've often talked to her. What can we possibly tell them about themselves they don't understand?'

'Friends can have a different slant. The advantage of some emotional distance.'

'So, you're a counsellor now, are you? Ready to preach to the less fortunate. I look forward to hearing it all,' and Carrie gave a laugh that held a passing element of belittlement as well as humour.

'You're probably right,' I said. 'Better stick to sympathy and support.'

'We're going into town together on Saturday.'

'A good idea. She'll enjoy that.'

'Kick the credit cards along and lunch at Pericles.'

'Good one,' I said. 'That'll do the trick.'

However, Rachel provided the opportunity for me to say something without the need to take any initiative, and so I thought expressing my opinion was okay. She rang me at the museum — from Portby, Portby and Tilling, the accountancy firm where she works.

'Touching base,' she said, 'about how Ryan's been in the last few days, how he's coping. Bernard said he was rather down the last time he saw him.'

'He's okay at work. It's a distraction for him — from his loneliness, I mean. He misses you so much.'

'He's never liked change. I don't know why.'

'He's drifting, isn't he?' I said. 'Who wouldn't be. All those years and now he's on his own. It's understandable.'

'Not at all easy for him, or me, but best for us both in the end. You can't hide from life. We'll come through the better for it, I'm convinced of that. We're in touch occasionally, you know. I just want to check on how you've found him recently — if he's managing better. He tends to bottle things up. You and Carrie have been there for him, and I really appreciate that. If I fuss over him now, though, it'll only make things more difficult, more drawn out.'

'Well, at work he seems okay. He does all he should, but there's no spark in it for him. He's a distant, sad man, who's pretty much at a loss.' I found it somehow easier to be direct on the phone, Rachel's face not visible. 'I don't want to pry, or interfere,' I said, 'but are you sure about everything, divorce and all?'

'Sympathy isn't enough as a basis for a marriage,' said Rachel after a pause. 'You stifle yourself that way, and I want us both to have full lives.'

'He thought he had, I suppose.'

'I don't want to get into all this on the phone,' she said. 'And you don't know the half of it, really.'

'Of course. I'm sorry,' I said.

'I'm only wanting to check to see how he is at work.'

'He's coping okay here,' I said.

'You're important to him now: you and Carrie. You can blame me. I don't care.'

'I don't blame you. I didn't mean to sound like that. It's just—' but she interrupted me.

'There's too much for me to cope with, let alone explaining to someone else,' she said. 'To be hurting someone you care about yet knowing it's the only way. A shitty place to be, believe me.'

'I'm sorry,' I said again. I wished that I had kept my mouth shut about anything except Ryan at work.

'I know you help him, and that's all that matters,' Rachel said.

I didn't help him much, and her call made me feel I should do more. I went through to Ryan's office. He was sitting on the carpet by his computer chair, absorbed in cutting his fingernails.

'What the heck are you doing down there?' I asked.

'I can put my hand in the waste basket so the clippings don't fly all over the place.'

'Looks odd.'

'Life's odd,' he said.

'Do you want to go to the café at lunchtime?'

'No,' he said. 'I know it doesn't look like it, but I've got a fair bit on. I've got a council presentation due on Tuesday.' He got up laboriously, levering on the chair and almost falling as it swivelled away. He isn't a nimble guy at all. Not a sportsman. 'Jesus,' he said, and then, as he steadied, 'I make my own lunch most days.' God knows what facilities and ingredients the Globus Backpackers provided. 'I've got to get the inventory site up to date too,' he said and began a painstaking, yet unenthused account of what that obligation involved. It occurred to me that here was a dull man, though not unpleasant. A dull, unsporting, conscientious guy with little appetite for change or challenge. An unremarkable, decent, rather boring guy whose son no longer needed his protection and whose wife found him a restriction to any flowering in life. When they were together, and he was buoyed up by Rachel's liveliness, none of that had been so apparent, but it was accentuated by his isolation and sense of defeat. I sat with him for a while, more to provide a listener than having much interest in what he said.

I'm not sure what I expected to be the outcome for Ryan. That he would suddenly run amok and shoot somebody — probably himself; be transformed through therapy and marry the sexiest of the museum women; retrench to being a permanent recluse in his two rooms in the Globus; immerse himself exclusively in his job to such effect that he's appointed director of the institution?

The reality was more humdrum, as is so often the way in life. Ryan became an eco-warrior, in his own subdued way, committed to establishing the causes of climate change, mitigating its consequences and preventing further global deterioration. He didn't appear on television, or star in the demonstrations he attended but competently managed the impressive database that gave credibility to the arguments and demands of the movement. Whatever conversation was begun with him, he always brought it around to this great threat the world faced in general. It was a refuge for him now that his life no longer had a personal heartland of family life. He left the Globus and bought a two-bedroom townhouse of pink Summerhill stone in Esther Crescent. A barren little place with a single heat pump and a single lemon tree slowly dying of thirst — symbol of a more general natural catastrophe. He still comes occasionally for a meal. Carrie and I haven't given up on him. He sits at the table with a false alertness and talks of hydrogen fuels, carbon sinks, glacier retreat and pending legislation to save the planet.

Rachel visits more often and radiates both gaiety and completeness. She has a new partner whom we've met: an electrician with his own successful business. A nice guy who's a keen squash player and always brings a classy bottle of cab sav. She asks after Ryan but doesn't see him now. She encourages Bernard to keep in touch with his father, but their son's become busy with his own life. Rachel's left Ryan behind but bears him no ill will. The climate-change movement is a really significant crusade, she says. Worthwhile stuff and vitally important for us all. Good on him, she says.

Recently, however, when Carrie asked me to drop off a gardening catalogue at Rachel's, I had a glimpse of Ryan without the protection of his public mission. I didn't take the car all the way because I wanted to combine the errand with an evening walk. I parked by the bowls pavilion so I could enjoy the quiet stroll along tree-lined Darwin Avenue towards Rachel's place. Dusk is a fitting time for both walking and reflection. It was almost night as I neared the house, but I recognised Ryan alone on the grassy berm and looking towards the lighted windows of the place that was once his home. I stopped by the corrugated trunk of an elm tree, for I realised the embarrassment my approach would be. As he stood, quiet and forlorn, staring at his own past, I felt my presence an intrusion, both physical and emotional, and back-tracked stealthily through the trees with the catalogue undelivered: left him there, solitary in the night.

Nothing was said of that the next day when I had a coffee with him in the museum café. He's got one of those short, jawline beards now, which actually suits him, but he's still the same dull, unremarkable and worthy man hiding behind a cause. He went on about energy resources, and I focused on his beard so as to appear attentive. I decided to ring Carrie and suggest we have a weekend in the capital. She likes spontaneous surprises like that, and you have to work at marriage. Ryan was solemnly explaining the distinction between fission and fusion in connection with nuclear power when the café sound system began playing an ABBA song — one of the great ones: 'The Winner Takes It All'. Outwardly it didn't seem to put him off stride a whit. Outwardly.

Charlie's Day

Charlie Wiles often slept with his socks on, and not just in winter. The back bedroom he shared with Aaron had no heating and was in the shade of a large magnolia tree. Their parents had an electric blanket, and so did Bella. No double glazing at 143 Burford Street. Old, red rubber hot-water bottles if the boys wanted them, though this was a morning in February, so they didn't. Charlie lay and watched the shadow leaves of the magnolia play across the pale bedroom wall. He'd had a dream about ostriches, or emus, but even as he tried to recall it, everything seeped away.

The house was quiet, as it was Saturday. Unless there was something special on, Charlie's family usually slept in on Saturdays, and Sundays too. There was nothing special on. Charlie, however, liked to make the most of Saturdays, so he got up quietly and put on a blue shirt his grandmother had bought for him, trousers that were a hand-me-down from Aaron and a jersey from the same source. Aaron was still asleep, and all Charlie could see of him was a thick tuft of dark hair between pillow and sheet. Charlie washed his face but left the rest of himself undisturbed. Bella had a shower every day, and he wondered how she could be bothered.

People got their own breakfast in Charlie's family, so in the kitchen he dished himself muesli. He hoped there might be fruit to have with it, but there wasn't, so he had more milk. Toast and Marmite too; he never went hungry. Food wasn't special in his family, but there was always something. He ate by the window to be in the morning sun and tried again to remember the ostriches, or had they even been moa and so much bigger? In his intermediate class on Friday, Mr Stanton had talked about moa hunters, so that was probably where the dream had come from. Charlie looked across the overgrown lawn to the clothesline and imagined a moa stepping out from behind the garage. The little, perched head, curved neck, fluffy body and thick, naked legs. Could there still be a moa hiding somewhere in the mountains?

Charlie didn't have a phone. He'd hoped to get one for his birthday but was given a new pair of sneakers instead. He wore them as he walked to Todd Beswarick's place. Todd was his best friend, or the closest anyway. Usually he liked Evan best, but he lived over the river and had music lessons on Saturdays. He was fun to be with and had this huge collection of Lego, but it wasn't easy to get to his place, even biking, and he often did things with his parents: trips away, meals out, linkups with other families. Charlie didn't have that sort of family. Another thing he noticed at Evan's place was all the books, whole shelves of them and sitting about on tables too. Some magazines came and went in Charlie's home, but there were hardly any books. Only those that helped his mother cook things or his father put things together. His father had more tools than books, and Charlie was proud of all that he could make and fix.

The quickest way to Todd's was through the scenic park, and Charlie liked walking among the trees and round the pond, seeing what was going on. It was still early, so there were just a few joggers and people walking their dogs. There were ducks and geese on the pond, and the small ripples they caused spread as arrows on the smooth surface. There were straggly lilies and thick rushes and a small concrete extension with two green benches. People often fed the ducks there, but no one had come yet. Once Charlie saw a big dog run to the pond and leap right in among the ducks and geese that had previously been squabbling over the bread thrown to them. Charlie stood by the benches for a time, remembering the flurry and confusion, the shouting, the explosive escape of the ducks, even though before him was just the quiet morning pool.

Todd's house was on a corner and had a veranda along the front with curved corrugated iron above it. Charlie didn't knock on the door because everything was quiet and he thought he must be too early, so

Todd's parents would be annoyed. He stood looking up to the sun. Mr Stanton said you could tell the time that way, but Charlie could only do it very approximately, not well enough to risk knocking, so he went onto the lawn and around the side of the house to Todd's bedroom. Todd had a bedroom all to himself, and Charlie was jealous of that. He and Aaron shared theirs, but Aaron's share was a lot bigger than Charlie's.

The curtain was pulled back on Todd's window, and Charlie could see him sitting in bed with his phone. Todd's dad had recently got a new one and given his son the old one, and Todd was still in love with it, and Charlie was still jealous. They both knew that but didn't say anything about it. Charlie tapped on the glass, and Todd came to the window, opened it.

'Do you want to go somewhere?' Charlie said.

'Where?' asked Todd. He still held his phone.

'I dunno. Maybe the skate park. Maybe hang out in town.'

'You got any money?'

'No,' said Charlie, but they decided to go into town anyway.

'Wait out front,' said Todd. 'I won't be long.' He was still in his pyjamas.

Charlie sat on the veranda steps in the sun and thought about the school sports day that was coming up. He was quite good at some sports, not those that required equipment or special coaching, but running and jumping. Sprints he was okay with, but the longer races he was better at, and he liked the 1,500 metres best. Mr Ogilvie said if he trained more he could make something of himself, and Charlie sometimes imagined himself coming first in a big race not just at school, but he never said anything to anyone. He wasn't much in the classroom. Aaron called him a fuckwit, but he wanted to do okay on sports day, and he decided that he'd go running later if he was by himself. As he thought about that, he pulled the petals off some yellow flowers by the steps without realising Todd's mum might be pissed off.

Todd brought a chocolate biscuit for him when he came out.

'Why so early?' he said.

'Just woke up early and it's Saturday,' said Charlie, and they walked down the path heading into town. They didn't have their skateboards, but the skate park was almost on their way and they had nothing better to do, so they went in to watch anyway. Bigger kids were there, a lot of loud noise, boards slapping on the concrete mounds, show-off shouts. Charlie and Todd walked out onto one of the flat tops and were abused.

'We're not hurting anything,' said Charlie.

'Shut up and fuck off.'

'We're only watching,' said Todd. Why shouldn't they?

'Drop dead.'

'Drop dead yourself,' said Charlie, but he and Todd scarpered when one of the boys ran at them. 'Pricks,' said Charlie when they were well away and heading for the shops again.

'That one in the red jersey is Matt Ramsey's brother,' Todd said.

They reached the tip and recycling station that was a block before the shops began. You were supposed to unload your stuff and leave, but Charlie and Todd knew how to get in unobserved and work their way behind the pits and sheds to a place where the recycling guys put stuff they thought was worth something. You never knew what would be there, and Charlie felt excitement that was part fear of getting caught and part anticipation. No one was around, but already stuff had been left: cabinets, containers, clothing, even a leaf blower and a metal window frame with the glass intact. The boys could take only small things, and they searched quickly, listening for the sound of anyone coming. Todd found a toolbox and a circular brass tabletop with dragons on it and also dents. Charlie found a good-looking garden trowel, a ceramic vase and a blue backpack. The first two went into the third, and Charlie and Todd crept away again behind the sheds.

Rummagers was a second-hand shop by the railway station, and they took the stuff there. The tall, bald man who walked funny remembered them.

'So, your uncle's still clearing out his shed,' he said knowingly. 'Not much I'm interested in here.' He always said that even when he took things. His bald head was shiny and had two large, dark spots on it. Charlie thought they looked like some sort of shit, but they were always there. The man worked the lid of the toolbox and checked the vase for chips. There weren't any, but he said hmmmmm, in a disapproving way.

'Twenty bucks for everything except the pack. I don't stock fabrics.'

'Twenty-five,' said Charlie hopefully.

'The pottery thing looks new,' said Todd.

'Twenty dollars,' the Rummagers man repeated.

Charlie didn't get any regular pocket money, and ten bucks wasn't to be sniffed at. Todd bought Turkish delight in town, but Charlie put his note deep in his pocket. They walked to the river and sat by the rowing club. Todd ate his Turkish delight, watched the rowers at practice and let Charlie play a game on his phone.

'They row at the high school too,' he said, but Charlie didn't answer. More than anything he wanted a phone. Most of his classmates had one, and it meant you were poor if you didn't. Evan did. Charlie was pleased with his new sneakers, but they weren't as good as a mobile. When Todd took the phone back, Charlie thought about what events he should enter in the sports.

'Do you want to go running this afternoon?' he asked.

'What for?'

'Get ready for the sports.'

'Nah, I'm going with Mum and Dad to look at a Honda Civic. They like one on Trade Me with low ks. It's for her.' Todd concentrated on his phone again.

A group of guys carried a skiff down the wooden ramp, and Charlie noticed how tall they were and wondered how much he'd grow. Aaron said he'd always be a short arse, but his mother said he'd get a spurt at about fourteen. She said there was height on her side although not his father's. Aaron was tall and Charlie wanted to be bigger than him. You don't get pushed around when you're big. He was looking upstream towards the bridge when he saw a kingfisher in a tree on the bank. He hadn't seen a kingfisher for ages, hardly ever, and he noticed how squat and brightly coloured it was and what a thick beak it had. It sat very still. Although Charlie hoped it would dive into the river, nothing happened. Often the things that Charlie hoped for didn't happen. He was starting to get hungry.

'What time is it?' he asked.

'Half-past eleven,' Todd said.

'So, what do we do now?'

'I need to be back by twelve because of the car thing,' Todd said. 'We could go past that empty place in Lowell Street where we saw those two guys bumming once. Could be stuff we can get for Rummagers.'

'I think it's being pulled down. There's a notice up about keeping out because of it.'

'Let's go anyway. It's on our way. I'm sick of it here,' Todd said.

The wooden place in Lowell Street was partly pulled down and had orange plastic tape along its frontage and a sign telling people to keep out, but because it was Saturday no one was working there and a bulldozer stood idle. Charlie and Todd ducked under the tape and ran into what was left of the building to be out of sight. The rooms were empty, even the bath had been taken out. Nothing was left small enough and worth enough to steal.

'Fucken useless,' said Charlie.

'Should've come days ago, at night,' Todd said.

'Yeah.' Charlie opened some of the cupboards and wardrobes, but there were just stained linings and junk fragments. There was a brass light fitting in what was left of the hall, and Todd was tugging at it in assessment when a man came over from next door and shouted at them.

'Get out of here, you kids. Bugger off,' he yelled, and he waved his arms as if in a swarm of flies. He didn't look as if he could run fast, and Charlie and Todd weren't scared, but they ran out and continued jogging down the road until well out of sight. Charlie still had the backpack that Rummagers didn't want, and he thought he'd keep it because it looked better than his own.

Big kids were still at the skate park, but not Matt Ramsey's brother with the red jersey.

'We could come here tomorrow with our boards,' Charlie said.

'Don't know what I'll be doing.' Todd didn't sound enthusiastic, and when they reached his place, he just said see you and went inside without suggesting anything for the next day. Todd wasn't his best friend, and it hadn't been a great morning, but Charlie was ten dollars better off than when he left home, and that was something.

Aaron had a banjo that their grandfather had given him years ago, but he never used it. Wouldn't even remember that it was stuffed away in one of the garage cupboards. Charlie knew, and he wondered how much it would be worth. He decided he'd take it out and hide it somewhere else and if no one said anything he'd be off with it to Rummagers.

There were more people in the park when he went back: parents with little kids at the play area; invisible people far off behind hedges and netting, their presence known only from the thudding of tennis balls and laughter; families feeding the ducks and geese. A few couples sitting, or walking. Aaron always said when couples got the chance they'd be feeling each other up.

Charlie sat by himself on the grass and inspected the blue backpack. The more closely he looked, the more pleased he became. No holes or damage, just slight scuffing at the base, the buckles were metal and all the straps there, and it had a tiger's head on it. He'd keep it for sure and flog off his own. When he put it down, he saw a monarch butterfly on the grass close by. Its wings were closed, so he hadn't noticed it before. He knew it was a monarch because they'd had some caterpillars at school and fed them on swan plant until they went into chrysalises and then hatched. Charlie touched it very gently, and it quivered but didn't fly. If it was old or sick, it would get walked on by people or eaten by a dog. He picked it up as lightly as he could and took it to the rushes at the pond, hid it there, hoping it would be safe. Its wings were a bit tattered, and Charlie thought yes, it was old. He hoped it would fly so he could see the colours, but it didn't. It seemed that beautifully coloured things died easily. Charlie used to have a budgie that had yellow, green and black feathers, but it had died one Christmas, and yet there're thousands of brown sparrows, aren't there?

He left the backpack in the hydrangeas behind the garage when he got home so he didn't have to explain it. Inside, the rest of the family were eating, none of them interested in where he'd been. His mother had made a green salad with sliced boiled eggs, and there were two rounds of luncheon sausage each. Bella and his mother said salad was good for you, but the others thought it rabbit food. Most of the talk was about Bella going with her boyfriend to his firm's staff dinner, and his mum wanting their dad, or Aaron, to cut the front hedge, which was poking out onto the footpath. The job would've been passed on to Charlie except that he was too young to be trusted with the electric clippers.

'Be careful with them,' Charlie's father told Aaron, 'I don't want them snagged on any bloody wire, okay?'

'Can't do it today,' Aaron said. 'I've got to get the Corolla going.'

'So, who and when then?' asked Charlie's mum loudly.

'I've told Graeme I'll pick him up and have a spin out to Sutherlands to look at—' began Charlie's dad.

'So, when then?' his wife interrupted.

'Aaron and I'll get onto it tomorrow, okay? I'll see to it, Jenny. Give it a rest, okay?'

'When it's done I will,' she said.

'I saw this monarch butterfly in the gardens this morning,' Charlie said, but nobody was interested. Bella told them that Liam would get promoted soon at Poulson Realty. He was doing really good.

'That's great,' said her mother.

'Big deal,' said Aaron.

'I'm going for a training run this afternoon. It's sports day next week,' Charlie told them, but only Aaron had a response.

'Big bloody deal,' he said. He was in a bad mood because he couldn't get the Corolla going, didn't have enough money to pay anyone else to get it going, and would have to ask his father and probably have to do the hedge in return for the help.

Charlie put on his PE shorts for the run. He decided to head up to the reservoir and follow the cycle track through the pines there. He liked running on his own. Things around him seemed closer then and had more meaning. He should be able to do even better in his new sneakers, because the shop woman said they were good for running in as well. Charlie had a certificate for the 1,500 metres, but what he really wanted was a cup like the one Evan had with his name on.

He jogged to the reservoir as a warm-up but really got going when he was in the pine trees. He liked the way the sunlight was cut up by the branches so there were stipples of brightness on the dark reddish ground beneath the trees. There were the occasional cyclists to watch out for as they swooped down the track, especially on the bends where he couldn't see them coming very well and his own open-mouthed breathing made them hard to hear. When it was him alone in the trees, he imagined himself being chased by wolves in Russia. He'd seen Russia's wolves and forests on TV and could almost see the wolves gaining on him, dark, silent cutouts, which helped him to go faster. He was glad after all that Todd hadn't wanted to train with him. Todd would've slowed him down. After running the whole track, Charlie even did some sprints when he was back at the reservoir. You need to have a sprint left in you at the end of the 1,500 metres, everybody said. Charlie had been pipped a couple of times on the line, and he didn't want that again. Not if he was going to win the cup.

It had been cool in the pine forest, and Charlie had been thinking of winter in Russia, so he enjoyed sitting in the summer sun by the reservoir. He took off his sneakers and waded in the water. There were no ducks, no families, but two separate strollers, each with a dog, who passed him and went on into the trees. Afterwards Charlie checked his pulse rate by holding his wrist, and it seemed fine, although he didn't know what it was supposed to be. He lay on the bank with his eyes closed, but his face up, and the sun was a red glow through his eyelids. He was thirsty, but he was warm and still, so stayed lying in the long grass and listening to the small sounds of summer. There were tests coming up at school as well as the sports day, but Charlie wasn't good at classwork and didn't want to think about tests. He didn't do his homework because he never did any good. Could be if you were born a fuckwit that was just it. Aaron had been a fuckwit at school, and yet he had a car of his own even if it wasn't going. Charlie could have fallen asleep there in the grass and under a full sun, but he was getting hungry after all the training, and he wanted to check if Aaron's banjo was still in the garage cupboard.

It was. Charlie wrapped the banjo in a sack and shifted it to the top of the cupboard, where there were only cobwebs and a roll of lino. Some of the instrument's strings had snapped, but it looked okay. He went back outside and watched his father helping Aaron with the car. His father gave the instructions, and Aaron carried them out. The two often argued, but on things mechanical Aaron knew to bow to his father. They even got it going, and as a tester Aaron and Charlie drove down to Hussley's Take-aways for fish, chips and sausages. It was Charlie's favourite meal, and how he liked a Saturday to end. Bella missed out because she was getting ready to go to the Poulson staff dinner with Liam.

'I don't want to stink of sausages,' she said and had a cup of coffee standing well back from the table.

'Anyone would think you're off to bloody Government House,' said Aaron, but he was in a good mood because the car was running again.

'Don't you two forget the hedge tomorrow,' said their mother.

'Yeah, yeah,' said Aaron as he took the last sausage while still holding the stub of another.

'Just give it a rest, okay?' Charlie's father said.

'As long as you both remember then,' she said.

The sun was still shining after they finished eating. Fish and chips meant few dishes, and Charlie soon had the plates in the dishwasher. He put long trousers on again and wondered what to do until it got dark. He looked up the TV programmes, but there were just game shows, cooking competitions and stuff about doing up houses in Italy. They didn't have Sky or Netflix. Evan and Todd often talked about programmes they watched there, and Charlie couldn't join in. He went to movies with them sometimes, though. He liked the ones in strange countries most: Iceland, Vietnam or Mongolia. He knew what *tundra* was, and even *veldt*. He'd be sure to go to those places, he told himself but nobody else. People thought you were a bullshitter if you said you wanted to do anything special.

Liam arrived to pick up Bella, and while he talked to Charlie's mother, Charlie went out to look at the Honda Accord that was Liam's new car. New to Liam anyway and only a few years old. Liam knew how to cherish a car. It had a plastic protective strip at the bonnet edge and the red paint glistened with turtle wax. When Bella and Liam came out to the street, Liam patted the bonnet as you would the head of a favourite dog.

'Not too bad, eh buddy?' he said to Charlie.

When they'd gone, Charlie went around to the big magnolia tree that shaded his bedroom but caught the falling sun full on itself. There was a plank nailed in the branches, and he climbed up and sat there and thought about what he could do tomorrow. Running of course but seeing Todd wasn't keen he should ring Evan on the landline and train with him. Evan was a good runner. Evan was good at most things, even class stuff, because of all those books probably, Charlie thought.

The Mallorys' cat walked calmly from the bottom of the section and sat in the sun by the clothesline. It wasn't the usual tabby like most of the neighbourhood cats. It was fluffy and blue, and its face was very flat. Aaron said it had to stuff its whole face into the dish to eat anything. Fucken freakish, he said, but Charlie thought it looked great — the colour and the light blue fur. Its name was Disraeli.

From the magnolia tree he could look into the Mallorys' section. He saw Mrs Mallory come out of the back door, and his father was with her. They talked briefly there, and then his father gave her a quick spank on the bum, and she laughed and pushed his shoulder. Charlie's dad walked off around the side of the house, and Mrs Mallory straightened the rubber doormat and went inside. The sky in the west was yellow and red, and the sun already behind the hills. Charlie was still warm, and he stayed there watching the sunset and thinking. He thought of the blue backpack, Aaron's banjo, the kingfisher and the butterfly, his ten-dollar share from Rummagers. He thought of his father and Mrs Mallory, the phone he didn't have and the cup he was sure to win on sports day. Mostly he thought about winning on sports day. Disraeli was still sitting by the clothesline, his flat face turned towards the magnolia tree. Could be he was thinking too.

Broderick and Riley

Broderick and Riley met five times during their lives, a total of less than nine hours, although they wouldn't have been capable of such exactitude. They were not friends and had little consciousness of each other, despite the occasions on which they interacted by whatever fate, or chance, you wish to believe in.

They were first together at the children's playground in the civic gardens when Broderick was seven and Riley six. Broderick's parents were some distance away, looking through the glasshouses. Riley's folks were sitting on a green bench, his father with face raised to the sun, his mother scrutinising a stain on her linen dress. The weeping willow drooped in full foliage and swayed gently in time with the breeze. A mallard duck was querulous because no one offered bread scraps.

The boys found themselves at one of the see-saws and not having companions of their own began a cautious and silent co-operation. First Riley climbed on, then Broderick reached up, pulled down and clambered on. They oscillated for a time, still without speaking, for they were strangers. Not only was Broderick older, but he was heavier and had to thrust his legs strongly from the ground to get his turn in the sky. He became aware of his superiority and so despised Riley on the other end of the see-saw. He stepped off abruptly, and Riley's end crashed down. Riley's face hit the iron hand grip, which chipped one of his front teeth. He cried loudly in both anger and pain, but Broderick jogged away taking no responsibility. Both Riley's parents ran quickly to comfort him. His father said they'd have ice-creams as consolation, his mother hugged him and said thank goodness they were his baby teeth. Broderick stood partly hidden beside a rocket ship and watched them.

He hadn't intended harm but was intrigued rather than feeling any guilt as a consequence of his action.

Eleven years later, Riley and Broderick were in opposing first-fifteen rugby teams. It was more than just the annual inter-school fixture: the final of a recently introduced college tournament and taken seriously, not only by the boys. School mana and parental pride were involved, as well as the self-respect of players, some of whom had dreams of representing the sport at higher levels. Frost was white on the field, and at scrums and rucks panted breath ascended in the still air, visible and drifting. There were many onlookers, including Riley's parents and Broderick's mother. She was not avid concerning sport but loved her son and was standing in for her husband, who was stranded and angry in Wellington because his ferry crossing had been cancelled.

There had been a reversal in their respective weights since the boys rode the see-saw, but both Broderick and Riley were hefty and muscular, one a lock and the other a prop. They were on the cusp of manhood, fit, strong and delighting in the smash and grab the sport demanded. They didn't know each other's names and had no wish to do so yet shared the close physical familiarity of a contact sport, butting their heads, pulling at each other's arms, clasping thighs in a passion of obstruction. Both earned the commendation of their coaches, but it was Riley who had the additional satisfaction of a win. He had also a swollen and bleeding eye socket from Broderick's left boot in a second-half ruck, although neither was aware who was responsible, and it was entirely accidental. In a school magazine photograph of that year, Riley is one of the players with a hand on the cup.

Broderick and Riley were first introduced at a Young Businessman of the Year event, the only time they heard each other's names. Riley was thirty-three and Broderick one year older, of course. Riley wore a grey jacket with a pink shirt open at the throat. Broderick wore a light suit and a striped tie and talked fluently of the innovative scientific equipment his firm had developed for the genetic improvement of livestock. Riley gave a screen presentation of the value and nature of distribution hubs, and despite the prosaic nature of such a business his commentary included asides that occasioned some amusement.

Neither of them received an award, or placing, and within a few days they had forgotten each other completely, busy with their respective enterprises, which had little in common. They were not to know that on the night their preferences for wine and mains had been the same — the dry riesling and *poisson du jour*. Whether that has any significance at all, there is no way of telling. Both men were accompanied by their wives, but the couples were not seated within a conversational distance, so Janine and Mia didn't meet. Had they known they both had language degrees and shared an enthusiasm for orchids, they may have made an effort to do so. The Young Businessman of that particular year was much later convicted for Ponzi-scheme fraud, but that's by the bye.

The fourth meeting between Riley and Broderick took place fifteen years afterwards at a farmlet nineteen ks outside the city. A little after mid-December, and they were there to buy Christmas trees. Juvenile pines were on sale closer to home, most offered by charity groups, but on the farm a purchaser could stroll the rows, observe symmetry, calculate the height, and make an individual choice, which would be cut on the spot, fresh, glitter green and without wilt. A good many people wished to make such choice, and various vehicles came and went, stirring dust from the unsealed track and the turning circle by the shed.

Broderick drove a BMW saloon with a small trailer; Riley a Mazda CX-5 SUV. It was a hot day and both men were casually dressed, which was unusual, for they headed successful enterprises, worked long office hours and had executive images to maintain. Riley wore stressed jeans, a short-sleeved white shirt and designer sneakers. Broderick wore knee shorts, a blue T-shirt and Tuscan sandals. They arrived at much the same time, and due to that coincidence found themselves briefly quite close together, walking among the Christmas trees that were not much taller than themselves. A sky blue and fathomless, hills pulsating in the distance. Broderick had reclaimed the weight advantage he had all those years ago on the playground see-saw. He was not a fat man, too much aware of self-image for that, but he was tall, powerfully built and, since Mia had left him for a parliamentary journalist, he had eaten out with greater regularity. Not that Riley was much behind in stature: he was also a big man, but one who found time for the gym, encouraged by

Janine. Riley was almost completely bald though, and to avoid the sun's assault he wore a hat rather like those favoured by lawn bowlers.

Despite the shared intention of selection, there was no conversation, or recognition, between the two, minimal awareness as strangers, and the only passing eye contact occurred on departure, when Riley's SUV briefly blocked Broderick's way as he walked to the shed to make payment for his Christmas tree, and two others as a donation for the Salvation Army. Broderick's divorce had a chastening effect, and he'd become more aware of those who suffered misfortune. His Christmas tree was to be erected at his daughter's home.

The last time our two protagonists were together, it was night, and they were travelling between cities in a bus. An unusual form of transport for both. Normally they used their own vehicles, flew when possible and favoured taxis when necessary, rather than buses. On this occasion, however, the plane had been turned back because of fog, and the alternative was a lengthy and tiresome journey by road. Riley was alone, on a trip to join a selection panel for the appointment of a senior executive. Broderick had remarried and was accompanied by Anna, his wife, on their way to visit her ailing father.

Both men were content with their lives, despite the temporary inconvenience of their situation. Healthy, wealthy and happily married with settled families, they had no reason to be displeased. The bus had been specially chartered by the airline and carried only its dispossessed customers. Riley sat towards the front, beside a snoozing, elderly man whose breath smelt faintly of peppermints and whose hands were like the talons of a hawk. Broderick sat towards the back with Anna, who was fragrant with French perfume and talked of new heat pumps that she said made no noise at all.

Rain began as they travelled over the hill road, not heavy enough to be audible within the bus, but a drizzle that gathered on the windows and caused a jewelled and shimmering fragmentation of the few lighted places they passed. Enough also to distract the driver so that he failed to gauge one of the tighter corners, and the bus rolled over the bank into the rocky gully. A well-known woman equestrian proved a hero by contacting the emergency services and going up to the road with a torch to wait for them. A Wellington chiropractor also distinguished himself by effective first aid to the injured before assistance arrived. Five people died, and Riley and Broderick were among them. Anna was fortunately unhurt.

The bodies of Broderick and Riley were taken away in the same ambulance, side by side, with their faces turned towards each other. Fitting in a way, for though unconscious of it then, or any time before, their lives had shown brief moments of synchronicity.

The Swansong Apartments

That wasn't the real name of course. No one in the accommodation business would use a name with such connotations. They were the Swannson Apartments because that's the name of the family who built them. They weren't really apartments either, not originally. They'd been motels years ago, in the chalet style that's out of fashion now. They'd dated and not been well maintained, so, when Edgar Porter bought them, they became units for permanent residents, who had less expectation than holiday folk and business travellers. Everyone who lived near called them the Swansong Apartments, and most who lived in them did as well.

There were nine apartments, and Bengy Rudd lived in number four. Bengy was the reason I visited Swansong, why I knew something about the place and what happened there. Bengy's son worked with my father at the council and said Bengy needed someone to get him out and about instead of moping at Swansong, and to do occasional jobs as well. Bengy's son said he just didn't have enough time. I was a second-year university student and had my full licence and a small Fiat. I had to be on the lookout for extra money, even in term time.

Actually, Bengy didn't mope. He had very bad arthritis, but all his wits about him and was positive in attitude most of the time, despite the pain and difficulty of movement. He'd been tall, but the arthritis made him sort of crouched over and slow, so that you tended to see as much bald head as face as he walked towards you. He said getting dressed took ages, so he liked clothes without buttons. As long as he was warm and dry and had something tasty to eat, he was happy enough.

'I've had a good spin,' he'd say. 'There's thousands worse off than me.'

He liked being taken to the supermarket, and as I waited beside him in the aisle with the trolley, he would hunt out the specials, or calculate weights and capacities and their relationship to price. 'They're cunning bastards,' he'd say. 'Too cunning to put the price up, so they reduce the amounts instead 'cause people don't notice that as much.'

Bengy's unit had altered little since its motel days, and I guessed the other eight hadn't much either, because all were only rented. There were those wooden cupboards with chrome handles that I remember from my grandparents' house, wooden-framed shower cubicle with a step-over lip to the shiny base, and a couple of small radiant heaters attached to the wall. The Porters had added a budget washing machine and dryer, the first constricted the bathroom, the other reduced kitchen space. But Bengy's place did face north, and that was a big advantage. It got lots of sun, and he and I would sit outside in worn cane chairs, or inside by the lounge window, with a view across the asphalt to units six to nine, which were less favoured.

Sometimes, I prepared Bengy's simple meals because even peeling a potato or screwing off a lid was difficult for him. Things like cottage pie, stew or sausage casserole were good because enough could be done for two days, even three. Left to himself, Bengy did things like cheese on toast, packet soup or splashed out at the Maccas, which he could walk to. No alcohol at all in unit four. Funny that, because Bengy had been in the navy for years, and it wasn't the cost, for early on I took Speight's around, but he didn't have any. I asked him once if he'd ever been a drinker, and he said booze kept you poor. Maybe that's why he'd ended up in Swansong.

When you're as old as Bengy and stuck in a place like that, it's no wonder you'd spend a good deal of time watching the neighbours and listening. Some were friends as well as neighbours, some were more observable than others, some remained strangers despite proximity. Bengy would talk about them, to entertain himself rather than me. Most of them weren't interesting people, just folk getting by as best they could. Alvin Ritter had a hooker with green hair visit once a fortnight. I saw her there a couple of times, but she didn't stay long. She was interesting, but he wasn't. Bengy said in the mercantile navy hookers would board ships in port and sometimes stay for days. Of course, arthritis wouldn't have been a bother for him then.

No, the most interesting one at Swansong was Mrs Geeling Liang. Her family had been here for generations, and she was a Kiwi in every way. She was in unit two and quite friendly with Bengy, sometimes ironing things for him or helping him to get Netflix sorted. But what made Mrs Liang different was that she had plenty of money and also how she made it. Bengy said no one else at Swansong had much money.

Mrs Liang was an artist. She slept in her main room and had turned her bedroom into a modest studio. I've been into it twice, and it was packed with stuff, including preserving jars with sprays of brushes, paints of all sorts, coffee mugs and art frames. The thing about those, the frames, is that they were all old and mostly showing wear. Mrs Liang bought them at garage sales and second-hand stores, or online. She wanted them because they matched the sort of paintings she did: dark-hued pictures of canals, windmills or someone in nineteenth-century clothes sitting at a window. All of them she signed with Dutch names, such as Hendricks, Verhoeven, or Van der Veen, and above them: Geeling. Nothing illegal, she told me, and there was always a sticker on the back that said *reframed*.

I don't know much about art, but they looked pretty good to me. She was especially clever with the clothes, using dark greens and rich yellows, and showing how the light affected the folds. She sold them to second-hand shops and advertised online. A couple of the local cafés were happy to have them on the walls for sale. I wouldn't have minded one at all, but they were seven- or eight-hundred dollars, even for the smaller sizes. Mrs Liang said she'd never been to the Netherlands, never been outside New Zealand, but she had art and travel books and watched TV programmes to get ideas.

Bengy said she could afford to live in a flash place but gave away lots of money to nieces and nephews for their education. She did have plenty of jewellery and used taxis a lot. Bengy said she wasn't completely self-taught and had done courses at the polytech. She'd worked for years as a school librarian but found she could make more money and be happier by painting of old times in far-off places. Bengy attended an art course himself but said he couldn't get the hang of it, and he had arthritis, of course. Probably he would've been better putting some of his navy stories on paper. Plenty there to hold your attention.

Yes, Bengy envied Geeling Liang, but his admiration was greater, and they got on well. There were others at Swansong Apartments who found her success, although not flaunted, to be too much a persistent reminder of their own failure and insignificance. Maurice Struddle said she was a fraudster and should be prosecuted. Maurice was divorced and lonely, often played a keyboard badly late at night. His trousers were extra baggy at the back, as if he had no bum at all. He feuded with Pita and Haeata Whatu next door too, and Bengy said the cops had even been called.

There were no garages at Swansong, so vehicles were just parked outside the units. Another sign of their motel origin. There was no congestion, for quite a few at Swansong didn't have a car. There was a yellow beetle parked outside number seven, where the Yestermans lived, but Bengy told me that in all the time he'd lived there it had never moved, though Don Yesterman washed it on Sundays. There're some odd people, aren't there? Celia Mulvanney in number nine was another one. She remained in her white dressing gown until lunchtime and would wear it to check the letterbox, or the washing line, but never acknowledge the existence of anyone until she was dressed in the afternoon. She had a small, ugly dog that slavered, walked with stiff legs and looked always on the point of frontal assault.

In a way, Swansong Apartments was like a little village, various in personalities but homogeneous in a lower socio-economic status, apart from Mrs Geeling Liang, of course. For nearly eighteen months before Bengy died, I went there quite often, and the two things that stand out in memory are the death of Mr Ploomer and the burglary of Mrs Liang's unit.

Mr Ploomer was a loner. I only saw him a few times and at a distance. A small, pale man, who rose on his toes as he walked and turned aside if people approached. Bengy told me that his wife and daughter had been drowned years ago when a bus went off the road and into Lake Dunstan. Mr Ploomer was in number eight, and once, while Bengy and I were seated at the window, we saw him throw something at Celia Mulvanney's dog. He missed, which disappointed Bengy.

Anyway, one Saturday after we'd been to the supermarket and I was taking stuff from the Fiat into Bengy's place, Betty Yesterman turned up wanting to talk. It was July and damn cold, so Bengy told her to come inside.

'It's just about Syd Ploomer,' she said. 'We haven't seen him for three days. Almost always he goes walking, even in winter, and we see him go past, always looking the other way. And there's been a courier bag on his doorstep since yesterday.'

'What have you done?' asked Bengy.

'We knocked on the door and the window. He never goes away and should be there.'

The three of us walked over to number eight, and Don Yesterman joined us from next door. 'I don't like it,' he said. 'Something's wrong.'

'Have you tried his phone?' I asked.

'Never had his number,' said Betty.

'I bet nobody has,' said Don.

There were no back doors to the Swansong units, but when I gave a good pull and twist to the handle of the front one, it opened, and the familiar configuration of the main room was revealed. Familiar not because any of us had ever been inside, but because all the units at Swansong were the same, apart from furnishings. We knew that if Ploomer had left the door unlocked he was probably inside somewhere.

'Mr Ploomer?' said Betty loudly. 'Are you here, Mr Ploomer?' But there was no reply, so we went in.

We found Syd Ploomer half under his old-fashioned bed. He had a shirt and jersey on, but only pyjamas lower down — striped ones. He looked very dead, although I don't remember exactly what gave that impression. None of us had known him really, but the Yestermans lived next door and saw him more often. Don was quite upset, but Betty took it calmly.

'Let's go back to the main room and leave him be,' she said.

So, we did, and Betty rang the police and we waited there. If it hadn't been so cold, we would have gone outside. Mr Ploomer must have been a very tidy man because the unit was clean and neat, though rather bare, or his death might have been intentional and so he'd done some housekeeping beforehand. I do remember that on his bedside table was a stuffed fabric kiwi with a long, yellow beak. I never mentioned that to anybody but guessed it must have been his daughter's.

Bengy told me that at the service in the funeral parlour days later, there were no relatives of Mr Ploomer, only the Yestermans, the Whatus, Mrs Geeling Liang and Kevin and Alison Gough from unit one. I don't think I've mentioned the Goughs before. They were comparative newcomers but made an effort to get to know their neighbours. They were originally from South Africa and said things just got too tough there. The Goughs were among the few at Swansong who still had jobs; they were younger than most of the others. Kevin worked at a car yard in Maltesse Street, and Alison helped out at a day-care centre. Both of them had a high-pitched yelping laugh that I thought might be a cultural thing in South Africa. Maybe just a coincidence, though.

Yes, the other main thing that happened in the time I knew the place was Mrs Liang being burgled. Not all that surprising, because she was almost rich, which Swansong inhabitants knew and likely talked about it to outside people. Also, she went away quite frequently to all those relatives that she helped support. Bengy was trusted with her key, and he'd go in to water the orchids and bonsai trees if she was visiting for more than a couple of days. It was on such occasions that I saw her studio and paintings.

The burglary was months after Syd Ploomer's death. A new guy had moved into number eight and summer had come as well. Not surprisingly, summer was the best time at Swansong Apartments, especially numbers one to five because they lay to the sun. Even the other units needed less heating then, and the evening light lingered on the old chalets in a flattering way. At the entrance was a magnolia tree with purple flowers among the glossy greenery: the only tree in the Swansong grounds and almost certainly there from the beginning. Celia Mulvanney in her white dressing gown would walk past some mornings to clip something from it for her vase, and her dog would piss and slobber in antagonistic fervour at the magnolia's base.

Mrs Liang flew to Wellington to the capping ceremony for one of the nieces she funded, and on the second night of her absence someone broke into her unit. Bengy didn't hear anything but saw the broken window when he went to water the plants. Alvin Ritter and the Goughs didn't hear anything either, and they were even closer to unit two. Bengy told me that apart from the window there were few signs that anybody had been inside, just a big dump unflushed in the toilet and the biscuit cupboard open, but when Mrs Liang arrived back she found stuff had been taken. Luckily, she had most of her jewellery with her, but two valuable channel-set rings were gone and a jade-and-gold necklace. One painting too, which she said was one of the biggest she'd done, and commissioned by Mrs Williams, who was on the city council.

The police came, of course, but there's not much chance of solving that sort of thing. No forensic disclosure, cryptic notes, or revealing surveillance camera footage. Merely another theft that goes unremarked and unpunished. I think Maurice Struddle did it, but I've never said that because there's no proof whatsoever, just the envy that he always showed and the comments about her art being fraudulent. And that he always seemed a prick. He would have sold off the rings and painting anyway and not kept anything incriminating. It could have been someone from outside Swansong, but how would they have known that Mrs Liang was away?

Bengy Rudd died a few months later, and I really felt it. It was more than the money. He was an interesting, decent and friendly old guy, and I enjoyed helping him. At the funeral, his son mentioned me, said how much Bengy had appreciated my companionship. I felt quite chuffed about that. All of the Swansong people attended the funeral except Maurice Struddle and Celia Mulvanney. Even the new man in Mr Ploomer's unit was there. I think Celia would have come if the service hadn't been in the morning. You don't go to a funeral in a white dressing gown.

Occasionally, I drive past the Swansong Apartments, but I've never been back since Bengy died. That's ages now, and I wouldn't know any of the people there. The chalets are looking their age, but the magnolia's bigger and more beautiful than ever. I still sometimes think of Bengy and the others at Swansong, and I still regret not having a rich-hued painting by Geeling Hendricks, Geeling Verhoeven or Geeling Van der Veen.

Touch and Go

Some staff wondered if Professor Oliphant had Covid-19, although the worst of the pandemic was well past and the vaccines readily available. The professor himself, who was inclined to pessimism, was concerned about the dry cough and said his food lacked piquancy. It was better, he decided, not to travel from Sydney to New Zealand to deliver his address centred on the Freycinet map of Australia.

The Professor's symptoms proved non-threatening, but by that time he'd already informed Massey University, which was hosting the conference, that Dr Laurie Philbin would take his place as a speaker. Laurie was happy enough to be a substitute. A senior lecturer, he received fewer such opportunities than his head of department, and nineteenth-century colonial cartography was not a field of study that received widespread attention even in the academic world. Acceptance entailed extra work in preparation and some financial cost — there were always incidental expenses on such trips not covered by the stipulated allowances. But Laurie was a single man who looked forward to the variety of experience the conference would provide, and also he was aware that having been a keynote speaker would provide heft to his CV.

'Don't hesitate to mention your own contribution to the paper,' said Oliphant magnanimously when they happened to meet in the reprographics room the day before Laurie left for the conference.

Laurie had been to New Zealand twice before, most recently to cycle the Central Otago Rail Trail with a male colleague from the anthropology department. Laurie considered he got on well with Kiwis, though he sensed a complacency that he attributed to insularity. He flew into Auckland and then on to Palmerston North: a flat city in the rain with wind turbines dimly visible on the far hills. At the airport, he was met by Kate Newton, an associate professor and his host. A small, friendly woman who blinked a lot. She was somewhat distracted because she had a sick cat in her car.

'I'm sorry,' she said, 'really sorry, but would you mind if we call quickly at the vet's. Agapanthus has puked up all over the house — not in your room, of course.' Agapanthus was crouched in a wire carry cage in the back of Kate's red SUV, but active enough to reach out and claw Laurie's case when it was placed beside her.

The vet's rooms were in a converted brick house close to the main square. Kate thanked Laurie for his offer to carry Agapanthus in but said it was no trouble, so he waited in the car and she bustled into the drizzle. He was surprised how cool it was, despite the summer season, and how lethargic the traffic seemed even in the city centre. He'd never been to this part of the country before. How quickly one's experience could move on. A few hours ago, he'd been in Sydney, and now he sat more than two-thousand ks away in a red SUV outside the premises of veterinarian Dr Bruce Bosset and newly acquainted with historian Kate and an ailing tabby cat named Agapanthus. The world has so many rooms, he thought, and how easy now to move from one to another.

Kate returned with the empty cage. 'He's given her a jab,' she said, 'and wants to monitor the effect.'

'Makes sense,' said Laurie.

'Anyway, it's probably best to have her there while the conference is on and there're visitors in the house. I'm sorry to be going on about the cat, but she's very much part of the family, and the kids are quite worried.'

'Pets are important, absolutely,' said Laurie. He thought of his boyhood love for Khan the Labrador, who presumably still lay buried under the golden wattle tree in Toowoomba, accompanied by Laurie's favourite plastic dinosaur in a Vegemite jar. 'What children do you have?' he asked.

'Two boys. Hugh gave the cat her name. He found her as a kitten in this agapanthus patch by the river. Years ago now.'

'How old are they?'

'Hugh's twelve. Sam's ten.'

Laurie met them both at Kate's home, and Graham her husband, who ran an employment agency, was almost bald and always seemed to be on his mobile.

'So, you're the map man,' he said cheerfully during a brief interlude from his phone. 'Welcome, map man.'

'I must confess, maps aren't my thing especially,' volunteered Kate, 'but I'm looking forward to a learning curve at the conference. Class and colonialism, though, that's my link to the programme.'

'Two books on it,' said Graham. Laurie was rather touched and pleased by his tone of evident pride. A successful marriage engenders a relaxed atmosphere for visitors.

'Maps served as both a means and a representation of imperial expansion in the nineteenth-century,' he said.

'I look forward to your talk,' she said sincerely with a spasm of blinks.

The Newtons had another guest: Graham's cousin, Natalie, from Auckland. She'd arrived the previous day but was still at the city gallery when Laurie had dinner with his hosts. She was advising on the setting up of a travelling Charles Goldie exhibition, he was told.

By the time Natalie appeared, the meal was over, the boys had gone to their rooms, their mother was clearing up and Graham had returned to his device. Natalie had already eaten, and she and Laurie sat in the lounge together as the normal routine of the house went on around them. Kate came briefly to give Natalie the most significant news of the day, before going back to the kitchen: 'Agapanthus is sick,' she said. 'She's at the vet's.'

Laurie didn't believe in love at first sight. He had the degree of cynicism commensurate with being thirty-four years old and the survivor of two relationships. Yet he felt powerfully drawn to Natalie as they sat and talked. It was initially entirely physical for she was an attractive, dark-haired woman with a ready smile. Her eyes were wide, and her high, curved forehead so smooth it gave her face serenity. He wouldn't have agreed with her own assessment that she needed to lose a little weight, for skinny women didn't arouse him. Other significant attributes soon became apparent. She was intelligent, friendly, proficient and confident in her own profession, interested in the lives of others and quick to see humour in the world. He valued all those things.

'I'd like to see the exhibition,' he told her. 'I know nothing about Charles Goldie, but the portraits sound interesting.'

'It doesn't open until Tuesday, but you're welcome to pop in tomorrow if you have the chance. We've got most of them up now. Lighting's been the major issue in placement. His paintings typically have subdued backgrounds.'

'I could skip one of tomorrow morning's conference sessions. My own isn't until the afternoon. The one immediately before lunch by Dr Hutcheson is on the influence nineteenth-century navigation methods had on colonisation. I'm pretty well up on that.'

'I don't want to be responsible for you playing truant,' Natalie said.

'It's the only chance I'll have, I think, before I leave. I could do with some relief from maps. A different memory to take from my trip.'

'The portraits are maps in a way, I reckon. Maps of physiognomy and the psyche as well.'

'You're right. Good argument. That'll justify a visit all right,' said Laurie. 'Tell me more about this Goldie guy.' He admired the way she could cross her legs and yet have both shins parallel and perpendicular.

He was somewhat disappointed when Kate and Graham finally rejoined them and the conversation became more general. They were pleasant folk, but he preferred being alone with his fellow guest. He had the rather odd, but authentic, feeling it would have been quite natural for Natalie and him to go off together to the same bedroom when conversation ended. In the night, Laurie did dream of her, but it wasn't libidinous. They were in a large artist's studio, old fashioned, as if from a film on Goya, and Natalie was teaching him to paint: she close beside him and the easel close in front. Lustrous globs of oil paint glistened on the palette; and the brush he held was very fine, a nib almost, rather than having bristles.

'Paint what you feel, rather than what you see,' she said to him, as he dipped the fine point into paint as green as a bullfrog and as soft as bird poo.

They had breakfast together and with their hosts. Laurie arranged with Natalie to go to the gallery later in the morning and then left with Kate for the conference. The cat cage was still in the back of the SUV, and he was reminded to ask after Agapanthus.

'I've been in touch,' said Kate. 'She's okay. I'm going to collect her at lunchtime, or earlier. I might miss Dr Hutcheson's talk like you and go then.' Laurie had a brief vision of an empty hall for Hutcheson, everyone having found more pressing business. His own session in the afternoon could meet the same fate.

The Massey campus wasn't traditional, but as Kate walked with him through the grounds Laurie enjoyed the variety in architecture and the abundance of trees and the garden plants left to proliferate in their own way. There was time too, before the conference began, for him to meet the academic who was to introduce him in the afternoon. A thin, listless man, who seemed peeved that his preparation to present Professor Oliphant had been largely wasted and extra time needed to acquaint himself with Laurie's background.

'We're disappointed Prof Oliphant couldn't come,' he said.

'So's he,' said Laurie.

'I do have to remind you to remain aware of the time limit. It's so easy for the programme to fall behind at these things.'

'Fifty minutes, visuals included,' Laurie reassured him. 'No problem.' The man was tiresome, but Laurie wasn't entirely unsympathetic. He'd been on committees organising such events and knew how cavalier some speakers could be about schedules.

The opening address was on the role of the military, specifically in South African colonialism. A Cape Town professor who was both learned and interesting. The second subject was 'Slavery: Impetus for Colonialism', and Laurie found both content and speaker less engaging. He retained a pose of professional attentiveness but thought of Natalie and the time soon to be spent with her in the gallery. He hoped she might have the inclination and the opportunity to attend his own session and imagined her in the audience: her natural poise, her quick smile, the habitual way she brushed hair from her smooth, high forehead with two fingers.

Kate was able to take him to the gallery on her way to collect

Agapanthus. They discussed the sessions and were agreed that slavery had proved somewhat disappointing, despite the potential of the subject.

'Too general,' she said. 'Not enough specific instances to bring out the personal tragedies, the callous inhumanity involved.'

'Exactly,' Laurie said.

'Only a hundred and fifty years ago, slavery was common in America. Amazing, isn't it?'

'And still exists in Africa today, according to UN reports.'

'We're lucky here in so many ways,' said Kate.

So we are, thought Laurie as he went into the gallery, and the good fortune of which he was most aware was his coming at that moment and at Natalie's invitation. The paintings had all been hung, but with the help of a pleasant young guy called Dougal she was placing the description cards on the walls and the exclusion indicator strips on the gallery floor. Laurie was impressed with the rigorous accuracy of it all: how often the tape measure was in use, the many fine adjustments.

'I can see you're a stickler for the rules,' he said.

'Curatorial efficiency is essential. You probably don't realise the value of these paintings,' Natalie said with mock seriousness.

'I thought art was all about originality and free expression.'

'Once that's achieved, though, you need a fascist exactitude in its display and preservation.'

'Do you agree?' Laurie asked Dougal.

'Can I afford not to?' he answered.

Natalie took a break so she could walk Laurie through the exhibition. The portraits were dark and traditional, but he liked them all the more for that. And he found the facial tattoos interesting. Moko, she told him. Perhaps because he lacked any art training, he preferred realism. Sometimes when he viewed modern art, he thought he could do just as well himself, though he knew better than to say so. Natalie told him that despite the prices achieved by Goldie's paintings there was still division among art experts as to his true significance as a painter.

'Some consider him too repetitive, too reliant on photographs, too inclined to romanticism.'

'What vivid detail, though, and rich intensity of colour,' Laurie said, and he was aware of a small, angry scratch on her left hand, which still held the metal tape measure; aware too of a fragrance she wore, faint, but utterly appropriate in ways he couldn't understand. He had a poor sense of smell and rarely noticed perfumes. He took this recognition as further proof of the affinity between them.

Maybe as they talked, Dr Hutcheson elsewhere was delivering the outstanding address of the conference, but even if that were so, Laurie preferred to be in the gallery with Natalie, enjoying a personal tour of the exhibition. He stood close by her side whenever they paused before a portrait and tried to avoid banality in his comments. Such sensitivity to the impression he made was not characteristic of him, for he was a confident man and secure in his good opinion of himself.

'Will you have much to do once the exhibition's in place?' he asked.

'I'm to give a floor talk at the opening,' she said, 'and other times also, and while I'm here I'm giving a lecture at the uni.'

'If I'd known I would've arranged to stay longer.'

'Oh, it'll be ordinary enough,' she said. 'Anyway, I'd better get on with things, I suppose,' and she hefted the metal tape measure as she said it.

'I don't suppose you would have time to listen to my own talk on campus this afternoon. A friendly face or two would be welcome. You'd be bored, of course, but we could have a coffee afterwards.'

'I'd like to. I'm almost sure I could fit it in.'

'It would be really good to see you there.'

'I've never thought of maps having any influence on colonisation apart from being a record,' Natalie said.

'Maps have authoritative appeal and served to legitimise colonialism and also incite it.'

'I'll come if I can. Ask a fatuous question that you can answer brilliantly.'

'I look forward to it,' Laurie said. He wondered why such a talented and attractive woman wasn't in a relationship. Though she might be. He'd never asked her — decided that in the afternoon he would. The gallery room was spacious and well lit, the portraits were serene and significant on the walls, Natalie was close and smiling at him. If all went well, he would delay his flight home. So much possibility, and all because cautious Professor Oliphant had experienced a cough.

'How about having lunch with me?' he said.

'I would,' she said, 'but if I'm to make it this afternoon I'd better push on here. Catch a bite and a coffee briefly when I can.'

'I'll get out of your way then and look forward to seeing you later. Did I tell you Kate's gone to pick up the cat?'

'You said. How will you get back to Massey?'

'I'll get a taxi,' he said.

'You could come with me, but you'd have to hang around here a fair while.'

'I'd like to, but I have to set up the visuals. You can't really talk about maps for long without giving people the chance to view them.' He would have preferred to stay, even if all he could do was watch Natalie as she worked. He could have spent more time in appreciation of the rich Goldie portraits: admiration that arose as much from her association with them as from intrinsic merit. 'See you later then,' he said and went reluctantly away. As he left, he wished he had touched her arm or shoulder, just to have at one brief juncture no separation between them.

Laurie's talk in the afternoon was a success — pertinent questions at its conclusion and appreciative applause, congratulatory comments afterwards, not all perfunctory, but he was disappointed. He was disappointed because Natalie hadn't turned up. He had scanned row by row as he spoke and as people looked past him to the graphics on the screen above, but he couldn't see her, and Kate said afterwards that she didn't think she was there.

'You were great,' Kate said generously. 'It's not easy to make such a specialised area of study accessible and interesting, even to fellow academics.'

'Thanks.' He waited about the doorway for a while, but Natalie didn't show up. He talked with Liam Laymann from Auckland, whom he knew a little. He had a coffee and afterwards sat with Kate and listened to Dr Belay-Willis draw out the fundamental differences between the colonial policies of Gladstone and Disraeli. The past was Laurie's profession, but in the circumstances even he was conscious of irrelevance.

When Kate checked her phone at the end of the session, there was a text from Natalie to say that her mother had collapsed and been admitted to hospital in Auckland, that she was in a very serious condition. Natalie had managed to get a flight north and was already on her way. She thanked Kate, apologised for disappearing, and asked her to pass on her regrets to Laurie regarding his conference presentation. There was no message from her on his own mobile.

Laurie was reunited with Agapanthus when he and Kate returned to her home, but it wasn't a fair trade for Natalie's absence. He could understand the reason for it and appreciate how upset she was, but disappointment was his predominant feeling. He'd allowed himself to imagine something personal and important would come of meeting her and that she shared that expectation.

At the end of the next day, he would leave the country with no more than wry recognition of this false assumption. Laurie sat with Kate and her boys, took his turn to pat an apparently fully restored Agapanthus and sought consolation in the stoicism of his academic training. He told himself that history is all about things that happened and that life is largely about things that didn't.

Freefall

Gordon was meant to be with him on that hike. It wasn't high mountain stuff, but it was rugged, and it's always sensible to have a companion when that far into the back country. They'd planned to do it in two days and knew each other's capabilities. But Gordon got Covid, and John decided to go alone. He was all set and didn't want to put it off. Another friend ran him up to the gorge and said he wished he'd time to come himself.

For the first couple of hours, John followed the river, but then he climbed up onto a main ridge as is usually best in high country, less up and down walking and the views more impressive. No trees and little scrub, tussock country and a few scabbed tors rearing through it. He didn't see any goats or deer, not even any merino, but there were birds for company, although they took no notice of him. Small birds close to ground that he thought might be pipits, and swinging high in the blue sea of the sky, a hawk. The sun was like the open and shimmering maw of a furnace, too fierce to look at. There was no wind. In the silence his own breathing and the sound of his boots in tussock or on stony ground was loud.

He stopped at an outcrop that gave him shade and adjusted his pack, which had become a bit lopsided. He had a drink and ate scroggin that he'd made himself, but nothing else. The big meal of the day would be at his evening camp. He tried to contact Gordon but was out of phone range, as he expected, so he briefly rested and looked into the gully where there were clumps of matagouri and dark stones.

As he clambered on, he kept gaining height until he stood on a bluff and could see far up the Ginty River. There was an outcrop on the bluff, and he had the sudden inclination to climb it and stand high there and be above it all. If anyone had been with him, he wouldn't have done it, but he was alone and gave way to the boyish impulse. He stood there and spread his arms out without conscious intention. The sun was hot through the soft fabric of his hat.

Schist rock can be crumbly, and a piece dislodged beneath his left boot, and he dropped to his knees to hold his place. Just briefly, though, he had the sense of a freefall from the rock, no part of his body was in contact with anything but air, and the visible world was in rotation. A displacing and powerful sense of absolute release. The dizziness passed, and he was on the rock once more. Silly bastard, he said to himself as a reprimand as he looked far down to where the fall would have taken him.

The going was easier after the bluff, mainly downhill and largely featureless, although he could see steep country again in the distance that he'd have to tackle early the next day. He followed a dry creek bed, and as the afternoon wore on and the sun languished, the first shadows began; those close were unremarkable, those in the distance had a purple tinge. He came around a spur onto a small flat, no bigger than a rugby field, and was surprised to see a man and woman sitting on the creek bank, close together and with no sign of packs. As he neared them, they remained sitting, relaxed and both smiling, almost as if they were expecting him there in that isolation. Neither of them wore tramping clothes, and John was surprised at that too, but the thought was superseded by an impression he had that they were familiar to him, although he couldn't place them. You don't walk past people in the hills without stopping, without a greeting. He took off his pack and sat down on the bank, conscious of the sun's heat through his hat and its indirect heat from the ground.

He gave his name, and they gave theirs — Passover they said, Alan and Eve. He made no reference to the obvious association of their Christian names because it would have been done so often before. He'd never met anybody called Passover, but there are lots of odd names around. They talked of their intentions, and basically John's starting point was their destination, although they seemed uncommitted. John talked with them of the landscape, and all three had experience in it that went back a good way. Alan was stocky, powerful, and when he briefly took off his hat, John saw that he was going bald. Eve was dark haired and fair skinned, and even when not talking her mouth remained slightly open, showing her top front teeth. They talked about changes that were taking place and the dangers to the environment they valued. They talked about places all three of them had been to, and the reasons for going there. There was a compatibility and ease in their conversation.

Alan and Eve seemed in no hurry to continue their tramp, and John enjoyed being with them, but he needed to move on if he were going to cover the distance he'd set for the first day. They farewelled him with smiles and a wave, and it was only when they were out of sight that it came to him why they seemed familiar. They reminded him of his parents, that was it, but younger, at an age when he had only indistinct recollections of them. He made a little noise of surprise to himself as that realisation hit him and then concentrated again on the terrain and his best route through it. Both his parents had died in their early seventies, and John's memory of them was a mixture of love and regret. There were things he wished he'd asked them, and things he wished he'd told them too. He had a feeling of closeness with them again, and it was a good feeling that sustained him as he walked.

One of the Ginty tributaries had a small, clear flow, so he filled his water-bottles. Water was scarce in the hills at that time of year. He also checked the map, looking up from it to the features it represented to reassure himself he was heading the right way. One hill looks much like another in such country. He gave himself fifteen minutes, leaning back in the grasses with his soft, blue hat over his face, and then he set off again to the west, once more gaining height.

As evening fell, he was in a tight ridge-and-gully landscape, looking forward to finding some sheltered nook where he could cook up a meal and spend the night. The country was no longer stripped naked by the direct sun but clothed in reaching shades and shadows as well as glancing light. John came over a promontory and walked down into yet another dry creek bed and around a spur onto a small area, no bigger than a rugby field. Alan and Eve were sitting together on a bank, much like the one earlier, and they were again unsurprised to see him. As he came closer, they stretched out their hands and smiled.

'You've had the freefall, John,' his father said as greeting.

'Stay with us,' his mother said.

Leon

When you're strong, it's hard to excuse the weak. Leon was thirty-six years old and had twice been within the top dozen in the Coast to Coast run despite not being a professional athlete. He was also one of the youngest senior policy advisers in the Ministry of Justice, happily married and with a son and a daughter. He felt on equal terms with the world.

That Tuesday, however, he was brassed off with a couple of colleagues he'd tasked with collating some statistics concerning the End of Life Choice Act 2019: Ryan Alpers and Cynthia Biddercombe. Especially Cynthia, for he'd emphasised the importance of having her information on schedule. It wasn't the first time he'd been disappointed with her, and he told her so, privately of course, not in the open-plan office where she worked. He was not by nature an unkind man. Cynthia apologised and said that she'd had to go home for an hour or so the day before and that had put her behind. There was always some excuse, wasn't there? If she'd had to take time from work, why hadn't she caught up at night? Leon didn't enjoy reprimanding colleagues but believed in high standards and expected folk to measure up.

'If you don't get your own stuff done, it affects other people,' he told Cynthia. 'A chain reaction, really, and that's frustrating for everybody, you see. I did say it was a priority, didn't I?'

'I'm sorry. I'll have it to you before the end of the day,' she said. Cynthia was older than Leon, but hadn't been at the Ministry long, only a few months, and before that she worked at the council, and before that at the registry of the University of Waikato where she'd taken her degree. A good degree, which was another reason Leon was disappointed. She should have been able to make more of herself in life. Leon was a not-so-quiet achiever, affable enough but with the assumption that those who couldn't match his own accomplishments and commitment lacked the will to do so.

'Think of it as a team thing,' he told her. 'What we do here is quite important, you know. Having a work plan is helpful, I find, so you don't get caught out for time. Is that something you have, a work plan?'

'I'll pay more attention to time allocation,' Cynthia said. 'It was personal stuff that cropped up unexpectedly. I'm sorry I held you up, but I had to deal with it straight away.' Her tone was quiet, even respectful, but she met his gaze.

Leon wasn't interested in her personal stuff, just wanted her to be efficient in her job. He wondered if he should suggest an afternoon course on task management and time allocation for all those who'd been in the department less than eighteen months. However, the efficacy of that would need to be considered alongside the time taken from ongoing tasks by those involved. The Ministry was a busy place.

Cynthia did have the figures to him by four, and they were competently assembled.

'Looks fine,' he said. 'Thank you.' He made no mention of the additional pressure on him as a consequence of the delay. He had those he answered to as well, and so he stayed on in the quiet after-hours building to ensure he was prepared for the presentation in the morning. Leon, though, had no fear of such challenges. He would be at his most impressive, especially as he knew there would soon be a vacancy for a senior managerial position.

Workday traffic was largely over by the time Leon finished, but already cars were flowing back into the city as people headed to the restaurants, theatres, petty gambling sites, even the supermarkets. Tuesday wasn't a big night, but there are always folk with reason to be downtown. Leon owned a Toyota Camry, his wife had a smaller vehicle, but usually he travelled by the number two bus, no changes needed. That Tuesday was one of the usual times, and he walked quite quickly because he hoped to catch the bus due soon and also because it was cold and already dusk. He made the stop on time, but the bus didn't, so he had to wait along with three other men, one of whom he knew: Hunter Christopher.

Hunter was a journalist who lived not far from Leon, and although they never visited each other or did things together, they talked with some familiarity when they met because of the bus route they had in common. Hunter was never probing in conversation with Leon, despite his profession, from courtesy or indifference or from awareness they were usually able to be overheard. Perhaps all three. On that Tuesday evening, the four men stood quite close in the shelter because of the July chill, and Hunter and Leon talked easily while the other two were silent. Even as he talked, Leon was thinking of work, the presentation he would give in the morning. And even as he talked and thought of work, he was aware of a full moon beginning to bloom.

Leon and Hunter had separate seats on the bus but briefly resumed talking as they walked together up the sloping street from their stop. They talked about the burgeoning interest in women's rugby and agreed it was a positive development, and then Hunter turned off at Wallace Street and Leon went on alone. As he'd worked late, his children would have had their tea, which disappointed him for he enjoyed the evening meal more when all of them were together.

It was dark when he reached the corner dairy owned by Mrs Purvis, but he turned in there to buy a packet of chips for Olivia and Sam. The bell sounded as usual as he slid open the door, but Mrs Purvis didn't need to be summoned as she was already tending to a customer: Cynthia Biddercombe. Leon was surprised to see her. He couldn't recall where she lived, but he knew it wasn't in his suburb.

'No,' said Cynthia, 'I'm much further out, but my mother's recently moved into the retirement home here. I'm getting one or two things for her.'

'Bella Montana Home?'

'That's the one. That's why I had to leave work yesterday,' Cynthia said. 'She'd just gone in and became upset. She was thirty-seven years in her own place and didn't want to leave. Tried to go home and was distraught when they found her wandering on the road.'

'I hope she settles in okay,' Leon said. 'It must be quite traumatic for some old people to make that shift, especially if they're by themselves.

Your father's no longer about, I suppose?'

'Died years ago,' Cynthia said.

Leon smiled at Mrs Purvis, but the bell had sounded, so she was looking towards the door. Leon turned in time to see a group of guys tumbling in, their faces obscured by hoods and masks, but their agility proof of youth. They were shouting, or rather chanting, but nothing that made sense. For a moment he continued to smile, but then saw they were carrying baseball bats and sticks. They headed through the small shop — to where Leon, Cynthia and Mrs Purvis had drawn instinctively close — and started hitting them.

Leon's hand, raised defensively, was walloped with force, and the pain was intense. He heard Mrs Purvis cry out as well. Leon got the worst of it because he was the largest and a man. All three of them were pushed to a crouch, held by many hands, and duck-walked into the small storeroom at the rear of the displays. The guys had obviously sussed the layout, possibly been customers for years, and they bundled the three into the room, paying little attention to Mrs Purvis because she was small and sobbing but briefly beating at Leon and Cynthia because they were bigger and unknown. Leon heard the door lock behind them and the shouting, the chanting, as they ran back to steal what they'd come for. A lot of noise but not for long and then silence from the shop and the sound of Mrs Purvis sobbing.

Leon found the light switch by the door with his left hand and held the other up by his face because it seemed to throb less that way and it wouldn't get bumped. Cynthia and Mrs Purvis sat on a carton of tinned fruit, and the shopkeeper wiped blood from her lip and stopped crying as Cynthia comforted her. Leon tugged at the door with his good hand but couldn't open it. As the man among them, he felt he should have been able to do more and was disappointed in himself, even though he'd been well outnumbered and taken by surprise.

'They've buggered off now anyway,' he said. 'How many do you reckon?'

'Five or six at least,' Cynthia said.

'They'll have the money and the cigarettes and trashed the place,' Mrs Purvis said. 'I never thought it would happen here, to me.'

'It's become a copycat sort of thing now,' Leon said. He clasped his right hand tightly at the wrist. It seemed to help. The knuckles were grotesquely swollen and almost purple.

'God, that looks really nasty,' Cynthia said.

'It was that first guy with the baseball bat,' Leon said. 'What about you? You got knocked about too?'

'Nothing too bad,' she said. 'My coat's pretty thick and took most of it.'

'I'm sorry about it all,' Mrs Purvis said, the words slurred somewhat because of her swollen lip.

'Nothing's your fault at all,' Cynthia said.

'You're not always here by yourself, are you. I've seen a young guy in the shop sometimes,' Leon said.

'My son, but he goes to music lessons on a Tuesday.'

'Those pricks would have known that,' Leon said. 'When does he get back?'

'Not for another half-hour yet,' Mrs Purvis said.

They were quiet for a short while, listening for any noise from the shop, the entry of a customer or a neighbour who had heard the din. Mrs Purvis explored her cut lip with a gentle tongue; Leon held his discoloured hand up like a baton; and Cynthia pulled her coat more tightly to her because the room was unheated. At the Ministry she had seemed to Leon an inconspicuous woman in appearance, conversation and performance. She was different in the storeroom of Mrs Purvis's dairy.

'I left my phone in the car. Have you got yours?' she asked, looking at Leon.

'I did, but it's in my bag, and I dropped that when those guys started bashing us.'

'Bummer,' Cynthia said.

'Mine's on the counter,' Mrs Purvis added.

'Bummer,' repeated Cynthia, and they were briefly quiet again.

There was one window in the storeroom, high up and small. Leon stood on a vegetable crate and pushed the frame with his good hand.

'It doesn't open,' said Mrs Purvis.

'I could smash it and shout out,' he said. 'Neighbours might hear. I'm actually surprised no one's come already.'

'Smash it if you want to. The shop will be smashed up, so something else won't matter.' Mrs Purvis's tone was both bitter and resigned.

Leon was still considering whether to break the window when they heard a voice from the shop. A loud, enquiring male voice saying, 'Hello? Hello?'

'In here,' Leon shouted, and he rattled the door. Footsteps, the key turning, and the door opened. A big man was there, in an orange hi-vis jacket and pale, heavy boots.

'Christ,' he said, 'how long have you been in here? Everyone okay?'

They were grateful for his assistance but expressed that only in passing as they hurried out to the shop: Leon still holding his right wrist, Mrs Purvis with a slight blush of blood on her face, Cynthia with her thick coat and dishevelled hair.

'Police,' said Leon, almost as an announcement, and bent down to grasp his bag, took out his phone and rang them, while Mrs Purvis moved about the small shop and tallied both loss and damage in a surprisingly steady voice.

Norris Sutch was their rescuer's name. 'I'd better stay till the cops arrive,' he said. 'Tell them I just stopped in for bread and Tim Tams and found all this and yous too.'

'We really appreciate it,' Cynthia told him.

'I never thought it would happen around here, but it's everywhere now,' Norris said. He pushed aside shards of cabinet glass with one boot. 'I assume there's insurance these days for raids like this, right?' he said, but no one answered.

Mrs Purvis's son arrived, followed by two police almost at the same time — man and woman — and a younger woman, walking a Labrador, who stopped outside and looked in on them all from the darkness. It started to feel crowded, and Leon's hand ached the more.

'You need to have it seen to,' the policewoman said. 'We've got enough for now. Just give me your address and mobile number and head off to hospital. You've got a vehicle?'

'I'll take him,' Cynthia said. She stepped back to Mrs Purvis and gave her a quick hug. As she and Leon went out to her car, he was sniffed at the crotch by the Labrador for the length of the leash.

'I should go home first, tell them what's happened and then Emma can run me to the hospital. That way you could still go on to see your mother,' Leon said. 'I don't want to be a bother.'

'Better you go straight to A&E, don't you think? Get some painkillers at least and find out how serious it is.'

'You're sure? That's really kind. I'll ring Emma and tell her what's going on.'

'I feel really sorry for Mrs Purvis. Maybe she won't be able to carry on in the shop unless her son's there all the time now.'

'What about you?' said Leon as he got carefully into her small car and clumsily reached for the seat belt with his left hand. 'You said about your coat, but you got bashed about too. You must be sore.'

'Nothing too much,' said Cynthia. 'Just my shoulder hurts a bit.'

As they drove, Leon felt oddments beneath his feet on the car floor, a small pottle, a rag, and he'd glimpsed stuff lying on the back seat. He disliked such untidiness but resisted his habitual urge to pick the things up. He needed to piss, but the hospital was quite close, and he thought he could hold on okay until there. He rang Emma and told her what had happened, toning it all down so she wouldn't get upset. And he spoke cheerfully to Olivia and Sam. It was fully dark, and as he finished talking and Cynthia drove over the hill, he noticed the city lights, sharp and glittery, some perched star-like, others from the cars streaming towards them, all a variety of colour and intensity. After the confusion and threat of what had gone before, it seemed oddly removed to be sitting there with his junior colleague as she drove. A time cut off from what had gone before and what was ahead. His hand still throbbed, but otherwise he felt okay, almost sleepy. A reaction perhaps.

'Something of a night, eh?' he said. 'You never know, do you?'

'They wouldn't have been all that old, those guys, would they?'

'Probably not. Teenagers, maybe in their twenties. Watching too many American programmes about neighbourhood gangs.'

'It's awful for Mrs Purvis. Do you know her well?'

'Hardly at all,' Leon said. 'Almost always we shop at the supermarket.'

'How's your hand?' she asked, turning her eyes briefly from the road to look.

'It's okay.' He was holding it close to his chest. 'How's your shoulder?'

'Not too bad,' she said.

There were plenty of people waiting in the emergency department, which was no surprise. They had their own apprehensive concerns and paid little attention to Leon and Cynthia. Leon made sure she had a seat, then went off to have a pee — a prolonged, clumsy task because of his hand. He returned and found Cynthia had kept a place for him. He was surprised how poorly dressed most people were, a few even with coats or gowns over nightwear. Hardly anyone talked. One woman had a small girl asleep on her knee, there was an old man mouthing and snorting, a couple leant together, clasped, murmuring and swaying. A young guy in work clothes had a blood-stained bandage on his hand.

Leon had never been to an A&E before, but Cynthia had several times when her mother suffered atrial tachycardia attacks, a sort of racing heart and feeling faint, Cynthia said. She told him that you get triaged first, so that they know who's in most need and can be sent through to the doctors as priority. It's an initial assessment, she explained. Leon said it sounded like an equestrian event, and they had a quiet laugh, but even that seemed rather out of place in A&E.

Leon was motioned up to the cubicle by the triage nurse, but he insisted that Cynthia come as well.

'She's been hurt too,' he said and told the nurse what had happened.

'A ram raid. That's nasty,' she said.

'Well, a raid without the ram,' Leon said.

'Neither of you lost consciousness at all?' the nurse asked. 'Painful, I bet,' she said after looking at Leon's hand and flexing the fingers gently, making him flinch. 'Nothing broken hopefully, but you'll need an X-ray almost certainly. I'll give you some painkillers while you wait, they'll help.' She examined Cynthia's shoulder and said there was only soft-tissue bruising and no real concern. 'What an experience though,' she said. 'You might like to consider counselling,' and she offered a pamphlet. 'Don't underestimate the emotional effects,' she said.

'I suppose there'll be a bit of a wait?' Leon said.

'I'm afraid so, yes,' she said. 'We're full on again tonight, and there's been that multiple accident on the motorway.'

Leon and Cynthia went back to find their seats occupied and had to take a place on a bench near the corridor. Leon found the water dispenser and took the painkillers. 'Why don't you go?' he asked when he got back. 'I'll be stuck here for ages. I'll call Emma when I've been seen, and she'll come and get me.'

'She'd have to bundle the kids in and everything. I'll wait an hour or so anyway, and if nothing's happened then I'll head off.'

'No partner waiting for you?' Leon was slightly embarrassed to ask that, not because it was personal but that he should have remembered more about her as part of his role at work. He found it easy to assume that once more junior people left the workplace they had no existence relevant to himself.

'What with work and my mother, there hasn't been room for much else. I've been living with her for over a year because she doesn't really cope on her own any more, and now it's got too much for me, onset of Alzheimer's and everything, so I had to agree on the Bella Montana.'

'No other family?'

'Just an older sister who lives in Brisbane. She said do whatever I think's best, but I still feel bad putting Mum in care when she didn't want to go. Mum blames me, I know: said my sister would never have done it. She'll have forgotten by now what I was going to bring, even that I was coming. I'll ring the place, though.'

It occurred to Leon that he could make a case that Cynthia was responsible for all that had happened to him, for if she hadn't been remiss with her statistical analysis he wouldn't have had to stay so late at the Ministry, wouldn't have been in Mrs Purvis's dairy when the louts roared in, wouldn't be sitting in A&E waiting to see a doctor. He knew all that was nonsense, however, and that any apology due was his to give.

'I need to tell you I'm sorry,' he told Cynthia.

'What for?'

'For this morning. For going on at you about not having the figures ready that I needed for the presentation. I had no idea you had all this personal stuff going on, and I should've asked, made allowance.

I get overly focused on my own deadlines.'

Cynthia looked at him appraisingly. 'Those meds must be kicking in,' she said. She smiled.

'Yeah, but I shouldn't have given you a hard time.'

'Do you know what the open office call you?' she said. Their attention was taken for a moment by a medic who came out and asked for Noel Rudd, who was the young guy in work clothes with the blood-stained bandage on his hand.

'So, what do they call me?' Leon asked when the two had gone.

'Buzz. That's what we call you.'

'Why the hell Buzz?'

'I'm not sure,' said Cynthia, 'I think it's a buzzy bee, busy bee, sort of thing. Always on the go.'

'Could be worse,' Leon said, 'but maybe it's buzz off?'

'Maybe that too. Could be.'

A couple hurried through the doors, both elderly, both agitated, the woman supported by the man and with her head down. They went straight to the triage cubicle and pushed open the glass door. Before it closed, Leon could hear the man talking urgently about her heart, her heart, but after assessment they too were quieter and required to wait with everybody else.

'I didn't realise you've had to look after your mother for such a long time with no one to help,' said Leon. 'That can't be easy.'

'She's quite young to have Alzheimer's. It's just got gradually worse and worse, and all day at work I'd be worrying about what she was doing at home, whether she'd even be there. She doesn't like the Home, but it's a relief for me, and I hope she'll get used to it. She'll have company there, and I'll know she'll be safe at least. She's been a great mum, but I'll be able to have more of a life myself. I'll still see her often of course.'

'I'm sorry for going on about the stuff you didn't get to me,' said Leon. 'I should've been more supportive. It's a pressured sort of place, the Ministry.'

'Yes, shape up, or ship out,' said Cynthia. 'Fair enough, and you've got the big presentation tomorrow, haven't you?'

'May have to can that. I'll see how I feel. Actually, those painkillers are really good, and I've still got two.' He gently flexed the fingers of his injured hand. 'I don't think there's anything broken. You should go home now. I'll give Emma a call when I'm seen. I might even piss off home if it's too long. I'm fine.'

'Are you sure?'

'Absolutely. And I don't think you should come in tomorrow after all this. Go to the doctor with your shoulder or rest up. Visit your mother.'

'Thanks, I'll see how I feel. I will go now if that's okay.'

'Absolutely,' said Leon.

'Good luck for tomorrow with the presentation.'

'We'll see.'

He watched her go and thought how much more he knew about her after just one accidental evening together. More in one night than in all the months she'd been working at the Ministry. For some reason, he thought too of Cynthia's mother, bewildered and feeling lost in a small room at the Bella Montana Home. He rang Emma and told her he was still waiting at A&E to be seen, but that he'd persuaded Cynthia to head home.

'I can drive over and be with you,' she said. 'I can take the kids over to Mum.' The medic appeared again, asked for Mrs Nannstead, who was the woman with her heart. She was led into the treatment area behind the doors, followed by the husband.

'Wait a while yet,' said Leon. 'If I'm not taken in soon, I'll come home. I'll let you know. I'm feeling okay.'

The policewoman rang soon afterwards. She asked how he was and said they'd like him to come in sometime in the next couple of days to say more about what happened at the dairy. Dramatic events were supposed to imprint on consciousness, but Leon was surprised how little of the raid was clear in his memory. He wouldn't be able to give even a facial description of the guy who hit him with the baseball bat, even though he'd had a hoodie not a mask. Mainly his memories of the night were of talking with Cynthia, finding out about her life and about himself. So, they called him Buzz, did they. But not to his face, for it was news to him. As he waited among the others seeking care, he thought about being Buzz and what it might signify.

Passing Through

Ryan saw Olivia naked even before he met her. It wasn't the intention of either. He was up a ladder cleaning windows at his uncle's motel units when she walked out of the bathroom, arranging a towel, but not fully draped in it. Both of them were surprised, but she knew there was no danger, that he had reason to be there and no access to the room. She turned quickly and went back into the bathroom, leaving him at the window with the squeegee at half arc. He climbed down, of course, and moved on, taking the ladder to another unit. He knocked on the door, as he always did, but this time someone answered, a youngish guy with a beard and a magazine who said it was fine for Ryan to do the windows. Ryan did wonder how long Olivia waited in the bathroom before coming out again.

Olivia was in the process of leaving her husband and was staying at Blue Sky Motels until he moved out of the family home as agreed. She had her four-year-old son with her and a fairly new Kia Seltos. Ryan only learned about the separation a good deal later, but he did meet her the day after the shower incident when she arrived with little Archie at reception and asked for advice as to the best local garage for a warrant. Ryan gave his recommendation, and although she'd given no sign of recognition, or embarrassment, he apologised for being at the window.

'I knocked before starting,' he said, 'but no one came.'

'That's okay. I was in the shower,' she said. 'Are there any playgrounds near here? Not schools, but public ones.' He was able to help her with that too.

As they were leaving, Archie turned and said with childish emphasis, 'I don't like it here,' and both Ryan and Olivia laughed.

'Nothing personal,' she said. 'He misses home.'

You get all sorts of folk in a motel, and Ryan had his share of experiences from working at Blue Sky part time. He'd ceased to be surprised by how squalid some people were, how little consideration for others they showed, how likely they were to shoot through or pilfer. Once the police came for a druggie, and they found him half under the bed and unconscious. He didn't die though. Most people were ordinary, decent and no bother. Olivia and Archie were unremarkable and undemanding guests, and she paid promptly. Colin, Ryan's uncle, rather liked such long stayers, less work for the team, he said. One nighters were something of a pain.

Olivia was part of the customer and communications team at the council and could do some of her tasks from the motel, which made it easier for her to work around Archie's kindy hours. Her pod leader understood she was going through a difficult time. Little Archie soon grew happier with the new life. He liked to follow the cleaners on their rounds, was always watching from the upper decking on the evenings when the bins went rumbling out and would call out the colours of their lids as they passed. He wandered into the office sometimes when Ryan was there and gave his view of the world with assurance.

'A girl at kindy spits at me,' he told Ryan. Olivia would seek him out, and they would go back to their motel.

It was a difficult situation for Olivia, and naturally she didn't talk about it much, but by the time she'd been there several weeks she felt comfortable enough to chat a bit with Ryan, even more so with his aunt — mainly about things other than her marriage. In age, Ryan guessed she would've been about midway between his age and Colin's. She asked him what he was doing at uni and said she wished now that she'd switched to law.

'I'd be independent now if I'd done law,' she said, 'and I'd be able to cut through a lot of the stuff that's bugging me now.'

'It's boring though, isn't it, law?'

'Right now, I'd settle for boring,' she said. She had a habit of looking away as she spoke, as if the words didn't matter or as if her eyes might betray her true preoccupation.

There were several women friends who visited her, and her husband turned up one Saturday when Ryan was in the office. Maybe he'd been before but not when Ryan was there. A short man, shorter than his wife, with receding soft hair and wearing a jacket, despite the summer heat. A polite man who asked which unit Mrs Alpers was in. Ryan knew he was the husband because as soon as he went up the stairs to Olivia's motel, she came down with Archie to the office.

'I wonder if you could do me a favour,' she said. 'Just have Archie with you for a bit while I talk to my husband. I don't want him upset by anything that's said.'

Archie quite liked being in the office. He could stack and shuffle the tourist brochures, ring the bell and play with Ryan's scooter helmet.

'Mum's been crying again, but Dad's here now,' he said, although no question had been posed.

'That's okay then,' Ryan said.

'Dad's got a present for me, for afterwards.'

'You're lucky.'

'We don't live in our house any more,' Archie said, 'and my toys are all there.'

'I've seen you with the flash little trike.'

'Most toys are there though.'

'There's not so much room here, and you'll go back to them sometime,' Ryan said.

'I like presents. It's not my birthday, but Dad's got a present.' Archie put on the blue helmet and stood in the office doorway, looking up towards his motel unit. The helmet rested on his shoulders but was still unsteady because his small head didn't fill it.

Half an hour later, Olivia and her husband came down the wooden stairs together but not in conversation. He waited there while she walked to the office. She lifted the helmet and stroked her son's hair.

'Run over to Daddy,' she said. 'He's got something special for you.' Archie trotted off without a word, and his mother and Ryan watched her husband take his hand and walk with him to the car. 'They're going to have the afternoon together. It's important they have time together so he doesn't get upset or confused,' she said. 'And I really appreciate you spending time with him. There's not a lot for him to do in the motel.' They watched the Lexus drive past, Archie smiling and waving, his father raising a polite hand.

'You didn't think of staying in your house with Archie, and your husband moving out?' As he'd been minding the boy, Ryan felt involved enough to be personal.

'Well, it's usually the one wanting the split who goes. At least in the first instance, otherwise things drag on. It would be so much easier if it wasn't for Archie, for what's best for him and not just us. You love him so much, but you can't have half each, can you?'

'Yeah, that must be tough.'

'We'll get through it,' she said with assumed briskness, conscious that Ryan was a part-time employee at the motel she lived in, not a confidant of her personal life, despite his kindness to her son. 'But thanks again,' she said. 'You're good with Archie, and he likes being with you.'

'He seems a happy little guy most of the time.'

'He doesn't realise what's going on. Kids are so vulnerable, aren't they? I hope we can go back to our own place soon, and he'll be more settled there. All his own stuff and everything. Anyway, I'd better tidy up and get off to the supermarket and do the chores while he's away.'

As she went out of the office, he wondered what it was that she needed to get away from, and the need so great that she was prepared to put so much at risk.

One of the risks was probably financial. Ryan's uncle told him that Olivia's husband wasn't just Mr Alpers, but Dr Alpers, an anaesthetist. 'Those boys make big bickies, don't you worry,' Colin said. 'Really big bickies. But if it gets nasty, she could find herself coming down a peg or two.'

'He doesn't seem nasty,' Ryan said.

'We don't know what's gone on though, do we? If he's playing around or she's playing around.'

'I haven't seen any guys coming round.'

'No, but she's not only here, is she? And she'd be extra careful while lawyers are on the job. And it could be him, with all those nurses at the hospital and him an anaesthetist. You just don't know, do you?'

Colin assumed that all marriage failures had a sexual cause. It was more interesting for him that way.

Ryan wasn't at the motel when Dr Alpers returned his son and wasn't there the next day at all because he was working on a tutorial assignment, but on the Saturday when he was cutting back the line of blue agapanthus close to the road, Olivia approached and said Archie wanted to show him the present from his father.

'It's set up on the table,' she said. As they walked to the unit, he thought she looked unwell. She was tall for a woman. Maybe her husband seemed short only because she herself was tall. Her legs were thin, and so were her exposed arms, the round wrist bones clear beneath the skin. She was pale too, even though it was summer. All that was going on was dragging her down, perhaps.

The toy was something called a marble run — brightly coloured blocks, funnels and spirals through which a silver ball bearing could career. Archie was doing that with much excitement when they came in.

'It has various configurations,' Olivia said. Archie wanted Ryan to have a go, and so he put in the ball, and they watched its convoluted descent.

'Do it again,' said Archie, so Ryan did. 'Do it again,' said the boy, and Ryan did.

'You play with it yourself now,' Olivia said.

'Dad gave it to me,' Archie said. He was jiggling with excitement each time he made it work.

His mother and Ryan stood a while on the narrow wooden decking at the door and looked down on the asphalt parking area, the office, other motels, the line of blue agapanthus partly trimmed.

'We won't be here much longer,' she told him. 'My husband's going to stay with his sister, and we'll go back home.'

'You'll be pleased about that.'

'In a way, and it'll be much better for Archie. The bummer is that Barry's going to contest custody.'

'I'm sorry,' said Ryan, 'but the mother usually gets priority, right?'

'It means lawyers, courts, antagonism. A lot of stuff coming out that's better not.'

'I'm sorry.'

'Well, it is what it is, and I want to thank you for the time you've given to Archie. It's been important for him, and you're patient with him. He wants to see you again today.'

'This afternoon,' offered Ryan.

'It's not a nuisance?'

'This morning I'll finish garden stuff, but this afternoon I'll be in the office. He can bring down the marble run if he likes.'

He did like and arrived with his new toy at two o'clock and set it up in a corner of reception, so, in between dealing with customer needs, Ryan looked after him, rolled the silver ball and feigned excitement, altered the configuration at the boy's request. A woman from Palmerston North, who was taking a unit, asked him if Archie was his brother.

Olivia and Archie moved out five days later, when Ryan wasn't there, so he never got to say goodbye. She left a card for him with his aunt though, thanking him for his help, especially his kindness to Archie. Although there was no personal goodbye, there was one last and indirect contact, of which she was unaware. The day before she left, the Wednesday afternoon, Ryan was in the unit below hers, replacing a microwave, when she and her husband walked out onto the decking above in tense conversation.

'Fuck you then,' she said.

'Okay, whatever. If that's the way you want it. It won't be pretty. Just remember he's my son too.'

'Who'd want you as a father.'

'I know you'd like me dead,' said Barry, 'but I love him too.'

'No, I've never wanted you dead,' she said, 'but I've often wished you more alive.'

'Yeah,' he said, the tone resigned rather than angry.

Ryan heard him walk down the stairs, and he passed the open door of the lower unit without a glance within, but Ryan could see there were tears on his face. Ryan never saw any of the Alpers again, never heard what happened about custody, or the division of assets, or anything else that was revealed in court, although Colin said there must have been some serious shagging somewhere along the line.

Hour of the Wolf

Dr Leong told me it was for my own good. I find in such circumstances the phrase invariably means that what is advised may be beneficial but will certainly be both a bore and a restriction. No, thank you, I said, I'll skip the optional communal session on the ex-All Black's story of overcoming impostor syndrome. The opportunity to pat a fat Labrador was also not irresistible, even though it might engender a flush of fellowship. Instead, I watched the slowly changing pattern the afternoon sun made across the dark carpet of my room. The lines and angles were reassuringly sharp, as if on an architect's drawing board, while outside was the contrast of colour frenzy and free shapes in the gardens. The pale clouds were languorous — creatures floating on their backs, appendages trailing into wisps — and on the blue, silent sky between them the narrow yet expanding streamers from invisible planes. That was my day really.

Many doors are locked here. I'm not sure whether the priority is to keep something in or something out. Overall, it is a voluntary incarceration, however, and by signing a few dispensations, and having family or friends to leave with, release is permitted, even if Dr Leong and his colleagues disapprove. So, a distinction between crime and illness is maintained.

In this place, we are a motley crew, in the archaic sense, and sad jesters much of the time. I consider myself to be displaced among these bottom dwellers, for I have a singular explanation for my condition. Dr Leong and Dr Milvance, however, tell me I have the typical traits of my condition — entitlement and denial — and so in the sessions I assume a guise of earnest rapprochement as Robbie Proctor sobs in his recitation of childhood neglect, or Olivia Mahaka in her soft voice links her descent to the experience of body shaming. Perhaps my favourite is little Casey, who has a faint, monastic smile and writes his doggerel on slips of paper that he places on the chairs before we have come in.

I have been in such institutions before and recognise certain core practices and tenets, although there is also individuality arising from proprietorship, governance, funding, location and the composition of both staff and patients. They are places marking the downswings of my life, but I have left them without subjugation and flown again.

In the entrance foyer is a large round of pounamu, highly polished on one side, the other in grizzled naturalness. It's the custom for most here to pass a hand across the smoothness, but LeRoy and I have the habit of patting the rougher side as a muted repudiation of allegiance. The greenstone rests on a kauri plinth, apparently untethered, but when LeRoy tried to lift it there was resistance. It must be attached from underneath. LeRoy intended no harm, his action was purely one of curiosity. Jade is enticing, and most of us reach out to touch it, look into its depths as if something might swim by. An addiction maybe.

At my individual meeting on Monday with Dr Milvance, I asked her which was my initial problem: depression or alcoholism? The Black Dog or the Grog? The chicken or the egg? It's a good one as a test for a therapist. Dr Milvance has a habit of fiddling with the hem of her skirt as she listens, as if uncertain whether it should be lifted. The origin of each is almost always the same, she said, but not necessarily manifested in tandem. Nothing new there. LeRoy told me that Dr Milvance has a son, Rory Piggot, who won a national kick-boxing title. Piggot because that's his father's name. I've never mentioned her son to her, but I like to imagine the pleasure she must feel at his accomplishment, for she's rather a clumsy woman. Dr Milvance has me on fluoxetine, but I'm familiar also with sertraline, paroxetine and citalopram. I can pronounce them and discuss with some authority the side effects of each.

I'm in this environment again not because of any personal inclination but because of Esther and Professor Ankkor. Esther is my third wife and Carl Ankkor is at least my fourth faculty head. I had given a rather declamatory lecture in E344, a large, tiered room, when I stumbled, fell, smashed my face on the iron lip of a step. I thought the address went rather well, but Professor Ankkor considered otherwise. The problem had begun earlier in the day when Paul came to say goodbye, as he was to fly to Melbourne the next afternoon to take up a visiting fellowship. Drinks and beer-battered cod in the Waka Restaurant with a view of the bay from our usual table. It wasn't beer that we drank, wine has always been my first choice, though the quality has improved markedly since the cardboard-enclosed bladders of student days. Later in life, I favoured full-blooded reds, especially Aussie shiraz. Brokenwood, now there's a name in reds. At the Waka with Paul it was dry riesling that I ordered — and reordered. The best Central Otago rieslings are now quite as good as those of the Rhine. I drank vodka alone after Paul left. Vodka, too, is an excellent companion and never has a pressing need to leave.

Hence the fall down the steps in E344, as I said, to hospital for brief admittance, and afterwards taken home with a face so swollen I could see much of it myself without a mirror. Esther came back from work early and looked after me with her usual dismissive solicitude. Carl turned up a day later and told me I was on leave until it was decided otherwise. He said, for Christ's sake and for my own, I should go somewhere and get myself sorted, and Esther agreed, saying I couldn't go on doing this sort of thing, that I was killing myself and hurting others too. Carl agreed.

Weeks I've been in this place, just as I've been weeks in other such places, each an underworld of denizens whom the world has abused and who abuse the world in turn. But I'll gather myself and go back to life outside, as I've done before. It was Carl who told me I should gather myself, and I nodded in solemn endorsement while wondering how exactly one gathers oneself.

Something interesting happened on Thursday a week ago. They cut down a large tree that I could see from my window. I'm not sure what species it belonged to, although I'd walked close to it often enough. It had dark, close foliage and was high and spreading. Maybe it was a macrocarpa; I'm not good with trees. Its execution was entertaining and instructive, but most fascinating was what happened afterwards in the evening. Groups of small birds swooped in, swirling in confusion in the space the tree had occupied. It had been a roosting tree. They returned by habit for two evenings, a bewildered vortex in the fading light. They might have cried, but I could hear nothing from within my room. Only a couple of days and they found a home elsewhere, and I didn't see them any more. I wonder how a roosting tree is chosen and whether birds mourn when it's felled?

A new guy is among us at therapy sessions now: Anton Miller, who is tall, scaly faced and has a voice of authority without apparent accomplishment as justification. Not many of us here speak with authority. LeRoy says a contrite demeanour is best suited to a recovery institution. Dr Leong asked Anton to tell his story, and as it drummed through the room I watched the faces of my companions for reaction. Most bore the subdued contours of inner pain, habitual when addicts imagine attention is elsewhere.

It was difficult, for me at least, to find connection to what Anton Miller said, despite its stridency. Anton is a two-handed addict — both drugs and drink — those mutual friends; whereas my attendants are depression and the bottle. If prescribed medication is excluded, then I can say I've never taken drugs, not even weed, which is now considered to be harmless by most people. No roll-your-owns, or cookies, no ice, acid or magic mushrooms, no injection kisses on pale skin. I don't boast of this, for it's just the mark of my path in life, my age and my appetites. Anton told us of time on container ships, in shearing gangs and in prison. I watched Nola pushing back the cuticles of her fingernails. She has an attractive face, except for the heavy pouches below her eyes, a store of unshed tears perhaps. Nola is non-residential and comes in for sessions but barely speaks. LeRoy says she was once married to a member of parliament and now works for a fishing company during long periods of sobriety. I suspect during these times she is a dry drunk — not drinking, but not committed to the recovery process and getting by on willpower alone. I don't know how LeRoy gets to know this stuff.

Having had considerable experience of rehab and read reasonably widely on my problems, it seems to me that three main explanations are generally put forward, individually or in combination: genetics, a troubled childhood, or a major life-change that triggers trauma. Genetics is a mystery to me, and to the therapists as well, I think, although they make no confession of that. A great many people have had addicts and depressives as parents, or siblings, and not succumbed themselves. I did have my DNA tested commercially just from general interest. Point-seven per cent North African was the only unexpected inheritance. I conjure in the distant past a single Arab on a loping camel amongst the shimmering dunes, but he is taciturn and sober.

As for childhood, which of us can unpack that box without joy and pain, instances of betrayal both inflicted and suffered, harboured resentments and guilt as well. Most of all, the loss of trust in others and the withdrawal into oneself. We recognise the experiences that have shaped us, shrunken and pallid exhibits, as if embalmed within glass bottles for our tuition.

I read somewhere that smell is the most evocative of all the senses. When my father walked into the kitchen with a suitcase and said he would be staying away for a long time, which meant for ever, my mother was at the bench cleaning tableware and filigree ornaments with a special cloth and Silvo, which is a liquid but forms and smells like a powder. I don't remember her reply, but she stood at the door to watch him drive away then came back to say we needed to get ready to visit Gran. We stayed on the farm several days, and except for a bee sting by the sheep dip I liked the time there. When we went home, the stuff was still on the bench with the blue-and-white tin of Silvo and the faintest powdery smell remaining in the room.

My father didn't entirely disappear, so I wasn't able to create some idealised figure from my past as emotional support. I met him very occasionally, which was sufficient to prove he was committed to other people and another life in which I had only a walk-on part. Just an ordinary, selfish guy, my father. He had no attractive qualities and the unattractive habit of spitting on the ground or in the sink. I can't recall him ever offering anything to me except an opinion. He moved from one useless job to another with hollow enthusiasm, and always bought a lotto ticket as salvation. The last time I saw him, years ago now, he asked me for money, saying he needed dentures and couldn't afford them.

LeRoy says men have to outgrow their fathers.

Now that the roosting tree is gone, I can see along Doyle Street from my favourite bench in the grounds, which is far enough around the west block to be out of sight from the majority of bedrooms. I sit there often, sometimes by myself, sometimes with LeRoy, and he sits there sometimes by himself too. Musing, he says. He and I spend a good deal of time musing. Also, I watch what goes on in Doyle Street, and no doubt some there watch us, for we are exhibits here: everyone knows we have cracked up and ended in rehab. Three houses down, in the place with a neat wood heap by the garage, a fitness fanatic lives. A small, square man who returns home in a suit earlier than most, has barely time to change and kiss his wife, before he emerges in dark track pants and runs towards me, then turns from Doyle Street into Liverpool Avenue and disappears for thirty minutes or so. He has an easy action and on those occasions that I witness his return, nothing of its impressiveness is lost. Most people are disappointed with their lives and the fit, square man seems an exception, although my observation is from a distance and incomplete.

Never jump from the Big Wheel at the top
For there's no way to survive such a drop

This was slipped under my door by Casey, and he waited out there until I came back from a talk with Dr Milvance, who was worried by reports that alcohol was being smuggled in. LeRoy and I are the obvious suspects and not without foundation. I like little Casey, the monk, but his mundane versifying has increased. No longer satisfied with chits on the session chairs, he comes directly to us with such offerings as this. I don't like to knock him back. There's therapeutic value, as we all know, and so I listened as he explained his processes — how the Big Wheel was a symbol for life and how he'd substituted 'way' for 'means' so that the lines would be of equal length. Craftsmanship is a significant source of self-esteem, Dr Leong says, and there are various activities available here, including origami and stone painting. Physical arts are encouraged rather than going online. Surely, what would be best is the carving of pounamu. I would sign up for that, but perhaps the material costs are too great for most, or the tutors unavailable.

I didn't invite Casey into my room. Conversed with at length, he tends to become maudlin, despite his engaging smile. LeRoy says he was a jeweller and twice the victim of ram raids, but he's never spoken of that in open session. I'm not sure how LeRoy gets to know these things, but he's a laid-back guy and listens well, so people tend to confide in him. It's such a southern USA sort of name, isn't it, but he says he's never been out of the country and that he's more Chinese than anything else. LeRoy has had his medication reduced and has begun a strenuous fitness programme to rid his body of impurities, spending much time on the exercycle with a towel around his neck. He said that personality should be more than a swirl of chemicals. LeRoy is a titular partner in a leading legal firm, but even the fine print hasn't been enough to save him. Not many people here have money, and he's given considerable respect because of it.

There's a tipping point in life, a time when you realise the past holds more for you than the future. It's not necessarily a matter of age. I think of my first wife more often now and with increasing guilt. Mary was collateral damage from the reckless selfishness I've never overcome. A first wife is maybe most damaged, the others know what they are getting into. And there are children with Mary, both men now and likely to come and see me only at my funeral. If you live just for yourself, then you likely die by yourself. I've pissed away a good deal of money and opportunity, but what's left will go to Mary. Esther has her own resources.

Dr Leong is interested in the dreams I have when depression hits. He thinks they may be of a cyclic nature that could be useful in gauging the entry and surfacing points of episodes. It's a facet of his clinical focus. I'm cold in the dreams, I tell him, always cold, and things seem far away and people's voices have an echo when there's no reason for it. He asked me about colours: which ones predominated and with what intensity. I told him that often a dark and glossy green is there, sometimes also sweeps of grey stretching like shore sand. It confirmed his opinion that green is the hue of depression rather than the black of conventional belief, and he told me I wasn't alone in experiencing that. He wished to know about smells too, those prevalent in my dreams when depressed, so I told him often the smell of fleece wool is strong, and he said no one had mentioned that before.

I said I didn't dream of sex when really down, but he wasn't much interested in that. Quite explicable, he said, because both alcohol excess and depression hammer the libido, and testosterone levels drop. He was more curious concerning what sort of people are in these dreams and how I interact with them. I was tempted to lie beguilingly, and so amuse myself by watching his reaction, but, because I respect the nature of academic research and value medical progress, what I told him was true, fragmentary and puzzling in a boring way. On his desk, Dr Leong has a sizable cactus in a yellow ceramic pot: one of those conventional plants, ribbed, light green and with white spikes. It reminds me of Santa Rosa, New Mexico, where I stayed for one night with my second wife while on a road trip. The town's mainly known for sinkhole lakes, but our stifling, faux-cowboy motel was stuffed with cacti.

Dr Milvance is a clever woman, intellectually and emotionally adroit, despite the physical clumsiness. She used the term 'whirlwind impulse' when we were talking of relapse. How apt and true. I can be sure in my resolve for weeks and then, when passing a restaurant or bar, be caught up with such a sudden urge that I feel forcibly propelled within and have a glass in my hand without conscious decision. Something destructive is always lurking, with the urge to take command. Not all of us have a unified personality. There's a sense of escape when I drink and also a brief time when pleasure and the senses are accentuated — the fragrances that fill out empty spaces, the glinting light through the movement of the liquid, the flavours as the return of old friends, even the feel of the round bottle in the hand. The fluids seem to have a molten nature as they're poured and a heavy luxury in the mouth. There's the sense of both relaxation and an increased comprehension of the world. All is entrapment, but even the knowledge of that is no prevention.

I haven't been great lately, and LeRoy tried to lighten my mood by telling me of a recent conversation with Anton Miller, who views women purely as a source of physical pleasure, like bouncy castles at the fairground. Anton's not really funny though. LeRoy and I agree he's suffering from Korsakoff Syndrome, though there's no confirmation from Dr Milvance or Dr Leong. They would never discuss one patient with another, and rightly so. As a recent arrival, Anton's still drying out, so the hallucinations will fade. Casey and Robbie Proctor are kind to him, as they are to us all, but Lloyd and Ravi challenge his delusions in what's here called 'levelling'. It's considered to be beneficial but not permitted to become personal during sessions. Nola and Jenny take no part in levelling, whether that's because of individual natures or their gender, I'm not sure.

A nor'wester on Friday, which is unusual at this time of year. I was encouraged to walk the three blocks to the botanic gardens and circled the pond there three times, thinking of Esther's last visit and her tolerance despite all that's happened. She deserves better companionship than I've been able to provide, although not without selfishness and presumptions of her own. I was wearing my brown corduroy jacket with metal buttons. My wives are united at least in a dismissal of corduroy in any form of clothing, but I've always had a fondness for it. It's a gentle fabric, yet hard wearing. When I was at university, there was a senior lecturer in the classics department who had a whole suit of it, top and bottom uniformly caramel, and I, perhaps alone, admired him for seeming impervious to derision.

There was a pond in the gardens of the city in which Mary and I lived years ago. It was called a lake but was really a pond. We would go there in the summer when the boys were small, feed the begging mallards and watch the dragonflies explore the rushes as small, living drones, although there were no drones then. I can't recall seeing dragonflies since, certainly not at the botanic pond on my walk yesterday. Winter now, of course.

The square man from Doyle Street has just arrived home, so I'll sit and wait for him to come out in his running gear and head off with assured athleticism in every stride. From his allegiance to strict routine, I imagine him a dogmatic man and so to be avoided. It's an assumption, I know, and based on insufficient evidence. Two houses farther down lives a guy with an electric scooter, and he swerves from road to footpath to maintain his speed when impatient in his coming and going. Often he has a yellow backpack, but he's too far away for me to see his face.

LeRoy is leaving soon, with the blessing of Dr Milvance and Dr Leong. We have pledged to keep in touch and to support each other. The friendship should be of benefit, but maybe a slip by one of us could also bring the other down. We both fear sadness more than the drink, yet there is a sort of serenity that accompanies hopelessness. Last night, I slept poorly and got up at five, went down to the side door and stood looking into the grounds. The time before dawn is the hour of the wolf in Russian folklore. It's difficult to be cheerful then. Something implacable was to be glimpsed, and the slow wind through the skeletons of winter trees whispered of futility.

After this morning's talk with Dr Leong, however, I feel better, for he considers I'm ready to go home and supports maintaining contact with LeRoy. I said nothing about the wolf hour and will sally forth into the world again. Esther is willing to have me back, and Carl Ankkor says when I'm ready there will be a place for me. The battle's not over. When rational, I acknowledge my own insignificance, yet somehow cannot imagine the world without me.

He and She

'Haven't we been here before?' he said, when the thin man had cleared the table of other people's dishes and withdrawn.

'No,' she said.

'You're sure? It seems familiar.' He took off his mask and smiled.

'Yes,' she said, 'I'm sure.' They were close to the sea, and even under the full sun a cool breeze blew over the water.

'Anyway,' he said, 'how've things been?'

'Ongoing inconvenience. I can't get used to it. The spells of working from home I'm okay with, but just so many things to remember when you go out that I can hardly be bothered. Other countries have it worse, I suppose. You'll know all about that.'

'Well, I was stuck there for months, began to think I'd never get home. Luckily, though, I always had work. The firm didn't seem to suffer and kept me on. For some professions, Covid is an opportunity not a threat, but you don't say much about that, of course. They even wanted me to stay permanently.'

'The place you're thinking of is further round the coast,' she said, 'by the marina. We were there not long before you went overseas.'

'And how's Duncan?' he asked after a pause.

'He's fine. Busy, as he always is. His brother died suddenly last June with no symptoms at all. Collapsed while washing the car. Heart failure, they said. The two of them were extra close and Duncan took it hard.'

'I think I met him. Leslie, wasn't it?'

'Lauchlan,' she said.

A sparrow landed on their wooden table with the impertinent

assurance of a practised scavenger. It found fragments of pastry, shat in gratitude and flew away.

'Bloody typical,' he said.

'That's why I always check the seats before sitting down at these outdoor places.'

'I'm sorry about Lauchlan. I remember now, it was at the races I met him. He'd had a good day and shouted a bottle of bubbly afterwards at that restaurant above the video shop.'

'It's gone now, the video shop,' she said.

'And he told amusing stories about the stuff that went on in the public service.'

'He was a manager at Foreign Affairs and Trade.'

'A nice guy. No wonder he and Duncan were close.'

'Less than two years between them. He wasn't even fifty,' she said.

'Is Duncan still mad keen on golf?'

'It's his relaxation, but he hasn't as much time as he'd like.'

'Golf's time-consuming. He'd be better with something like squash. In a couple of hours, you can sweat heaps, shower, have a quick beer and be home.'

The breeze fluffed her loose, dark hair across her face. She brushed it back and looked to a horizon that was all sea and sky.

'It always mystifies me,' he said, 'why it takes so long to bring a couple of lattes.'

'But you're an instant man, aren't you?'

'Maybe that's it.'

'I heard nothing from you at all when you were over there.'

'No,' he said, and with one finger lightly tapped her wrist. 'After what you said, I thought it was for the best.' In the pause that followed, they looked steadily at each other, and he smiled slightly.

'And where're you staying here?' she said.

'I've rented an apartment in Usher Drive. In that white high-rise close to the corner, but it's just temporary. A few jobs are on offer, so I'm not sure where I'll end up. I wouldn't mind staying here, but it depends.'

'We'll have to have you round,' she said.

'Sure. I'd like that,' he said. 'You were going to extend the decking from the lounge. What happened about that?'

'Yes, we did that, but now there's a close up of the garden weeds.'

'Come on. I know you. Everything will be in order.'

'You know me only in a biblical sense,' she said.

'I know you'll be happy, and that's the main thing. That's what matters.'

'So, we're moving on,' she said calmly and with a twitch of her lips that wasn't quite a smile. The thin man brought their lattes. 'Thank you,' she said.

At a table not far away, three young guys started laughing. Loud laughter, obviously for the purpose of drawing attention to themselves, rather than from spontaneous amusement. The long-haired one raised a fist above his head and said, 'You fucken betcha.'

'Someone's having a good time,' she said.

'Aren't we all?' he said. 'You can't let Covid rule you.'

'So, these job offers. They're good prospects?'

'Yeah, I think a couple of them are. There's a legal firm in Palmerston North that's pretty keen for me to go, but whether that's the place for me I'm not sure. I've always lived by the sea, even when overseas — especially overseas. The sea makes me feel comfortable. It's the friend I like to be close to.'

'And the other offers have the sea?'

'I'm weighing up one in Dunedin. I've got friends in Dunedin,' he said.

'And you've got friends here too.'

'Yes, I have, and I may well stay. I could even go back to Sanhepe Legal, slot pretty much into the old job.'

'Okay, let's get out of here,' said the long-haired guy, as the three of them sauntered past.

'Would you still be a partner?' she said when they were gone.

'I don't see why not. I know even more about corporate and commercial law now than I did when I was with them before.' He smiled to show he was being jocular rather than vain. New people settled at the table two away: an older couple obviously easy in each other's company and without the need for constant conversation. The man sat well back in his chair, his face raised to the sun and his eyes closed. The woman concentrated on her phone and massaged the lobe of her ear absently as she did so.

On the shingle beach, a woman wearing baggy shorts was picking up seaweed scraps and putting them in a plastic bag.

'What's that about?' he said.

'It's good on the garden.'

'Ah,' he said and told her about the Luxembourg Gardens and those at Versailles, which she knew better than he did.

'So, you're happy with your apartment,' she said.

'It's okay. A bit poky, only one bedroom, but it's fine for now. A woman on the level below has a cat named Terence. She roams the building calling for it at all hours. It brasses me off. What a name anyway. Nobody's called Terence, not even a cat.'

'Terence Rattigan was.'

'True, but he's been dead for ages now. Anyway, an apartment building's no place for pets.'

'Have you caught up with many people since coming back?' she asked.

'Not so much, no,' he said. 'What with restrictions and getting sorted back here, I haven't had much time for socialising. I did go into Sanhepes and have a chat with friends. They're having a big revamp of systems. Almost everything online.' He went on at some length about it, especially his reservations about security and retrieval. She listened, holding the green leather strap of her handbag, moving her thumb on the smooth surface.

A middle-aged woman jogger came towards them with a shuffling gait and no greater speed than that of a walker. She paused by the low stone wall, adjusted the visible bra straps on her soft shoulders with a sense of accomplishment and ambled back the way she'd come. They watched her go and looked at each other. No comment was necessary.

'It'll be great to pick up again if I stay,' he said.

'Some things aren't possible,' she said. 'Not in themselves, but because of what's gone before.'

'That's it then?'

'We're not going through it all again,' she said.

'Even if I told you I've decided that not having someone to love is worse than not being loved yourself?'

'Enough's enough,' she said.

'I'd still like to keep in touch. I look forward to coming round, as you said. I'm comfortable with it. We've been friends for a long time.'

'Oh, we can be friends,' she said.

'That's okay then. I'd like to visit, but only when it suits you. I missed you when I was overseas. It's not the same there. Anyway, are you good to go?'

'Yes,' she said. She stood and picked up her soft leather handbag, cradling it under her arm as French women do a lapdog. They began walking to their cars. The sea wind was behind them and seemed to encourage departure.

'That breeze is coming up,' he said.

'I always think that wind's the voice of nature's indifference.'

'How very profound you are this morning. I'm impressed.'

'You know you're welcome to visit,' she said.

'Great. I'll be in touch. Give Duncan my regards,' he said. 'Mention the squash to him. It's ideal for busy professional guys.'

'I will,' she said.

'You know,' he said, before they parted to go to their own cars, 'Whatever you say, I still think we've been to this place before.'

The Batman Drop

The devil is kept busy in other parts of the world and gives cursory attention to Te Tarehi. There was the Tamahana's piebald horse that disappeared, of course, Brian Rickles, who took undeclared cash for his carpentry, so defrauding the state, and widespread growing of cannabis, but of that it was said legalisation was coming and people just smoked it or made cookies anyway. Very little hash.

Burglary was different, especially of Mrs Pomare's store, because her husband had drowned while out for crayfish only seven months before and she was coping with that and the care of two little girls. And days after the store, someone stole the batteries from Guy Fomison's tractor and Ford Ranger. Worst of all was old Mr Mulgrew being beaten up in his own crib, and his tinned food stolen. He was pretty much an invalid before it happened and a good deal worse afterwards. Everyone knew he relied on tinned stuff and had something of a hoard. Old Mulgrew wasn't the most popular resident of Te Tarehi, bit of a boozer and bully in his day, but no one deserves what happened to him. Marjorie Camell was the local stirrer but had a real concern for what happened in Te Tarehi. She rang the police station.

'Rampant,' she said. 'Crime is rampant here, and what are you doing about it? Absolutely rampant, I'm telling you.'

The police station is in Warrington and has responsibility for Te Tarehi. Normally that necessitated little action, but after the burglaries and bashing, Sergeant Reg Hall told Constable Hamplar he was in charge of finding out what the hell was going on in Te Tarehi.

'You drop everything and concentrate on Te Tarehi, okay Kevin?' the sergeant said. 'And you're part Māori, so that should be an advantage.'

Kevin's mother had said there was Ngāti Raukawa blood, but they'd never followed up much on that, and a policeman is a policeman anyway as far as most people are concerned, but he did feel slightly chuffed that he was singled out to deal with Te Tarehi's crime wave. Sergeant Hall made it sound almost like a mission. Warrington's police force was just the sergeant and four constables, individual missions were rare, and Kevin Hamplar was the youngest of the team.

Kevin decided to spend all the next day at Te Tarehi, interview Mrs Pomare, Guy Fomison and old Mulgrew, maybe even a reassuring call on Mrs Camell, although she hadn't suffered directly from any crime. He was disappointed when Sergeant Hall told him he'd have to take his own car because there were only three police vehicles available, and he didn't want one out of town all day. There would be reimbursement for petrol, of course, but Kevin thought it would have been better for Te Tarehi to see an official car, know their problems were being taken seriously. There were complaints that not enough attention had been paid initially to the incidents. Kevin put this case to Sergeant Hall but was told to just get on with it, and with his own Corolla.

Most of the road to Te Tarehi is close to the coast: abrupt headlands and sweeps of dark iron sand, the sea matching its colour to the weather. It was a route that Kevin quite enjoyed. As he drove, he looked for spots good for fishing, although he never seemed to find much time for that, not solely because of his job but because he and Sharon had a year-old baby daughter. Sandcastles and nappies, and he wouldn't have it any other way.

He thought about the goings on at Te Tarehi too. The evening before, he'd read through the files, especially that about the burglary of Mrs Pomare's shop. He didn't know her, but according to the initial enquiry everybody liked her, which made Kevin think that it wasn't a local responsible. Someone drifting through perhaps, and a drifter wouldn't be interested in batteries, so he didn't think the offences were necessarily related. He was thinking about the third thing, the bashing of old Mulgrew, when a woman in a loose red dress appeared on the road in front, waving her arms, not hysterically but rather like an airport guy guiding in a plane. She was a good way off, and Kevin had time to slow and pull to the side. She came to the driver's door as he got out.

'Thanks for stopping,' she said. 'And it's so good you're a policeman,' as she took in the uniform. 'Couldn't be better when I need a bit of help.' She put out her hand and said, 'I'm Frieda Menzies. We farm just up from here.'

'Constable Hamplar,' Kevin said. As they shook hands, he found it oddly formal. 'What's the trouble?'

'My ute won't start. It's down on the beach. It'll be the battery again. We've been meaning to do something about a replacement. You've got leads maybe?'

'As a matter of fact, I have,' said Kevin. He had them always in the car.

'Great. If you're not going to some emergency, I'd really appreciate it,' she said. 'Normally I have my phone with me and could call my husband, but it's always Murphy's Law, isn't it?'

'Usually, yeah. No, I've got time if it's just a jump start. Otherwise, I can ring in for you.'

So, Frieda got in and they drove off the road, down the track through the scrub to the beach where the Hilux was parked. On the way, she explained that she'd been collecting seaweed for her garden. Kevin drew up nose to nose with the ute, and Frieda got out purposefully. She had long, grey hair, loose on her shoulders, but was agile and strong. She popped the hood of the Toyota and attached her end of the cables as efficiently as Kevin did his, talking all the time about her garden and the benefits of seaweed. He noticed she had big feet, or she might have borrowed her husband's brown sneakers to wear on the sand. The ute fired on the first try, and she left it running while Kevin put away the gear.

'Have you got time for a cup of tea?' she said. 'We're just down the road a couple of miles.'

'Thanks, but no, I'd better push on. I need to be in Te Tarehi.'

'Well, my thanks to you. I really appreciate it,' and she put out her hand again to shake his in an almost masculine way. 'I probably won't admit to my husband I was silly enough to get stranded, but I'll make sure a new battery's on the way.' She got into her vehicle, waved and went bouncing through the scrub towards the road.

Kevin didn't follow straight away. He needed a piss. Although there was nobody about that he could see, he walked away from the dirt turning-circle towards a clump of broom along the beach. You have to be more aware of possible scrutiny when you're a policeman. As he stood in the scrub, a small single-engine plane flew over from the south, dipping low to the sea, and something fell from it into the water, quite close to the shore, splashed and floated. The plane gained height and continued north, but almost immediately a powerboat jetted around the headland. It was clear enough what was happening. Kevin's police belt was in the car: the belt heavy with radio, retractable baton, pepper spray, gloves, et al. His duty bag was there also. He thought of running back to get the belt, but the powerboat was bearing down on the object floating just beyond the small breakers, so he ran down the beach and waded out, relying on his uniform as deterrent and protection. He reached the small package before the boat, which circled around him, the two men aboard staring, assessing, holding a hand before their mouths to prevent identification. It was a brief face-off, nothing shouted, nothing signalled, until the outboard motor roared, and the boat sped off again.

He waded to the dark sand, walked awkwardly up to his car with shoes squelching and the heavy uniform trousers clinging to his legs. He radioed in and got senior constable Brian Eccles, told him all about it, although they both knew there wasn't much that could be done immediately. There was no chopper, or drone, at Warrington.

'I'll go straight round the headland to check up there, but they'll be long gone, I reckon. Then I'll drive back in and change, 'cause I'm drenched. I'm going to tell the Te Tarehi people I won't be coming today.'

'Makes sense. Okay,' said Constable Eccles. 'I'll tell Reg when he's back.'

'I've got the drop though.'

'Good one. Bloody good work,' said Eccles.

Nobody, of course, was at the small beach around the point when Kevin drove there; only the vehicle and trailer tracks and the drift of marram grass in the sea breeze amid the scrubby dunes. It was uncomfortable driving in wet uniform, and he was keen to get home and change, keen also to see Sharon and baby Isla.

When showered and in a dry uniform again, he sat with them in the toy-strewn lounge, Isla on his knee, and told the story of the morning. It didn't need much embellishment, the reality had interest enough, and although there had been no arrests, no identifications, there were the two wads of what was almost certainly cocaine, not much bigger than supermarket meat packs.

'These alone are worth bloody heaps,' he told Sharon. Two-hundred thousand or so, I'd say. The dealers here often cut it with other crap stuff.' He put his daughter down and showed Sharon the Batman logo on the packages. 'It's South American, almost for sure. That's where Batman drugs originate. People here will be highly pissed off, and the pilot will get the hammer.'

'How come it doesn't sink?'

'I don't know. Cocaine just doesn't.'

'Let's keep one and fly to Paris,' Sharon said. It was quite exciting, more so than any other things Kevin had told her about his work. Being with Isla almost all the time was the most rewarding thing, the most important, but not exciting.

'It'll be the gangs here,' said Kevin. 'Anyway, I'd better go in and make a report. I'm glad I got the stuff otherwise there'd be nothing to show for it all.'

'Did you have to swim for it?'

'No, but the water was up to my chest. Any further out and the boat guys would have scooped it up. Would've too if I'd been just a bit later getting to it. Being in uniform was the clincher, I think.'

'You could've been shot,' Sharon said, suddenly serious. She was thinking of the TV programmes with people getting knocked off all over the place because of drugs.

'These guys weren't expecting anything, and they probably thought I had backup with me.'

'You're okay. That's all that really matters,' she said.

Not only was Sergeant Hall keen to hear about it, but Brian Eccles and the other two constables were there too. The whole four-man and one-woman Warrington police force in the main office as Kevin detailed his clash with the bad guys. He kept to the facts, omitting only that he'd been having a piss when he saw the plane. After all, Constable Hinewai Hapeta was present, and it was a detail not relevant to an official report. The two Batman packs were on the long table, and Kevin's colleagues regarded them with interest. Sergeant Hall said he'd seen the same sort of stuff before and wasn't surprised.

'I've actually been following up a couple of leads recently,' he said. He did give Kevin due credit, however, and even mentioned that Frieda Menzies had rung him to say how much she'd appreciated Constable Hamplar's help with her ute. 'You going down to the beach to help was what made it all happen really,' he said. 'Otherwise, we'd be none the wiser.' Kevin had experienced his share of mistakes and embarrassments as a young cop and found the day's success a pleasant affirmation. Sure, much of what had happened was coincidence, but he'd made the right choices along the line, and he knew that.

Warrington doesn't have a fully fledged newspaper, but there's a local give-away that includes news items. Sergeant Hall got in touch with the editor and also the city papers, so there were interviews with him and Constable Hamplar. Even a short clip on television, with Kevin and Sergeant Hall standing on the beach where it happened. Much was made of the Batman motif and links to major-crime syndicates. Marjorie Camell told everybody she wasn't surprised — so many bikies around recently, she said.

The whole thing kept the police team busy for several days, but they weren't able to turn up anything that led to arrests, just a few minor offences unrelated to their enquiries. There were too many rough landing strips on farmland where the plane could have left from. When Kevin finally went up to Te Tarehi, he wasn't able to make any breakthrough there either, except that the Tamahana's piebald horse was found wandering on Māori land by a local.

Kevin was three years at the Warrington station before being posted to New Plymouth. Nothing else in that time came up to match the Batman drug seizure. His colleagues even called him Batman for a while. The whole thing was forgotten in the end — except by Kevin and his family. It cheered him whenever he drove up that way.

Sophie Headlong

Sophie was a widow at forty-three, which is unusual in the twenty-first century, at least in peaceful countries. Blake, her husband, was the same age when he drowned while piloting a Cessna 152 that crashed into the sea in the Marlborough Sounds, only a hundred metres or so from the shore. He was a hobby pilot, with a full-time job as manager of the online side of a large distribution hub. The accident featured on the television, so everyone knew about it, and Sophie received a great many expressions of sympathy, which she appreciated, but they made the loss no easier to bear.

The suddenness of it, the unexpectedness, the perceived unfairness blunted her emotional responses for months, and she could recollect little of that time. Mourning came later, when she was more often by herself or with those who had known Blake, especially her daughters Freya and Esme. She was able to think of the good times without crying, and most of their marriage had been good times, or difficult times that they countered together. Her work helped. Sophie was in a government department and concerned with strategy and infrastructure, the concentration on which was a healthy distraction. Only fourteen months after Blake's death, she was promoted to team leader with responsibility for eleven well-qualified people.

Sophie had friends, but almost all of them were married and with teenagers, busy people who were supportive but also often preoccupied. Freya and Esme were old enough to feel some responsibility for their mother and encouraged her to try new things. That's why they were interested when the invitation to the Headlong family reunion arrived, and why they wanted Sophie to be interested as well. Sophie was

Mrs Duval, but her maternal grandmother had been a Headlong, and so she could claim to be one too. She'd never been much interested in family history. Her parents never talked about it, for them the present and the future were more immediate. She knew Headlong was of English origin and unusual but hadn't been sufficiently curious to investigate, although Google and ancestry sites had made that relatively easy.

The invitation was quite formal, detailed and contained in a card that had the Headlong crest on the cover: animals standing on their hind legs and lots of wreathing foliage. A committee had been set up to organise the reunion: five enthusiasts, two of whom still had the Headlong surname. One of these was Norman Headlong, a retired clergyman who lived in Wellington, which was where the reunion was to be held.

'Go on, Mum. It's something different,' said Freya, who was in her first year at university.

'Yeah, go for it,' agreed Esme, who was two years younger. 'You could find we're all related to a duke or a prime minister. We might've had an abbey or a castle. Bluebloods for sure.'

'Mainly poor people came out to the colonies,' Sophie told them. 'If you were doing well, why would you leave for the other side of the world? Most family crests are made up.' Nevertheless, she decided to go, even though her mother wasn't interested. She was aware of her own tendency to withdraw since Blake's death and knew that was unhealthy, so perhaps the reunion would be a good thing. She could share with the girls what she discovered about family origins, maybe even expand in time to research the Duvals, whom Blake had said were originally French. The Headlongs were ample for the time being, though.

As preparation for the reunion, she did a minimum of research, almost all online. She didn't want to appear completely ignorant to others she met in Wellington. Probably many zealous, enquiring Headlongs would be there. No wonder the term 'family tree' is used — among her grandparents alone there were O'Sullivans, Neckermanns and Quills as well as Headlongs. Given the proliferating complexity, Sophie stuck just to Headlongs and only a few generations back. There aren't many Headlongs in the world: a rare name with no authoritative account of meaning and seeming to have originated in Berkshire.

Two months after replying to the invitation, Sophie was sent more information, including a schedule: the Friday evening enrolment, welcome drinks and nibbles; a Saturday morning visit to the home once belonging to one of the first New Zealand Headlongs; a graveyard homage in the afternoon for the same individual; video, speeches and dinner in the evening; and on Sunday, photographs, exchanges, conclusions and then dispersal. Accompanying the schedule was a much reproduced and deteriorated photograph of a nineteenth-century Berkshire Headlong. A staring, rigid man with a soft, ploughman's hat and a seemingly dark, thunderous sky behind him.

Sophie flew to Wellington on the Friday morning, checked in to her hotel, shopped in the afternoon and in the evening went to the reunion session at the RSA in Thorndon. She knew no one and so busied herself selecting something from the nibbles table and briefly talking to the woman pouring wine. By the time Norman Headlong asked them to be seated, Sophie had counted sixty-three people and wondered to how many of them she was related and how many were merely companions to people who claimed a Headlong connection. She sat well towards the back, on one of the blue plastic and chrome stackable chairs and was joined there by a woman of about her own age, who introduced herself as Catherine Aimes. Catherine was also by herself, although married.

'Chris said he'd come,' she told Sophie, 'but he'd be bored silly. The details of your own family are often quite enough, without the ramifications of someone else's.'

Catherine wore a light pant suit, ideal for summer, yet a precaution against Wellington weather, and her blue leather handbag was just like those Sophie had most admired in a main street boutique that afternoon. There's something about genuine Italian leather. The shoulder bag Sophie had bought in Sienna years ago was still serviceable. They talked together of handbags and Italy, until Norman stood up on the small portable dais to welcome them all. An elderly man with large features on a very thin, tendon-strung neck. He said there were only seven people present with the surname Headlong, and he seemed pleased with the exclusivity, as if it bestowed more Headlong genes, rather than, say, an indication that daughters had been prevalent in the lineage.

'Some Headlongs might have chosen to change their name,' Catherine said to Sophie quietly. 'It's a bit of an oddity, isn't it?'

'The suggestion of impetuosity or intransigence,' said Sophie. 'I've been accused of both at times.'

'I don't see one Māori or Chinese Headlong. Not a one.'

'They know better,' said Sophie.

'Continental names have more class. Duval, now that's French, surely. A château or two there, I'd say.'

'I'm working on it,' said Sophie. Both of them enjoyed their surreptitious, mild mockery of the reunion they'd nevertheless chosen to attend. And Norman Headlong was making a meal of it, reciting his own connections and asking them all to contribute both content and money towards a Headlong family history to be privately published. Perhaps he missed the pulpit time of former years. Ten minutes also of explaining the location of Saturday's venues and the best ways of reaching them.

Afterwards, when drinks and mingling resumed, Sophie and Catherine knew they should be meeting and greeting as many of the others as possible, establishing facial recognition at least for the weekend to come, but they'd already instinctively formed a small cell of their own within the body of the reunion, and they remained apart, talking together. Sophie felt an affinity, and not just because she was alone, and she sensed Catherine felt it too. They asked questions of each other that grew increasingly personal. As the crowd began to thin out, Catherine asked Sophie where she was staying, and when told she said, 'You must stay with us not by yourself in a hotel. Hotels are soulless places when you're by yourself.'

'I'll only be there to sleep. It's a full weekend schedule, but thanks.'

'I mean it, truly. You haven't a car, and we can drive to venues together. Company for us both.'

'I'm not going to turn up with you tonight as a stray. No way. Your husband's probably watching the TV in his pyjamas.'

'Okay, but you best be checked out of that hotel by nine-thirty tomorrow, and I'll pick you up there to go to this Headlong house we're seeing in the morning, and you'll come home with me when everything's over. Headlongs stick together.'

'Are you sure of this?' asked Sophie.

'Absolutely.'

'Your husband will be fine with a stranger for the weekend?'

'You'll like Chris,' said Catherine. 'He's a very easy guy. He'll be happy I've got someone to do the Headlong thing with.'

In the morning, Sophie was waiting with her case at the hotel, and Catherine arrived promptly to collect her. Sometimes when two people have met for the first time and felt especially compatible — clicked, Freya would say — a second meeting is a disappointment, revealing less attractive aspects of personality or reducing by familiarity those that initially appealed. It wasn't so with them. Talk was easy and so were silences. They found they were not closely related but had much in common. Catherine also worked in a government department, involved in support services for diplomatic staff. She too had children near adulthood. She still had a husband, though, and as they drove to Lower Hutt Sophie explained why she didn't.

'I'm still not used to it,' she said. 'You have a boyfriend, next a husband, then you have kids and become a family, and that's supposed to just carry on, isn't it, unless you start hating each other? Nothing's ever perfect, but we were happy until suddenly he was gone. I even blamed him for a while. He left me.'

'How did your girls get over it?'

'Okay, I think. We don't talk about it now. Not because it doesn't matter but because we can't change anything. A few times we've been to the grave together. Freya wears his tracksuit top when she goes jogging, but we haven't talked about that.'

'A hell of a thing for you all,' said Catherine. She was a confident driver in the city traffic, overtaking others with verve and continuing to talk as she did so. Sophie noticed the pink nail polish and the two rings on her left hand, one a ruby flanked by diamonds, the other channel set with large, coloured stones.

'Tell me more about your children,' Sophie said, and as she listened she wondered what Catherine's perfume was called. It was unobtrusive, hints of sandalwood, but apparent within the confines of the car. Sophie liked it, and when it wasn't too much a break from the topic of family, she asked about it, and they talked about fragrances, finding agreement there also. Catherine's hair was blonde, heavy and short, faint parentheses formed at the edges of her mouth when she smiled, which was often, and Sophie liked looking at her. She knew she could travel a long time with Catherine without wishing to be anywhere else, but the drive was soon over.

The Headlong house in Lower Hutt wasn't special, no architectural features of note, no particularly attractive garden. A wooden bungalow, with a much more recent corrugated-iron garage largely obscuring it. Headlongs hadn't lived there for nearly a hundred years, but owners Jean and Maurice Staples had agreed the reunion folk could visit. The Staples had never heard of the Headlongs before being approached but felt a certain pride in their home being of interest, and satisfaction in the five-hundred dollars given to them for making it available. The Headlong committee had arranged for tables and forms on the uneven lawn, and that's where everyone had morning tea, and most spent the majority of their time there because there was so little of interest to view within the house. Norman Headlong did claim that an old, dark-stained wardrobe in the main bedroom would have been there in Headlong days, but there was no provenance in support of that. Jean and Maurice Staples joined the morning tea, and the next-door family of five stood a little back from the fence to observe, with the occasional pretence of gardening. People cycling and driving past stared too. Such a big group of people gathered so publicly on the front lawn of the small, old house.

A middle-aged guy in jacket and jeans sat down, without invitation, with Sophie and Catherine, introducing himself as Nigel and asking them where they came from. He had good posture and a ready smile. He was obviously looking for someone to spend the night with but was prepared first to tell them in a falsely self-deprecating way of his business trips to Dubai and New York. The women soon tired of him, fully understanding what he was after, but they weren't rude, and when he realised they weren't interested he moved on.

'I'm off for another sandwich,' he said, 'and might pop into the house again. Can I get you ladies anything?' Their reply, of course, was that they were fine, but thanks.

'Do men realise how obvious they are?' said Sophie when he'd gone.

'Do they care?' said Catherine. 'Do many come on to you now you're single again?'

'I'm usually with people I know.'

'And does that make a difference?'

'That's really cynical.' said Sophie.

'Realistic,' said Catherine. 'Take Nigel now. Either of us would have done for tonight. It always amazes me how indiscriminate men are.'

'Well, I suppose he wasn't after a life partner.'

'And now he's propositioning a sandwich,' said Catherine. They had a laugh at that. Catherine was an attractive woman, and Sophie thought her knowledge of men could be considerable. The bob-cut fair hair suited her, and she was naturally graceful in movement. Sophie felt she herself had a tendency to neglect makeup, although she'd kept her figure, despite two kids and a dislike of gym workouts.

'You know what,' Catherine said.

'What?'

'I don't think we should bother with the cemetery this afternoon. Let sleeping Headlongs lie, I say, and Norman will have a set speech that keeps us standing about for ever. Who was this Headlong guy again?'

'Tobias Frederick, I think.'

'Why don't I take you round the bays instead? Too nice a day to spend in a graveyard. Sun without wind. You take advantage when that happens in Wellington.'

'Sounds good to me,' said Sophie.

'After all, nothing's compulsory, is it, and we'll be back at the RSA for the dinner and everything tonight. For now, though, there's a place I know in Eastbourne that has wonderful salads and a view of the sea. And if you like we can go back into the city for shopping later.'

'As long as you don't mind all the driving, and it's my wine shout. You know, those people are still standing at the fence and watching everything. All these Headlongs crowded on the lawn and yacking. We must seem an odd bunch, and the Staples aren't even related to us, knew nothing about old Tobias Frederick building their place.'

'Everything about the Headlongs seems an oddity though, don't you think? A Headlong reunion just has to be farcical. I mean, a name like that.'

'Novelty value, perhaps,' said Sophie, 'rather than humdrum Smith, Jones and Brown, and neither of us have to use it day to day.'

'Aimes is my own name,' said Catherine. 'Women don't need to take their husband's.'

'But isn't that from your patriarchal line, though?'

'True, time for a change.'

'I was an O'Sullivan.'

'Get back to it,' said Catherine. 'Sophie O'Sullivan's got a ring to it. Like in an Irish movie. A colleen with a sparkle in your eye.'

'I just might,' said Sophie, not only to express agreement but because the idea appealed to her. Ireland was a country she'd never been to, and so she was able to sustain agreeable myths.

People were beginning to leave the Lower Hutt house, most in a manner that suggested it wasn't a high point of the reunion. Norman Headlong started talking with Maurice Staples about the truck coming to collect the tables and chairs. Of the neighbours at the fence, only two young girls remained, steady in their scrutiny. Norman saw Sophie and Catherine walking away and broke off talking to Maurice to call after them, asking if they knew the way to the graveyard for the afternoon gathering.

'All set,' Sophie called back.

'We'll be truants,' Catherine told her as they walked to the car. 'I used to enjoy being a truant, and no one will notice we're not there.'

'Nigel might.'

'I don't think so. He was chatting up that tall woman with the purple top and very white teeth. I've been thinking of getting my teeth whitened. Meaning to look into it, but there always seems something else to do. Work's quite mad at the moment. I'd like a job all by myself, counting kiwi and kākāpō in a forest somewhere.'

'White teeth wouldn't matter at all there,' volunteered Sophie.

'Exactly,' said Catherine.

They talked about their jobs and their families as they drove around the bays to Eastbourne. Important things, and they spoke without reservation. They continued to talk at the café by the sea as they ate the salads Catherine recommended and drank the Marlborough cab sav Sophie chose. The sound and undulation of the sea had a lulling effect, and the only stridency was of the gulls. It would be good to live by the sea, Sophie thought, close enough to hear its voice and have its strong, feral smell. Blake once told her that it was when you flew that you realised how much of the world was ocean. Sophie had rarely experienced that with him, despite a private pilot licence permitting him to have passengers. He'd never discouraged her, but Sophie formed the impression that solitary flying was what he enjoyed the most.

Catherine and Sophie decided not to go to the city shops but farther on to Catherine's home in Roseneath. There was no sense of guilt because they were fully paid up for the Headlong reunion, and Tobias Frederick in his Headlong grave would never know they were absent. Normally, Sophie's life was quite structured, but the weekend was becoming increasing unpredictable, which gave her a sense of freedom and possibility, emphasised perhaps because Catherine was happy to take the lead.

Roseneath is an admired suburb, but Catherine's place wasn't especially impressive from the outside: a brick home with a sunroom added and only one garage. The interior, however, had been extensively remodelled, and the bedroom into which they took Sophie's case was spacious with pale-blue walls and white drapes. From the lounge, there was a view across the bay and, more immediately, houses stepping down the hill. No street noise, just a distant thunder sometimes from planes leaving the airport.

'We're in the city without being in the city,' Catherine said.

Having a Headlong family connection had brought them together, but Sophie said they should try to find the closest physically they had ever been before, unknowingly. They hadn't lived in the same towns, hadn't gone to the same university, or attended the same concerts by touring stars. The best they could come up with was that in mid-June 2004 they were both in Paris, but that's a big place and probably they didn't pass each other on the way to the Musée d'Orsay or be part of the same waiting crowd on the platform of the Gare de Lyon.

'Chris and I want to go back,' Catherine said, 'but we'll wait now until Scott's settled at uni. And we won't want to bum around the way we did in our twenties. I want to stay in decent places and not queue for a shower. Too many special places still to visit that previously we couldn't afford to go to.'

'People say everything's so expensive now.'

'Would you go by yourself anyway?'

'I think I would,' said Sophie. 'I don't fancy a tour itinerary, though, but it's not a plan for me for a while. I'd quite like to go to Japan, Korea and Vietnam. Never been to any of those. And back to Italy, of course.'

Sophie had always found friends, some of them close, although, once married, family was her emotional centre. She was drawn to Catherine, however, and aware their personalities and attitudes were complementary, and there was a certain physical attraction. Catherine's skin was great, her movement agile and her smile had a twitch that suggested an ironic detachment of view. Her hips were not pronounced, which could be why she favoured pant suits.

'We could still go to the shops,' Catherine said. 'But it's coffee time already, and I'm easy. What do you think?'

'I'm happy just to blob out, and we've got more reunion tonight, haven't we? I did all the shopping I needed yesterday afternoon, so I don't mind.'

'It'll give me time to get something for Chris and Scott's tea. Chris is cycling. God knows where Scott is. Generally, he's home before six. They can scratch around for themselves in the kitchen and don't mind, but I might make wraps or a pasta for them.' Catherine went into the kitchen but only to make coffee. When she returned, they began talking of travel again and both the satisfactions and irritations of their jobs.

They were still there when Chris arrived home. A guy well over six feet, with a firm handshake, balanced stance and the faint smell of sweat.

'So, another of the Headlong clan, welcome,' he said. 'How's it been going?'

'Good,' said Sophie, 'although we decided to miss this afternoon's session.'

'Tombstone worship, so we skipped it,' added Catherine, 'but tonight's the big feast.'

'I'll just have a shower and then we can talk.'

'We've got to be there by half-past six, so there's not a lot of time. I thought I'd do a salad wrap for you before we go.'

'Sounds good,' he said.

'Do you know when Scott's coming home?'

'No idea,' Chris said.

The women went out to the kitchen, and they talked as Catherine made the wraps. Chris soon joined them, but there was little time together as both Sophie and Catherine wanted showers themselves before getting ready for the reunion dinner.

'If you want to drink tonight, I'm happy to run you down to the do and pick you up afterwards,' Chris offered.

'Thanks, but from what we've seen of the Headlongs, I don't think it's going to be that sort of night,' Catherine said.

'A single chaste glass of Prosecco to toast with if we're lucky,' said Sophie.

'We paid enough, though,' said Catherine.

Turned out they were entitled to two glasses of an unidentified and undistinguished bubbly that may well have been Prosecco, and there was no provision for the purchase of anything more or different. The food, however, they had to admit wasn't half bad: no heavy meats or stodgy, overcooked vegetables, but ham from the bone, couscous, bean and green salads.

Norman spoke between the main course and dessert, which meant there was ample time for the main to go down. He talked about the challenges of colonial times for both immigrants and Māori, with emphasis on the role of missionaries. He was almost sure the first Headlongs here were chapel people. Norman managed to include a good deal of his own ecclesiastical background in his talk, and there were no questions on its conclusion.

After the meal, the tables were cleared, but everyone remained seated to listen to Associate Professor Claibourne talk entertainingly about a pre-Victorian novel called *Headlong Hall*. A satire of manners, he said, and as far as he knew the only time that the Headlongs had surfaced in English literature or any literature. Sophie and Catherine had never heard of it, or the author — Thomas Love Peacock. With a name like Thomas Love Peacock he had no right to be making fun of the Headlongs, Catherine and Sophie agreed, but nevertheless they decided it was a book they'd like to read. The more they experienced the family reunion, the greater pleasure they found in mockery.

A video was the final item for the evening. Filmed by Norman Headlong, of course, during a trip he and his wife made to Berkshire while visiting the UK. Shaky frames of Headlong homes and grave-stones, the insides of small churches and three brief interviews with local Headlongs, who seemed quite bewildered by Norman's attention, and to whom he could prove no greater connection than a common surname. One lank-haired woman stood in her doorway to talk, not even inviting Norman inside.

'I've had enough of the effing Headlongs,' said Catherine as they drove home. 'Do you think we really have to go tomorrow?'

'Farewells and photos,' Sophie said, 'but we haven't really been part of it, have we? We've been aloof and mocking, I suppose, and not made the effort to get to know the others. I can hardly remember a name, just the faces. I do feel a bit guilty.'

'So what?' said Catherine. 'I've met you, and that's been the best thing of all, and it's so relaxing not to feel a responsibility to make sure an event goes off well. It's liberating to be irresponsible every now and then. You get sick of being the organiser, holding things together.'

'Know what you mean. We needn't go, and Norman will be wanting us all to cough up for the proposed family history book.'

'I'm easy,' said Catherine.

'Let's see how we feel in the morning. Maybe we'll have an attack of conscience or Headlongs will appear in our dreams as enforcers.'

'Two days of it,' said Catherine, 'and we still have no idea where the name came from.'

Chris was up when they got back, but Scott still not home. Chris showed a dutiful interest in the dinner event, but Sophie was more interested in his job as a vet.

'I do just about anything except fish,' he said. 'I have a block about fish. Birds aren't my favourite either, but they're part of the deal in a city practice.'

'I enjoy those TV vet programmes,' said Sophie. 'Such a variety.'

'But they're always hauling calves out of cows' backsides with a rope around the hooves,' said Catherine.

'Done that,' said Chris, 'but mostly for me it's cats and dogs and horses. I do get called into the zoo at times, though. I've even fitted a prosthetic hoof to a giraffe.'

'Neat.' Sophie was impressed.

'Well, the anaesthetic was the biggest danger. And there's less pressure than being a doctor. Losing a giraffe is better than losing a person, even though there are far fewer giraffes in the world.'

'The good thing', said Catherine, 'is that our jobs are so different we find common ground in subjects unrelated to them. We can leave work at the office.'

It seemed to Sophie that they had a good marriage. They were relaxed together, and later from her room she heard them in their bedroom laughing. Always a true sign when a couple laugh together. Sophie was happy for them, but it made her think of Blake, so there was sadness too. She remembered how sometimes when talking, just the two of them, they would reach out their hands and clasp each other's — interlocking fingers even — and keep on talking. There was some compensatory benefit in him going when he did, she told herself. She could remember him in his prime, when they were in the fullness of their love together, and she'd never have to see him become weak, old and silly, a doddery man heading into death with her. It was still sad, though, and she thought about her husband, and for the umpteenth time she worried about the effect his loss might be having on Freya and Esme. She should talk to them about him, but she didn't know how to begin or once begun how to end.

She lay in Catherine's guest room, the faint light from the street sufficient to show an occasional shiver in the curtains and glint from the metal base of the bedside lamp. She might sign up for the Headlong history and try contributing a small piece detailing their own family — Sophie, Freya, Esme and Blake, deceased. She fell asleep thinking of them all, but if there were dreams she had no recollection of them when she woke.

Catherine's elder son was flatting, but Scott was with them at breakfast, despite what must have been a late night. In fact, he was finishing his breakfast as they began theirs. A year-thirteen student as tall as his father, but unlike either parent in appearance and in constant movement. He talked briefly to Sophie as a courtesy and then was gone, loud on his phone even as he left the house.

'He'll go to the waterfront,' Catherine said. 'We won't see him now till teatime.'

'Have you decided about this morning? Whether you're going?' asked Chris.

'We haven't really talked about it, have we?' said Catherine.

'I don't mind,' said Sophie. 'I've Headlonged enough. Last night was fine, but I could leave it there.'

'We might hang out, as the kids say, or go into town. What about you?'

'I think I'll do the hedge,' Chris said, 'and this afternoon I should make an inventory of medications at the clinic. There's a mandatory monthly check, and I need to get onto it. So, I doubt my exciting day will be any better than counting Headlongs.'

'Go for it,' said Catherine. 'Get the hedge done, and there's a bacon-and-egg pie we can have for lunch.'

'I need a better incentive,' Chris told her.

'Dream on,' she said.

It was another warm day, but the Wellington wind was there, though not strong enough to dissuade Chris from cutting the hedge on the sloping southern side of the section. He used battery-powered clippers. Sitting close together in the lounge, facing the window, Catherine and Sophie could see his head and shoulders as he worked, the arc of the trimmer like a windscreen wiper. No noise penetrated the lounge, and the clippings fell away without a sound.

'We keep it down mainly for the neighbours' sake,' said Catherine, 'otherwise it blocks their sun. So, what do you think about today?'

'I'm happy to flag it.'

'Good, so am I. I'm pleased about the reunion, though, mainly because I met you. I wonder how much common Headlong DNA we have?'

'It's been fun,' said Sophie. 'It is fun.' She stretched her hand out, and Catherine took it, pressed slightly.

'Don't fly back tonight,' she said.

'I have to get back for the girls.'

'Come up again soon then.' Catherine pressed Sophie's hand again, turned to smile. 'I might fall in love with you,' she said.

'You don't fall in love in two days.'

'But you might know you're going to.'

'And what would Chris say about that?'

'Why would he care?' Catherine said. 'It's a different love you have with guys, and not necessarily an opposition, or an either or. With men you have pleasure in the compatibility of difference, with women it's all compatibility, don't you reckon? Anyway, being in love is something in itself. You don't have to do anything about it. And I read somewhere that a lot more women are bi than men.'

Sophie smiled. She'd never fallen in love with a woman, but she recognised that she might with Catherine, although what form it would take she didn't know and didn't especially care. Was she just lonely but hadn't admitted that to herself? She thought of Eva, a flatmate during her first year at university. She thought of her because Eva was someone else to whom she'd felt a physical as well as emotional attraction. No awkwardness, or consummation, but sometimes, as they lay talking on the bed, one of them would smooth the other's hair back, or finger tap on a breast, and sometimes — even as they talked of men with unguarded assessment — they were pleasurably aware of each other's bodies. They painted each other's toenails and shaved the bikini line. They lay close together and sometimes even slept that way on winter evenings, with their swot notes scattered beside them. They always kissed when they were parting for a few days and kissed too when they met again.

Sophie and Catherine continued sitting together in the warm lounge with the far view across the deep water of Evans Bay, a few clouds stretched by the wind, and in the foreground the top third of Chris as he sliced the new growth from the hedge. With her thumb, Sophie gently stroked the back of Catherine's hand.

'We could all have a holiday together sometime and see how it works out. The three of us and any of the kids who want to come.'

'Mine wouldn't want to,' said Catherine.

'Probably mine wouldn't either.'

'What about Europe?'

'Why not?' said Sophie.

'Headlong for Paris then?'

'Why not?' said Sophie again.

The Ferris Wheel

'I've been asked to go to the February course,' said Rianna. 'I wanted to tell you myself before Conrad posts it. I know you were interested.'

'Good on you,' said Wynne. 'Congrats.' He knew she was being considerate, but what he wished to say was, 'Fuck off, Rianna, and leave me alone,' but that would be an open expression of his disappointment and envy. 'I expect it'll bring a good many new ideas and practices into the department,' he said. 'And good you'll have a break away, too.'

'You'll have to suffer through my presentation to the full staff afterwards. Conrad insists on me giving one.'

'Looking forward to it,' he said. Rianna waited to see if he wanted to continue the conversation, but he didn't look up from the screen, so she walked back to her own.

His desk was close to the large window, and he could look down to the walkway and the narrow riverside park. From five storeys up, the view of people was mainly heads and the extremities of arms and legs working beneath. Very few faces, unless they were raised to the sun by folk sitting on the green benches or on rugs spread on the lawn. It was a familiar and pleasant sight, but he'd never taken his lunch and sat in the park there — probably for the very reason that he could then be observed by his office colleagues, as he observed others.

Wynne knew what it meant that Rianna had been chosen to attend the senior management course. It meant that she would soon be appointed to lead the Capability and International Services team. Nothing surer. Six months ago, there was nothing surer than Wynne himself getting the position, but then the Ministry head was diagnosed with a malignant brain tumour, resigned, and Conrad Poone became

CE. Conrad was progressive and wished to increase the number of women in senior management positions. An irony of timing. Wynne acknowledged that Rianna was quite as capable and experienced as himself, but had the tumour held back for even a few months the outcome would have been different. Happenstance can be a cruel arbiter of success and failure.

As he watched a small boy throwing stones into the fountain, he admitted to himself that he was highly pissed off. Things usually went his way, and he'd developed no stoicism in regard to failure or rebuff. Especially, he coveted the office that Rianna would inherit: a spacious room with a view of the harbour and a door to close out lesser colleagues in the open-plan work areas beyond. Bugger, he thought. Couldn't the tumour have been discovered a few months later? Such a selfish view of how things should be, and he'd admired the former CE, but the wish came even so.

A walk, that's what he needed: to be out of the workplace and away from Rianna, yet he smiled at her blithely as he passed on his way to the lifts. No doubt she was thinking of the upcoming course, or already planning the arrangement of personal items within the office that would come with promotion. The photograph of her clustered family in a silver frame, the delicate flute of coloured glass she'd bought on a visit to Singapore, the pounamu carving presented to her after the symposium on immigration reception facilities.

With him in the lift was one of the workers installing new heat pumps on the fourth and fifth floors. Young, round faced, thick, tousled hair and with a slouching jocularity to which Wynne had little interest in responding.

'You'll be well set up with these new Mitsubishis,' the guy said. He idled a greasy, yellow bucket in one hand. 'Heat in winter and cool air in summer.'

'Right,' said Wynne.

'They're a big bloody improvement these ones. Cheaper to run and not half as noisy.'

'Let's hope so.' Wynne was wondering if he should start looking for new career opportunities now that Rianna had blocked his promotion.

Improved air conditioning was no compensation.

'Have you worked here long?' the guy said, but Wynne was already facing away, ready to be first out of the door.

He headed down towards the walkways, cafés and open spaces close to the sea. There was a summer carnival, and without conscious choice he drifted with others towards it, thinking he'd been hard done by. His wife would be disappointed too. They had been talking of bathroom and kitchen renovations, maybe even a new home. He didn't dislike Rianna. They'd been colleagues for years and worked well enough together as equals, but to be under her jurisdiction would be different. A constant reminder of her preferment and the check to his own ambition.

It was a weekday, but the carnival was still popular. Even some youngsters in school uniforms, and mothers with pushchairs strolling in the summer warmth. There wasn't, however, the jostling urgency of Christmas or New Year, and Wynne walked the lines of stalls and sideshows pleased to be free of the office. The Ferris wheel dominated all else, rising above the merry-go-round, the octopus, the dodgems, the food stalls and the haunted house. It had a stately rotation, and people looked up to it. How long since he'd ridden on a Ferris wheel? Surely not since his sons were children, and without questioning the impulse he joined the small queue at the ticket booth. It took quite a time for people to disembark, chair after chair descending. Even longer to fill again, as the operators waited to have at least two customers in each seat before fastening the iron restraint that made them safe.

Wynne's companion was an elderly man in a Harris-tweed jacket and dark suit trousers, both patently outdated but clean, and his brown shoes shone. His face was the colour of kauri wood, his soft, grey hair like rabbit fur. He smiled at Wynne as he got in, and they sat silently together as the Ferris wheel filled up and they rose higher, jolt by jolt. When the ride finally began, both of them gripped the bar to keep their balance and looked down to the diminished fairground. Most on the wheel were content to sit and enjoy the privileged perspective it gave; only a few youngsters threw themselves back and forth to make their chairs swing violently and so prove their daring.

The circular repetition, the altering perspective were comforting to

Wynne and a distraction from his disappointment and sense of grievance. Life had treated him badly though, hadn't it? His qualifications were among the best in the department.

When the Ferris wheel came to an abrupt halt, he thought it the clumsy ending to the ride, but only the people in the lowest chairs got out and the wheel made no further movement. The three operators clustered around the engine for a while, and one of them shouted up something about a temporary problem and not to worry. Wynne's chair was almost the highest, and he could barely hear what was said. Suspended and isolated there together with no further movement, he and his companion felt an awkwardness in not having yet acknowledged each other.

'Well, there's some hold up down there by the sound of it,' the old guy said as way of introduction.

'Seems like it,' said Wynne.

'I'm Trevor.'

'Wynne. Just our luck to be too high to get out before things are fixed.'

'We've got about the best view though. That's something,' Trevor said. 'I don't suppose it'll be long.'

But it was long. After ten minutes or so, the chief operator got a megaphone from somewhere and pointed it upwards to blare out that he was sorry about the mechanical problem and they were doing their best. No risks to anybody, but there would be a delay and they were getting expert advice. It could take a while. No worries though, he said.

'It doesn't bother me much,' said Trevor, 'but there'll be people on board who need to be places, won't there: appointments and so on. What about you?'

'It depends how long we're here. I'm taking a break from the office.'

'I'll need to piss, though, if it's too long. That's one of the things when you're old.'

'They should have us down fairly soon,' said Wynne.

'There's always something, isn't there?'

No one on the wheel displayed any panic. The sun shone, the chairs felt secure, the world went on below, and farther off the calm sea pulsed.

It wasn't an atmosphere of threat. A small crowd gathered at the ticket office to gaze up at the suspended chairs, but elsewhere the carnival continued. Distant sounds of laughter and impact from the dodgems, squeals of mock alarm from the haunted house.

'What do you do in your office?' asked Trevor.

'It's a government department,' said Wynne. 'I deal mainly with immigration issues and policy development.'

'Do you like it?'

'It's very busy and can get quite stressful at times.' He never thought to explain how it was he had time to be riding a Ferris wheel during a weekday afternoon.

'It sounds important stuff.'

'It's necessary and quite precise work.'

'Good on you,' said Trevor.

Wynne felt an obligation to show some interest in Trevor after this exchange, though he would have been content to sit in the sun and look down on the carnival without conversation. An old guy dressed in such clothes was unlikely to offer anything worth attention. 'What about you?' Wynne said, his gaze on the crowd gathering below.

'I'm a free agent. I live in a caravan without wheels in the corner of the Lynley camping ground.'

'What did you used to do?'

'I was a shearer then a musterer. I had a fall on a cliff at the head of the Rangitata and buggered my back. Finished off what the shearing started. I've been on a benefit for nineteen years.'

'No family at all?'

'Never kept in touch. Dad fucked off, my mother married another loser and my brothers and sisters left as soon as they could to make lives for themselves. We don't have reunions. I was married myself at one stage, but —' Trevor was interrupted by the megaphone with a message that there was a serious fault with the Ferris wheel machinery, but that a fire engine was coming and would get everybody down okay, so there was nothing to worry about.

'More waiting,' said Wynne. 'All this can't be doing your back much good.'

'Sitting and walking's not bad. It's the seizures with bloody awful pain that's the bugger. The cogs get out of alignment, the specialist says. It happens out of the blue: putting on my socks even or opening a door. The thing right now is that I'm going to have to pee. Good thing is that it's a solid floor and won't drip on anybody below us.'

Wynne didn't have a response to that, so looked away while Trevor clumsily undid his fly and pissed onto the floor of the chair as inconspicuously as he could. The smell was strong.

'I'm really sorry about this,' Trevor said.

'It's not your fault.'

'Sorry though,' said Trevor.

Wynne took his cell phone out and rang Rianna. 'I've been held up a bit,' he said. 'There's nothing urgent is there?' He moved his feet a little so they would be clear of the metal floor.

'Nothing special here,' she said.

'I'll get back when I can.' He thought of telling her that he was stuck at the top of a Ferris wheel and awash with piss, but it was too absurd. When he finished the call, he asked Trevor if there was anyone he needed to get in touch with — offered him the phone.

'No, I've got no one to tell. I don't even have a phone. Everything costs money, doesn't it?' There was no self-pity in his voice, no appeal. Having had his pee without much embarrassment, he was interested again in the unusual situation he found himself in.

'Money's tight, is it?' Wynne asked.

'It's all about choices,' said Trevor. 'I like a beer or two, nothing over the top, and at the weekend I go once to McDonald's or KFC if there's the dollars. I've got heating in the caravan, but it eats up money. Most days in winter if my back's okay, I go to the library or the city information centre. It's warm there. The library's the best. There's even places on the higher levels where you can stretch out and sleep. Whole rooms of books that nobody much ever bothers about. My favourite possie is by the poetry stack. There's a padded window seat, and I can watch the street below. You'd be surprised the odd things you see. Even a bag snatch once.'

They sat in the summer warmth and talked about heating for a time.

Wynne told Trevor about the new air-conditioning units being installed at his work. Trevor said his back was bad in the cold. He had a brace, a sort of corset, that he had to wear most of the time.

'It's a bit of a bugger sometimes, getting old,' he said.

Wynne phoned his wife at her work at the dental clinic. 'Guess where I am,' he said.

'No idea, but you should be at work.'

'Stuck at the top of the big wheel at the carnival.'

'You're kidding!'

'No. Something went haywire, and we're stuck. A fire engine's supposed to be coming any time to get us down.' Trevor was grinning beside Wynne as he spoke.

'What the heck are you doing at the carnival anyway?' Penny said.

'I took a breather from the office. Rianna's been selected for the senior management course, so you know what that means.'

'No surprise really, though, is it? Just look after yourself and get down safely. Call me again when you're down. I can't let you out of my sight, can I?'

'My wife,' he told Trevor when the call was over.

'You're lucky. Any kids?'

'Two boys. One's doing the big OE; the other's at uni and flatting.'

'Good for you,' said Trevor. 'I sort of missed out on family and kids. I had good mates, but it's not the same, is it? You do stuff with your boys?'

'We used to do a lot: taking them to play sport and so on. They're both quite keen on gaming too, and I joined in. Not so much now, of course. They've pretty much got their own lives and friends. They still come home, though. Shaun's in Vietnam, but we hear all about it. You can keep in touch from all over the world now, no problem.'

'I've never been away,' said Trevor. 'I watch a lot of TV, though. It takes you just about everywhere. Those nature programmes show you more than if you're there.'

'You're right.'

He was right, but seeing more wasn't everything. There was smelling, tasting, touching. There was meeting people and talking with them. There were the epiphanies experienced when you stood in places of wondrous association. Although, thought Wynne, there would be places in Trevor's circumscribed life just as special to him as the Acropolis or Central Park were to others.

In the chair immediately below them, a young woman was trying to placate two small children. Not much of any of the occupants was visible, but Wynne called out to ask if they were okay, and she called back to say they were.

'All these kids will have a story to tell, won't they?' Trevor said. 'Maybe they'll get some free tickets when everything's fixed, as compensation.'

Wynne was surprised that the merry-go-round, the octopus and other rides continued. Perhaps they did so to emphasise normality, despite the motionless Ferris wheel and its dangling customers. A large ship was passing, with containers piled so high it seemed it must capsize, despite the calm sea. Perched in the sky, Wynne felt an odd detachment from all he saw. He had no awareness of danger, merely a feeling of stasis and inconsequence.

'How the hell do we end up here?' he said, more to himself than anyone else.

'How the hell do we end up anywhere?' replied Trevor, not fazed by the question. He ran a hand through his grey, soft hair and stroked his thin throat. 'You have to take what you get dished out,' he said. 'No use whining, and everything's over sooner or later.'

'True.'

'I reckon you need a bit of luck,' said Trevor.

'So, you've been lucky?'

'I've had my moments. I eat and sleep as much as I like, don't I? There's the pension. I even get to ride the bloody Ferris wheel.' He gave a small laugh. 'There's millions and millions of poor bastards overseas a lot worse off.'

'I guess so,' said Wynne.

'It's my back really. That's the bugger. And I've got these specks always in my eyes — like seagulls in the distance. Floaters, the doctor calls them. But I don't drive now anyway. Always far-off seagulls, but it doesn't bother me that much when watching tele.'

'Do you watch much sport?' asked Wynne.

'Only if it's on ordinary channels. I haven't got Sky or Netflix movies, none of those. On fine weekends, I can walk from the camping ground to the sports fields and watch local footy and stuff.'

The fire engine's arrival wasn't dramatic. It came slowly, without siren, nosing through the fairground towards the Ferris wheel. The crowd at the base of the wheel gave way reluctantly.

Wynne had expected a vehicle with extension ladders, but it was one of those appliances with a small platform that could be raised and rotated to allow firemen to direct hoses on a blaze — much better than ladders for the need at hand. It began with the lower chairs and worked upwards. A slow process because the chairs tended to sway as people were taken off, and the fireman on the platform was careful to have a grip on each as they stepped over.

Some of the children were fearful, and the crowd murmured in sympathy as they were passed hand to hand. Each time the platform was lowered, the people released were clapped and acclaimed — minor and temporary celebrities, although they had been in no real danger. It was a drama that the onlookers could witness and talk about later with a sense of authority.

Wynne and Trevor were almost the last to be taken down. Wynne helped Trevor onto the small metal platform.

'He's got a bad back,' he warned the lanky fireman, who was enjoying his role, but with a smile that showed he understood no true heroism was required. Having waited until the final family group were landed, Wynne and Trevor walked away from the wheel and its crowd, towards the carnival gates.

'Well, that was something a bit different, wasn't it?' Wynne said.

'Sure was.'

'I wonder if they'll get it going again today and if they do whether people will want to go on it.'

'I want to apologise for pissing when we were up there,' said Trevor. 'I haven't got a lot of control now. It's another of the things that's come with my buggered back.'

'It's not your fault. Sure you're okay now? Will you head home?'

'It's nice and warm. I'll go along the sea front and sit in the sun. What about you?'

'Back to the office for me,' said Wynne. 'Anyway, good luck.'

They shook hands at the gate, and that seemed quite natural. Wynne watched his Ferris wheel companion walk away. Trevor, in his op-shop sports jacket and mismatched suit trousers, with a broken back and not much else, going off purposefully into the world.

Ghost Christmas

That year, Danny was in Palmerston North, working for a removal firm and living in a flat with people he hardly knew. It hadn't started that way: originally there were his close friends Josie and Rohan, and later Peter moved in when they advertised for a fourth flatmate. The wooden bungalow had only three bedrooms, but to make it cheaper for them all the lounge was given over to Peter and when they congregated they did so in the kitchen. The three friends didn't see much of Peter, who kept mainly to his room and took his mates there when they came around.

Only a couple of months later, however, Josie left to live with her boyfriend and Rohan decided to move back home. Following minimal discussion with Danny, Peter roped in a couple of his own friends, guys who partied hard, high-fived and kept the place in a mess. Toby and Dylan. Danny didn't take to either of them and realised that he'd become the odd man out in the flat, as Peter had been before. Danny was now the one that kept largely to his own space, ate take-aways there rather than joining in communal meals. Danny became aware that he was out of step with the others and out of sympathy too. No unpleasantness or overt exclusion, but he lacked a history of companionship with those guys and was just the Danny who had a room and paid a quarter of the rent and with whom they made desultory small talk in passing.

Early in December, a Sunday evening, Peter knocked briefly on Danny's bedroom door as he opened it.

'Hi,' he said.

'Hi.' Danny looked up from his screen. He could have been watching porn or learning Portuguese, but he wasn't. He was checking on Massey courses because he'd pretty much decided to go back to university but switch to an agri-science degree. Things were better for him financially after a year working, but he didn't want to be lugging furniture from house to house all his life.

Peter was a large, soft, long-haired guy, who filled the doorway before entering and sitting on the bed, as there was only one chair. His ears were like emerging mushrooms within his dense, mulch-like hair.

'Got a moment?' he said.

'Sure.'

'About Christmas.'

'Yeah?'

'The three of us were thinking,' said Peter.

'Yeah?'

'Thinking of having it here. Having a full Christmas blow-out. And New Year party as well, and we just wondered about your plans. You're welcome, of course, but we wondered if you'd be going home to family, or whatever?'

'Actually,' said Danny, 'I'm going to have to leave you guys and move on. Next year I'm back to uni and might try the hall. I've been meaning to say, but you won't have any trouble at all getting someone in here.'

'So, you'll go when?' said Peter without surprise or regret in his tone.

'The hall opens late in Feb. I'll settle up and be out of here then.'

'So, you're on for Christmas here?'

'No,' said Danny, making up his mind as he spoke.

'You've got somewhere to go for Christmas? Home?'

'Yeah, home,' said Danny, although he knew he wouldn't go home for Christmas. Home was a long way away, in distance and also in time. In fact, there was no home, but none of that was any business of Peter's.

'Okay then. That's fine,' said Peter, heaving himself from the bed. He glanced around him, taking in the unpainted kit-set bookcase, the second-hand desk and bed. 'A hostel room would be furnished, wouldn't it,' he said. 'We could make an offer on this stuff if you like?' They both knew a room already set up would be more attractive to prospective flatmates, and more could be asked for possession of it.

'I'll see,' said Danny. 'I haven't sussed anything out yet, but I'll get onto it. Might be things I don't need.'

'Hey, we'll miss you man. What are you thinking of at Massey?'

'Agri-science,' said Danny.

'Way to go,' said Peter without enthusiasm, and he padded from the room.

Danny had an enjoyable catch-up with Josie and Rohan before he left at Christmas, but there was little notice taken of his departure by the other three, who were too busy preparing for their Christmas rave, which would pretty much roll on to New Year's Eve. When Danny left, Dylan wasn't even there. Danny had his aging Honda Civic fully packed before lunch. He was twenty-two years old and happy to head off into the blue. Peter and Toby did come out to the car to see him leave.

'So, where is it you're off to again?' asked Toby.

'Auckland.'

'Family, right?' said Peter.

'Right,' said Danny, but it wasn't, of course. 'There'll be quite a lot of us, but Mum and Dad have a big place. Should be great.' Why should they think themselves the only ones having a special Christmas?

'Whereabouts in Auckland?' asked Toby.

'Devonport,' said Danny, but it wasn't. It wasn't anywhere. 'I hope your Christmas do's a blast. Don't burn the damn place down before I'm back, though.'

'It'll be fucken awesome,' Toby said.

'See you then. Hope all goes well,' said Peter. Both he and Toby had gone back inside before the Civic reached the gate.

Danny had made no plans whatsoever about Auckland. He was taking off to be somewhere else for a time. You don't need plans when you're twenty-two. Every place in the world's a possible destination. You're nimble enough and cocky enough to handle what life throws at you. Rohan had told him that it would take about six hours to reach Auckland, but with pre-Christmas traffic and stops at Taumarunui, Te Kuiti and Hamilton, it was dusk when Danny joined the vehicle queues of the city. A warm dusk, and humid too.

Auckland was a city unfamiliar to him. He'd been there a few times before but never for long. Eventually, he found himself on Ponsonby Road and recognised the name although not anything of the surroundings. He turned off at the shops and drove past houses until he found a space to park without charge. The walk back to the shops took longer than he'd expected, but he had no deadlines to meet. There was a KFC in the centre, and he liked fried chicken and chips. Other places were more expensive and better looking, but he wasn't tempted. Ambience wasn't something he was prepared to pay for.

He sat at a small white table inside with a view of the street. As soon as he settled, rain began. He hadn't noticed a build-up of cloud and was surprised by how quickly the squall came and how heavy it was. People on the street were equally unprepared and scuttled past to seek shelter. Danny was only a window away but was able to stay dry, eating his chicken and chips, watching the flurry outside that was increasingly caught in the spill of variegated colours from vehicles, shops and streetlights as night fell. It occurred to him, though, that he didn't have his coat and his car was a good distance away. For the moment, however, he had advantage in the world, and he sat relaxed, eating and drinking, watching others less fortunate. He was a young guy with more curiosity concerning the future than fear. There was a black SUV parked close: no one inside, but a small, brindle dog thrust its head from the half-open window to join Danny in watching the people passing, and then turned to regard him as a fellow observer.

The KFC was busy, and Danny soon had to share his table. A young Chinese guy, tall and slim, who sat down with a grin as introduction and began to eat quickly, his face close to the food. Danny was in no hurry, for it was still raining, and his random companion finished before him, stood up, gave his smile again, but this time as farewell, and left hurriedly. Danny watched him draw his jacket lapels together as he stepped into the street and hunched into the rain. Only when he was out of sight and Danny's attention had returned to his drink, did he notice the wallet on the seat. A large wallet of black leather with a chrome zipper pocket on the visible side. He didn't dash after the owner: it was too late and the guy would surely return when he realised his loss. Danny could hand the wallet to someone on the staff before he left if necessary, but for the moment he indulged a natural curiosity and took the wallet and opened it. Credit cards, driver's licence, three twenty-dollar notes, among other usual items, but the one thing that interested him was a small, laminated head-and-shoulders photograph of an elderly Chinese woman in European dress and with a gap-toothed smile. A warm and natural smile, nevertheless.

The rain stopped as suddenly as it had begun, so Danny decided to hand in the wallet and leave, but he was still seated when the owner returned, coming quickly inside and towards the table. Before he could say anything, Danny held up the wallet.

'I was about to hand it in at the counter,' he said casually. 'I decided not to steal it.'

'You would've buggered off with it smartly if you'd wanted to do that.'

'Not in the rain,' said Danny, handing the wallet over. The owner smiled and sat down without checking it.

'Thanks mate,' he said. 'Just about shat myself when I realised I'd lost it. I was rushing to get to the supermarket. I stack shelves there most of the night and should be there now, but when I realised it was gone I told them I was off back here. There's not much money, but it's your credit card and all that other stuff, isn't it? That's the thing.'

Calvin Lowe was his name. A quick-talking, quick-moving guy, who genuinely appreciated Danny's honesty and was interested to know more about him. When he found that Danny was a student like himself, but not an Aucklander and with not much going on for Christmas Eve, he wanted to keep in touch.

'Look,' he said, 'I got to get back to work, but give me your number, and I'll be in touch tomorrow afternoon. We could hang out if you like. You don't want to be knocking around by yourself on Christmas Eve.'

'I know a few people here,' lied Danny.

'I'll ring anyway. Even if we just have a quick drink. The least I can do.' He put the number on his mobile, slapped the table lightly in a gesture of farewell, smiled and hurried off to his job. Danny used the toilets, then left in a leisurely way, pausing at the SUV to gurn at the dog in the window, who barked in retaliation. He began the walk back to his car parked in Summer Street. That's what the sign said, and he thought it appropriate and propitious, for the air was still warm and the footpath already drying. Would he have taken the money, he wondered, if there had been hundreds of dollars and not just sixty?

He was surprised by how quiet it was once he was a couple of blocks from the Ponsonby centre, walking past houses ordinary in appearance, yet hugely expensive to buy. Most drew no attention to themselves, but one, not far from his car, had an artificial Christmas tree on its veranda with coloured lights blinking in the darkness. A family place, he could tell, because a plastic pedal car was close to the door. He remembered a Christmas when he was still at primary school: Todd Mackle next door got a pedal car, and he got striped pyjamas and a colouring book.

Christmas Eve night he'd stay at a motel or a backpackers, he decided, but he'd doss down in the car for the first night. He put the front seat as far back as it would go, opened the window slightly, took off his shoes and relaxed in the semi-darkness of the suburban street. It wasn't much after ten o'clock. He should have gone on to a bar after KFC, he told himself, but he was tired. What would Peter, Toby and Dylan be doing? Drinking and gaming: probably already had someone keen to take his room. He sent an email to Rohan and Josie, saying he was in the big city and wishing his friends all the best. Although several houses away the blinking Christmas tree lights still cast soft colours that flickered on the windscreen and mirror, they were no distraction in Danny's final drift to sleep.

Passing cars woke him a little after six. He put on his shoes, had a surreptitious piss with the door ajar and then drove back towards the shops before residents would be about to notice him as a transient. Because it was early, he was able to find a free park closer than he had the night before. He sat with his tablet, playing Brick Puzzle to while away time before places began to open. Also, he googled local motels to find the cheapest accommodation. It wasn't that he was particularly short of money but that he had his own priorities as to its use. It was too early to ring anyone, but he jotted down several motel numbers to try later.

He hadn't forgotten Calvin Lowe and the wallet. Perhaps he'd never hear from him, and even if he did it would be much later in the day when Calvin woke after his night's work in the supermarket. Danny thought stacking shelves would be easier than lugging furniture from house to truck and truck to house but didn't fancy working nights.

Somewhere in the muddle of his stuff were three packets of chips, but they weren't visible, and he wasn't hungry enough to start burrowing. He knew KFC wouldn't open until ten, but other places would much earlier, so he walked to the shops to find one in which he could have a coffee and freshen up in the toilet. It wasn't a difficult search, and he was soon at a bench in Becky's, looking out on a different stretch of the last night's street. He admitted to himself that he was bored. He had come to the city not just to avoid his flatmates but for new experiences. Finding a wallet and giving it back wasn't all that exciting. He thought of Frances, his girlfriend until three months before, when he told her that he didn't want anything serious. Danny was accustomed to girlfriends, and he missed having one, not Frances specifically but someone. He looked forward to a remedy when he was back at uni: it wasn't easy working as a removal man to meet women. Auckland was full of women, he told himself.

The first two motels he rang were fully booked, and so was the third until he emphasised that anything would do.

'There's a studio unit being renovated that's not finished,' the woman said. 'It's fully functional but not carpeted. It was supposed to be done weeks ago, but the tradies let us down. You couldn't have it long because they may turn up any time.'

'It would be one night. Two at most. How much?'

'Hundred and thirty, and only night by night.'

'I'm okay with that if I can bring my stuff straight after midday,' Danny said.

'All right, I'll get the linen done. Only night by night though.'

'I'm okay with that.'

Danny sat around most of the morning, idle amidst the bustle of other people on Christmas Eve. He had an early bar lunch of burger and beer and then drove to the motel — a two-storeyed, Summerhill stone, U-shaped building in Grey Lynn. His small unit was on the ground floor and complete, except for carpet, the bare particle board still with wisps of underlay beneath the few tacks remaining.

'Everything's here,' the woman said, giving him a small bottle of milk. 'Just remember we can't guarantee more than a night.'

'That's fine. Thanks,' said Danny. Little chance surely of any carpet guys turning up on Christmas Day.

He brought in what he needed from the car, including a change of clothes. He showered, made a coffee and sat looking through the glass sliding door across the car park to a wall on which were a large, white-painted arrow and a blue neon sign: *RECEPTION*. It wasn't paradise, but he was pleased to be in a space of his own and one more roomy than his car. He would go into the city later, he decided, to the big shops, entertainments and Smith and Caughey's Christmas window. He'd tell himself that it wasn't important that, although there were people related to him, there was no family in the way others had a family. A white van pulled in opposite, and a tubby man in shorts got out and carried a shopping bag into his unit, returning for two packs of beer. Danny was reminded of the flat and Peter, Toby and Dylan. They'd be stocking up too, wouldn't they?

Calvin Lowe rang when Danny was about to leave for the city. 'Is that wallet man?' he asked.

'That's me,' said Danny.

'Where are you?'

'A motel without carpet in Grey Lynn.'

'Why without carpet?'

'It's a long story.'

'Anyway, if you haven't got anything jacked up, I wonder if you'd like to come with us tonight. A beach party at a mate's in Kohimarama. Should be fun, and you're invited.'

'I'd thought of going into Queen Street, Aotea Square and the stuff going on there,' said Danny.

'Yeah, yeah, we could do that before, but it's not like New Year's Eve, you know. You wouldn't hang out there late. Up to you, though.'

'No, I'd like to come. Thanks. Where and when?'

'Probably best I pick you up,' said Calvin. 'How about six-thirty or so?'

He was only twenty minutes late, arrived driving a well-kept Falcon and came in to see the novelty of a motel unit with no carpet.

'I was lucky to get anything at all,' Danny told him.

'We'll need booze,' Calvin said as they went back to his car. 'We'll get it on the way. What do you drink?'

'I'm not fussy. Most beers and port and brandy.'

'Jesus, port! I don't know anyone who drinks port.'

'I drink cheap port sometimes,' said Danny. 'What about you?'

'Stella Artois's my beer. Sav blanc's my wine. I'm not much into the hard stuff.'

They stocked up at a supermarket on the way: chops, sausages and salad packs as well as liquor. Calvin said if Danny wanted to see Christmas lights, they could check out Franklin Road, but it was better when dark and would mean a detour. It was the sort of invitation a parent would give a child, but Danny knew it wasn't meant as sarcasm and said he was happy to just head off for Kohimarama, which was a drive in itself.

Although interested in Calvin's heritage, Danny found he quickly forgot his new friend was Chinese for his voice and his life were entirely Kiwi. He was doing law: third year already over and cruising. 'I don't want to do court work or anything though,' he said as he contested the lines of traffic with the resignation of a local. 'Maybe a government department, and anyway I want to go overseas when I graduate. A working holiday around Europe for a year or more.' Danny was keen on that himself, and they compared the places that most interested them. New York was higher on Calvin's list than Beijing. There were no close family links in China, he said.

Kohimarama beach — Kohi beach, as Calvin called it — was very urban and so different to the natural coasts Danny was familiar with from his Whanganui boyhood. No dunes, lupins or driftwood stacks: a manicured seaside of pavements, low concrete walls and grass plots and a great many people in the evening sun.

'We'll come down here later from Jordon's place,' said Calvin. Jordon's place was a couple of blocks back from the beach. Two-storeyed, wooden and recently painted. Jordon himself was dark haired, muscular and with the indolent ease of an athlete. Danny never got to know his surname but did learn that his parents were away.

'So, you're the honest guy with his wallet,' he said when Calvin introduced Danny. 'He never has any money anyway.'

Danny had expected a crowd of people, although Calvin hadn't talked of numbers. There were nine when they arrived and only two more came later. Jordon was tinkering with a large, wheeled barbecue with a chrome top, and the others sat about on the decking talking and drinking. There were no individual introductions, just a general 'this is Danny' from Calvin, and some lifted hands in acknowledgment. Later Danny got to talk to some of them as they stood about the barbecue. All of them seemed to be students, except for Jordon's girlfriend, who worked as a vet's assistant. It was well after eight o'clock, but the sun was still ablaze in the sky, and Danny, with his plate of charred sausages and coleslaw, sought the shade close to the house, where he sat with Danusia Smaill, the similarities of their Christian names the first link between them.

'It's Polish, a feminine form of Daniel, apparently,' she said.

'I like it.'

'Isn't that just an oblique way of admiring your own name?'

'For a long time, I wanted to be called Brad or Cliff, like a cowboy.'

'I rather like exotic names like Talullah or Celeste,' she said.

'So do I, and Danusia's one of them.'

'Flatterer.'

She had a round face and a narrow body. She wore tight jeans, which accentuated her thin legs, and yellow canvas shoes without socks. Danny liked her straight away, although she wasn't especially good looking: not like Jordon's girl. She was at ease, though, not striving to make an impression, yet with a natural engagement.

'I bet you're doing law,' said Danny, and he raised a sausage to Jordon who wasn't far away.

'No cigar,' said Danusia. 'I'm doing English honours. What about you?'

'I took a year off from Massey, but I'm going back to do agri-science. I can switch most of my passes.'

'But you come from here?'

'No,' said Danny, 'I'm just cruising around for Christmas. Hanging out in a Grey Lynn motel. I'm from Palmy.' He liked her naturalness, the slight smile on her round face and the freedom of her long, dark hair.

'So, who do you know here then?'

He told her about Calvin and the wallet, and she seemed less impressed by the randomness of it all than he was himself. He could well have been in the party flat with Peter, Toby and Dylan, or more likely at Rohan's home, but instead he was at a Christmas Eve barbecue in Kohimarama, among strangers and in a place unknown to him, yet he was happy. Sometimes it's better to let life happen rather than try to impose yourself upon it. And he'd met Danusia, was sitting in the sunset with her and had nowhere else he needed to be. They drank his beer together: she sparingly, he with a generous sense of occasion.

'Christmas is a bit odd when you've grown up, don't you think?' he said. 'When you've grown up but still by yourself. You're not excited as you were as a kid, and you haven't got kids yourself to be excited with together. It's not like New Year's Eve, is it? New Year's a real blast.' He wondered if Danusia had come with some guy. He thought how trusting it was of Jordon's parents to allow their place to be used for a party. It would've been beyond the comprehension of his own parents.

'Christmas is family time. New Year is party time,' said Danusia.

'So, we'll have double party time.'

'I don't know where I'll be for New Year.'

'Nor do I,' said Danny with conscious on-the-road casualness. Long shadows cast by the setting sun stretched across the well-kept lawn, and the voices of the others seemed to have a more noticeable reverberation than before. No one interrupted or joined his talk with Danusia, and he was glad. Maybe she hadn't come with anyone special. She had her hands clasped around her knees. Large hands for a woman, with short, unpainted nails.

'Do you play netball?' he asked.

'A bit, but tennis is my thing.'

'Any good?'

'Club level. I like grass courts best. Are you sporty?'

'Not really. I always seemed to have a job, even at school.' He was quite a good shot, but he didn't hunt any more, and it wasn't a sport in the opinion of most. Not a team thing. Not something that would interest her. He'd start drinking his port soon, he thought, after another beer or two. He watched Jordon's girlfriend going into the house and wondered what she'd be like in bed. He watched the darkness stealing in and the light withdrawing. He watched someone he thought was called Liam — the last to still be using the barbecue. A seagull perched on the wooden fence. Danny found concentration difficult when he'd had a few.

'Why are you changing your course?' Danusia asked, and his answer had as much of the truth as abbreviation and personal reserve permitted. 'I just think it's best to do what you find most interesting,' she said. 'Not be too bothered about a meal ticket. Knowledge for knowledge's sake, that's how universities began, right?'

'I guess so. You've got to have a qualification for everything these days, though: looking after kids, working in a massage parlour, giving out library books.'

'They say people change occupations a lot more in a lifetime now anyway.'

'I'm all for some variety,' said Danny. 'Different things in different places with different people.'

'See that guy there with Calvin?' said Danusia without a pause, as if it followed naturally from what he'd said.

'Yeah. With the yellow T-shirt?'

'Yeah. He got bitten by a shark surfing at Muriwai.'

'A surfing shark?'

'No joke for him,' she said.

'He doesn't look too bad.'

'His shoulder's a mess.'

'You wouldn't want to swim again after that, would you?'

'What are the chances, eh? One in a million or more, like being struck by lightning or having a satellite fall on you, yet it has to happen to someone,' she said. They began a list of the most improbable individual catastrophes and rated them according to their personal phobias. The worst fears are safely mocked in the abstract, and they laughed a lot.

Later in the warm dusk, Jordon led everyone down to the beach. The families who had been there earlier had gone, but adults in couples and groups walked or rested in the gathering darkness. A few even swam. Danny and Danusia sat on the low wall, she with a bottle of Heineken, he with his bottle of cheap port, for he'd drunk or given away all his beer.

'I don't know anyone who drinks that stuff,' she said. 'Isn't it just a dark sherry?'

'A fortified wine. I got onto it through my uncle, who used to drink it in the maimai in duck-shooting season. No one else seems to like it.'

'Hardly trendy,' she said but without judgement. A woman called out to her. An indistinct figure close to the water, and Danusia struggled to take off her jeans. 'I should've worn shorts,' she said. She ran off, and he could hear her laughing and talking as she waded into the sea. She would come back though, he knew, for on the wall beside him were the crumpled heap of her jeans and her Heineken beers. Briefly, Danny thought of joining her, but he couldn't be bothered taking off his trousers and sneakers. He just sat and drank his port and thought that he could be spending Christmas Eve in a lot worse places than Jordon's Kohimarama. Someone in another group farther down the shore had lit a fire, and people stood around it, outlined in the glow. It was forbidden, he supposed, but it seemed to complete the scene. If he were to walk up and join them, would they notice his arrival, and would his departure be marked by those he was presently with? He supposed he was getting slightly pissed and told himself to lay off the port. He wanted to be coherent when Danusia came back. It was a pity she was skinny, but he liked her: the round face as contrast to the rest of her physique, the flowing hair, most of all the naturalness and the intelligence.

He lifted his head and sang out her name twice, prolonging the syllables, then stopped, embarrassed, having no recollection of his own intention, but the figures flickered in the firelight without pause, small waves continued to slap, people were loud in talk and laughter, and behind it all was the noise of street traffic.

'I missed you,' he said when later she returned.

'Was that you calling out?' she asked.

'I didn't want you to drown. There'll be sharks out there too.'

'Time to knock off the port.'

'You're right,' he said.

Getting her jeans back on was even more of a struggle for her than taking them off because her legs were wet, and afterwards she perched on the wall to brush sand from her feet before putting her shoes back on.

'I'm hungry again,' he said. 'I should have brought one of those sausages down.'

'A sausage is just a penis confirmation,' she said.

'Very clever. Who was that with you in the water?'

'Anika.'

'She at uni too?'

'Yeah,' Danusia said. 'And Calvin was asking about you.'

'There seem to be lots of Chinese people up here.'

'Calvin's family's been here for ages. Gold rush times. Probably longer than yours and mine. Right?'

As they talked, Danusia took the port bottle from his loose grip and, without any comment at all, poured what was left in it onto the ground. Danny offered neither rebuke nor resistance, just listened to the story of her mother's people coming from Poland after Hitler's war. He was on the cusp of drunkenness, still able to realise that and wish not to go beyond it. He'd found that getting pissed rarely endeared him to women.

'What about your family?' she said. 'You're not with them for Christmas?'

'My mother's dead, I always fight with my father, and my sister and I don't bother with each other.' Danny was rather pleased with his succinctness, and at the same time he became aware that after a lull the breeze was shifting, flowing out on the sea as the land cooled. A horizon was no longer discernible, and hearing had become more significant than sight as gauge of what surrounded them. 'How about you?' he said. The small fire on the beach was dying down: fewer people stood around it. Fewer people were anywhere.

'My dad died at only fifty-six — pneumonia — and Mum married a guy who's turned out to be a bit of prick. I think so anyway, though she's okay with him. They're in Nelson now.'

Danusia was telling him about her elder sisters, both of whom she loved, when Calvin came looking for him.

'I'm heading off,' he said. 'You okay to go?'

'Sure,' but Danny remained seated and relaxed, in no hurry to leave.

'I can drop him off if you like,' Danusia said. 'Grey Lynn's not that much out of the way for me.'

'Okay,' said Calvin. 'Hope you both have a cool Christmas. You've got my number, man, so keep in touch if you want, eh.' Danny watched him fade into the night and thought they would probably not meet again: a KFC and wallet introduction, a barbecue and beach farewell, and casual goodwill in between.

'Do you want to see Jordon before we go? Say something to him?' Danusia asked. Danny couldn't be bothered. Courtesy fades with the increase of alcohol.

'He could be anywhere,' he said.

'Let's hit the road then. It's after midnight, and we'll turn to pumpkins.'

They walked back into the streets to find her car. A blue Corolla with a sheepskin on the driver's seat. 'You know your motel address, don't you?' she said.

'Yeah, of course.' He'd written it down before leaving, which was a relief because he had no recollection of street, or number, and they weren't on the key tag. The city was still brightly lit as they drove back, cars still passing. Danny admired the calm assurance with which Danusia drove and was pleased not to have that responsibility. He liked her. He made an effort to be entertaining by exaggerating the defects of his Palmy flatmates.

At the motel, she pulled up close to his car. He pointed it out, and she peered in its window.

'King of the road,' she said.

'She's never missed a beat,' and he patted the Honda's bonnet. 'Anyway, come in for a coffee.' And she did.

'What the hell's gone on here?' she asked as soon as they were inside.

'They're supposed to have a new carpet, but it hasn't turned up. It's all they had, so I was lucky to get it.' Beer, port, sausages and the sea air had made him weary, and he half lay on the bed propped with pillows, instead of doing anything, so Danusia went to the bench and made the coffee herself. 'There's a packet of chips,' he said complacently, and she brought that over as well and sat on one of the wooden chairs. 'Thanks,' he said. 'It's officially Christmas Day now, isn't it? The only present I can offer is a packet of chips.'

'I miss family Christmases, but I like to hang out with friends. It was cool tonight, wasn't it? It was good to have Jordon's place to meet up.' She took her phone from her purse and busied herself with it briefly. 'I'm letting my flatmate know I'm okay,' she said. 'She's probably not home herself, but we check in.'

'Only the two of you?'

'No. There's three of us, but Emm's gone home for Christmas.'

'My flatmates will be plastered by now.'

'Why did you drive up here by yourself?'

So, Danny told her about them not being real friends, about not being keen on their Christmas-to-New-Year binge with a crowd he didn't know. About Rohan's parents being happy to have him for a few days between Christmas and New Year if that would help out, and about his resolution to take his studies more seriously this time around.

She told him she had nightmares about failing exams but almost always got A grades. 'I work like a bugger most of the time,' she said. Danny liked that admission. It was nerdy, and most students didn't like to confess to that.

When the chips were finished, she washed her hands in the sink, then lay on the bed beside him.

'Don't think you're going to get into me,' she said. 'It's just that it's more comfortable here. These studio units never have a soft chair, do they?' Her long hair spread over the pillow, and she told Danny that she'd broken up with her boyfriend only a few weeks before. 'I'm not sure I did the right thing,' she said. 'We were together nearly two years.'

'Why ditch him?'

'It sounds so shallow, but I think we got too used to each other: so familiar it wasn't exciting any more. Other couples seemed to be doing better than we were.' Her head was close enough for Danny to smell her hair. Part natural fragrance, part some shampoo.

'Your hair smells nice.'

'You stink a bit,' she said cheerfully.

'Not fair. I had a shower and changed shirts before Calvin picked me up.'

'It's sweat and sausages and that bloody port.'

'Well, you can always sit on the chair again if you can't take it,' he said, but she didn't move. 'Why do you have your hair so long? It must take a hell of a lot of looking after.'

'Short hair doesn't suit a round face.'

'Round faces are okay.'

'How many film stars do you know with round faces?' she said.

'I don't know any film stars.'

'Because you smell.'

'What's strange is that you've got a round face, but you're skinny.' He'd drunk enough to not think that might give offence. 'I don't mind round faces, though,' he added.

'I've always been thin.'

'I don't know any skinny film stars either.'

'Because you smell,' Danusia said. She pushed off her shoes by using one against the other and her bare feet were pale, lying close to his in their green socks. 'I should go soon,' she said, stretching back on the pillow.

Danny thought this was the way it should be: letting life find its own uninhibited way, as the wind does, instead of always trying to direct things to some preconceived end; instead of having expectations, so many of which wouldn't come to anything. He was happy enough to be lying there with the blue reception sign showing through the curtain of the sliding door and Danusia talking with him of the favourite places she'd never been to.

'Paris most of all,' she said. 'Paris and then Dublin. Dublin's a writer's city. I'm going to do my thesis on Anne Enright.'

'Never heard of her,' said Danny. His tone wasn't dismissive, rather an apology for his own ignorance.

'Freaking marvellous. You must read her. The Prof says I should be concentrating on a Kiwi writer, but I don't care,' she said, and after a pause, 'I'm feeling pooped. I might stay here the night, but you're not going to get into me.'

'That's okay. You're all right here.'

'You know what?' she said.

'What?'

'I've always wanted to play the violin really well. Not just average, but really well.'

'Yeah. You've got big hands. I can see you in an orchestra.'

''Cause music's the only universal language, isn't it? Somebody said that.'

'I wouldn't know,' said Danny. 'It's good to be young, though. I know that for sure. Older people always seem to be disappointed.'

'They've sold out, I suppose.'

Danny wasn't sure what she meant, but he was content to lie there, half drunk, half asleep, and regard their feet sticking up at the bed end, hers palely bare and his in green socks. Two o'clock in the morning of Christmas Day and Santa hadn't been with any carpet or promises for the future.

Stepping Down

He and Joanne had taken a cruise after he left the firm. A two-month Mediterranean voyage that was part of the generous package he received on retirement. And on his return he'd taken his time before visiting his former colleagues, even though Nikora, his successor, emphasised that the door was always open. Tony remembered his father's advice when he went to boarding school: 'I don't want you to come home for a month,' he said. 'We'll all miss each other, but it's the best way to deal with homesickness, believe me.'

The situation was different, but Tony felt the advice was still relevant, and he didn't go back to Marples Foodstuffs until months after his return from Europe. However, when he thought the time right, he rang and was told he was welcome, an open invitation and no more than he expected. He chose a summer morning with a sea breeze to ensure the heat wasn't oppressive.

'I'm quite looking forward to going,' he told Joanne.

Nikora greeted him in the outer office, took him into that of the CEO and asked if he preferred coffee or tea, although Judy, who stood with a smile in the doorway, of course knew what the answer would be. Tony noticed the new, large, slatted venetian blinds and the leather sofa with a glass-topped coffee table in front. The office had assumed a greater ambience of executive ease since his possession of it. Different personal items on the desk also: a photograph of a smiling woman, presumably Nikora's wife; an award plaque set in a varnished wooden stand; a pounamu koru with a high polish. Tony experienced a sense of dispossession as he followed Nikora to the sofa. The CEO's manner was altered too, in a more subtle way since their time together during the handover. He'd always had presence; Tony had noticed that at the first board interview, the calmness and the attention paid when others were speaking. Tony had given his support to the appointment without reservation.

'Great to see you,' said Nikora. 'I hope you'll have the time to have a good wander around later. Anyway, tell me about the cruise. That must have been really something?' Nikora had been to some of the places on the cruise itinerary but used that familiarity merely to encourage Tony's own impressions. Judy brought the coffees and biscuits, said she was pleased to see him, and Tony asked after her husband and children, using all their names. 'You bequeathed me a first-rate PA there,' said Nikora when she left.

'Finding the right people is the most important thing,' said Tony.

'Absolutely.'

'And not just a management team. A workforce on board from top to bottom.'

'Absolutely,' said Nikora and he offered the biscuits once again.

'I'm interested to know how the plans for the new refrigeration units worked out,' said Tony. 'One of the last major projects I had on the go.'

'Actually, we put that on hold. There was a consensus that there might be financial advantage in the use of available space in the facilities at the wharf. It could yet happen in the future, of course. We have made changes in the supply chain that will interest you,' and Nikora elaborated on those and on the restructuring of the management team to prioritise technical innovation.

Tony was interested, responded politely, but wasn't convinced that any alterations made were improvements on his own set-up when in charge.

Nikora didn't look at his watch but said, 'I'd like to stroll round with you, but unfortunately I've an appointment at eleven-thirty. You'll know so many people anyway.'

'That's fine. I won't keep you. It's good to see you well settled in.'

'Feel free to pop in again before you leave. I should be here. I'd be interested to get your impressions of the place again. After all, this was your working home for a long time, and the affiliation's still strong, I imagine. The greater the responsibility you have for an enterprise, the closer your engagement with it.'

Something else was different in the office, something missing, and as he shook hands with his successor, Tony realised what it was: the aerial photograph of the plant that had hung on the wall behind the desk. Nothing had replaced it. There was just a pale, repainted surface that would not detract from the person seated before it. In the outer office, he paused at Judy's desk to talk at greater length with her, but they'd barely begun when she received a call. Taking it, she raised a hand in apology and exasperation, so he walked on.

Solly Minogue was financial officer and visible at his desk through the glass section of his door. A tall man, stooped not with physical labour but attention to screen and keyboard. Solly could see Tony too and motioned for him to enter.

'I heard you were coming in today,' Solly said, and they shook hands.

Tony talked of his trip again, then asked Solly how things were going. It was a superficial conversation, for they'd never been close. Early in Tony's time as chief, they'd clashed over roles. Solly had maintained that he was entitled to direct access to the board on major financial matters, had lost the battle on that and afterwards preserved an impersonal efficiency to disguise his resentment. Solly now praised Nikora's management style as an indirect criticism of Tony's own, but Tony responded only with affable interest.

'I'm going for a wander around the plant,' he said as he stood up. 'I'll notice changes no doubt.'

'We're on the up and up now.' Solly gave the last word a slight emphasis.

Tony walked across the lawn from the admin building towards the main processing plant. When he'd been appointed as CEO, that lawn space was roughly gravelled and used as a staff-parking area, sometimes even by mobile harvesters and trucks. He'd had lawn put down, garden plots and a modest plinth with a granite commemoration of Cedric Marples, founder of the firm. It remained well maintained. Tony was pleased to see that Nikora, too, understood the importance of first impressions.

A cube-shaped, double-door entrance enabled the main processing building to be kept at the optimum temperature, and he felt the chill as he entered. In the first bay, they were working on peas, and he went to the conveyor belt where five women and one young guy were picking any damaged peas or detritus from the flow that passed them. It wasn't easy to distinguish the workers from each other because of their hygienic smocks and hair coverings, but Tony prided himself on knowing at least some of the long-serving people on the factory floor. The thin, older woman with a nose that flared somewhat at its end was surely Megan Posswillow, and he stood closer so that he was noticed, despite the background noise and the transparent cap covering her ears. Megan half turned on her stool and smiled.

'Still here, Megan?' said Tony, then wished the comment less obvious. She smiled again and nodded, her hands briefly stilled. 'Good to see you again.' His voice slightly raised because of the machinery.

'Yes, you too Mr Weymouth,' she said, slightly embarrassed, yet pleased to be singled out.

Tony walked on over the concrete floor, veering from the conveyor belts and blanchers towards the freezers, where he saw Anton talking to a guy with a clipboard. Anton was assistant factory manager and well known to Tony and their meeting was cordial. The clipboard guy was newly appointed to a distribution role. Anton introduced him, but the new man soon realised the other two were talking of a past in which he had no place, so he excused himself to get on with work. Tony enjoyed the catch up, and Anton seemed pleased to see him, although obviously too busy to invite his former chief to sit in the comparative quietness of the glass-panelled office to reminisce.

'Absolutely full on,' he said. 'You're well out of it.' But he smiled. Tony asked him about the deferment of the plans for the additional on-site refrigeration. He'd spent a lot of time on the project and was disappointed to find it shelved. 'Yeah, I thought of you,' said Anton. 'Solly and Nikora came round to the view that it was better to take advantage of cheap storage capacity at the harbour, and the board went along with it.'

'We need to be self-sufficient though, for god's sake.' The inclusive pronoun still came naturally to Tony.

'I'm with you there, but that's the way it went. Long term I think you're absolutely right.'

The clipboard guy had returned and stood at a little distance, waiting for Anton's attention. Some issue at despatch had arisen.

'I better go and sort this,' Anton said. 'There's always something, isn't there? Who knows that better than you, eh? Well, you can sit back and smile now. You've earned it.'

'Stick with it,' Tony advised him, and then, 'Khadi about?'

'He's checking crops at Lointon, I think,' said Anton. He shook hands and walked off briskly in conversation with the distribution man. Tony stood for a while looking about him. Khadi was field manager and a long-time friend and colleague. In his disappointment, Tony decided to go no farther in the factory and walked back towards the main entrance, feeling the familiar slight vibration of the plant and hearing the habitual melody of its light machinery.

Everything was as he recalled it, yet different somehow, and he began to understand why. The deference he'd been accorded at Marples Foodstuffs had been the result of his position, rather than his nature. That realisation was unsettling, deflating even, and diminished the pleasure he had in returning to an organisation whose success owed so much to him — at least in his own estimation. He'd assumed that his reception would be much as it had been formerly when he was in charge. He should have known better. It wasn't that there was animosity, just that he was no longer an essential part of the team, wasn't part of the team at all. People were busy, and although most greeted him warmly enough, their preoccupations and loyalties lay elsewhere now. He was no longer important — that was it, and he'd become accustomed to being important. All this was reinforced when he went back to the admin building to see Nikora again before leaving.

'I'm sorry,' Judy told him, 'but he's got the board chair with him now. You're welcome to wait here.' But he had no wish to wait outside an office that not long ago had been his own.

When Tony was again in summer warmth and crossing the neat

lawns, this time toward the car park, a woman passed him, turned, smiled and said, 'Mr Weymouth. I thought it was you.' Was her face familiar? Maybe so, but he had no idea of her name. An upright, well-built woman with short, blonde hair and a small, resolute mouth. 'Nina Necklermann,' she said.

'Ah, yes,' he replied, as if much had come back to him.

'You probably don't remember me, but I was the first woman here to be a full-time driver. The truckies weren't all that keen. It seemed odd to them, I suppose, but you decided it was down to who could do the job, irrespective of sex.'

'Of course, yes,' he said, but had only a hazy recollection of that decision — one among so many.

'I'm still driving, you know, tankers too, and I'm not the only one now. There's three of us women on trucks.'

'Good on you.'

'I wanted to say thank you.'

'I appreciate that, Nina,' he said. 'I'm pleased you're still here and happy with the work.'

'I am. I just saw you and thought, that's Mr Weymouth, and I wanted to say thank you.'

Tony watched her go. He felt better than at any other time during his visit, and most of it had been fine. He wouldn't come again, though, for he was ordinary at Marples now.

Jasper Coursey in Nice

Jasper arrived from Marseilles to Nice by bus. The inland route, though he was sorry to miss Toulon, which the train passes through, but the bus was cheaper and only a little slower. A budget is important when you are twenty-four and having the big OE year in Europe. It was raining in Nice, and Jasper hoped the next day would be fine because that was all the time he planned in the city, and he didn't want rain to be his enduring memory of the place. It's like that when you're a flitting traveller in foreign countries: Turin for Jasper is always in the grip of a rail strike; Albacete closed for a religious holiday; Tirana merely a nest of thieves, one of whom stole his phone. Capri, on the other hand, is bathed in eternal aromatic sunshine; Vernazza has the best paella in the world; and women of Viborg are all beautiful, fair haired and called Freja. Ah, Freja.

The rain wasn't heavy that evening in Nice, so Jasper walked through its drift in his red nylon jacket until he reached a backpackers not far from the beach. He was to find it had various deficiencies, as such places always do. His was an eight-person dorm, and neither the light nor charger above his bed worked, but the linen was clean and the individual security locker sound enough. There were cooking facilities, but free of his pack Jasper went again into the soft, grey rain and had frites and yellow cake in a small café away from the tourist streets. Rosé wine too, which was the cheapest on the Cote d'Azur and weak as a cordial. The only other customers were an elderly couple who spoke not a word to each other but seemed perfectly at ease. Jasper wondered if in a long and compatible marriage words finally became unnecessary.

There was a communal room at the backpackers, which he went into when he returned and talked for a while with two Australian women and an older guy from London who said he spoke both French and German. Jasper couldn't test the assertion and had no reason to doubt it, but he thought it unusual that someone with such linguistic skills should be reduced to backpacker accommodation. As a Kiwi Jasper was only recently aware of how multi-lingual many Europeans are. The Englishman had been in Nice for several days, had visited at other times and he willingly gave advice as to how time there was best spent. You must go to this gallery, that restaurant, such and such an alpine village.

When he tired of such instruction, Jasper retreated to his dorm and had a shower. There were five other occupants, and after brief acknowledgement he went to bed. Some of his fellows read, wrote, or used their phones when the main light was turned off, but Jasper had no bed light. A bearded guy offered him the chance to charge his phone, and he took it. He lay listening for rain but was asleep before he could decide if it still fell.

The blue sky in the morning transformed the city. Jasper parked his pack, headed for the sea and had a frugal breakfast at a café close to the Promenade des Anglais, which curved around the pebbled bay. He watched the walkers, joggers, dogs with owners, even a few early swimmers whose posture showed awareness of their own audacity. At the next table were a young woman and an old man. All was peaceful until, in a flurry too rapid to allow prevention, a speeding, dark-skinned boy fell from his skateboard, which careered into the couple's table, Jasper only partly able to slow it with his foot. Food and dishes were flung aside, the noise was great, but no one was hurt, not even the boy, who took the retrieved board from Jasper, shouted what was presumably an apology and ran off. Jasper assisted in the clean-up, and when the café staff had gone inside, he sat with the two and asked if there was any other help they needed. They were mainly concerned about their clothes, especially the young woman.

'There's stuff all over my jeans,' she said, 'and coffee on my top. Jesus.'

They talked about the suddenness of it — seeing it coming but without time for avoidance — before they introduced themselves: Gerald Bigelow and his niece Lucy Jaye. Jasper was to learn later that it was Dr Gerald, but that made no difference. They were English and having their own European tour — a first time for Lucy, a swansong for Gerald. Jasper judged him to be in his eighties but decided not to enquire. Gerald had taught at Warwick University and was also a genealogical researcher.

'What do you know about your name?' he asked Jasper.

'I assume it's from that green gemstone, isn't it? That's what I've always believed.'

'I wouldn't think so. Jasper means treasurer and derives from a Hebrew word and further back from Persian. Not sure about Coursey. I'd say French, but I'd have to check it out. You can find almost anything on Google now. I'm becoming redundant.'

'I'll have to go back to the hotel and change,' Lucy said. 'I stink of scrambled egg.'

'Off you go then. I'll stay with Jasper — and don't be all day.'

Lucy was attractive in a conventional, blonde way. Her cheeks were streaked with sun lotion, her forehead high and smooth. Jasper would have preferred she were the one staying, or that he could go with her to the hotel, but he didn't wish to be rude, and Gerald was intelligent and interesting enough for an old guy. Besides, he ordered more coffee and cakes. Jasper had become quite fond of pastries at breakfast. They talked of what each wished to do in the city and compared choices. Some of Jasper's were the consequence of his talk with the multi-lingual Londoner the night before.

'I've got just the day here,' Jasper said. 'I'm booked this evening on the bus to Ventimiglia.'

'How's the money holding?' Gerald asked as he watched Jasper take a third macaroon.

'I need to get some work pretty soon,' Jasper said. 'I'll ask around some restaurants tomorrow. I'm okay at washing up and washing out. You don't need much of the language for that, but mostly I get field jobs. I'm used to animals and crops. In Italy I'll work a while if I can, but today I'll enjoy being here.'

No doubt they appeared an odd couple there at the outside café table, close to the beachfront of Nice, the sun already ablaze, all sorts of people with all sorts of intentions passing on the Promenade des Anglais. Jasper tall, even formidable, a guy on the road with his brown hairy legs and yellow boots; Gerald thin, frail, but well dressed in a very English sunhat and light jacket over a blue shirt. An old man whose hands trembled slightly on the sunlit table and whose lower eyelids drooped, showing moist, pink linings. He studied Jasper as they talked and then took advantage of a pause.

'I have a proposition,' he said. 'Not, however, an improper one,' he continued with a smile. 'I'll tell you before Lucy comes back. She's my niece but also what the Victorians used to call a paid companion. We like each other, and she's been great, but she needs some time to herself. I suppose, I do too. I'm old and slow and particular about things. Last night at the hotel, she got talking to some American girls, and they invited her to join them on a trip to the Fragonard perfume factory at Eze. She'd love to go, I know, but won't leave me by myself, and I don't want to spend the afternoon sniffing from bottles. Anyway, the proposition's this — you and I do our thing together so she can have her trip. You'll be guardian, and I'll be guide. Food on me and a hundred and sixty euros if you bring me back alive.'

Jasper was surprised — being carer and companion to an old geezer wasn't how he'd envisaged his day in Nice — but a hundred and sixty euros was a good deal of money to him, and he didn't imagine much effort being involved. He did have conditions, though, and told Gerald he'd do it, but there were some places he definitely needed to see.

'We'll work out an itinerary, but first I need to contact Lucy so she can check that it's still okay with her friends,' said Gerald. 'They'll still be at the hotel if she's lucky.'

They weren't, but easily contacted by Lucy, so the trip to Eze was on, but only after Gerald reassured her that he'd be fine. After talking with him, she asked to speak to Jasper. Gerald passed over his phone and sat happily in the strong sunlight with his eyes closed, like a well-dressed lizard.

'This is all pretty sudden, isn't it?' she said.

'Yeah, it is,' said Jasper. 'He seems keen, though, and we'll work out the places to go. He's been here several times before, hasn't he? He wants you to have the chance to see the perfume factory.'

'You have to remember all the time how old he is, no matter what he says. He can talk like a young guy, but he's eighty-two. You need always to take it easy and know where the toilets are. Put my number on your phone, and we'll keep in touch during the day. Make sure you have a long lunch hour and he has cold drinks. And don't let him climb on things. This afternoon, we can arrange a rendezvous time at the hotel.'

'We'll be fine. We won't be going far, just a few places around the city. The Chagall Museum and places like that.'

'It won't be a picnic, you know,' said Lucy. 'There's responsibility and thinking ahead. Are you sure about it? Are you up to it?'

'Yeah, absolutely.'

'How much is he paying you?'

'Privileged information,' said Jasper, then, 'Just kidding. Hundred and sixty euros.'

'So, lucky you. We'll keep in touch during the day. Make sure you look after him and remember about the toilets.'

'You have a good time too. Soak up those perfumes.'

'Okay. See you this afternoon.'

'Sure thing,' said Jasper, who began putting her number on his own phone. He had no hesitation in being Gerald's companion but was a little surprised that Lucy agreed to hand him over to a stranger, even one who had proved to be of assistance. He wondered if her hotel acquaintances included a guy, but Gerald said no, they were all women.

'So, what's first?' Jasper asked him.

'I like the historic places best,' said Gerald.

Although Jasper was young, he did too, maybe because he came from a country where nothing was really old. They decided to go to the original part of the city, to the Castle Hill with its ruins, gardens and views.

'The ancient Greeks settled here,' said Gerald. 'That's how it got its name, Nike was the Greek goddess of victory.'

Jasper would have walked — distance was nothing to him — but a taxi was necessary for Gerald, otherwise he'd be buggered by the time they got there. He had some French and talked a bit with the taxi driver about the fare to let him know he wasn't to be overcharged. After they were dropped off at the bus station, at the foot of the hill where the old town began, Gerald handed his sizable man-bag to Jasper to carry.

'I'll keep up better without it,' he said. 'It's like I have a handbag now — glasses, wallet, phone, passport, tissues and pills, lip salve, even a puffer. I travel like a woman now.'

'I could just take off with it, money and all,' said Jasper as they began on the incline into the narrow streets, lined with small shops and the old buildings in faded shades of pink, yellow and grey.

'Indeed, you could, Jasper. Yes,' said Gerald, but absently as his attention was on the precinct they were entering. 'Nothing much seems to have changed,' he said with satisfaction.

No doubt the shops and apartments were inconvenient, difficult to maintain and unsuited to modern use, but they had charm, and there was profit to be made of that. Boutique tourist places, side alley cafés, flowers in window boxes, uneven cobbles. Churches too and buildings with dark interiors and heavy external ornamentation that once had municipal purpose. Wherever there were steps, Gerald took scrupulous care, as if he suspected they were booby trapped.

'Have you bought any gifts for your people at home?' he asked.

'Not much. I can't cart a lot of stuff around,' said Jasper.

'That's right. That's why you should buy some soap here. The place is famous for it, and the bars are cheap, small, long lasting and don't damage easily. You may even need to use one yourself.' Gerald stopped at a small shop devoted entirely to soaps, some in fancy packaging but most loose in large baskets. They were shaped like lemons, very hard and brightly coloured. Jasper bought a green, a purple and a yellow. 'Miriam used to buy soap here,' Gerald said. Jasper assumed her to have been his wife.

They had coffee close to a flower market. On going inside, Gerald had taken off his hat to reveal sparse, grey hair and hearing aids, also grey. He talked of earlier visits to Nice, on one occasion to attend a symposium at the university.

'We used to walk up to the ruins and the park and look over the city and the sea,' he said.

'We'll do that soon. I'm looking forward to it,' said Jasper. Had he been alone, he would have been up there already.

'But I'll have to use the lift now. You could walk up, Jasper, and I could meet you there.'

'No, I'll come with you.' This recognition of responsibility made him think of Lucy, so he rang.

'Where are you?' she asked, and when told she said that she was on the bus to Eze. 'Send me a photo from the top,' she said. Then she talked to Gerald, and he said that he was completely satisfied with Jasper so far.

'So far,' he repeated with a smile for Jasper. 'He's obliged to listen to me, and I don't have to listen to him. Not only is he my paid companion, he's no relation. Anyway, buy a bottle of the best perfume in Eze, and I'll give it to you for your birthday.' That made a pleasant conclusion to the call.

'Teaching and family research must pay well,' Jasper said.

'Not really. My grandfather had a pig farm on the outskirts of Nottingham. No great living, but as the city grew the land became more and more valuable. He wouldn't sell and dug in there until his death at ninety-three. I owe a certain financial ease to my grandfather's pig farm.'

'So, you've been able to travel anywhere you like?'

'But I was busy at the university,' Gerald said. 'There are responsibilities. I should have travelled even more. I've never been to South America, for instance.'

'But you've been retired for years, haven't you?'

'I should have taken more advantage then. Mind you, that whole Covid business would put anyone off travel. I couldn't be bothered with the hassle of it. You think you have for ever, but the years tick by and you find old age is a prison of reduced capability.' Despite what he said, Gerald didn't seem to be suffering unduly from degenerative incarceration. His smile remained, and he was happy in surroundings he recalled. He told Jasper of a trip he'd made to the mountain village of St Agnes some twenty years before.

Although Jasper looked around, there was no indication of a customers' lavatory in the café, but Gerald fronted up to the proprietor, a woman considerably larger than himself, and she reluctantly led him away to relieve himself. Jasper also felt relief, remembering Lucy's instructions. From the café, they walked on through the narrow streets, Gerald occasionally pausing for a breather, until they reached the lift, which took them to the ruins and gardens at the top of the hill, where they sat together to see the city and ocean spread below. It was just as in a tourist brochure, but with fragrances and soft sounds from the movement of the breeze. Jasper took some photos, and Gerald sat with his hat pulled forward to shield his face from the sun.

'What are you going to do in life, Jasper?' he asked. He had the habit of including the name of those he addressed, even when there was no risk of confusion.

'I've got a BSc. I think I might take a job with the Department of Conservation. I've worked a bit there and quite enjoyed it. Mainly I'm interested in the regeneration of native plants and the retirement of land unsuitable for farming.'

'I wish I'd been to New Zealand. I did go to Australia a couple of times but never got out of the cities, except to vineyards. My father had a good deal to do with Australians in the war and talked about them sometimes.'

'I like Aussies,' said Jasper. 'They're straight shooters.'

'He said in the war they were great foragers. I think he meant thieves, but that's what war's all about, isn't it, just on a grander scale?'

Jasper was a practical guy, not much given to flights of imagination, but he experienced a sense almost of epiphany, sitting there with the city and ocean spread below and with Gerald as companion. He'd taken photos of the view but none of Gerald, and so he took his phone, asked the old guy to push his hat back and took a selfie with him. Jasper might return to the views from Colline du Château but not with this companion. In the photograph, they'd be together always.

'I'll send this one to Lucy,' Jasper said.

'What a pleasant breeze,' said Gerald. 'Ideal here in so many ways. No wonder they built the castle on this spot. They could be safe, cool and keep a look out for invaders all at once. All these coastal settlements were often attacked by pirates and Saracens.'

'But they had to cart every bloody thing up the hill — not easy hundreds of years ago,' commented Jasper.

'True, Jasper.'

'I'm getting hungry. Do you think we should eat in the old town, or head back into the city, find a place there and afterwards go on to the galleries?'

'There's a couple of really good couscous restaurants here. I've been to them, and I suspect they're still thriving. Why don't we go there?'

So, they wandered back down to the old town and after enquiry found a couscous place, although Gerald wasn't sure it was one he remembered. They sat at a small metal table on the street close to the door but shaded by the two storeys above them. Gerald ordered them couscous with smoked sausage and peppers, which Jasper didn't think much of, but he kept that to himself for he wasn't paying and the white wine was much better than the rosé he'd drunk the evening before. Gerald was a slow eater and paused often to scrutinise anyone arriving, as if he expected to recognise someone from his past.

He was showing Jasper a photograph of Eze sent through by Lucy, when a dog fell, or was thrown, from a balcony above them. It didn't bounce but rather crushed on the cobbles like a very large egg. The only noise was of the impact, and some blood from its snout was cast across Jasper's bare legs. That's how close it was.

'Christ!' Jasper exclaimed, scrambling up from his chair, which caught on the uneven cobbles and toppled. Gerald's reflexes were less responsive; he just sat with the phone still in his hand and his face wrinkled up in disbelief.

It wasn't an especially small dog: medium sized with short ears, brownish with a white patch on its neck, quite dead. Its lips were drawn back from the teeth as if in defiance of fate even as it fell. No one else seemed to have witnessed the incident, so Jasper had to go inside, call out in English — knowing he might well not be understood — and motion with his arm to get the proprietor to follow him. The restaurant man nonchalantly pushed the dog's body away from the shop front into the gutter with his foot and covered it with a tablecloth. He was more concerned with the effect on trade than where the dog had dropped from, or how Jasper and Gerald were feeling. Gerald had to draw his attention to the blood on Jasper's legs before he took them inside and offered help.

'Someone's after us,' said Gerald when Jasper was cleaned up and they sat at an inside table with complimentary coffees. 'First the skateboard as a missile and now a dog thrown from the heavens.'

'Poor bugger,' said Jasper. 'I wonder what happened.'

'I never heard or saw anything. You were lucky it didn't land on you, it was so close.'

'No one's come down.'

'Don't want to have to get rid of it, I suppose, or else no one's home.'

The dog was still there when they left, the front paws with black pads protruding from the red-and-white chequered tablecloth. They decided to say nothing to Lucy about what had happened, at least not until reunited with her at the end of the day. It was after two in the afternoon when they left the old precinct for the bus station and the modern city. They sat for a while for a reassessment, knowing there was no longer time to do all they'd planned. Jasper's bus left at half-six for Ventimiglia, and before that he had to deliver Gerald back to the hotel and Lucy's care.

'It becomes a question of priorities,' said Gerald, 'and compromise.'

'You can choose,' said Jasper. After all, he was being paid.

'But I'll be here tomorrow, Jasper, and maybe the day after. I've other opportunities, and besides I've been here before. What do you most want to see?'

'We talked about the galleries, didn't we? The Matisse and Chagall museums.'

'I don't think there'll be time for both. You make a choice. I don't mind.'

'In Paris, I saw the Chagall ceiling in the Opera house. I liked that,' said Jasper.

'There you are then, decision made,' said Gerald.

For most of the taxi ride, Gerald slept, or appeared to, and Jasper didn't disturb him. For an old guy, he'd already done quite a lot during the day, and the falling dog and the walking would have sapped him, even though he hadn't been as close to the dog as Jasper and didn't seem at all traumatised. A certain detachment had come with his old age.

The Chagall Museum was an attractive place, set in gardens and walkways, and with the artist's paintings, drawings, prints, even ceramics and stained glass. Most paintings were large, and the vivid blues and reds were accentuated by the severe, white walls. Drifting animals and angels, strangely elongated against an indistinct, wonderfully colourful background. It was odd stuff. Jasper enjoyed looking at it, although he wasn't sure why, and Gerald made most of the comments. He said Chagall was influenced by both Fauvism and Surrealism. Jasper had no idea what Fauvism was and only a hazy conception of the other.

The gallery had a café, and Jasper and Gerald took coffees outside to the gardens and paths. Olive trees and cypresses stood green against the throbbing blue of the sky. Jasper liked trees; liked most plants and hoped to make his occupation among them. He wondered what the native vegetation had been when the Greeks arrived all those years ago, as Gerald had said. The climate could have been different then. Plants adapted too. Most people were only interested in the evolution of creatures, dinosaurs and other monsters, but Jasper knew something of the history of plants, which had their own struggles to survive and rule.

Gerald enjoyed the heat and sat with his big hat and light jacket in the sun. Jasper would have preferred the shade.

'You feel the cold when you're older,' Gerald said. 'There's never enough sun in England.'

'I thought there might be more people here,' said Jasper.

'It's the sleepy time of the day.'

A hawker with shiny belts and purses approached them, but Gerald told him politely they weren't interested.

'Algerian, I'd say,' he told Jasper when the man had gone.

'Your French must be pretty good.'

'Not at all, but I can make myself understood. Like most who haven't been taught, I understand it better than I speak it. I don't like to use French with people I know, but when you're travelling it doesn't matter how much you embarrass yourself with strangers. You can move on.'

'I wish I could speak French or German. You can't get to know locals much without their language.'

'I suspect in the end we'll all have the same one. I wonder what will win out — English, Hindi or Chinese? It'll be a battle to the death.'

'There must be more Chinese speakers, so that's an advantage.'

'It's not just a numbers game though, Jasper,' said Gerald. 'It's about cultural dominance and political power.'

And so, they sat in the sunlit gardens and talked of languages, and later of Chagall's paintings, and they watched the hawker being successively rebuffed by others in the grounds.

'It must be great to be able come back like this: get to revisit places special to you,' Jasper said.

'Yes, pleasant enough,' said Gerald, 'but it's not the same. The world is always at its best when you yourself are in your prime. You reflect your own condition on what you see.' The sun shone as if the day would never end, and the flowers shone too, and the trees were sketched against the sky, and a consciously beautiful woman in white slacks stood by the entrance.

Gerald was in no hurry, but Jasper had a deadline, and not only did they have to rendezvous with Lucy before that, but he had to reclaim his gear from the backpackers and reach the bus station.

'I better go and arrange a taxi for us,' he said. 'They speak English at the desk. Can you give Lucy a call and say we'll be there by five?'

Lucy was waiting, and they sat together in the hotel lounge to share their experiences of the day. She was on a high, and Jasper thought that not only a consequence of Eze's attractions and the perfumes bought there, but the time spent with women of her own age and predilections, free from responsibility. She wasn't entirely preoccupied with her own experiences, however, and enjoyed being told of the falling dog at the couscous restaurant and the gardens and paintings of the Chagall Museum. She asked to see the soaps Jasper bought and said she must buy some for herself. For Lucy and her uncle, it was time to relax, reflect and share, but Jasper had to move on, and he experienced that unavoidable emotional transfer that occurs when you must concentrate on your own future, which doesn't involve those you are with. There is a slight but nagging sense of loneliness and loss.

'I have to be on my way if I'm to get the bus before six-thirty,' he said.

'Have a drink with us before you go,' said Lucy. 'We've hardly talked, and it's been a fab day.'

'Yes, a quick drink,' added Gerald. 'I'll give you extra for a taxi, so you won't be late.' He took his wallet, somewhat clumsily assembled the notes, and proffered them. 'Thank you, Jasper. Thank you. I've enjoyed it all.'

'Hey, I don't get that much for one day,' said Lucy in mock accusation.

''Cause it's casual rates — but yes, this is really generous, and I've had a day to remember,' said Jasper. He found the leave-taking slightly awkward. It had been fun, and he liked them both, but he'd been paid to do a job, hadn't he, and he would never see them again. 'I better dash,' he said. 'I've still got to get my pack and so on.'

'All the very best, Jasper. May life be kind to you,' said Gerald, and he leant forward to shake hands then relaxed back into the lounge chair, his mouth slightly open, but still with a smile.

'See you. Thanks,' said Lucy.

When he turned at the door, they were looking towards him, and both raised an arm. Jasper knew they would talk about him for a bit when he was gone before taking up their own plans together again.

He wouldn't take a taxi, Jasper decided. The fare would be extra in his pocket to be spent on more important things. He would lope to the backpackers and hurry on to the bus station. He would soon be on his way to Italy, with almost two hundred euros more than he had the day before. There were places he'd hoped to see in Nice that he'd missed, but there might be other opportunities, and he'd spent time with old Gerald — hadn't he? — learnt that Jasper meant treasurer, and came from Hebrew and Persian, and he still had traces of blood on his legs from a dog that fell from a balcony above a couscous restaurant in the old precinct of the city. The sun shone as if the day would have no end, and Jasper sped cheerfully through the streets of Nice to reach the point of his departure. To travel on.

Up at the Nancy

If you had been with us then, as we moved out of the bush and onto the snow tussock of the mountain side, you would've thought it was going to be a pretty good day. Jacob, Doug and I after deer, or feral goats if they came our way. It's not a good idea to do too much hunting on your own, and three's not a crowd when you take turns carrying a carcass out or a trophy head. It's good to know who you're with too, rather than hunting with strangers. We have a lengthy history together: Doug I've known since primary school; and Jacob since I joined Goliath Transport. We go out when we can. They're best with rifles, while I like shooting over water more. The shotgun, I think, suits the more instinctive shooter.

We hadn't seen much game at all that afternoon, but mainly we just wanted to get up to the Nancy hut and get settled there with our gear. It's not great hunting with a full pack. The Nancy sits on a bit of a ridge, so is mainly clear of snow in winter, and it's close to a creek that usually has water even in summer. It was summer that day, and a bit of slog in the heat, but four hours after leaving the ute we reached the hut, which is all tin and timber and only one room. We sat by the door with bare feet, our boots and socks in the sun beside us to dry. My feet were pale and wrinkled from crossing that damn river so often on the way up. We chewed on scroggin and debated whether it was worth going out for what was left of the day. Doug was keen, but the sun was already low, and Jacob and I wanted to rustle up a decent cooked meal.

'I'll go over the ridge a bit,' Doug said, 'see if there's anything doing along the creek. I'll bring back some more water too.'

'We'll eat in an hour or so,' I said.

'Yeah, okay.' He put his boots on again, took his rifle and left. He's an odd build is Doug: very long legs without much muscle, but I don't know anyone who could outwalk him, and he's going bald at twenty-nine. Maybe already having two children and running his own hire business has been aging.

'He's that bloody keen,' said Jacob, who for the moment was more interested in resting and eating than shooting things. For that matter, so was I. Rice-and-bacon curry was what we decided on, but there was time enough for that, so we sat in the sun with our backs resting on the corrugated iron of the hut and had a laugh and a grizzle about things at work. They were rearranging the teams at Goliath, and we weren't fussed on how it was turning out.

We had our cooker going on the hut bench when Jacob saw Doug coming back.

'What the fuck!' he said, because Doug wasn't alone. He had a carry bag and walking beside him was a woman in a blue dress. A dress, for Christ's sake. It was like something in a Jane Campion film. Bean-pole Doug in hunting gear in the wop-wops returning with a woman in a blue dress. We could see them on the treeless alpine slope, and stood at the door, gobsmacked, watching them draw closer.

It was a strange introduction, there at the hut, with the sun low and the temperature already dropping. Her name was Rhona, and she seemed remarkably composed for a woman discovered wandering along a creek in the mountains.

'It's so good to see somebody,' she said, 'and a hut too. Maybe I would've passed this way and seen it before dark. A relief though. It'll be cold up here at night even in summer.'

'Rhona got left behind by a helicopter,' said Doug, who knew we were wondering where the hell she'd arrived from, and he raised his eyebrows to show his own disbelief.

'How so?' I asked.

'I came up with my husband to take photographs, and we had a row. A heck of a row, and I wouldn't get back in, and he said he'd teach me a lesson then and flew off and left me.'

We hadn't heard anything, but Rhona said it was in the morning, and she'd been wandering ever since. What sort of a husband would leave his wife alone in the mountains just because they'd had a row?

'He'll come back before dark, right?' said Jacob.

'He won't before tomorrow,' Rhona said firmly.

'So, he must know about the hut here?' I said.

'No idea. Probably not,' she said.

So, we ended up having a rice-and-bacon curry with Rhona in the Nancy, and she ate well and talked well — not about her husband at first but camera work. That was their job: freelance photography with a chopper, mainly for DOC, coffee-table book publishers, or farmers who wanted an aerial picture of their property for the lounge wall. Even film people looking for locations.

She showed us a cut on her leg from speargrass, and Doug told her the best thing to do was to leave the cut to scab up but wash around it. Although in a dress, she was wearing sturdy sneakers. Rhona wasn't young; I'd say she was in her fifties, but it's difficult to tell with women. Her dark hair, tied back, had a tinge of grey above her ears. A compact woman of medium height who moved well and so didn't seem all that out of place in the mountains, even if she did wear a dress.

No husband appeared to claim her, and it became obvious that she'd spend the night with us. There was awkwardness in that initially. The hut had four bunks and a long drop a few metres away. Jacob pointed it out and put our roll of toilet paper tactfully by the hut door without comment. Rhona's carry bag held mostly camera stuff and a couple of cans of Sprite that she offered up. There were just palliasses on the bunks, no bedding, and so she needed a sleeping bag, although she said she didn't. Mine was almost new and didn't smell as much as Doug's or Jacob's.

'It's summer, and I've got a jersey,' I told her.

'Are you sure? That's really kind,' she said. 'I'm being a nuisance here, I know, and I've eaten half your food as well.'

'No probs,' said Doug. 'We'll have venison steaks by tomorrow night.'

'Take the low bunk,' I told her, 'so you don't have to be clambering about.' I put her bag there. 'Tomorrow one of us will walk you out if your husband doesn't turn up. You'll be okay.'

'I've got my cell phone,' Rhona said. 'I've already tried to get him. Is there coverage?'

'Not up here,' Jacob said. 'You can't use it until you're almost out of the valley. Hours away.'

Rhona wanted to help with the clean-up, but we had our own ways that didn't use a lot of water, and Doug did most of it because he hadn't been there for the meal's preparation. We talked for quite a while: Rhona was interested in the hunting, especially that we'd done it together for years. She'd never photographed hunters and thought it would make a good book — scenic, yet with a topic for focus at the same time — but we told her there were oodles of hunting books. I found it strange that after being abandoned in the mountains she could seem so unconcerned. And being in an isolated hut with three strange guys would have made most women pretty quiet, I'd say. I think she talked about her work at first to avoid having to explain what had gone wrong with her marriage.

We turned in soon after ten. There's not much you can do in a candle-lit hut once you've finished talking. The three of us went outside so that Rhona could take off her dress and get into the sleeping bag. There was a moon, so more light outside than in. No wind, the tussock country palely passive between the dark mountain cut-outs and the dense bush further down.

'This is an odd bloody thing, isn't it?' Doug said.

'Let's hope her guy turns up tomorrow,' I said. 'We can hardly go off and leave her stuck here.'

'Why would she run off in a place like this anyway, without any gear or anything? Must have been some god-almighty, bloody shouting match.' Jacob seemed half irritated, half sympathetic. He was the only one of us not married and unused to compromise.

'Her husband's sure to turn up first thing in the morning,' I said. 'The noise of the chopper will wake us. I wonder where he puts down?'

'There's those flatter bits further round the second ridge,' said Doug.

I was fully dressed, and the hut was dark, so there was no embarrassment as I climbed into the top bunk. After the afternoon's hike up with a full pack, I didn't expect to be awake long, but once I'd settled Rhona began to talk.

'I don't want to be a nuisance to you all,' she said. 'You should just carry on with your plans as if I wasn't here. Keith will come for me tomorrow, and it'll all be okay. We've been married more than thirty years and had our ups and downs. We get through things and carry on.'

'He shouldn't have left you here like that no matter what happened,' I said.

'He blows up easily.'

'You've got no gear or anything to stay up here. He didn't even know about the hut, I'm guessing. You could've been in the open all night.'

'We haven't flown here before and came up from the other side.'

'It's really stupid and dangerous. Who the heck acts like that?' I said.

'He's got some issues. Always has, and they've got worse not better.'

'He doesn't knock you around, does he?'

'Nothing like that. No.'

'If he hits you, you should go straight to the police. Even once. There's no excuse.'

'Nothing like that. He's okay in most ways. He didn't want to have any kids, and I did. We had that argument for years. Although it's too late now, it's something I can't forgive, and he knows it. It's always there between us.'

Weird really, to be lying in a top bunk there in the Nancy, and have Rhona's quiet, disembodied voice coming up to reveal the intimacies of her marriage. Probably Doug and Jacob on the other side of the hut couldn't hear, maybe they wanted to stay out of it. Rhona didn't stop there; she went on to other things equally personal, and all I had to do was listen. She told me that Keith had been a fireman in Aussie, and they'd also spent time in Singapore.

'There's always something better for him somewhere else,' she said. 'Always the pot of gold at another rainbow. And he won't put his money in the bank. Won't wear wool next to his skin. Never wanted any children. Wouldn't have children. I've got no children at all and never will now. How sad is that?'

'Why was he so hung up about it?' I asked her.

'Because of something when he was a kid that he doesn't talk about. It must have been a really peculiar family, I think. I've never met any of them; they didn't even come to our wedding. He did once tell me his father had killed the neighbour's dog with a spade.' She had a lot more to say about Keith and their marriage, but it all began to blur, and I fell asleep. Did she keep going half the night, talking to herself in the darkness on and on as the rest of us slept? I don't know.

It wasn't a chopper that woke us in the morning but someone banging on the door. Barely light. As I was fully clothed, I climbed down, Rhona looking at me, just her head visible from the sleeping bag. A tall guy wearing jeans and a beanie, and holding a pink puffer jacket, was at the door. It had to be Keith, surely: a stranger I knew a great deal about, more than he could ever be comfortable with.

'Thank god, thank god,' he said when I told him, yes, Rhona was with us. 'Where is she? Is she okay?' I could have told him she was in my sleeping bag, but it didn't seem the time for that sort of humour or any other. I opened the door fully so he could see her; she was now sitting up in the bunk with the blue dress draped over her shoulders. Keith hurried straight to her and gave her a hug, which she seemed happy enough with. He put the puffer jacket around her and said how relieved and sorry he was, that he'd been looking everywhere for her.

Jacob and Doug, having slept in their underpants as usual, were able to put on their clothes without embarrassment, and the three of us went outside for a bit to give Rhona and Keith time to sort things between them.

'Well, she'll be okay now,' said Doug. 'We'll be able to go off for the day as we planned. Bloody odd business though.'

'We'll have to give them breakfast. A coffee at least,' said Jacob. 'All of this is pretty weird, eh. What was she talking about half the night over there, and where's this guy come from? I can't understand why we didn't hear anything before he turned up.'

I found out why that was later, when Rhona, in blue dress and pink puffer jacket, had walked off to the long drop and left Keith and I sitting on her bunk while the other two got muesli and coffee ready.

'No, no,' said Keith, 'I never went anywhere. I stayed with the chopper all night, waiting for her to return. Before first light, I set off to find her, and bloody worried, I can tell you. She was lucky to link up with you three. I appreciate that. What did she tell you all?'

'She said you had a hell of a row, and she buggered off, basically. And that you did too. Just left her. She told me there's no children because you don't want any, and she can't get over that. She went on about it.'

Keith put his head back and closed his eyes briefly in a sort of exasperated resignation. 'Ah, yes. Jesus, yes. Always the usual spiel about no kids and it's my fault. It's sad and crap at the same time. Can I tell you something? We had a daughter, and we had a granddaughter. Our granddaughter died when she was ten months, and Steph committed suicide ten months afterwards. That's what all this is about really. Rhona won't see anyone for counselling, and she keeps saying we didn't have any children and it's because of me. She's okay some of the time, and we get on with life and the photography, but it all bubbles up sooner or later. It's always there for her. For us both really. Stuff like that doesn't go away. It's really damaging, that's what it is.'

I didn't ask any more questions. The answers had become too confusing and too personal, their stories too far apart. Rhona and Keith had a coffee but nothing else. She showed us again the Spaniard cut on her leg, and it had scabbed up well. Keith said he had a first-aid kit in the chopper, but Doug said it was best left open to the sun. I wanted to ask Rhona if she was okay with going back with her husband, but there was no opportunity and she seemed happy enough. It would've been good too if there was a chance to ask her if it was true she'd never had children — no Stephanie, no granddaughter.

'I'm going to take a photo of you outside the hut,' Rhona said, and she put Doug in the middle with his rifle, because he looked the most unusual, I suppose. 'I still think there's a place for a really good hunting book,' she said. 'I haven't given the idea up.'

As she put her camera gear back in the bag, I edged close. 'Are you happy with going like this?' I asked her softly.

'As happy as I'll ever be,' she said without looking up.

We went out to see Keith and Rhona leave, and they again said thanks and walked away quite close together. Comfortable with each other, or so it seemed. Rhona in her blue dress and pink puffer jacket and her hair pulled back. An hour and half later, when we were well away from the Nancy, the chopper came looking for us and circled above, close and slanting so we could see both Rhona and Keith. They waved, and then the chopper gained height again and swept away downhill. It spooked any deer for sure, and we didn't have much luck that day, not until the evening. We had three days at the Nancy on that trip, but I only remember it better than other times because of Rhona and Keith and their versions of each other that didn't match.

Legacy

I knew Albie was dying, but it still hit me when his daughter rang to tell me he'd gone. Albie was my cousin and only a year older than me. As kids, we spent a good deal of holiday time together on their farm in Central Otago. My family was in Dunedin then, and we'd stack up the car and head off towards the lonely expanse of the Māniatoto. I hardly saw Albie after I left uni, but those early years remained a bond between us.

'You should fly down,' my wife said. 'You'd probably be the only one from your side of the family.'

'I'll hardly know anyone,' I told her.

'You'll know those who matter. Your mum and dad would've liked you to go,' she said. She was right about that.

There were colleagues and friends in Dunedin I needed to catch up with, so I flew there and spent three days with them before renting a hybrid and driving early in the morning through to Central the Middlemarch way. It's easy time on those quiet roads. An hour passes with less stress than a few minutes in the traffic of Sydney or Auckland. Landscape rolls out before you, and the sky above. You can slow and notice things or throttle up if that's your choice. I like that sort of driving — when the urgent dictates of other people are diminished and you possess the world.

Albie's house and outbuildings are on the flat, but the farm stretches back into the Rock and Pillar Range, where the tors stand like Titans and the wagon tracks of goldminers can still be seen. The house had been renovated and enlarged yet seemed smaller than I recall from boyhood, and the shearing shed too. Albie's daughter, Anna, and her husband own the farm now. He hails from inland Marlborough, country not unlike the Māniatoto. Albie's son, Connor, is a pilot and never wanted to take over the family property. He was there, though, when I arrived, with his mother Raewyn, Anna and her husband and Albie's older sister Margaret and her partner. None of us are all that old, for Albie was barely sixty when he died.

'It's not fair,' said Raewyn as she watched Margaret and Anna put out the cold lunch, the sun glaring outside.

'If only they'd caught it sooner,' said Anna, 'but Dad hated going to the doctor. It was like admitting you were sick, so if you didn't go you must be okay.'

'He was always that way,' said Margaret. I couldn't remember Albie being that way, but in boyhood we had no fear of doctors, no fear of much at all. Life is endless when you're young.

Albie was lying at the undertaker's in Alex, ready for the funeral the following day. Raewyn said I was welcome to go in to view the body, but having known him alive I had no wish to see him dead, and besides it was more driving. For me, Albie never really grew up, and I've no enduring impressions of him as an adult from my few fleeting visits. Albie's alive in the past of boyhood for me.

In an unobtrusive and natural way, Anna seemed to lead us all that day, maybe because it was now her house that we were in. 'Why don't we have a stroll for a bit,' she said to me when the dishes were done, and so she and I went over the brown lawn, through the wire gate and walked down the track towards the yards. 'When did you last see Dad?' she asked. A light, warm wind was coming from the west and brought the dungy smell of the shearing shed and yards with it. Thistledown too.

'Must be seven or eight years ago. We called on our way back from a Queenstown holiday when we lived in Sydney.'

'I don't remember.'

'I think you must have been away.'

'You're mentioned in the will,' Anna said with a smile. 'Just about the only one outside the immediate family. A bequest. It's the moa bone Dad found. Not valuable enough for a change of lifestyle. Connor and I had a bit of a laugh.'

'I wouldn't sell it,' I said. 'As long as it's not too big for the plane.'

'There's conditions though,' she said. 'I think Dad's having you on.'

The first condition was that I had to turn up for the funeral, and I'd fulfilled that. The second requirement was that I climb up to The Dick, which was almost the highest point on the farm. You could see for miles from there. The Dick was a penis-shaped tor that Albie had christened when we were kids. All the family use the name now, and even some of the neighbours, Anna said.

'Bit of an embarrassment really,' she added, 'but you know Dad.'

'It's a fair hike that,' I said.

'No one cares if you do it or not. It's just Dad's way of reaching out, isn't it? The lawyer will never know if you go or not and won't care either.'

But I knew the requirement had purpose — a request rather than condition. I didn't try to explain that to Anna, or Connor, when we were back at the house, but told them I was going to climb to The Dick anyway. To be honest in my claim of the moa bone, I said, and I was going to do it that evening, straight after tea if that was all right.

'Leave it till tomorrow, when the funeral's over,' said Anna. 'You don't want to be bothered after the drive.' But I told her that I'd be in good clothes then, and I'd be driving back to Dunedin in the evening.

'Better I can be at the funeral with all Albie's conditions fulfilled. All present and correct,' I said, making something of a joke of it. 'And I'll drive to the track end anyway and walk up from there. It's light for hours in the evenings here. Tons of time.'

'Well, no use taking that rental,' she said. 'Take the ute. It's four-wheel drive, so you can get into the hills a bit.'

'You townies get lost easily,' said Connor. 'Fall over, sprain things, and reception's dicey up there, so we can't rescue you. Last time I went up, there was a rogue steer that turned pretty nasty.'

'You can stop the bullshit,' I told him. 'I used to whip up to The Dick and back no trouble as a kid. An hour's walk from the track end — a good deal less if I take the ute on a bit. Your dad and I used to bike to the end of the track.'

We talked about Albie while eating the homemade beef burgers for tea. He would have enjoyed those. We talked about his affection for sheep and dislike of dairying, his conviviality and his compatibility with solitude as well. There was talk of his illness too and the unavailing treatments. I could take no part or pleasure in that, but I knew it was a measure of catharsis for the others. I disengaged when I could do so without seeming abrupt and asked if I could borrow a pair of sneakers for the hill climb. Connor's were too big, which didn't surprise me. He's well over six feet tall and his hands are large too. Anna's husband, Lucas, had a newish pair that fitted though, which he was happy for me to borrow. He came out with the keys for the ute and told me that if I went through the gate at the end of the track I could drive another k or so on the left side of the gully before needing to walk.

It's easy to overstock in Central, seasonal country, and I didn't see many sheep or cattle even on the flat of the farm. It was a dry summer, Lucas had said. I did go through the gate and bumped up the gully for a bit until I found a place where I could turn around without hassle, so left the ute there. The sun was still well up, but the heat of a Māniatoto summer is a dry heat and easier to work and walk in than the oppressive humidity of the far north.

The hills were both strange and familiar. The outlines and inclines were still the same, even a hawk suspended on a lazy circle, but there seemed more groundcover: blue tussock, cushion plants, daisy clumps, hebes, even the menacing Spaniards. Maybe Albie had been encouraging regeneration. Maybe it was climate change. Maybe it was just the waywardness of memory.

Schist outcrops are common in that country, many of them banded in muted variation and grotesquely weathered. Some seemed to struggle to escape the ground, or make gestures to the sky, some humped and somnolent in the heat. The farther I climbed, the more clearly the times with Albie came back to me. How we would scamper onto some of the tors, stand there and shout, or creep about their fringe in search of skinks. I could see The Dick long before I reached it. Outlined against the blue vellum of the sky, to the adult eye it looked more like a spire than a cock and seemed to lean to the north more than I remembered. I had a sweat up when I reached it, sat in its shade and made no repeat of the efforts to climb it that had marked our boyhood visits. I could see a long way, and everything was quiet and still. Even the harrier hawk had been released from orbit and was gone. Small butterflies or moths, without much colour, fluttered close to the ground.

Albie had wanted me to climb up, knowing that he would be dead when I did so. He knew that the place would bring back the time when we were close and active together, thought in the same way, trusted each other. It was there, high up in the Rock and Pillar Range, that I said goodbye to Albie, although the next day I joined the others at the funeral parlour in Alex, where a grown-up Albie I knew little about received a more formal leave-taking.

Ring around the Rosie

'I wish I didn't have to land this on you,' said Richie in a voice dripping with insincerity. 'I really do, but there it is, you see. The powers that be have asked that we have a proposal to them by Thursday, and there's no one else free, I'm afraid.' His use of the inclusive 'we' was purely conventional and not an offer of assistance.

'What about Elaine?' Toby asked. 'She's finished with the Medlicott thing, hasn't she?'

'I need Elaine to help with an upcoming appraisal of the Majestic Vibratory Recliner ad. The Majestic people aren't all that happy,' Richie said. Toby could have given an appraisal in one four-letter word but refrained.

'Mason then?' he said.

'Mason's not up to it. You know that. He'd just fart around with a script, no visual nous at all. I don't know that we can carry him much longer.'

'I'm filming both the short and long versions of Huxtable Homes tomorrow. I'm flat out, for god's sake,' Toby said.

'I know, I know, but there it is. The powers that be. I'll get Fleur to drop the stuff to your desk.' Richie lifted a hand that was at once a gesture of helpless sympathy and a dismissal. Richie was a guy of considerable talent who had exploited it strenuously until he'd reached a position in which he didn't have to work hard any more. That's where he was determined to stay.

Fleur brought the Orleons Supplements file and brochures not long after Toby returned from setting up for the Huxtable shoot in the studio. The usual stuff about natural oils, fragrances, alkalising greens, bee pollen and Sumatran root ginger. There was also notification and a photograph from the Orleons management concerning the new ribbed product bottles coming soon. Orleons were committed to a policy of refreshing their television and online advertising, and the contact details for their promotions director were included.

Glenn walked into Toby's small office without knocking, seeking an opinion on a jingle that he and Kate had created for a fast-food franchise. The verse referenced a video-game superhero, and Toby suggested maybe they needed to ensure they'd targeted the most appropriate consumer group. When Glenn had gone, Toby was reluctant to return to the realm of Orleons Supplements. He wasn't where he'd hoped to be. He made an appraisal as he sat at his desk with a view of a seven-storey apartment block across the street.

Soon a thin, elderly man would appear in the sixth window from the right on the fifth floor and begin a series of exercises. It happened almost every day at much the same time, and usually the guy wore track pants and a singlet, although the exercises were undemanding. Toby had hoped to be working in feature films or TV drama series by this stage in his career. Thirty-four years old, married with two children, a degree in film studies — and overworked and underwhelmed at Ferrent Visuals, which specialised in corporate advertising. Toby and most of his fellow employees called the place Ferret, and in common usage it had largely lost its innuendo. Toby felt that nothing he did at Ferret had any lasting value or gave him a sense of achievement.

The elderly man in the apartment window arrived and began his exercises. Toby made his assessment of the guy's age because, even at that considerable distance, his bald head was obvious and his movements were awkward. Perhaps, though, thought Toby, he was younger but in recovery from some major illness.

Toby made the decision not to take the Orleons file home, even though he knew he should. Within him, resistance was forming, and he felt both apprehension and hope because of it. It was well after five o'clock, but Toby was noted for being conscientious: a reputation that was almost his sole satisfaction in his employment. He was thirty-four and disappointed, despite a wife and children who were everything he wished.

Ros was his wife. Miles and Oliver were his sons, both at primary school. A happy band, and he entrusted with their love and care. That happiness had no noticeable fragility, but Toby didn't wish to put it at risk. When the boys were asleep that evening, he told Ros about Richie and the Orleons task, the latest example of treatment he considered unfair.

'It's not just him though,' he said, 'not just the loading me up with stuff. Ferret isn't where I want to be, not the work I want to be doing. It was only going to be a start, wasn't it? And now it's where I'm bloody stuck.'

'So, you need to do something about it, don't you,' said Ros. 'You've been unhappy there for ages, but nothing changes.'

'I could have it out with Richie. Tell him I'm sick of having stuff piled on me all the time.'

'But, as you say, that's not the real problem. Not Richie. The thing is you don't want to be there. You don't want to do that commercial work any more.'

'I never did really, but it's what I could get. I thought I'd soon be able to move on to more creative stuff.'

'Then move on now,' Ros said quietly. They were sitting in the small lounge of their small house, but it was a well-kept home in a reasonable suburb. They owned it and were driving down the manageable mortgage. Through the window, in the deepening summer dusk, they could see the new wooden paling fence that Toby and his neighbour had built and the shadowed shrubs that Ros had spaced along its length.

'But move on to what?' said Toby. 'That's the crunch, isn't it? No one's come knocking, and I'm too busy to follow things up myself. And there's all these young graduates coming out prepared to work for peanuts, even as so-called interns for just the experience. They think they'll be the next cinematographer for Jane Campion or Taika Waititi.'

'If you're really unhappy at Ferret, then you need to get out and look for something you find worthwhile. A job's a big part of your life.'

'If I toss it in, though, without anything else to go to, can we make it? Ferret pays okay at least, and we've got the boys to consider.'

'I could increase my hours at the hospital,' she said. 'They keep asking me. You could pick the boys up after school and so on. We'd manage until you found a decent opportunity.'

'I should have done law or IT. What mug thinks you can walk into full-time camera work for ongoing projects in New Zealand?'

'You just need a foot in the door,' Ros said.

How many women would show such understanding, he wondered? How many would, with such equanimity, encourage their husband to toss security aside in search of personal satisfaction when there were children and debts to consider? Her unqualified support had the odd effect of making his own selfishness more apparent, the dangers greater, and he found himself arguing against his own cause.

'Probably most people don't like their job much but know they have to stick it out, find compensation in clubs, holidays and sports,' he said. 'All those people playing golf in the weekend to forget what's waiting Monday to Friday.'

'They say people change jobs far more often these days. The whole workforce thing's more fluid. You could even retrain if necessary. You need to have more faith in yourself.'

'Do you like nursing?' he asked. It was almost fully dark outside, and high in the sky above the blackness of the wall was a scatter of stars. The southerly crooned at the garage guttering.

'I do actually. Most of the time, anyway, because it needs doing and most people appreciate care and attention when they're not well.'

'It's the boys really,' said Toby. 'What happens if I can't get something worthwhile that also gives them the support they'll need?'

'Well, if it doesn't work out you could always go back to Ferret, or some place like it. You'd be snapped up. At least you'd know you gave it a shot.'

'You could well be right,' he said. He had a passing impulse to hug her because she was so supportive but had a heightened sense of family vulnerability, his responsibility for them all, and he didn't wish to become emotional. 'We'll talk it over. You make me feel better about it and not so selfish,' he said. 'It's quite a big call to let go of Ferret with nothing lined up. And maybe I'm just a bit pissed off with Richie loading more jobs onto me. Or rather, more pissed off than usual.'

'They know you're good at things, so they push work your way.'

'I wouldn't mind being so busy if I could feel better about it. It's just the same routine techniques over and over. I'm not learning anything new, and I know that nothing I do has any lasting value. It's merely work, you know, rather than creating, rather than being challenged.'

'A job's a big part of your life,' Ros said again. 'So, it's got to be meaningful, surely.'

Toby thought about that quite a lot over the following few weeks. Meaningful? A pragmatist might say that any job that provided a livelihood was meaningful and that expectation of a sense of fulfilment in addition was selfish, even unrealistic. The great majority of people had to accept that a job was a means to an end rather than an expression of creativity.

He completed the new advertising for Orleons Supplements, and their satisfaction and that of Ferret was evident only in the absence of criticism. He and Ros talked more, and she encouraged him to look about, perhaps make some approaches to production companies and TV networks regarding cinematography opportunities. There were jobs advertised for camera operators to join TVNZ's news and current affairs operations team, opportunity for a videographer with a company specialising in wildlife programmes, Fire and Emergency New Zealand wanted someone for their media and communications team and a digital advertising and social media firm was seeking a motion graphic designer. Nothing from established TV series or companies currently filming in the country.

'It's all about who you know. I don't have to tell you that,' said Ros. 'You know lots of people in the industry. Put some feelers out. Be positive.' Ros was positive. It was another of her virtues, even if it did sometimes lead to temporary disappointment. They were sitting in the public gardens, a seat on the terraced bank, from where they could watch Miles and Oliver mucking about at the edge of the duck pond, old enough now not to need close supervision. There were peonies flowering in a plot close to Toby and Ros, and she said they smelled like climbing roses and she wanted to steal some. 'What would be the punishment for stealing the council's peonies?' she asked.

'You're right. If I'm serious about a switch, I need to get onto people. I always find that sort of thing awkward, though, trading on friendship and time together.'

'All you're doing is sussing things out. Nicky at Wētā Workshop, for instance,' she said. 'You've helped her enough times.'

'Yeah, but I don't know that Wētā would be quite a fit for me.'

'It gets bigger and bigger and does just about everything now, doesn't it?' Before Toby could answer, she called out loudly to the boys, telling them not to pick rushes from the edge of the pond and not to throw anything into it. 'We're going to the playground in a minute,' she shouted. She stood up and made a snipping gesture at the closest peonies. She brushed her hands over the back of her jeans, as was her habit when she'd been sitting outdoors. 'You should make a list tonight of people who might know of something,' she said. 'We need to say goodbye to bloody Ferret.' She was short, blonde, purposeful and they had been lovers for a long time. Toby put his hand on her shoulder as they walked down the stone steps from one level of the terraced garden to the next.

'Let's go to the café on the way home. Chips for the boys,' he said.

Toby did make a list and also sent emails to those on it that he thought were most likely to be helpful. The most promising reply was from Anna Fresnan at Meteor Visual Productions, which had the green light for a three-part thriller series. Toby and Anna had been at university together and later on a couple of shoots. There was a senior camera operator/edit assistant vacancy to be filled, and she said she was happy to support him, though pointing out she wasn't all that advanced in the hierarchy. The job was still not officially advertised, but Toby rang the guy that Anna suggested and was offered an interview in Wellington — and remuneration for his air fare.

Should he tell Ferret about the interview? He talked about that with Ros. 'It's really none of their business,' she said, 'but the Meteor people are bound to check with them anyway, to ask how good you are at your job.'

'That's the thing, and they could be brassed off if it comes out of the blue.'

'And why shouldn't you be looking for new opportunities? It might give Richie and Gavin and Brenda a wake-up call, even if you don't get the job. They might think about your value to the place.'

'I'll probably get a lecture about loyalty to the firm,' Toby said.

In fact, Richie didn't seem surprised or much interested. 'Oh okay, but I'd be careful,' he said. 'These frothy drama things often fall through. It's the commercial stuff that sustains the industry. Anyway, what's the latest on the Riband Realty account?'

'All good. So, I'll be away all day on the ninth.'

'Yeah, okay,' Richie said.

On the ninth, Toby flew up for the interview. Meteor had a facility in Lower Hutt — a large new studio shed and small prefab offices and storerooms alongside. He didn't see Anna, and that disappointed him, but was met by Stefan, who was a partner and production manager. They went into one of the prefabs that smelt of newness and had its metal skeleton exposed on the inside. A desk, three plastic chairs, two cabinets, computers and a copier, one small louvre window that sectioned the blue sky.

'Can I get you a coffee?' Stefan asked. He was tall and slightly overweight. In his fifties, Toby judged, but with abundant tussock hair. He wore pale linen trousers and a blue jacket of similar material. His eyes were almost hidden by heavy lids.

'I'm okay, thanks,' Toby said.

'Anna said she trained with you.'

'And we were on a couple of wildlife docos together.'

'Who are you with now?'

'Mainly I've been doing commercial advertising,' Toby told him. 'I'm the senior graphic designer and camera operator at Ferrent Visuals.'

'Any work on drama series?'

'Only filling in, but I'm keen to get into it.'

'Isn't everyone?' said Stefan.

He told Toby about the upcoming three-part series: the local and Australian leads; the script writers; the funding; and the inner-city settings. 'We're more than lakes, mountains, valleys and bush, and we want to show that. It's gritty urban stuff.' Stefan was enthusiastic, and

Toby liked that. Their talk broadened to a discussion of films, series and camera techniques, and they found they were largely in agreement. Forty minutes or so they spent together, at which point Stefan said he had somewhere to be.

'You told your people you were coming up?' he asked. 'Because I'll need to get in touch with them, of course.'

'Yes, I told them,' Toby said. As he left, he admired the large new studio shed and wished Stefan had taken him for a tour, but the interview had gone okay, hadn't it?

That's what he told Ros after the flight home. 'Seemed to go all right,' he said. 'Stefan's the production manager, so will pretty much have the say, I reckon. I quite liked him. I didn't get to see Anna, which is a pity.'

'Fingers crossed for you,' she said. 'When do you hear? I'll have a bottle of bubbly ready.'

The bubbly proved unnecessary. At least Stefan rang to give the news personally. He seemed somewhat embarrassed and said the decision was a timing thing and no reflection on Toby's abilities. They'd decided to take a more considered and overall look at staff requirements, he said. It was Anna who told Toby the real reason for his rejection. Ferret had given a less-than-enthusiastic recommendation, said that his attitude wasn't conducive to good relationships in the workplace. Even a sense of entitlement at times. Anna said Stefan had liked him, but others considering the appointment had been put off by Ferret's comments.

'It's not fair,' Ros said. 'It's that damn Richie. He's worked out that the only way to keep you is to tell everyone else that you're hopeless. Cunning, cunning.'

'Maybe it wasn't him that Stefan spoke to.'

'Whoever it was, they had the same reason for putting you down. You don't want to keep working at a place that treats people like that.'

'Well, I've got nowhere else to be.'

'Tell Richie where to stick it,' she said. Did she have more courage or simply less realisation of the risk in leaving? Definitely more courage and loyalty, and he loved her for that even though he was diminished in comparison.

Richie hadn't mentioned the Wellington interview since Toby's return, but the day after Stefan's call, Toby went to Richie's office. 'I didn't get the Wellington job,' he said.

'Bad luck,' said Richie blandly. He wrinkled his face and pursed his lips in perfunctory sympathy then glanced down again to his computer screen. 'There's plenty of work for you here,' he told it.

'They asked you about me, I suppose.'

'Who's that?'

'The Meteor people. They got in touch for a reference.'

'Yeah, they did, I think,' said Richie. 'Couple of days ago.'

'With you, was it?'

'Gavin asked me to deal with it,' said Richie, and he lifted his eyes, leant back and moved his swivel chair slightly from side to side. 'I told them you were good at your job.'

'And that I didn't fit in.'

'That you had your own opinions. That's what I told them.'

Toby left it at that. What was the point of any argument with Richie when the Wellington opportunity was gone. Toby still had to work at Ferret, at least until he and Ros considered alternatives. As he walked back to his own office, Toby wondered how common was the situation in which he found himself — someone held in a job by the employer's refusal to recommend them for any other.

'As long as I'm there, they'll keep on doing their best to scupper anything I go for,' he told Ros that evening. The boys were bringing plates from the table, he was stacking the dishwasher and she, having cooked both a casserole and a lemon-meringue pie, was watching the news on the television.

'We're going to talk about that later,' she said. 'When the boys have their screen time, we'll talk about it. I feel like having a go at Richie myself and Gavin too. You can't treat people like that and expect them to care about what they do.'

'In business, it's the law of the jungle,' Toby replied.

The boys were allowed half-an-hour's screen time when in their beds. Miles said it wasn't fair because he was fourteen months older than his brother and so should get longer. They were in the same room, though, and Toby said sometimes practicality outweighed entitlement.

'He might have a lifelong grievance about it,' Toby said when he'd rejoined Ros.

'If that's to be his worst memory of growing up, then we've done a good job.'

'I'm actually pissed off with Gavin and Richie. I thought the Meteor interview went okay and I had a good chance.'

'They'll probably do it every time you apply somewhere,' Ros said and turned the television off.

'There's not much I can do about that though, is there?'

'Well, you could tell people at the interview what to expect from Ferret and why, or you could tell Ferret to stick their job and not mention them at all. I think if you really want to move on, you've got to commit and go for it. You can't be the best dad, the best husband, if you're unhappy.'

'What if I can't find anything better?' Toby said.

'I've already told you I can ramp up my hospital hours for a while.'

'It could be bloody ages, though.'

'You're not going to make the changes you want without taking risks. And if nothing crops up you can always go back to being unhappy and making TV ads about dishwashing liquid.'

'Been there, done that. I do remember that Auckland outfit offering me a job selling visual media equipment.'

'There you are, then,' said Ros. 'Opportunities everywhere, and they'd give you a fancy vehicle to drive around in.'

'My dream job.'

'If you're serious about all this, I think you have to leave Ferret first. Tricky, I know, but that'll free you up to go all out on getting something else.'

'I worry about the boys.'

'The boys will be fine,' Ros said. 'And I wouldn't give up on Meteor yet either. Sound Anna out again about what's happening there.'

Given such reassurance and support, Toby decided to resign. He'd sometimes wondered what would be Richie's reaction if he did so, but the reality was not dramatic. 'Is it money?' Richie asked.

'Not really,' Toby told him.

'What's the problem then? I think we've treated you pretty well. If it is money, we could talk about that with Gavin and Brenda.'

'I'd like to get into film, or TV docos and drama. I did a bit before coming here. That's why I was interested in Meteor.'

'We can't all work for Peter Jackson, Toby. On and off, on and off, that's the life of freelance camera operators. You know that. And who knows how long Hollywood's love affair with our scenery will last. I'd have a good think about it, man, before anything hasty.'

'I have,' said Toby. 'Ros and I have talked it out.'

'It's not news we like to hear, but it's up to you. I hope it works out. Have you said anything to the Ferrents?'

'Just to you.'

'You should go in right away,' said Richie. 'The sooner they know the better.'

Gavin and Brenda, who were partners both in life and in business, asked him for a month's notice so they could begin a search for his replacement. They were sorry to lose him, they said, and wished him well. Toby wondered if perhaps the assessment of him given by Richie was accurate. Do you ever really know how you appear to other people? His farewell from Ferret, when it came, was modest. Cupcakes and wine in their own cafeteria, a framed Siddell print, a short speech of thanks and best wishes from Gavin — Brenda had a dental appointment. Mason, the least talented of his colleagues, seemed the most affected.

'You helped me a lot,' he said. 'It's not great here. If you see creative opportunities where you're going, let me know.' At least Ros had been invited, and Toby witnessed again the ease with which she mingled and joined in conversations, the rapport she maintained with folk she seldom saw.

There was relief in leaving Ferret. During his final month, he had a sense that he was fading from his colleagues' view, already deleted from their future. Consultation dwindled, the in-house gossip no longer reached him, competition ceased and his approbation was no longer sought.

He expected to feel relief, even excitement, after he left but instead found himself anxious, preoccupied with the search for new opportunity, fearful of failure. Having no job diminished him as husband and father in his own estimation. Some of the friends he contacted seemed surprised that he'd left his job before securing another. He woke some mornings with a sense of shock to find himself unemployed but said nothing of his insecurity to Ros, yet she knew, of course. In a successful marriage, there is a mutual aura of emotion that provides understanding, even when nothing is said.

With her assistance, Toby compiled a list of possible placements, but before he made any approaches Anna got in touch again and said he shouldn't give up on Meteor. The three-part series was almost sure to go ahead, and they hadn't got a full crew yet. She thought Stefan had quite liked him at the interview. 'Why don't you fly up again. Ask for a chance to show your skills. Have some names who'll give you a better backing than Ferrent Visuals.'

'Go for it,' Ros urged. 'You need to show you're hungry and that you've got the skills. Tell them what you were making at Ferret, though, so they don't think you're a pushover.'

'I don't think my position or salary at Ferret will impress them seeing I've quit,' said Toby. 'But I could give it a go. The airfares won't be cheap. At least Anna's keen, and I'd be working with her.'

'Yeah, why the hell not go for it?' said Ros again. 'You've got time now.'

He rang Stefan and told him that he'd left Ferret. 'I know you still haven't got a full team for the drama series,' he said. 'I'd like to send you up some of my better work: even ads sometimes provide opportunity, and there's wildlife docos. I've got other referees too that you might be interested in contacting. I dare say, Ferrent Visuals didn't go overboard.' Toby was tempted to say that was because they didn't want to lose him, but that sounded too self-serving. 'I'm happy to come up and have a few days on set during anything Meteor's got going at present. Just a basic rate, but you'd get an idea of my work, and I'd get the feel of your outfit. No promises either way.'

'We wouldn't be able to pay for flights again,' Stefan told him.

'Understood.'

'Not for accommodation either. It would be the basic rate for the days you're with us.'

'That's okay,' said Toby. 'I appreciate the chance to be there.'

'We'll be doing some preliminary street shots for the series and checking sites,' Stefan said.

Anna was happy for Toby to stay with her, extending the invitation, though he'd made no request. She and Logan also had two sons, much the same age as Miles and Oliver. Toby had met Logan once before, when he and Ros had called in while on a North Island road trip. A tall, thin man with a slight stutter and an interest in vintage cars. He and Toby had little in common except fatherhood and good will, but that was sufficient for a stay of a few days. Toby was even spared the need to bus to the Hutt Valley, travelling with Anna in her quaint little Fiat.

It was a small team for the preparatory shots. Stefan wanted footage of the central city that could be interpolated later and so not hold up full production shooting. There was emphasis on moody late-night and early-morning footage, and they tried to keep as inconspicuous as possible to avoid members of the public showing awareness of the camera. Light angles were important to Stefan, and they did quite a bit at both sunset and sunrise, surface-water reflections after rain, streaked storeroom windows, headlight and traffic-light montages. Toby and Anna were behind the cameras and worked well together. Toby suggested taking some footage from a double-decker bus, and the results were pleasing. He also impressed with some slo-mos of seagulls around the Beehive. Four days in all, and Stefan said he was considering using some of it with the opening credits as well.

'I can't promise anything yet,' Stefan said when they parted. 'I think you get the idea of what we're after, though, and you and Anna work well together. I'll have to talk to my partners when it comes to forming a full crew, and we can't do that until the final go ahead from the backers. But we really appreciate you coming up. I promise to let you know as soon as I can. You won't be left hanging around.'

The night before his return south, Toby took Anna and Logan to Barbarossa, a noted restaurant in Courtenay Place, as a thank-you for their support. Anna was optimistic of his chances, saying that Stefan was impressed with his rapport with lighting and tech stuff and his ability to follow camera scripts.

Toby also felt positive, although when back home he was careful to stress to Ros that it wasn't a done deal. And so it proved. Three days later, a blue-sky Saturday when he was playing cricket with his sons, there was a call from Stefan to say that the funding had fallen through at the last moment. There would be no three-episode drama series for Meteor, and consequently no hirings, rather job anxiety for existing staff. Toby was a small part of collateral damage, and he knew how hard Stefan and his colleagues were hit. It was the sort of unpredictable, boom-or-bust industry they were in, with big money being so crucial.

'So,' said Ros defiantly, 'there'll be other things that come along. Other opportunities, and Meteor will give you a good reference to add to all your others. You'll see. I feel sorry for Anna and hope she hangs onto her job.'

'She'll be okay. She's well in there: been there for ages. A hell of a disappointment for them, though, and after so much work in preparation that's all wasted, including the stuff Anna and I did. Devastating really. At least they do have a bunch of other ongoing projects, though not as exciting or on that scale.'

'What happened to the bloody funding?'

'I think it was supposed to be coming from some outfit in Australia,' Toby said. 'They missed out on the Film Commission here.' His boys were calling for him from the lawn, so he rejoined them in cricket. The sky was still blue, his sons still happy to have him in their game, but apprehension and disappointment were a throb deep within.

Ros took on more work at the hospital, but after five months it was obvious that more money was going out than coming in, and Toby had found no promising opportunities. He even contacted the Auckland outfit that had offered the job selling camera equipment, but it was commission payment and involved a lot of travel.

'I'm going to go back to commercial work,' he told Ros.

'You shouldn't give up yet. It's just a slack time. It's always an up-and-down business, isn't it? I read that at least two American feature films are going to be shot in the South Island this year.'

'It's not fair on you and the boys.'

'The boys are fine. They don't understand what's going on, and they don't care. They're happy.'

'There's responsibility though, isn't there?' said Toby. 'Real life isn't about living some dream. It's more about obligation when you come down to it.'

He got in touch with several companies specialising in visual services and advertising. Two were keen to talk with him. He had something of a profile within the industry. The prospect of moving to another city didn't faze him, and Ros's skills were in demand everywhere. Ferret got to hear, of course, and Richie rang, careful to sound understanding.

'I'm sorry about the Meteor series not working out,' he said. Such information seemed to travel by osmosis without requiring a specific source.

'Worth a try,' replied Toby.

'Hell, yes, and there'll be other things. I've often thought of having a go myself. Anyway, what I want to say is that we'd like you back with us. There's a lot on and Steven's off overseas and we've had to let Mason go, just not up to it. You're missed, buddy, that's for sure.'

'I feel it's time for a change anyway, though.'

'If it's money, we can have a talk,' said Richie. 'Gavin and Brenda told me they're on board with that. Why don't you come in and see us?'

It was oddly gratifying — leaving and then being offered more money to return, but Toby didn't fool himself, a return was still an admission of failure. He'd left in search of greater challenge and fulfilment and would go back to what he'd hoped to leave behind.

Ros thought he should at least work for a different company. She said Richie would still be a prick and load him up with stuff again. 'If it means you'd be happier, I don't mind moving, and it could work out for the best.' How could such love and loyalty be repaid, except by the sacrifice of his own conceit. Toby didn't want to disrupt his sons' schooling, leave the friends he and Ros had made and the home they owned, take Ros from a workplace in which she was happy. You can't have everything you want, he told himself.

So, he went back to Ferret for a meeting with Gavin and Brenda

Ferrent in their office, an impressive office with a view towards the hills instead of an old man exercising in an apartment window. An office with matching sofa and chair as well as two desks and a compact red-and-silver coffee maker.

'Thanks for coming in,' said Gavin, who motioned towards the chair, while he and Brenda sat on the sofa as a statement of informality and rapprochement.

'We're not going to say we're sorry you didn't get the Wellington job,' Brenda said. 'That would be insincere. Actually, we need you here and we're hoping you'll come back.' She was a good deal younger than her husband. A forceful woman and practical. Toby had never heard her giggle and assumed she never did. Ros said she had excellent dress sense, but Toby was no judge of such things. He sensed a mercantile preoccupation and found it unattractive.

'It would be the same work,' admitted Gavin. 'We know you've wanted to stretch your wings in more imaginative stuff. It would be the same work here, let's be clear, that's who we are, what we do, but we want to make it worth your while.'

'It may not be high art,' said Brenda, 'but it has its skills and usefulness, as you well know, and it doesn't come and go like the film and TV work.'

'I'd still be on the lookout, though, apply for something else in time.'

'We understand that,' she said.

'And we know you'll give your best here. You always have,' Gavin said.

'Richie and I haven't always hit it off,' said Toby. 'That's another thing.'

'We've talked with him about that, and he sees that he's sometimes pushed too much your way. I think you'd find it better now.' Gavin glanced at his wife as a cue for her to add enticement.

'We'd like to offer you a newly created position of team leader,' Brenda said. 'You'd have five or six reporting to you and greater scope for artistic direction.'

'Richie still there, of course, but more flexibility and choice.' Gavin leant forward with a smile. His hair was dark and heavy, although he was in his sixties. It made his face seem smaller.

'And we're open to talk of salary if it's within reason,' Brenda added.

So, there was talk of salary within reason and flexibility and team leadership. It sounded almost like a victory when later Toby laid it out for Ros as they sat on their small deck with a coffee, the slanting sun, and enough breeze to set the neighbour's willow tree talking quietly to itself. 'We'll be able to boost the mortgage payments anyway,' Toby told her with a smile, but she knew that for him the return to Ferret was both a disappointment and a failure.

'It's not for ever,' she told him. 'There'll be other opportunities.'

'Glenn said I was a cunning bastard. I met him when I was leaving, and he said I was a cunning bastard who'd fooled the bosses into making a better offer.'

'They didn't realise all you did there until you weren't there any more. That's what it was. Typical. Richie took the credit for everything, I suppose.'

Richie seemed much the same when Toby resumed work at Ferret. 'You having your own team suits me,' he said. 'I'm spread pretty thin, and the staff keeps growing. 'You'll report to me, though: you realise that? I'll be there for you.'

'I'd like a say in what projects come my way.'

'Sure, sure. Might be that your team specialises in the bigger ticket items. More artistic leeway, but we'll see what works out.'

'I'll give it a hundred per cent. You know that.'

'I've always said you're not a slacker. Always said that.' Richie put out his hand, as if some deal was to be struck, and maybe it was. They didn't like each other much but realised that they needed each other — at least for the present.

Toby did work hard: it was his nature. More money and the promotion within the firm made it somewhat easier to commit. He took up golf, joined a film club, had the kitchen refitted with German-engineered oven, fridge and dishwasher. Ros reduced her nursing hours, and she and Toby became active in the school community to which their sons belonged. After all, family life is what it's all about, surely. Ros stopped exhorting him to give priority to personal ambition, not because of any change of mind but because she understood intuitively that he'd made the decision so many arrive at when faced with the persistent compromise that is life. At the end of his first year back at Ferret, they were able to have a family holiday in Sydney. Among other excursions was the trip across the harbour to the zoo, and the boys thought that the best thing of all.

'Cool, cool,' said Miles. 'Those bears, eh.'

'Tons of wild animals,' said Oliver. 'Let's go back every year. We should. Every year.'

'Why not?' said Toby. 'Maybe not the zoo, but every year we'll do something extra special — all of us together.' Good to have something special once a year, and Toby was becoming reconciled to practicality.

Cloud Drift

Michael's bed in the ward faced the large glass door to ablutions, but at certain times of the day if the light was right, he could see reflected there the sky that was visible from the small window high above his head. Birds sometimes passed, he had seen the medical emergency helicopter slanting down to the landing pad out of his sight, but mostly it was just the sky. Michael saw all sorts of skies and had professional knowledge concerning them, but what he liked best was that powder-blue background and white clouds drifting across it. There was a distanced serenity to it that alleviated his pain and gave him a sense of peaceful travel, even as he lay static between the hospital sheets. Sometimes the blue sky seemed like a deep ocean and the cumulus humilis clouds massive, pale whales in a steady migration across it.

There was plenty of time for such fancies. Michael wasn't going anywhere. The small, four-bed ward had become his world, and he, Wayne, Max and George were the sum of its semi-permanent inhabitants. Each bed could be curtained off for privacy, but that was done only for 'procedures' or 'incidents', such as the fouling of a bed. The life of each of them was bare before his fellows: the low-voiced pleas to Doctor Robbins, the observations of Nurse Gemmell or Nurse Roche, the somewhat laboured conversations of visitors, even the unintended revelations of sleep talk. Max was most prone to that, even though he was much younger than the others. His bed was next to Michael's, and sometimes in the long nights he would talk with the wife who had left him, and always of cheerful things, never the tumour that was his daylight preoccupation. Once he even gave a quiet laugh while speaking of their honeymoon — the one occasion Michael ever heard him voice amusement. Max had one eye blue and one brown, and Michael never got used to it. Most medical staff commented on it in an admiring way, as if it were a personal achievement. Dr Sunge said it was called heterochromia. Other scientific terms the staff used in reference to Max were less innocuous.

Michael had thought of warning his wife that all she said would be overheard by his fellow patients unless they had visitors of their own, but he decided that he should allow a contribution to the general knowledge of the ward, for distraction or novelty were scarce enough there. Illness is sufficiently isolating without encouragement, and although his wife was candid she didn't say foolish things.

George was a large, gaunt man who'd once been overweight, as his skin folds evinced. A retired academic but still engrossed in his specialist study of the Hittites, which he was happy to share with his fellow patients and also visitors, when not woozy from medication. Maybe as his own world closed down, George saw that of the Hittites as refuge.

Before admittance to the hospital, Michael had never heard of the Hittites, but gradually, in the absence of many alternatives, he became both interested and informed. He had known nothing at all about ancient people, even biblical ones, had never needed to, but he felt the better for learning of this Anatolian race with an empire centred on Hattusa. George spent over an hour on Easter Monday describing the great battle of Kadesh against the Egyptians. It occurred to Michael that he'd joined the select few worldwide who knew of the event. Because of the almost-certain outcome of his own illness and the consequent sense of emotional suspension, the battle of Kadesh assumed a significance quite equal with his years as a meteorologist, his stents or the embossed silver cup he had twice won at the Saddle Hills Golf Club.

'It amazes me how much of this stuff you can remember,' Nurse Roche might say to George, and Michael was envious of the compliment. Nurse Roche was the favourite: small, plump, unhurried and with a gentle touch. Wayne said you never ever felt the needle going in.

Despite his name, Wayne was Māori. Short, thin and with straight, grey hair that accentuated his dark skin and eyes. Michael had read somewhere that there were no full-blooded Māori people left, but he didn't believe it. Wayne bolstered that opinion by saying he was Ngāi Tahu one-hundred per cent, even if he couldn't speak te reo. He'd been a fisherman, owned two boats and lived at Moeraki, where the tourist boulders were. Michael had been there a couple of times. Wayne had also lived in the Chathams and told of being caught at sea in weather that took no prisoners. There wasn't sufficient medical care on the Chathams, though, he said, not for his condition, and he'd known it was progressive in the worst way. Wayne was a keen card player on his better days and disappointed with his ward fellows in that respect: George thought it a waste of time, Max couldn't seem to get the hang of poker or five hundred and was a sore loser, Michael found an upright posture maintained for a long time became unpleasant, and his medication necessitated frequent use of the sick bowl.

Although Nurse Roche was the favourite, Nurse Gemmell provided greater distraction for she had allure, was constantly romantically involved with different men and talked with Nurse Roche of their persistent attentions, standing with her in the annex, which was little more than a walk-through cupboard, within earshot of the four who lay like caterpillars but with no hope of winged transformation.

'Anyway,' Nurse Gemmell might say, 'this guy wouldn't leave me alone, keeps putting his hand on my knee. Kevin his name was, yes, Kevin, and he wanted me to go out with him to get some air.'

'Typical,' Nurse Roche might say.

'You go get some air, I told him. I don't need any more air. He kept hanging around until Liam collected me, then disappeared.'

'Does Liam like to get some air?'

'Oh, yes,' Nurse Gemmell might say. 'Oh, yes.'

Cuisine is not a high point of a hospital stay, but in Michael's ward appetites weren't great, not even for life itself much of the time. Max said he didn't like eating pug, George ate the desserts and flushed most first courses, Wayne preferred the food smuggled in by his wife, Michael had Jaffas in his locker next to Marcel Proust's unending recollections of the past. Michael did sometimes think of food, not because he was hungry but because it served as a distraction. He would ask his daughter what she had in mind for her family's evening meal in the open-plan kitchen with the sliding glass door to the patio.

'I've got some really nice loin chops, and we'll have baked potato and kūmara,' she might say, or, more prosaically, 'I've had a busy day, so it'll be homemade burgers with onions. Are you eating everything they give you? That's so important, you know, keeping your strength up.' Proust had a wonderful memory for food. Not just the taste or the smell or the colours, but the way something broke apart, the light from a doorway across its texture as a voice came from another room, the piece of gristle left opaque and glistening on the plate.

When Max was feeling especially down, he would lie on his back and pull the sheet over his face, even if someone was talking to him or he'd been talking to them. Michael didn't take it personally. They all had means of removing themselves emotionally, and only Max required a physical barrier. George would close his eyes, open his mouth and withdraw. Wayne would rock slightly, as if to regain the motion of his fishing boat. 'Wind from the west,' he might say or, 'Back before dark if we move her along.'

The nature and conversations of the regular visitors became commonplace for them all. Michael's wife and daughter, Max's parents, George's wife, daughter and sister, Wayne's wife, two sons, daughter, fishing mates Jodi and Stan, and Stan's wife Mary, who had been Wayne's girlfriend before her marriage. Not all Wayne's visitors arrived at once but in various combinations and frequencies. In time, however, even they became routine.

A new visitor to the ward gave a lift to them all, even the staff. 'I'm sure Mr Ledgely will be pleased to see you,' Nurse Roche might say.

'It's the third bed, with the oxygen machine beside it,' Nurse Gemmell might add and wait in the doorway to see what reception the person was given.

One very hot day, when the helicopter had just landed outside, a Cambridge professor came to see George. They'd become friends when George was a visiting Fellow. Professor Kannasse was his name, a Hittite scholar with a small beard and a forward-jutting face like a highly intelligent ruminant. There was little mention of the symptoms or treatment of George's illness, but an intense discussion of King Šuppiluliuma the first.

Wayne's most interesting stranger was a representative of the fisheries section of the Ministry for Primary Industries, who wished his opinion on a proposed dolphin sanctuary. Wayne was able to be helpful on the seasonal distribution of dolphins and which nets caused the most fatalities among them.

'I've never understood the difference between a porpoise and a dolphin,' Nurse Roche might say. Michael's most appreciated contribution was Sandra, a well-endowed young woman who was contemplating a balloon flight from Australia to New Zealand and wished for his advice concerning the prevailing wind patterns over the Tasman. He was of some note as a meteorologist, which was an additional reason for his customary perusal of the sky reflected in the glass door of ablutions. No doubt Max, Wayne and George all imagined themselves floating high with Sandra. Michael did.

'Men,' Nurse Gemmell might say without bitterness. 'They're all the same.'

Earphones were a means of both solitude and transference. Michael listened often to Sibelius but wasn't judgemental when Wayne said his favourite was ABBA. ABBA was fine for almost everybody. George liked best to listen to cricket, which seemed initially to Michael an odd choice, but he learned that George had been born in Yorkshire and emigrated to New Zealand when he was twenty-eight. Max said Justin Bieber was the greatest singer in the world: none of the others had heard of him.

Books, too, provided alternative worlds if the reader was well enough to concentrate. George read scholarly studies of ancient peoples, Wayne favoured Stephen King, and Max confounded his companions' expectations by asking his mother for the autobiography of Michelle Obama. Michael had Marcel Proust at his bedside, as you know, but as *In Search of Lost Time* has seven volumes there was locker space for only a selection.

Dr Sunge and Dr Robbins were the regular specialists, but very seldom did their visits coincide. Michael wondered if they didn't hit it off, though realised it may have been a matter of shifts.

'Good, good,' Dr Sunge might murmur as he did a check, or else a less reassuring and drawn out 'hmmmmm'. Sometimes he had junior doctors with him and made mild requests for their opinion as disguised interrogation. He had a slow smile and once accepted a giant Jaffa Michael offered him. 'Thank you, thank you, very kind,' he might have said.

Dr Robbins was portly. That's what George said of him but not in his presence. Michael was intrigued by the description. He couldn't remember any Kiwi using the word portly. George was originally English, of course. He gave that description quite naturally and only the once, but whenever Dr Robbins came into the ward after that Michael remembered it. Despite his bulk, Dr Robbins moved swiftly and with authoritative purpose, almost seeming to burst through the entrance, and his exit, too, merited a roll of thunder.

'Mr Truckler,' he might say from within the curtain, 'we must, I think, consider another colonoscopy because there is further bleeding.' Dr Robbins had warm, short-fingered hands and was particularly dexterous with any medical apparatus, even showing a slight vanity in such accomplishment, as a gunfighter twirls his revolvers. 'Just the necessary skill of one's profession,' he might say following the insertion of a catheter.

Illness affects even time, and Michael came to learn that the nights are much longer in a hospital than elsewhere, even though darkness is never complete. Always, there is subdued light, as well, winking red or blue eyes, the hollow whisper of the air conditioning, the squeaking shoes of a nurse passing in the corridor, a snore, a cough, an inexplicable doleful murmur from the ablutions room, as if previous inhabitants have gathered there with nowhere else to go. Even the throbbing of one's own pulse and the slothful white clock on the wall. Sometimes during the night, Michael wondered how long he would live, although he knew it was a morbid line of thought and not helpful at all.

'Remember the hotel room in Queenstown with a view of the lake,' Max might say to the wife who had left him. His tone of voice was quite different when dreaming, revealing new facets of personality. 'We shared the pyjamas. Top me and bottom you.' And on moonlit nights, Michael could see the reflected ablutions sky, often with a few wispy cirrus scurrying by.

'It's a good forecast for the morning, I think,' Nurse Roche might say, smiling in the dim-lit room before continuing to other wards on her night round.

Many thousands died at the great battle of Kadesh, yet it was indecisive, George told him. Michael could lie and think of lives wasted so long ago. Possibly, the largest chariot battle ever fought, and he could imagine the charge across the dusty Asian plain and the desperation of both humans and horses as they clashed.

'Men,' Nurse Gemmell might say, 'they're all the same. Nothing changes.'

The Old Story

Andrew was cutting the front hedge when the man approached him. An escallonia hedge on his frontage that provided privacy, but which he never allowed to grow much above head height. He released his finger from the trigger of the electric trimmer, and the noise died.

'Mr Lugard?' the man said. He was wearing jeans and a thick, dark jersey with a zip at the neck.

'Yes.'

'My name's Cyril Withers. Can we talk a bit?'

'Have we met?' Andrew asked. It wasn't the ideal time or place to talk. Late autumn, the breeze was cold, the hedge unfinished.

'We haven't met,' Cyril said. 'I could've phoned, but it's better face to face, I think. This first time.' He was a tall man, as was Andrew himself, and they stood eye to eye in brief assessment of each other. 'Mason's your son, right?' Cyril said.

'Yes.'

'Has he said anything to you about Noleen?'

'I don't think so. Who's Noleen?'

'Noleen Withers, my daughter. She and Mason have been seeing each other, and now she's pregnant. That's why I'm here.' Noleen's father seemed sad rather than angry. Sad but with a sense of duty and determination. 'Your son doesn't seem to want to front up to it,' he said.

That's how it began. Cyril didn't press to come into the house. He wasn't surprised Andrew knew nothing about it and said that once Andrew had a chance to talk with his son, the two families should get together to agree on things. He said he'd expect to hear pronto and that Mason knew how to get in touch.

'It's not a simple situation, is it? We've got past a shotgun wedding as the only solution these days, I suppose,' he said. Andrew hadn't heard the expression shotgun wedding for years.

'I know nothing about it,' he said. 'Mason's never mentioned anything about Noleen to us. He flats with friends. I'll talk with him today and see what he says. See if you're right.'

'I'm right all right,' said Cyril. 'It's not what anyone wanted, but it's a situation we have to deal with. No use going on about it until you've had a chance to sort things with Mason. It's sudden for you, I know. Anyway, I'll expect to hear back in a day or so. We need to help them find the best way to go, don't we? I'll let you get on with the clipping, but I needed to come and see you. Noleen's nineteen years old, Mason's, what, nineteen or twenty?'

'Just twenty,' said Andrew.

'There you go. They still need their families, don't they, Mr Lugard? Okay now, I'll let you get on but expect to hear from you.' Cyril turned and walked away, tall and with his thick jersey dark against the glossy green of the hedge.

Andrew waited until he was out of sight, without any conscious reason for doing so, then walked into the house to find Pamela, who was cleaning the inside of the dishwasher.

'Why are you bringing the hedge trimmer in here?' she asked him. In his preoccupation with what Cyril had told him, Andrew had forgotten he still held it, and he went back and put it outside the door.

'I've just been talking with a Mr Withers,' he said as he returned. 'Did you know Mason was seeing a girl called Noleen Withers?'

'He never says anything about girls he goes out with. Never says anything much at all about his life, you know Mason.'

'Cyril Withers says that Mason's got her pregnant.'

Pamela put the cleaning fluid and cloth on the bench, set the machine to a quick cycle and took off her rubber kitchen gloves, all without a word, but her face assumed a certain intentness and her movements greater deliberation. 'Start again,' she said. 'Who's Cyril Withers and what's he saying?'

'I've no idea who he is, but he reckons Mason and his daughter have been going out, and now she's pregnant and he wants us to meet with him and work out what's to be done about it. He turned up when I was doing the hedge.'

'Why didn't he come in?'

'He wanted us to have a chance to talk to Mason first, and that's fair enough. We need some time to get our heads around it.'

'Is it some sort of con? Did he ask for money or something?'

'He just said we all need to meet very soon and sort things out. I'm going to phone Mason now and tell him to drive straight over.'

'It's Saturday, so he'll probably be at rugby,' said Pamela.

'I don't care where he is,' said Andrew. 'We need to talk to him.'

'No, talk with him; there's a difference. Don't assume anything. We don't know, do we.'

Mason was at the park, but his game was over. He was drinking with his teammates, although he wasn't a great boozer, and Andrew gave him credit for that. Andrew didn't mention pregnancy when he spoke to him, only that Mr Withers had come round and there were things to talk about. 'Come home as soon as you can. You can have tea here if you like.'

'Don't say anything to Hugo,' Pamela told her husband when the call was over. Hugo was year twelve at Ralton College and already something of a talent, with aspirations greater than his older brother's Poly electricians' course.

'Yeah, okay. I'd better clean up at the hedge first. Might be nothing much to all this. It's shot out of nowhere, though.'

Andrew put the trimmer away, although the job wasn't finished, and raked the clippings onto a tarpaulin, which he carried to the bin. Less than an hour before, his main concerns had been poor badminton form and whether to increase his holdings in the power companies, and then the accusation from Cyril Withers that Mason was responsible for impregnating his nineteen-year-old daughter. It was a very old story and an unwelcome one, made more so because it prompted Andrew's recollection of Fran Swann.

He hadn't thought of Fran for many years. A smiling, ginger-haired girl, whom he'd shagged beneath a bridge on their way back from an open-air musical-talent contest. They were both second-year uni students, both semi-drunk and only casual acquaintances. They'd taken no precautions, and afterwards he worried she might be pregnant and tended to avoid her, as if that would somehow favourably affect the outcome. Worried for himself rather than her, when Fran had greater reason for concern. Yes, an old story and, because she proved not to be pregnant, one of little consequence.

The evenings fall early in May, and the temperature too. Andrew was aware of the chill as he finished raking up and lingered outside only because he thought Mason might be on his way. Nobody came, so he joined Pamela.

'I looked up in the phone book,' she said immediately. 'They've still got a landline, I think. C. L. and A. Withers, 29 Broughton Street. That'll be them.'

'Where's Broughton Street?' It was an automatic query more than anything else.

'No idea,' Pamela said, 'but it's the contact, isn't it? Mason will only have the girl's cell phone.'

'I wonder what sort of a girl she is.'

'A pretty upset one, I'd say. At least she's told her parents early.'

'Do we know that?' said Andrew.

'Her father wouldn't have been talking about options if it was too far on.'

'I hope it's got nothing to do with Mason. Where the hell is he anyway?'

'I guess he knows why Noleen's father turned up.'

'Aren't things different now, with the pill and everything? It's like some damn joke, something from a TV sitcom. I just want Mason to come and clear things up. Things are different these days, as I say, aren't they?'

'People are still the same,' said Pamela.

The rest of the family had already begun their macaroni cheese when Mason rode in. His arrival on the Honda 125 was clearly heard and dimly visible too through the large window by the dining table. Andrew hurried out to meet him.

'We won't talk about it until after tea,' Andrew told him. 'Hugo doesn't need to be brought into it.'

'Okay,' said Mason, who was taking off his yellow-and-red jacket. He left it folded on the seat with his blue helmet, signs that he didn't expect to be long. He was dark haired, like both his parents, but not as tall as Andrew and with the balance and agility of a young man. He seemed slightly more off-hand than usual, but Andrew told himself that was his own imagination. Everything had shifted somewhat since Cyril Withers' visit, aspects subtly altered. And Andrew was still accustoming himself to having an adult son. He remained more familiar, more comfortable even, with Mason as a boy rather than a man.

Hugo showed little curiosity concerning his brother's visit and after the meal went off to his room where he could soon be heard laughing and talking with friends, although alone. Gaming. He was good at gaming and even better at French and maths. Andrew stacked the dishwasher, Pamela and Mason watched from the table.

'Mr Withers talked to your father,' she said.

'Yeah, so he said.'

'I guess you're not surprised,' said Andrew. He set the timer and joined them at the table.

'It'll be about Noleen,' Mason answered.

'You're right there. How come we haven't heard about Noleen Withers before?'

''Cause it's my life, isn't it? I'm not at home now. I've got my own stuff going on.' Mason wasn't sullen, almost patient in giving his explanation.

'Her father says she's pregnant and you're responsible,' said Pamela. 'Is that right? She's your girlfriend?'

'We've hung out a bit. I wouldn't exactly say girlfriend.'

'You knew she's pregnant though?' said Andrew. There was an unreality to the conversation that seemed to bleed it of emotion and intensity. It wasn't at all as he expected to feel.

'She told me only the other day. I don't know if it's me.'

'Stop it!' said Pamela. It was a brief abruptness, then she was restrained once more, 'You've got this girl pregnant, haven't you, and you're not doing anything. Her father's come here, and we know nothing about it.'

'I don't know if it's me or not. I don't see her all that often. How do I know?'

'You know because she says so. She and her family will be quite aware that these days parentage is easily enough established. DNA and all that. No doubts at all. For god's sake, Mason, wake up. There's even tests that work before birth.'

'I didn't know that,' said Andrew.

'I googled it,' said Pamela. 'Science can do anything these days.' She looked steadily at Mason, as if to determine how honest he was being, as if she realised how much of him she didn't understand. 'We haven't asked you the most important question yet,' she said.

'What?' Mason said.

'Do you love her?'

'No,' said Mason after a pause. 'I like her, but I don't think I love her, and she doesn't love me. She's not on at all about getting married or anything. She's working out what to do. She could just take something. There're medicines, aren't there?'

'What've you told her?' Andrew asked.

'Nothing much. I wasn't sure it was me, was I?'

They were back where they started. All three recognised that, although the talk continued with decreasing engagement. Andrew said he'd ring Noleen's father and arrange a meeting, maybe as soon as the next day. He said they all needed to do the right thing.

'Do you want to do a test?' Pamela asked Mason, and he said he wasn't sure. 'You're all right?' she asked him, and he said he was okay.

'I wish you'd confided in us,' Andrew said. 'Instead of this. Anyway, I'll ring Mr Withers. Do you want to talk to him or Noleen?'

'Not now, no,' Mason said.

'Think how she's feeling,' said Pamela. 'She's nineteen and pregnant by someone who doesn't love her. Great place to be, eh?' Mason didn't reply. 'Oh, Mason,' she said softly. It was part admonition, part disappointment, part love.

'We've seen Mason,' said Andrew when he rang Cyril Withers. He didn't say his son was sitting close by and picking at his lip as a release. 'Would you like to come around tomorrow? Noleen and your wife too, of course. A good talk to see what's best to be done.' But Cyril said it was better that they meet at his house. Mid-morning, he said, if that suited. He maintained a gruff courtesy, which made the situation seem to Andrew even more unreal. He'd hoped to finish the hedge on Sunday, even begin a protective coat of deck oil on the outdoor furniture. Sundays for Pamela and Andrew were for relaxation or for chores. Neither of them attended a church. A visit to the Withers family would be no relaxation, he supposed, and almost certainly of much greater significance than a chore.

Mason left as soon as the morning visit was arranged and the phone call over. Listening, Andrew reckoned his son revved the Honda to an angry pitch.

'My god, this is something out of the blue, isn't it?' Pamela said.

'Happy Days,' said Andrew. 'What do you think's the best thing to do?'

'Well, they're hardly going to get married, are they? Not loving each other and so young. I suppose the choice is abortion, adoption or a solo mum. It's free and legal now, abortion is.'

It's an ugly word, abortion. Pamela used it as an ugly word, and he received it as such.

'It's a real bugger for everybody.' He still hoped somehow that it wasn't true.

'We've got to think of the girl as well as Mason. Until I meet her, I don't really know what to think.'

'There's a balance, isn't there? I mean between making them face up to it, take responsibility, and us being there for Mason, for both perhaps. And there's the thing about whether it's his, as he says. Whether some proof's needed.'

'Don't go in there challenging her, Andrew. Don't do that.'

'No, but it's a fair question. Has to be asked, doesn't it?'

Later neither of them found it easy to get to sleep, and each was aware the other would be thinking about the same thing, but they didn't want to start talking about it again. Not before it was a new day and they could find out things by going to the Withers' place. In the morning, Andrew said he'd had a dream of an endless icy waste with polar bears and flabby seals. Pamela said she'd had no dream at all. Both were surprised not to have dreamt of Mason and Noleen. Pamela said it was probably some sort of protective psychological evasion.

At ten-fifteen, they picked up Mason, after a short delay because Pamela sent him back into the flat to put on a better shirt. Broughton Street wasn't in a favoured suburb of the city, the house wooden, conventional and with a garden neat but unremarkable — except for a variety of brightly painted plaster gnomes. Cyril Withers met them and led them into the lounge where his wife, Alison, and Noleen waited. Strangely, the most awkward meeting was that between Mason and Noleen, despite their familiarity. Coming together under the auspices of their parents and in such circumstances was embarrassing, belittling even.

Alison was a thin, rather gracious woman and eased the initial conversation to generalities rather than some declaration concerning the reason for the visit. The gnomes were not restricted to the garden, and one had found a niche in the lounge. Pamela remarked on it as her contribution to civility. Alison explained that when Noleen was fifteen she had a craze on the making and painting of them, and the selling of them too.

'She actually did very well, hundreds of dollars, but after a while they weren't the fashion any more.'

'I hate them now,' Noleen said. 'They need dumping.'

'But they're a reminder of something you did well,' said her mother. 'Something you made a success of and enjoyed at the time.'

'They're stupid,' Noleen said. 'No one has gnomes now.' Andrew and Pamela were interested in Noleen but didn't want to make that obvious, didn't stare. Andrew had expected a quiet, even submissive young woman, one caught up and overwhelmed by events, but she was tall, angular, attractive, with long fair hair. She wore jeans ripped fashionably at the knees and a yellow jersey. There was something of latent defiance about her.

You can't sustain a conversation of gnomes and the weather for long with strangers, not when there is a pregnancy as an issue. Cyril came to the point when there was a pause in the exchanges.

'We felt we needed to get in touch. Noleen says she doesn't want to lose the baby, and she doesn't want to get married,' he said. It wasn't at all what Andrew and Pamela expected.

'There are people desperate for a baby,' said Noleen. 'Lots of good people.' Andrew had the thought that she wished to sell the baby but quickly dismissed it.

'So, if she has the baby, the adoption people we talked to say it's best that the father's name is known, for various reasons, they said. Saves complications later. So that's where we're at, why we got in touch really.' Cyril looked at his daughter as he spoke.

'I'll be part of deciding who the baby goes to,' she said firmly.

Andrew felt things were moving too quickly past one of the basic questions, which was challenging to pose, but he did so. 'Are we sure Mason's the father?' The use of the plural pronoun made it seem less antagonistic.

'Noleen is,' said Alison. 'And that's good enough for us. And there're tests now, we're told. If you want, there're tests.'

'I told you about those,' said Pamela to her husband.

'What does Mason say?' asked Cyril. They looked at Mason, waited.

'I guess so,' said Mason.

'Guess so what?' asked Cyril.

'That it's me,' said Mason.

'I'm happy to take any test,' said Noleen.

'You've considered termination?' said Pamela. A good word, termination. It meant no other more confronting need be used.

'I'm not having anything killed in me,' Noleen said.

'We feel it's her decision,' said Alison. 'We'll support her all the way.'

'All the way,' affirmed Cyril.

'And Mason will too, won't you, Mason?' said Andrew.

'Yes,' he said, striving somewhat for Noleen's tone of resolve.

'And Pamela and I will too,' continued Andrew. He was going to go on to say that they could all get through it if they worked together but checked himself.

'Mainly it's just any interruption of her studies that's a worry,' said Alison.

'She's on a top scholarship and everything,' said Cyril warmly and then coughed to check himself.

There seemed little in common between Mason and Noleen as they sat there. It was hard to imagine them coming together, bonding, making love. Andrew thought of himself and red-headed Fran again. How little of personality is sometimes involved in sex.

Alison insisted that they have morning tea, and so what may have ended in confrontation was in fact concluded with a slightly formal but well-intentioned talk over coffee and biscuits. All under the ironic gaze of Noleen's gnome beside the television set.

'Mason will keep in touch for any paperwork that might be necessary,' Pamela said as they left. 'And, Noleen, we hope that all goes well. Don't hesitate to get in touch. Someone's going to get a wonderful baby out of this, and that's the important thing.' She leant forward and pressed Noleen's hand with her own.

'Thanks. I think so too.' Noleen smiled for the first time since they'd met.

'Bye,' said Mason awkwardly. He'd seemed almost incidental to the meeting of the families and was aware of it. An instigator and then sidelined.

'Where did you meet Noleen?' Pamela asked him as they drove him to his flat.

'She does the night stint stacking shelves at Countdown like me. I started dropping her off afterwards on the bike. She's keen on music gigs too.'

'What does her father do?' asked Andrew.

'I think something with the bus companies. At the maintenance place or somewhere.'

'You realise you'll be acknowledging you're the father?' said Pamela.

'I haven't got much money or anything,' Mason said.

'I don't think Noleen has either, but if the child's adopted not a lot of money should be involved,' said Andrew, 'and we're here for you: for you both. It's a lesson though, isn't it? You've got to do the right thing. Do you still want a test done?'

'Suppose not,' Mason said.

'I imagine they'll do one anyway as part of all the rigmarole of adoption. You'll be asked for a sample or a swab,' his father said.

'Okay,' said Mason. He clearly wanted it all to go away.

'Do you want to come to us for lunch?' Pamela asked.

'No thanks.'

So, there was only Hugo with them for lunch. He didn't ask anything about their morning, and they said nothing of it. He talked a bit about the trip to New Caledonia that his French teacher was organising for the next year. He assumed his parents would pay, and his assumption was correct. He was a bright kid, and they'd been rather disappointed with Mason's school record. Both Andrew and Pamela were achievers, and Mason fell short of their expectations. Although they'd never told him that, he knew well enough.

'I think I'll finish the hedge,' said Andrew when Hugo had gone.

'Maybe Noleen's made the right choice,' said Pamela. 'She's different to what I expected. I can't imagine her having much in common with Mason.'

'He's good looking like his father. That's all you need.'

But Pamela remained serious. 'She seems older,' she said. 'She's thought it all out. You have to respect that. As she said, there will be couples desperate to have a baby.'

'I thought Cyril and Alison were pretty good about it all. I don't imagine they've got much money, but they just want to support her. They don't seem judgemental. Will she be able to keep her university subjects going? Exams and that.'

'Depends on when the baby's due, I guess,' said Pamela, 'and these days there's various dispensations and online options. She's a bright cookie, I gather.' Andrew started to say something about Mason, but Pamela talked over him. 'We'll have a grandchild we won't know and who won't know us. We won't be part of any of it.'

'The baby will be loved and happy. That's what matters.'

'Tough, though, isn't it? Although Mason doesn't mind now, he might feel differently in time. I think we will.'

'Do you want to talk to Noleen and the Withers again? We can if you're unhappy,' said Andrew.

'No. We go with it because it's Noleen's call. I admire her really. We just need to give support — money maybe as well. It's probably the best decision. I'm only saying there's a sadness in it too.'

Soon after, Andrew went out to the hedge again. He put the trimmer on the tarpaulin and stood for a time before starting. It was colder even than the day before, and he could feel the skin of his face and neck tightening as the breeze brushed by. The smell of the injured escallonia was strong, and where he had cut the branches back from the gateway the woodwork was stained. One chore had revealed another. Only a day since he'd been there, doing the same task with the same tools, blithely self-absorbed. Now he had apprehensions he found difficult to identify. Pamela was right, he thought, and no matter what support they all gave each other, sadness was there.

Transitions

Karen sat with a cup of peppermint tea and looked at her hands. The backs were true to her age, finely wrinkled, slightly mottled and easily bruised, but when she turned them, the palms were pale and firm, just as they had always been. Her hands were telling two different stories, she decided. Interesting that and something she would mention to Mia, who would be arriving soon.

Mia came most weekends, the Saturday or Sunday, cleaned the bathroom and talked about her family and her job. Sometimes during the week, she called in too. Karen enjoyed hearing about her daughter's family — she loved the two children, Ella and Charlotte, and didn't dislike Jono the husband. Mia's talk about her job, though, was rather boring, although Karen sometimes paid attention, even made supportive comment, not just because she appreciated the visits but also because she knew Mia's grizzles were a form of release.

Many daughters surpass their mothers in career achievement. It's part of a major shift in the female role in society, but that wasn't the case for Karen and Mia. Karen had been a lawyer. Not a barrister or a solicitor but a senior legal adviser to government on constitutional matters — if you could say the country had a constitution. Mia worked at Herb's Nursery: plants, not children. Karen took some responsibility for that. She had left her husband when Mia was only two, and her daughter had been brought up by a succession of caregivers, almost all pleasant and responsible women, but without a duty to advance her in the world. In what time Karen had found for Mia, she'd indulged her rather than assisting with homework or instilling goals. Yes, she set an example of diligence and attainment, but provided little assistance for

Mia to achieve them herself. Mia had never reproached her mother concerning her upbringing, and Karen had resisted any sense of guilt, for at the time she'd done what she thought was best. In retrospect, however, the significance of her career diminished and the importance of motherhood increased.

Through the full-length sliding glass doors of her unit, she could see Mia coming up Tulip Lane. Absurd really, the names they gave to the access ways in the retirement complex, some of them only a hundred metres or so in length. Daffodil Crescent, Holly Close, Buxus Drive. Unless it was raining, Mia parked by the community centre and walked to her mother's place. She liked the gardens, and Herb's Nursery was sometimes the source of the plants, although owner Herb Pugh gave her only a reduced role in the selection, which was one of her grievances. They were just pretty flowers and greenery to Karen, distinguishable by colour rather than name, their main advantage being that she didn't have to tend them.

'The azaleas by fourteen A and B are doing so well,' Mia said as she came in. 'I'll leave the door open a bit. It's getting hot.'

'I've been looking at my hands,' said her mother.

'And?'

'The backs look so old.'

'They're as old as you are, Mum,' Mia said. 'I hate to think what mine will look like at your age, after all the garden work.'

'Don't you wear gloves?'

'Usually. They make you clumsy, though.'

'I did the bathroom yesterday,' said Karen, 'so sit here with me and talk. Tell me about the kids and Jono. Perhaps the vacuuming before you go, though.'

But first Mia made herself an instant coffee. She didn't like peppermint tea. Cradling her mug, she settled beside her mother so she could look down Tulip Lane, the units of which mostly had the same floor plan but were placed differently on their small sections to give the impression of individuality. A few had a tiled roof, and a few others had a small, glassed addition at their entrance called a conservatory. Karen's had both.

'Tell me how the kids are and Jono,' said Karen again.

'Jono got a bonus. Three-hundred dollars.'

'Good for him.'

'It works out at six dollars a week,' Mia said ruefully.

'It's extra, I suppose.'

'And did I get any bonus?' Karen didn't answer. 'Not bloody likely,' added Mia. 'Herb wouldn't know the meaning of the word, just keeps moaning about the cost of everything.'

'I FaceTimed Ella,' Karen said. 'She's excited about going to university, isn't she? Don't say anything to her, but I thought I might give her some money, some help.'

'She could do with that. It's kind of you. She'll have to get a student loan at some stage.'

'Has she got a boyfriend?'

'Who knows? No one special, I think, but who knows?'

'See, the palms are just the same. I could still be thirty.' Karen was looking at her hands again.

'Well, they don't get all that much sun, do they? They don't get burnt. No one walks or lies around with the inside of their hands to the sun.'

'Maybe that's it,' said Karen.

A green car drove up Tulip Lane and turned into eleven C, which had an ordinary steel roof and no conservatory. The Andersons lived there. A fat man in shorts got out and went to the door.

'I've never seen him before,' Karen said.

'Actually, Mum, I wanted to ask about my dad.'

'You don't remember your father. You were two when we separated.'

'I know,' said Mia, 'that's the point really. Charlotte was asking about him the other day, and I knew hardly anything.'

'There're photos and stuff. You know that.'

'Yeah, but we don't see him, do we? The girls have never met him, even though he's alive.' In fact, her daughters weren't much worried about an absent grandfather, but Mia felt mention of them gave added weight to her own curiosity.

'He lives in Auckland,' said Karen. 'You know that.'

'But we never see him, maybe we should. For the girls' sake and mine too. I don't mean prying into what happened between you, but just being on speaking terms with a father and a grandfather. Do you keep him away, or isn't he interested?' The man in shorts returned to his car and drove away. Presumably the Andersons weren't home, or he was delivering.

'We're not in touch now, Mia. Martin married again. There's a child, I gather, but if you want to contact him that's okay. There's no mystery. It was a long time ago. You've never been much interested before.'

'What's he like?'

'I don't know now. Then he didn't smoke, didn't drink, didn't do anything really. He avoided as much of life as he could and concentrated on algorithms.'

'What the hell are they?' asked Mia.

'Rules for solving problems on computers. I never really caught on.'

'So why did you marry him?'

'He was quite good looking as a young guy. That'll be gone now.'

'So why did you two divorce?'

'We just grew apart. In a marriage, you either grow closer I guess, or you grow apart, and if you're too far apart what's the use of pretending to be together?'

'Okay,' said Mia. She knew her mother didn't want to go there. 'I'd still like to get in touch, though. Do you mind? You've got a phone number or an address?'

'Both,' said Karen. 'I'll give them to you before you go. I assume they're still living in the same place. Is Charlotte doing a family project at school or something? Most teenagers aren't much into grandparents, are they?'

'It's me as much as anyone,' Mia admitted, 'and Jono said if I didn't watch out my father would die before I had any memory of him. It got me thinking, that. You may have grown apart, but he might like to see me. If he doesn't, there's nothing lost, and none of this is any reflection on you, Mum. It's for me, and the girls, so there's a chance for something more than photos. How old is he anyway?'

'Eighty-three. He'll be eighty-three. Three years older than me.'

Karen got up and hunted in the drawers for evidence of her ex-husband's present existence, and as she did so she talked, not of him but of Ella and Charlotte. How she was going to sell some of her SkyCity shares and give a couple of thousand dollars each to the girls and to Mia too. 'I might as well now, when they need it,' she said, 'and when I lose my marbles and have to go into care it'll be all gobbled up anyway.'

'Don't feel you have to,' said Mia.

'I don't.'

'Well, it's very kind. You're sure there's nothing I can do here before I go?'

'Nothing urgent. Forget about the vacuuming.' She found Martin's contact information on the back of a lawyer's letter — Hawkinson and Balfour — and gave it to Mia. Hawkinson had once come on to her, many years ago, and she'd rebuffed him. A tall, pompous man who didn't take rejection kindly. 'Go ahead and get in touch by all means,' she told Mia. 'I don't hate Martin at all. There's nothing unresolved. Let me know the response you get. I can't remember his wife's name.' That was true. Martin hadn't remarried until quite a few years after the divorce, and Karen had never met her. It was Karen who had initiated the separation, and she'd felt no resentment at his remarriage, a mild relief even.

'I might not get around to it,' Mia said as she left. 'The girls may forget all about it.'

Karen rarely thought of Martin. Although she'd never remarried, there had been men in her life more important than him, one in particular whom she missed a lot. Dreamt of him sometimes and awoke to desolation. Mia's query, however, got her thinking of Martin. She wished she'd never married him, except that they'd had Mia, of course. He'd been a handsome man and without vanity, without awareness of it. An agreeable, intelligent, good-living man, honest and hardworking, all of which made him seem from the outside of the marriage to be suitable as a partner, whereas over time Karen found him boring, contained, inspired by nothing and inspiring nothing. An unexceptional man when she required more in a life partner. Passive, when life isn't meant to be a passive experience. It hit you fast, so you had to grapple with it, force it to yield the best it has before it's over.

Karen remembered their European trip when Martin's objective each day seemed merely to reach the security of the next hotel, where he spent hours in meticulous planning to ensure nothing of raw experience could intrude, when he always seemed to have a cold, or cough, or toothache that overrode the opportunity and enjoyment of them both. In Venice, he'd said the seat in the gondola was sticky, and in Istanbul his wallet was stolen in a café. He was a person to whom things happened rather than someone who made things happen. His friends were as humdrum as he was himself. When they first married, she'd worked to awaken enterprise in him. She was successful in most things but not in that and had given up on him.

Mia didn't forget about her father. She said to Jono she wondered why she hadn't done anything before. All those years without knowing anything much about him and only now reaching out.

'You realise he's old now, that's why. He could die anytime soon,' Jono said. 'Eighty-three's a good innings. And you only get interested in family stuff when you're older yourself.'

'Should I ring or write, do you think?'

'I'd write. Less embarrassment if he snubs you.'

She did write: a short letter saying she hoped he was well and that he might like to know that she had two girls and that Karen was in her own unit at Pounamu Retirement Village and well settled. She gave her own address and said he'd be welcome to call any time he came south.

The reply arrived nearly three weeks later. Martin apologised for taking so long. He'd had a bout of Covid and his wife, Linda, too. Interesting, he said, that Mia had two daughters as he had two himself, including her. Must be a family that produces daughters, he said, and that daughters are best. 'As it happens,' he wrote, 'we have been planning a trip south,' and he gave the dates but said they weren't final at all. The only mention of Karen was a conventional request to pass on his regards.

In all her growing up, Mia had asked very little about her father, although there was never an explicit rule to avoid the subject. It seemed natural somehow, just as when walking you move round a boggy patch without need of comment or instruction. There had been one photo of the three of them in the lounge of the house she grew up in, with her as a two-year-old, a small figure between them and a hand in each of theirs. That photo never made it to a public place in the retirement unit, but there were others in the album, and Karen had no problem with that. Mia couldn't remember her father, which made it easier to forget about him. Sometimes, especially after she had been in the two-parent homes of her friends, she'd taken out the album and looked for her father. He had appeared relaxed enough, not laughing but not unhappy. Nevertheless, the images seemed sad because everything they represented was over. In several of the pictures, he wore a corduroy jacket that made it seem even more a distant past. Occasionally, Karen mentioned him, but always in connection to an ongoing subject not one in which he was central or essential. She'd forgotten him.

Late May they came. Her father and Linda without their daughter, who was married and lived in Wollongong. Mia was glad of that, not because she had anything against the daughter — in fact she was curious about her stepsister — but too many strangers would surely make the meeting more difficult. May isn't the ideal time to head south, but Martin had a university reunion in Dunedin. Mia wondered what subjects would prepare you for a career in algorithms but couldn't think of the answer, and Jono wasn't any help. They would all have lunch together, and then Martin and Linda would go on. It seemed about the right amount of time to Mia because most of it could be taken up with eating if the conversation wasn't easy.

The visit was at Mia's place, and her mother played no part in the arrangements, showed no enthusiasm but wasn't antagonistic. Mia invited her, and she said she'd come but might be slightly late because Pounamu's bridge group met on Tuesday mornings. Karen had an outside partner, a retired judge, whom she didn't like letting down and who often brought tomatoes and silverbeet from his garden for her.

'She doesn't want to seem too interested,' said Jono. 'She hasn't kept up any contact at all. Might be odd.'

It was cold the day they visited and dull too, but it wasn't raining when they arrived. The flight was on time, and Martin and Linda picked up a rental car at the airport and drove to Mia's place. From the window, she watched them park and noticed how her father struggled slightly to get out of the car, as if some suction was being exercised from within. She moved out of sight as they walked up the path to the wooden house, and she waited briefly after their knock before opening the door so they wouldn't think they'd been observed. Yes, it was a rather awkward greeting — an adult daughter meeting a father she didn't know and his wife who wasn't her mother, her husband acknowledging strangers. Smiles, rather formal and conciliatory laughter, thanks for the invitation and thanks for coming. No one risked embarrassment by offering an embrace. Handshakes, though, with goodwill expressed and compliments made — what an attractive skirt, how beautifully the dining table was laid, what a pleasing view past the neighbour's garage. These from Linda with endorsement from Martin's smiles and nods.

Mia had hoped for some striking sense of connection with her father. Not just a commonality of features or mannerisms but the more subtle recognition of the genes themselves. Something almost spiritual, but no, there was nothing special on meeting Martin, except the knowledge of who he was. Karen had said he'd been good looking when they married, and he was okay for eighty-three, still a thatch of grey hair with a neat parting and a pleasant face with white teeth, but his posture was simian, legs slightly bowed and his body leaning forward, as if he were about to begin a race or fall forward. She wondered if he'd ever thought much about her, or whether the new daughter now in Wollongong had entirely replaced her.

'Mum said she might be a bit late 'cause she has something regular on Tuesdays,' she told him when they were seated.

'She's in a home, I gather?' said Linda. She wore cream slacks and a close-fitting green jersey. Although her face was heavily lined, she looked younger than Martin, younger than Karen. She was slim, and Mia thought that was probably why she looked younger. You couldn't ask, of course. She was making an effort to relate, so Mia felt no animosity towards her, and there was no reason why she should.

'It's a village really, as they call them, and she's got a three-bedroom place of her own with grounds. A very small lawn and garden, and Pounamu look after it. The best of both worlds.'

'Mind you, they charge plenty,' said Jono.

'Are you still in an ordinary house?' Mia asked. 'I mean, not in a village or anything.'

'Still in our own place on the North Shore, but I suppose we'll have to make that sort of shift in the not too distant,' said Martin. 'Too much ground, and I can't do what I used to.'

'We have a chap who comes in, but it's more Martin's health really,' added Linda. 'He's got this heart condition and really needs to be somewhere with a nurse handy or a doctor. Does your mother keep good health?'

They were talking of Karen's health when she arrived, letting herself in and taking off her winter coat as they watched. How does a couple long divorced greet one another when they meet after so many years? Mia didn't hold her breath, but there seemed a cinema-like focus as her mother walked towards Martin and he stood up. Something of an anti-climax, though.

'Nice to see you, Karen,' he said.

'You too,' she said, and her manner was easy. No restrained hug, not even a handshake.

Although he was saying something about Mia's kindness in inviting them, Karen's attention had already turned to Linda. 'Welcome,' she said. 'I would've liked to have had you all at my place, but it's bridge day and my partner's an ex-judge and severe on any dereliction of duty.'

'Mia is looking after us so well,' Linda said.

'She's even taken the day off work,' Karen said to emphasise her daughter's kindness.

It's always that way with mother, Mia thought. A poise, a confidence in her ability to have language clear the way. Eighty and gripped with arthritis, yet still able to build a case for whatever view she chose. Mia recalled the only time that Karen came to her secondary school. It was in response to a request from the guidance counsellor and concerned Mia bunking classes. It was the counsellor who ended on the defensive, and Karen who handed out a rebuke concerning the school's failure of motivation and supervision. Karen was never summoned again, but Mia had suffered afterwards, not from her mother but the counsellor. Empathy wasn't one of Karen's strengths.

'Let's move to the table,' Mia said. 'You'll understand if Jono has to go early.'

'Work, always work,' said her husband, who held up his hands in mock dismay. Linda politely asked him what work he did, for he'd had little part in their talk, and he described his job at Parks and Recreations, which no one was much interested in.

Martin watched Karen looking down at her hands, turning them, palm up, palm down, for scrutiny. What was obvious to Martin was how the conversation during lunch stayed in the present and the recent past, and no one went back the many years to the time when he and Karen had been married and Mia just a child. They talked of occupations and concerns, health and politics, the new world of electronics that young people were comfortable in. Computers had been very much part of Martin's career, but even he admitted to being now left behind. As he talked of that, he was looking at Karen and thinking of the life they'd had and the life they hadn't had. She'd always been an intellect and attractive when young, but in the marriage he'd found that almost all her ambitions were concerned not with him or Mia or domesticity but personal achievement. And she'd taken no interest in his friends. Other couples that he knew all seemed to have friends in common, but Karen had made no effort to engage with people he liked. Mostly quiet, unobtrusive people and mostly guys. People who didn't see life as a stage on which to present themselves. People like himself really. She once told him she liked people who sparkled, people who made a difference for goodness' sake, she'd said. She did lots of things with her friends, with no particular encouragement for him to join in — no sparkle, he supposed — so he joined them less and less.

The marriage had little reinforcement from a common acquaintanceship, and often in their conversation the person not talking wasn't listening either. A mutual physical attraction had faded as they realised there was little else they admired about each other. Martin knew that was a cruel summary, but true in essence. He watched his ex-wife, covertly, during the meal. She talked more than others at the table, assured and competent, always with herself at the centre of the story. He could see the inconspicuous leads of her hearing aids and probably wouldn't have registered them at all except that he wore them himself. He noticed that her voice had altered in old age, still strong but breaking briefly at times into an odd falsetto, and the tendons of her thin neck were as taut as violin strings.

He was sorry he didn't know Mia, sorry he hadn't pushed for at least some small part in her life after the divorce. Karen hadn't wanted that, and he'd acquiesced too easily perhaps. He disliked confrontation. Sorry too that he'd have no meaningful relationship with Ella and Charlotte. Too late for all of that. Yes, he'd taken the easy way, turned to Linda with so little regret and closed the door behind him. He knew that of himself. His daughter was providing him with lunch. She seemed a good sort but was a stranger to him. Whatever the future, he couldn't reclaim the role of father in anything but name. All he had was the memory of a lovely two-year-old child, his child, and she was gone for ever. He was glad his granddaughters were at school, not because he didn't care about them but that he would mean nothing to them, and he feared in their adolescent brashness that would have been evident.

Not long before their divorce, he'd gone with Karen to a New Year's party at the home of the local member of parliament, and on arrival she'd gone off to her favourite people as usual and left him to drift on the fringes of the gathering, making desultory conversation with those as ill at ease as himself. He looked at her now, her head up and talking fluently to Linda, giving advice without reservation on whatever subject came up. After that party, the one at the politician's, he'd said that he would have appreciated it if she'd made some effort to include him, introduce him to her friends, so he wasn't left at a loss, hardly knowing anyone. After all, he'd gone only to accompany her.

'Oh, stay at home, for god's sake, if you can't find your own way in the world. I'm not your big sister,' she said. Yes, she'd been drinking, but he'd never forgotten that, and there was something about her friendship with that guy. Martin had never followed that up because they decided to divorce not long afterwards.

It started to rain when they were having dessert. Heavy rain slanting in from the south, which was where he and Linda were heading. It made him slightly anxious and keen to be on the way to Dunedin. He'd never enjoyed driving, and in old age he tended even more to imagine the worst — flooding of low stretches of road, traffic banked up — and he understood he had a reduced capacity to cope with such events.

'Not ideal travel if this keeps up,' said Karen with equanimity. 'The worst of our weather comes from the south.'

'We haven't got a deadline,' said Linda. 'We'll take it easy and drive to the conditions.'

'It's not forecast to be all that bad,' said Jono, and Mia said they needed a coffee before anybody left and that everyone should move back to the comfortable lounge seats. Everyone did, except Jono, who excused himself and left for work, pausing at the door to say the rain seemed to be easing and how much he'd enjoyed the chance to meet Martin and Linda, all of which was ignored. The four were left sitting, drinking and talking some more of the present world, topical things, until Martin said that it had been a great catch-up but they'd best be on their way.

'I almost forgot,' said Linda. 'I brought something. Nothing much, but a small thank-you for having us,' and she took from her bag a box through the cellophane windows of which could be seen three small jars of jam — strawberry, apricot and marmalade.

'Thanks so much,' said Mia, 'and I nearly forgot something too. We need a photo, and I should've done it while Jono was here to take it, but the main thing is to get the two of you with us.'

So, they stood close together, and Mia picked up her phone, stretched out her arm and took several selfies. None of them was great, but a record nevertheless of Mia and her father, smiling strangers, and Karen and Linda too, whose only link was a husband in common but at different points in their lives. They said goodbye at the door, for rain was still falling though less than before. Yes, Martin and Mia hugged, briefly and without pressure but also without embarrassment.

'Visit us any time,' he said.

'You'd be welcome,' said Linda, 'and thanks again for everything.' They went down the path in the rain to the car, Martin seeming more stooped as he hurried. Before he got in, an entry as clumsy as the earlier exit, he turned and waved, and Linda did too.

'My god, he's aged,' said Karen, quite dispassionately.

'I'm glad he came and Linda too,' said Mia. 'I'm glad because now I know what he's like.'

'You need more than a lunch with someone to know what they're like,' said Karen dismissively.

Mia let her mother have the last word. It was easier that way. She had her own opinion, however.

The Enemy Without a Tail

Barry didn't mind meeting someone at Taronga zoo. Even if it was a no show, he could enjoy the ferry ride and time with the animals. He liked the camels most of all. They knew they weren't cute and took no notice of an audience. They stood peacefully together, and that pleased him too because in Afghanistan he'd seen them forced to wrestle and so provide a grotesque spectacle, worse than dogfights.

It was time-consuming going to the zoo: much quicker to meet at work, at a pub, or an associate's house, but the cops were increasingly into surveillance and the less camera time he had the better. Notoriety wasn't something he sought. He wanted to be left alone to do his job and look after his daughter. Play a little golf. You don't need a team for golf. You can even play alone, or run early in the morning through the grounds, and he was happy with that. It's relaxing to be alone when you have an occupation that keeps you wary in the presence of others.

It seemed even warmer at the zoo. Maybe it was just he was less exposed to the harbour breeze than when on the ferry. The primates were close to the entrance but drew too many visitors to suit Barry. He'd arranged the meeting at the kangaroo enclosure and walked the considerable distance to get there, standing to watch their idleness.

'There's some really big bastards, aren't there?' said Pauley, who joined him quietly. He wore knee-length, dark shorts and a white linen shirt with a soft, expansive collar.

'Some big bastards all right.' Bloody stupid name, *Pauley*, he thought. He still found it hard to get used to. No one else he worked with felt the need to have a name like that. And it wasn't only the name he disliked: he'd clashed with Pauley several times concerning how things should be done and had no trust in him.

'There's to be a pick-up at the Wilberforce property somewhere round midday on Wednesday. Are you okay for that, Bazza?'

'No problem.'

'Patrick says better not to take it straight to the cutting house. Better to take it to Shaun's. He's expecting it.'

'Yeah, okay,' said Barry. The kangaroos were close, most of them chewing. Barry came from a farm but not in kangaroo country. 'Do you know much about these guys?' he asked. 'When I was overseas people always asked about kangaroos. It's all some people know about Australia. Kangaroos and boomerangs.'

'Useless fucken animals, kangaroos,' said Pauley. 'Like most animals. I ate some kangaroo once. In a place out past Birdsville, and it wasn't good. Like pig's snout. Anyway, as long as you're fine about Wednesday. There's containers coming in soon too, but we'll let you know about that.' He talked a bit about the containers and about some bikies who'd been selling ice and badly cut heroin in places they shouldn't and might need to be dissuaded. It wasn't a long conversation, and at the end of it Pauley handed him two envelopes without addresses, but Barry knew the thicker one was for the pilot and the other for himself. 'All right?' said Pauley. 'Let us know how the pick-up goes.'

'Will do.'

'See you then.' After a quick, unfriendly look into Barry's face, Pauley turned to go. It was obvious he thought Barry was an arrogant fuck and a rival in the organisation, but a dangerous fuck.

'Yeah, see you,' said Barry and he watched Pauley pad off, his brown legs so thin the shorts were almost a skirt. Barry put the envelopes into the small bag he carried without any check of their contents. Money's a private thing.

He stopped for a few minutes on his way out to watch the baboons. All sizes and some with swollen, angry-looking arses. He remembered that when he was overseas there was this particular guy who was convinced the Taliban were training monkeys to be soldiers. He'd seen one, he said. Barry had seen worse things in Afghanistan than gun-toting monkeys.

He was back in the city in time to pick up his daughter, Tracey, from her work at Hazlitt Associates. Tracey lived with him but was soon to get married. Although he wanted her to be happy, he didn't look forward to her going for he had no other family. He'd played little part in her upbringing, but she didn't resent his abandonment They talked as they made a salmon salad together and took it outside to eat beneath the sun umbrella. Ryan was coming round later, she told him, and then they were going out to meet friends in the city. So, Ryan might be at breakfast with him the next day, but he was okay with that. Ryan was an all right guy, and for Tracey's sake Barry made him welcome.

'I need to go up-country to Wellington on Wednesday,' he said, as the breeze freshened from the sea.

'Again?'

'Yeah. The Wilberforces need parts for a harvester. They're in a pretty big way up there now. A lot of machinery. Important clients for us. I'll have to be away early, but I'll come back the same day.'

'That's a long, tiring drive,' Tracey said.

'That's just the way the job is.' He enjoyed sitting there on the deck of a decent home that was mortgage free. His home. He enjoyed even more being close to Tracey and knowing she was happy. 'Might call into one of those orchard places', he said, 'and get some fresh fruit.'

'That would be good. Nectarines especially,' she said.

He was away by six o'clock on Wednesday, and so avoided the worst of the morning traffic. Without the radio on, or any music playing, he drove fast, but not recklessly, and he thought about the work he did and especially about Patrick Caputo, whom he didn't fear but didn't trust either. Another couple of years and he could finish up with Patrick and the whole drug thing. He wasn't a user, never had been, although some he'd served with had been into it. There's a lot of money around the stuff, though, and that's why he worked for Patrick: why he was driving to Wellington for a rendezvous with a light plane at an outback landing strip.

In Orange, he stopped for a pie and a beer at the small pub run by a friendly Scottish couple. The novelty of that proprietorship and the quality of the pies made it his stop off for any trips to the Wilberforce property. He didn't pause at Wellington, which was known by police and within the drug trade as Little Antarctica because of the amount of ice bought and sold on its streets. Better to have no direct contacts there. He drove on out to the isolated station owned by Hec Wilberforce, who always made sure to be away when deliveries were due. He passed the homestead and equipment sheds, the yards and small reservoir, and went on a good way to park by the landing strip, which was just a stretch of ground without obstacles and no indication of its occasional purpose.

Barry sat in the shade of some gum trees to wait for the plane. He'd given up smoking three years before, but in quiet times he still felt the urge to light up, to draw in and experience that initial hit deep in the lungs. But he'd given up and wasn't going back to it: never carried smokes with him or accepted them from others. He watched a flock of galahs fossicking in the sparse grass, their pink fronts glowing in the sun, and he thought of the dry landscape of Uruzgan province, where he'd served. Country sometimes serene, sometimes threatening, the barren beauty so often fought over. It was tough country and bred tough people. A desperate country in which many people were desperate in various ways. A dog-eat-dog country.

He heard the plane before he saw it, dark and small like a beetle in the sky. It flew in without circling: a Beechcraft Bonanza that he recognised from the last visit. The pilot was new, though. Barry didn't know any of the pilots by name, but the guy the last couple of times had been tall with his hair combed back, not short like the man Barry approached.

The pilot was in a hurry. They always were. He checked the money and helped unload the boxes. There were several cars parked together in the trees beyond the creek, he said, and he didn't like the look of it. He had no questions for Barry, and Barry had none for him. The transfer of money was all the communication required. It wasn't Barry's job to make a detailed check on the stuff, just take delivery and bring it safely in. It was mainly ice, he knew, and a lesser amount of ecstasy.

'I'd piss off straight away if I was you,' the pilot said. 'Those cars are about twelve or fifteen ks away. Anyway, I'm off.'

'Me too,' said Barry. He didn't wait to watch the plane taxi, but he could hear it as he drove back along the farm track to the road. There, he kept to the speed limit and checked his rear-vision mirror, but nobody came in pursuit. Probably those cars at the creek were teenagers swimming and shagging together. He was just a guy driving a conventional red SUV on a Wednesday afternoon. Nothing to see here. He stopped only once, at a petrol station on the outskirts of Orange, which had local fruit for sale, so as well as filling up he bought peaches and nectarines for Tracey.

It was a long trip, and he was pleased to reach Sydney, more pleased to arrive at Shaun Hopper's house in Baulkham Hills after sending a text that said: *nearly there.* A modern home with a flower garden that suggested a woman's enthusiasm. Barry got on well with Shaun. Of those people Patrick liked to call business associates, Shaun was the only one Barry had formed anything approaching friendship with. Even that was guarded.

The large garage was open, and Barry drove straight in. Shaun was waiting, and they unloaded and went through to the house. They had a beer in a spacious, uncluttered room looking out on the lawn, where a watering device undulated, its spray spangled in the sun.

'A good job done,' said Shaun, 'and everything in order.' He was smaller, darker and older than Barry, and had a habit of licking his teeth. 'Always a relief to get it home,' he said.

'A different pilot, but no snags.'

'I think Patrick's going to shift to another landing strip for a while to be on the safe side.'

'It's hardly a regular service.'

'Yeah, but there's always some bloody local who notices what comes and goes, isn't there?'

'We don't need it any further away, that's for sure,' Barry said. 'Closer would be a good thing; I'll tell him that tonight.'

'He's really pissed off at the moment.'

'Surprise me,' said Barry.

'Stuff's been going missing, tallies not right, and he's not sure where along the line it's happening. Pauley's been stirring things up about it too. The shit'll hit the fan sometime soon, I reckon.'

'Nothing to do with me,' said Barry. 'I'm clean.'

'I'd watch it, though. You know what he's like. Fires up that easy.'

'Tell me about it. And how does an Italian come to be called Patrick, for Christ's sake?'

Shaun just laughed.

They talked a bit about what they did in the business, about the edginess of it and the difficulties in predicting how Patrick and Pauley thought, and how they reacted. They talked of less significant guys too, none of whom were friends. They shared misgivings, without either of them confiding anything that might be used against them. They agreed that their business wasn't one in which you stayed longer than you needed to, but where else was money so readily made?

On his way back from Shaun's, Barry passed the street where Stan Pooke used to live. Stan had been with him overseas, and they'd kept in touch when they returned, meeting occasionally for a drink and a yarn, the races perhaps. Stan drowned one night at Byron Bay, close to where his in-laws lived, leaving a wife and three sons. It was thought that he'd got into difficulties in a rip, but Barry knew that he'd been drinking more and more since coming back and didn't seem to want to go on. Barry felt guilty that he'd been to see Stan's wife only once afterwards, but she'd never been enthusiastic about her husband's army mates. Stan had been a close friend and deserved a better end than had eventuated, even if the choice was his own. As he passed the Connell Street sign, Barry remembered how Stan would sleep lying on his stomach, with his hands stretched above his head, and how resolute he was when bravery was called for. Barry could imagine him swimming steadily out into the deepening and darkening water of Byron Bay. There weren't many real friends left.

After reaching home, Barry had a shower and enjoyed a late tea with a note from Tracey for company. He knew Patrick would be waiting to hear how the delivery went but let him wait. Patrick hadn't done the job after all, just sat on his arse while Barry took the risk.

'I've been waiting to hear, haven't I?' said Patrick later. 'Why the fucking hold up?'

'No hold up. I'm not long back after a bloody long day, aren't I?

Anyway, the stuff's all at Shaun's now.'

'No problems?'

'No problems.'

'The suppliers want a different location next time,' said Patrick. 'Reckon we should give the Wilberforce strip a rest for a while.'

'Not a bad idea but make it closer.'

'You know it's got to be well away from anything and anywhere. Let's try that old mining strip at Sandringham again for a while. Sus that out for us, eh? See that guy. What's his name?'

'Rivers.'

'Yeah, see Rivers. Find out what the situation is and whether it's good to use again.'

'Okay, I'll check it out. Shaun said there's been issues with distribution. Product going missing and so on. So, what's up?' Patrick didn't reply for a time, deciding how much Barry knew, or how much he needed to know. What he was up to maybe. Pauley had been saying things.

'Yeah. Some bastard's been helping himself somewhere along the line. How were the boxes when you got them?'

'All present and all sealed.'

'You're sure?'

'Looked okay to me. I just passed them on. Shaun will do the check.'

'Well, someone's fucking with us, and I'll find out who,' said Patrick. There was something in his voice that made Barry aware that the warning was to him as well. People like Patrick Caputo trust nobody, not even their mothers. He allowed a pause — his steady breathing audible — then he changed the subject and his tone too. 'A container's coming in soon. It's been sent via Seoul so it shouldn't attract much attention. Pauley will be in touch.'

The conversation worried Barry somewhat. He knew better than to be involved in any siphoning, but the business he was in was such that problems were dealt with in a way that accepted collateral damage: people ended face down just to cover eventualities. Patrick had no compunction about anything, and that made his decisions both easier and less fastidious.

Soon after the call, Tracey returned home, and Barry was able to put Patrick out of his mind and relax, talking with his daughter. He asked after Ryan to show he liked him, he asked after her work and listened attentively to her minor and passing grievances concerning her office job at Hazlitt Associates. He asked her if she needed any money, because he equated generosity with love, having experienced very little love himself.

'Oh, Dad,' she said. 'I don't need more money.'

'When you get married you will,' he said. 'When you get married, I'm going to help you get a place of your own. Renting's a mug's game.'

'That's kind, but Ryan and me are doing okay. Anyway, we'll see. It's good of you.'

'I can help. I haven't got anybody else.' He had more money than it was easy to explain, so he didn't try. He'd just do it when the time came. As they talked, he took pleasure in looking at her as well as in what she said. She was a bit overweight perhaps, but attractive and composed, and he was proud of her. He loved her. She reminded him of her mother, who was now with someone else, and who could blame her?

'When did you last see your mother?' he asked.

'I've been in touch. I'm hoping to go up in a couple of weeks. For one night. You know I don't go much on him.' She knew Barry liked hearing that, but he didn't respond, instead he reminded her to have her car checked for the trip.

'You're as bad as Ryan. Women can look after cars, you know.'

'Good for you,' he said. 'Tell me if you need anything: anything at all.'

'Dad, I'm fine,' she said.

He headed to the golf course early next morning. He was a member, although a very average player. He valued the access his subscription gave him and the proximity to his home. Often, as on that morning, he went without clubs and jogged there in running gear, through the trees around the ponds and sand traps, over the undulating fairways. It was early and cool, no one was playing, and he enjoyed the running and didn't think about much at all. At the back of his mind, though, was concern about Patrick's discovery that there was someone in the organisation helping themselves to merchandise they weren't entitled to. The shit would hit the fan, as Shaun had said. You didn't try that on with Patrick Caputo.

Six days later, Barry got the call from Pauley. 'The parts shipment from Korea's coming in Thursday, or Friday,' he said. 'Wharf three. I'll let you know when it's unloaded and the right man's at the desk.'

'And it goes to Shaun?' Barry asked.

'No, straight to the storage shed at the shop site. Drop it there. After a check and sort up, we'll probably need you to take it on further. Not sure. Keep both days free, though, and the Saturday.'

'Wouldn't it be better to move it on straight away? Get it off the premises?'

'Just follow the plan, eh Bazza,' said Pauley. 'Just follow the fucken plan.'

The front for Patrick Caputo's business was a machine and parts shop: rotary hoes; ride-on mowers; chainsaws; water pumps. The parts side of the enterprise was the more developed because drugs could be brought in that way with least risk. Thousands of containers come through Sydney each week and they couldn't all be checked. One-hundred billion dollars' worth of trade passes through NSW ports each year. Only mugs tried to bring in stuff through airport customs. Crime works best within a cloak of legitimacy. Barry wasn't always riding shotgun on ice, ecstasy, or cocaine, not even mostly. Often he delivered sprocket sets to other shops, maybe a leaf blower to a widow in Waverton. Sometimes he demonstrated Husqvarna chainsaws and recommended them as a reliable brand. Most of his life was ordinary. Ordinary is good. It draws less attention. It passes by unnoticed. Premier Machines was a sizable, reputable business — much bigger than it appeared and with undisclosed interests.

Early Friday, he got the call that their shipment had been unloaded at the Botany Bay terminal and he took a company truck down at lunchtime. In the movies, stuff came in late at night: shadowy figures in the drizzle, fog horns, car lights flashed at a distance as a signal, but Barry went in the sunlight, in a quiet lunchtime. Ordinary is best. He knew the storage man by sight and knew his Christian name: Ray. Patrick paid Ray to unload from the container and had someone observe from a distance to check on any customs intervention. Ray had no inkling of what was hidden within some of the machines and parts in the crates he handled. Barry gave him his cash in an envelope and signed for delivery. He took the time to have a chat and pretend interest in Ray's assessment of the Rabbitohs. He stopped on his way back to the shop for a beef burger and ate it sitting in the sun by a skateboard park.

How would anyone guess that within the bulk of the parts in the crates stacked in the back of the Premier Machines truck were drugs worth more than a million dollars? How could they guess that the driver taking time out for a burger by the skateboard park was a former army sniper with an honourable discharge from a past he had no wish to revisit? A past that had cost him his marriage and several friends and rewarded him only with cynicism and the ability to look after himself and deter others.

There was a woman walking through the park with a Labrador on a leash. The dog was barking and pulling towards the concrete basins where two guys on skateboards clattered and swooped, but it was the woman Barry watched. She moved well, and her figure in the short dress was outlined against the green of the park trees. He wished he knew her, that he could walk to her and be greeted as a lover, go with her somewhere beneath the trees. His job, however, wasn't one that suited relationships. As he went back to the truck, he decided to visit the Blue House in a day or two and have time with Monica, or Dok Mai, maybe Celeste. It didn't much matter which: he liked them all.

At Premier Machines, Barry called young Ricky from the showroom to help unload the crates into the shed. Ricky had no idea he was employed by a criminal organisation: he slept easy at night and was one of the city's best badminton players.

'Just leave the load as is,' Barry told him. 'Don't bother with it. Probably I'll be back later.' Even if Ricky had bothered with it, he wouldn't have noticed anything untoward unless he knew what he was looking for and where it was hidden.

'Did the Stihl stuff arrive?' Ricky asked.

'Yeah, I think it's on the inventory,' Barry said.

'About time. We've got people getting angsty.'

'You should be okay now.'

'The parts from Korea have arrived,' Barry told Patrick later, sitting in his lounge, looking across to watch his neighbour manhandling a ladder to reach the guttering of his house.

'So, all at the shop?' Patrick said. Although it was a phone call, Barry could visualise his employer with exactness. The long, thin body; the long, even thinner face with a stubble of dark hair like a horseshoe above his ears. When he smiled, you saw the gaps between his oddly square teeth: not just the front ones but between all that were visible. 'I said everything's at the shop now?' Patrick's voice held exasperation at Barry's delay in replying. Patrick Caputo isn't a patient man.

'Yeah, all there. Do you want me to have a check inside later today, or tomorrow?'

'No. We'll leave it tonight. I'll need you to go with whoever I get to distribute stuff tomorrow, though. Make sure it all goes smoothly. There's a group of the Rebels I want to talk to you about as well, pricks who've reneged on the deal made about territory.'

'Pauley said something about it. Bikies pushing their luck.'

'Yeah, but we'll get round to that. Let's get this shipment out first.'

'Okay,' said Barry.

'So, nothing unusual at the port and no sign of anything being tampered with?'

'All went smoothly at the wharf, and the crates looked fine to me, but I didn't dig around at all.'

'Sounds good. Anyway, I'll let you know about the drop-offs. Make sure you stick around home in the morning for my call.' Patrick cut off, having said all he wanted.

What he didn't say was that he'd pretty much decided that Barry was the one fucking the system. More and more things pointed that way. Patrick had deliberately told Barry he knew someone was siphoning stuff off: that way he wouldn't think himself under suspicion. He's a cunning man, is Patrick. He got in touch with Pauley, who had already been at Premier Machines and who said he'd found signs someone had been in the crates.

'Some bugger's been ratting in,' Pauley told Patrick. 'I don't like to say it, but it's pretty clear to me.' That was the clincher for Patrick, and he made it plain to Pauley what had to happen.

'I've told him to make sure he's at home in the morning,' he said. 'That I'll be calling him.'

'How did he sound?' asked Pauley.

'The same,' said Patrick. 'No reason he shouldn't be, is there? Just get done what has to be done.'

'I know the right boys.'

'Get it done tidy,' said Patrick.

'Tidy it is,' said Pauley, careful to keep satisfaction from his voice. He wouldn't make as much money in the future, but good things come to an end. And he'd never liked Barry, who could be a dangerous bugger.

Even Patrick doesn't make such decisions often or lightly, but having done so he knew the best thing was to keep things normal. He put on his second-best suit from a choice of five and with his wife attended a fundraiser for a local politician — a man he despised, but who was useful. Patrick has no time for anyone unless they're useful.

Tracey had Ryan with her when she came home. Often he shared their evening meal on a Friday and occasionally stayed over without any permission sought from her father and without awkwardness as well, for Barry saw the home as much hers as his. The three of them talked together, and Barry was made aware again of how idealistic they were in their view of the world and how cynical experience had made him. His pleasure was her proximity and affection. Later he left them in the lounge together as they wished to be and went to his room to watch television. He could hear their occasional laughter, and that pleased him too. There had been no laughter in the house he lived in as a boy.

The three of them had breakfast together the next morning. As it was Saturday, Tracey and her boyfriend were still at the table in dressing gowns when Barry drove to the shop. He knew Patrick might need him, but he had his phone and wouldn't be long or far away. He thought he should have a closer look at the new shipment after all. Ricky and Ben were in the showroom, both busy with customers, and Barry took the shed key from the office and crossed the yard. The crates had been opened, which surprised him. He asked Ricky about it when he returned to the shop.

'That Pauley guy came after you left yesterday,' Ricky told him. 'Said he needed parts urgently for some neighbour of Mr Caputo's. He wanted to know if anyone else had been in the workshop, and I said you'd just dropped the stuff off and would be back.'

There was something up, something badly wrong, but Barry smiled at Ricky and raised a hand to Ben as he left. With difficulty, he resisted the urge to drive home. If something was planned to happen there, it was already over. He phoned Tracey. No answer. He drove to the PEG parking building, where he had a rented locker. When there he phoned again, and again without response. He sat in his red Honda SUV looking at the concrete ramps and low, concrete roof, and he listened to the radio. He saw the lines of the parking spaces had been recently painted and that there was a dismembered bird's nest by the stairwell. He listened to the radio for a long time, until there was the news that two people had been shot dead in a house in his suburb and his street. Both found still in their dressing gowns the radio said. He didn't make any noise, continued to view the concrete, the newly painted lines and the bird's nest as before, but there were tears on his face that he took no notice of, not even to wipe away.

Barry knew he couldn't go home, for Patrick would have realised a mistake had been made and have people out, instead he sat and thought about his daughter when alive, although he knew she was dead. He felt anger, sadness, guilt and despair. He felt that hopelessness that settles when you have no one left who matters. After a time, he left the car and went down the stairwell to his locker and took from it a good deal of money and one rifle case, and he drove off to find a quiet, ordinary place in which to concentrate on the means of retribution, for that was the only motivation left to him. For no reason, he thought of his friend and fellow sergeant, Stan Pooke, who, when asked his opinion of the country they were serving in, said, 'In every fucken village there's always dogs barking.'

'You know what you've done, don't you?' said Patrick, his voice barely kept in check. He stood so close that Pauley could see the grey stubble on his jaw and the redness of his eyelids, could smell tobacco on his breath. 'You pricks have put me right in it. As long as his daughter was alive, we had him, and now he's out there — fucken enemy without a tail.'

'The guys thought it was him sitting with her.'

'Well, they were bloody useless. You should have done the job yourself.'

'We'll catch up with him. We're watching the house, watching the police station even,' said Pauley.

'What bullshit. You think he's as thick as you? The fucker's out there with only one thing on his mind,' and Patrick looked over the groomed slope of his grounds towards the street and moved out of the line of fire of anyone watching there. Patrick Caputo wouldn't go down easy, but he knew that he would probably go down, because out there was his enemy, an enemy without a tail.

Marjorie's Mushroom

Marjorie Ketle was an ordinary person with an ordinary life, neither a conspicuous success nor an obvious failure. A member of the largely unremarkable mass in between. Marjorie was a receptionist at the legal firm of Purcill and Pugh. Simon, her husband, with whom she'd lived without serious dispute for almost forty years, had died of pneumonia, and their daughter, Roseanne, had married a poultry farmer and lived in Dubbo, New South Wales.

After Simon's death, Marjorie took up bowls and Pilates, which she enjoyed despite their failure to compensate for the loss of her husband. Financially, she wasn't in bad shape. The modest house was mortgage-free, she had limited savings and her place with Purcill and Pugh. Lots of widows were worse off, and many better provided for. Marjorie was in reasonable health for her age, although her doctor had her in the queue for a hip replacement. She was too honest to exaggerate her symptoms and faced a considerable wait in the system.

It was a mushroom that finally made Marjorie distinctive, elevated her above all the other ordinary people with whom she'd been perfectly content. She first noticed the mushroom after several days of light autumn rain. It emerged in a small triangle of grass between the path and the garage. An ordinary mushroom in appearance at first but astounding in the rapidity of its growth, reaching fourteen inches within a week, three feet before a month. People turned up to see such a curiosity: first her friends and neighbours, then a widening circle. She would come out of her front door to find folk clustered at the gate to catch sight of the mushroom, some even walked down the path uninvited for a closer inspection. A local know-all, Bevan Preece, said it wasn't a mushroom at all but a toadstool. He was put in his place by a horticulturist who said there was no scientific distinction between mushrooms and toadstools, just a popular assumption that the latter were poisonous.

The mushroom grew to be over five feet tall, lost its initial perfect pallor and gained a slightly yellow, crazed surface to its head. There are always those, however, who harbour schadenfreude, and a retired primary-schoolteacher with long-Covid came shouting to Marjorie's house one Friday night and attacked the mushroom with a pair of scissors, claiming it exalted masculinity. Marjorie was upset but didn't press charges because the woman was unwell. Oddly enough, the damage only increased the mushroom's singularity and the interest in it, for the damaged portion of the crest developed an excrescence with a remarkable resemblance to a human foot: toes and all.

A botanical curiosity, people said, and it was viewed on national television and around the world on YouTube. Marjorie had to put a *no trespass* sign at her gate. She became a familiar face to her fellow citizens. The director of the city gardens visited her and in a rather presumptuous manner suggested the mushroom be re-located to one of the conservatories under his jurisdiction. Marjorie agreed to consider the proposal, which the director said was in the best interest of the plant and community, but when she mentioned it at her work Mr Pugh took a contrary view.

'No, no, Marjorie,' he said. 'It's unjust appropriation of something that could be of significant value to you.'

Denis Pugh was a shrewd man, as lawyers often are, but the advantages he could see in the situation were not for himself. Marjorie had been a good servant of the firm for many years, and he appreciated her loyalty and quiet efficiency, wanted her to have all the benefits available from the fortuitous sprouting of a giant mushroom on her property.

'Take advantage while you can,' he told her. 'Who knows how long a mushroom can last. I can help you if you like.'

'I'd appreciate that if you've got time, Mr Pugh,' Marjorie said. 'Thank you.'

The gardens' director was rather put out, but there was nothing he could do except grumble in private about selfish exploitation. He knew better than to take on Purcill and Pugh. Mr Pugh contacted tradies, and a neat alley was built from the street to an enclosure surrounding the mushroom, so that it was no longer visible from the gate. The mushroom itself was completely covered with a ventilated Perspex dome, and an information plaque was placed at eye level, including the fact that the largest living organism on earth is a fungus. A giant *Armillaria ostoyae* that covers 965 hectares in Oregon's Blue Mountains. Denis Pugh arranged it all and paid for it all, saying that Marjorie could reimburse him later. He even suggested Peter Bovate as someone to collect the entrance money. Peter was a large, cheerful man, who walked with a stick because of a motorbike accident and was known to be honest.

The giant mushroom with a human foot was available for viewing seven days a week between ten in the morning until four in the afternoon unless it was raining. The cost was five dollars, and there was no additional charge for taking photographs. Marjorie thought it a bit steep, but Mr Pugh said such a curiosity had to be taken advantage of while the opportunity was there. 'No one knows how long your mushroom will last,' he told her, 'or whether people's interest will persist as well.'

Even with one foot, the mushroom lasted pretty well, and people travelled there from all over, even though know-all Bevan Preece said, as a naturally occurring phenomenon, access should be free. Bus tours made Marjorie's place a regular stop, and she was even visited by fungi scientists of note, including a very attractive African American woman from the University of California and a rather monosyllabic withdrawn fellow from Aberdeen. Mr Pugh agreed that anyone with academic credentials should be allowed a free viewing, even have the dome removed, but he was adamant that no tissue was to be taken from the mushroom itself. More than a dozen film crews arrived at one time or another, one even from a BBC nature series. Marjorie had several new dresses she could choose from for such occasions and had pat answers to such questions as 'What did you think when you first saw the mushroom?' and 'What difference has it made to your life?'

The difference it made to her life was very considerable. She was now well-off financially and able to visit her daughter in Dubbo whenever she pleased, but more significantly she had become famous, through no endeavour of her own. She was The Giant Mushroom Lady and so no longer ordinary.

The mushroom withered and died in less than a year. Mr Pugh arranged to have corpse specimens available to interested laboratories — for a price of course. Private individuals bought samples too, hoping there might be spores that would strike in their own gardens and bring renown and wealth.

Even with the giant mushroom passed away, the viewing paraphernalia removed and honest Peter Bovate let go, Marjorie didn't revert to ordinariness. The mushroom may have been fortuitous, but it had happened to her, and so she possessed the aura of one chosen. Her opinion was valued on all sorts of matters of which she knew little, and her acquaintanceship was prized. She had no need to continue being the receptionist at Purcill and Pugh, but she remained loyal, and her salary and mana there were increased because of the additional clients she attracted.

A lesser person may well have assumed that such success and status was of their own doing and so become proudly superior, but Marjorie understood that she'd just been lucky. Perhaps that realisation in itself is proof that she had never been ordinary to begin with.

Elspeth and Lloyd George

'And you are again?' the receptionist said, having failed to find Rhys's name on first perusal of the booking list.

'Rhys Griffith. I made the reservation from London some days ago.'

'Ah,' exhaled the man, as if a riddle had been solved. 'Ah, yes, here you are,' as he transferred his attention to another page. There was no Welsh lilt to his voice.

'Yes, here I am,' said Rhys.

He was in Criccieth, checking in to an old-fashioned, rather looming hotel with a strong wind buffeting the main doors as if resentful at being denied entry. He had no formal business in Criccieth, he hadn't visited before, but he was there on behalf of his dead father. His father had never been there either but claimed their forebears came from the place. His father was as much English as Welsh, but it was the Celtic twilight that had claimed his allegiance and where he'd chosen to roam in imagination.

'Do you want help with your case?' the desk man asked.

'No thanks.'

'Number thirteen. You've got a view of the Bay.'

'Good. Thank you.' Rhys wheeled his case to the lift, went up to number thirteen — unperturbed by its association with misfortune — and stood at the window to look out over Cardigan Bay. His father had talked about Cardigan Bay, about the long-ago Griffith folk who had lived in the small town, although he'd had very little evidence of the association, mainly hearsay passed down by his own father.

Seen at such distance, the sea seemed merely ruffled by the strong wind, but Rhys knew the waves would be challenging and decided not to go to the shore on what little was left of the first day. He didn't like walking in the wind. He walked happily in winter frost or summer heat if clothed suitably, but not in strong wind, which he found a distraction from reflection. He put his case on a stand with straps on the top and folding chrome legs beneath and began to unpack. During overnight hotel stays, he often didn't bother, but he planned to spend two days in Criccieth. His father deserved that.

It was a plain room, old fashioned and with no sign it had ever been anything other than an ordinary room for ordinary people: travelling salesmen, school inspectors and local honeymoon couples, rather than folk from the continent. By the door, there was a framed photograph of three loose-maned Welsh ponies grouped at a wooden farm gate. He sat down in the one armchair and looked through the hotel folder with its instructions for Wi-Fi and the television, check-out times, local sites of interest, menus. There didn't seem to be room service. Taking out his journal, he wrote about the day's trip while it was still fresh in his mind, including impressions of the rather bland Offa's Dyke and the far more impressive Harlech Castle. The one annoyance of the latter visit had been the difficulty in finding a parking space.

Rhys's father would have enjoyed both places. The older things were, the more they had interested him, possibly because fewer facts allowed greater scope for imagination and supposition. His father often said that he would travel to Wales, to Criccieth, and find relatives there. He never did; did he know in his heart that only disappointment awaited? There would be municipal records and chapel ones too, he claimed. His own father had told him that the Griffiths were chapel folk. Rhys decided that tomorrow he would make enquiries, but he didn't have great expectations or particular enthusiasm. Their family had been in New Zealand for a hundred-and-fifty years, so he was all Kiwi. He'd come to honour his father, not in search of ancestry. And Griffith was such a common Welsh name that finding any personal link was unlikely without sure provenance.

Journal entry completed, Rhys went again to the window and looked over the houses to the sea. Modest homes, drab if one's mood was low. He thought of southern France and Italy, where small, old places often glowed with pink and yellow even if neglected. Where people felt no embarrassment in drawing attention to themselves.

The sun shone. After his long drive, he had hoped for a walk, but the wind was still strong and whined at the corner guttering not far from the window, so he decided to go down to the bar.

The barman was friendly, and the cadence of his speech left no doubt he was Welsh. He suggested a local beer that he said was rather like an Irish stout. They talked a little before his duties took him away, but Rhys didn't say that he had links with the town. Locals would be bored with tourists claiming some sort of affiliation. He did ask for tips as to places worth a look, an even more common topic, and enquired as to Lloyd George's childhood home and museum.

'No distance at all hardly, no distance hardly at all. Just a short drive to Llanystumdwy if you've got a car. Oh, yes, the only Welsh Prime Minister and a great one,' was the reply.

Rhys's father had talked often of David Lloyd George and read a great deal about him too. He said no doubt his Griffith relatives would have known him, for the town population was even smaller then. He'd emphasised that Lloyd George came from a humble background, yet eventually sat with presidents to decide the fate of Europe. Such upward mobility had impressed Rhys's father, especially as — despite being bright and industrious and starting almost from ground zero himself — he attained merely the moderate success of middle management.

Cardigan Bay was not visible from the ground-floor window of the bar where Rhys sat, but he could still see the unobtrusive houses and the blue porcelain sky above burnished by the wind. Close outside, the glossy green leaves of a magnolia tree flipped in the gusts to flash brown bellies, like a shoal of fish in a sudden turn. No, he wouldn't walk before dinner: maybe afterwards in the summer evening if the wind abated.

A woman was farewelling her companion outside by the main entrance, both slightly distracted by the wind. The man was tall, the woman holding her blonde hair back with one hand, her dress whipping at her legs. They kissed quickly, and the man waved his arm back towards the hotel door, not as dismissal but as consideration for her, before getting into the red Audi and driving away. Rhys watched only because he happened to be at the window and wasn't to know he would see the woman again, that she would become part of his life for far less time than he wished.

Their meeting later was an accident, both in the sense of coincidence and a cause of injury. Rhys was coming back from the dining room, where he'd had the lamb as a main and apple crumble for dessert. There was no Welsh rarebit on the menu, but perhaps that was a breakfast dish, and his father had told him it was originally a derogatory term. As the lift door opened following ascent, Rhys found the farewell woman waiting to go down, and he held the door open for her to go in. Turning to thank him, she caught her foot on the small lip and fell into the lift space, hitting her face. Her nose bled, smudging on to her long, fair hair, which had been flung forward.

Rhys said he'd go down with her in the lift to get help at the desk, but she wanted to go to her room — number fifteen. So, they headed there, and at the door he asked if she'd be okay and if she wanted him to come in, but she didn't. She thanked him and said she was fine and just needed to clean up and hurried through to the bathroom without looking back, one hand and a handkerchief to her nose, the other briefly flourished at her side in gratitude. Rhys closed the door and went to his own room. He felt sorry for her, assuming her partner was still away, but that in itself was a reason not to bother her.

'This bloody wind,' he said to himself, looking out to the town, where outlines were softening as the sun set. Beyond the town, seeming somehow above it, the sea was rough, white crested because of the wind.

It was gone in the morning, the wind, but the clear sky and sun had returned. He was in a good mood when he went down to breakfast, already planning things for the day. It was unusual, and so especially pleasant, to have a whole day before him with no obligations whatsoever. The farewell woman was there before him, by herself, and he stepped over to her table and asked how she was feeling.

'Fine,' she said, 'and I want to thank you again. I dashed off, didn't I? But I needed to get to the bathroom. I spent the night with tissue plugs in my nose though didn't really need them. I get nosebleeds so easily. All fine now.'

'That's good.'

'I had a look when I came down this morning, and there's hardly any lip to the lift at all. I don't know how I tripped on it.'

'As long as you're okay.'

'I'm Elspeth,' she said and stretched up her hand, smiled. There was no sign of bruising on her face.

'Rhys,' he said.

Elspeth didn't ask him to sit down, so he went to a table close to the door, near a middle-aged couple with a Coronation Street accent so pronounced that he had to repress the inclination to congratulate them on their mastery. The man was cheerfully explaining to his wife that with such a breakfast they wouldn't need lunch. Rhys had only egg and toast himself, then a coffee, and he was still sitting with his drink when Elspeth left, lifting a hand to him and smiling as she passed. An attractive woman and relaxed in her own awareness of it. Maybe late thirties, he thought. She was wearing jeans and looked good in them, and he remembered the evening before and the strong wind moulding the yellow dress around her as she stood by the car.

When he walked from the dining room into the hotel lounge, she was sitting on a large leather sofa, focusing on her cell phone, but she looked up and smiled again. 'So much better now,' she said.

'Nosebleeds can be nasty,' he said.

'No, I meant the weather today,' and she laughed.

'Oh, of course, yes. You're right. I'll be able to see the sights of Criccieth and be blown away only metaphorically.'

'Sit down if you want to,' she said. 'Tell me the places you've got sorted.' The invitation was delivered with casual naturalness, so Rhys sat on the sofa, stretching his legs beneath the low table in front of it. 'Have you been here before?' she asked.

'Never.'

'You're Australian, right?'

'New Zealand. I'm a Kiwi.'

'A long way from home then.'

'What about you?' he asked.

'We live in London but like to visit Wales when we can.' She knew

Criccieth and its surrounds well and endorsed the selections he'd made, suggested others in the area as well, especially Caernarfon. Her husband was a keen yachtsman, and they liked to hire a boat and go out on the bay. Criccieth was never swamped with tourists, she said. She told him that her husband had needed to leave suddenly for Chester the day before because his mother had suffered a heart attack. She didn't say why she hadn't gone with him. 'Yes, today would be good for the train ride to the top of Mount Snowdon,' she said. 'The right day for it. It's all a bit Noddy and Big Ears, but quite fun. You'll be close to what's left of Dolbadarn Castle and could do that afterwards if you're interested in that sort of thing. Anyway, I'd better get on.' She stood up and gave her attractive, direct smile again.

'Watch out for the lift,' he said as, without turning back, she walked away.

Snowdonia — that was what the brochures called the area he drove through, and it was pleasant enough, less manicured than most of the English tourist spots, more like his own country. Quite a crowd waited at the little station at the base of the mountain, and after a relaxed chug up to the top of what was really just a high hill, he found almost as many people at the summit, some of whom had hiked up. He rather wished he'd done the same but didn't have the gear. He took photos and sat with a coffee at the café and then boarded the small train to return. The exorbitant charge for parking was the only grievance, and a small one. He was a wise enough tourist not to allow such things to rile him.

As Elspeth had advised, he next drove to see the remains of Dolbadarn Castle. Because of his profession, buildings interested him whatever their age. It was obvious the fortress had never been large and little of it remained, only the keep intact. Nothing of the grandeur of Harlech Castle but with a sense of dour tenacity of claim, nevertheless. The country smell of the place was relaxing after London, and he was conscious of breathing deeply.

Criccieth also had a castle, so on his return to the town Rhys walked down to see it after a pub lunch. It was better situated than Dolbadarn — on a headland between beaches with a view across the bay — and better preserved too. Only three other people came to view it during his time there: a bearded backpacker who clambered up where he could, stood with outstretched arms and shouted, and an elderly couple in town shoes who took selfies with their eyes half closed in the sun. Rhys knew the castle had been assaulted and captured several times in its history, but in the warm peace of that afternoon it was hard to imagine savagery and desperation. His father would have talked of the past, would have known which Llywelyn or Glendower had built the place. Rhys felt regret that he'd never brought his father to Wales. The inclination and means had been there, but not the opportunity, or so it had seemed. He'd never done enough to repay his mother and father for their love and support, except to give the same to his own son.

In the small shopping area of the town, he found a place for a coffee — a tearoom really, rather than a café. While he sat by the window with his flat white and a date scone, Elspeth walked in. At first, she didn't notice him and stood at the counter to make her order. Her hair was tied back in a ponytail and her jeans flattering without being clingy. When she turned, she noticed Rhys watching, gave her easy smile and came to sit with him.

'You'll be thinking I'm a stalker,' she said.

'I could live with that.'

'So, where did you go? You took my advice, I hope.'

'I did, absolutely,' said Rhys. 'I travelled up to the top of Snowdon in the Noddy train and then to Dolbardan Castle.'

'Dolbadarn,' she said as correction.

'Right. And when I got back, I went to the castle here. What a great view it's got and the best defensive position, obviously. What about you? What have you been doing?'

'I spent most of the day in the hotel. I've got a presentation coming up. With Philip away, I might as well get on with it. I've done the local things here over many visits.'

He asked about the presentation, and she told him it was to do with nursing qualifications. He asked too what her husband did, and Elspeth explained that he headed a company that specialised in insurance for pets. 'It's become quite a big thing these days,' she said. 'Booming almost, and Philip's always busy. Amazing what some people are prepared to do for their pets. What's your line?'

'Commercial architect. Offices, boutique hotels, restaurants, unit blocks, things like that and a good deal of basic renovation. We've had some really nasty earthquakes at home in recent years, so there's a lot of emphasis now on precautionary design and structural integrity.'

'Is this just a holiday?'

'It's a sort of sabbatical, I suppose,' said Rhys, 'but I'm going on to a conference that starts in Manchester the day after tomorrow.'

'And you have a thing for castles on your way?'

'Not really. My father always said the family came from here originally, so I'm having some time to feel the vibes, maybe find some Griffith with a common ancestor.'

'Any success?' Elspeth asked.

'I haven't really tried. It's my first full day, and I'd rather get out and about than scratch around in baptismal and marriage registers. We've been away far too long for any meaningful connection. It's a sentimental pilgrimage more than anything, for my father's sake, and a break for me from work.'

'Your father couldn't come?'

'He died a year or so ago,' Rhys said, and he spoke of him for a time, explaining his father's interest in the Welsh connection and in Lloyd George, the pleasure he took in imagining the life of forebears.

Elspeth was a good listener but talked too, about her nursing background and the growing dissatisfaction she and Philip felt about life in London. No mention of children. She sat with her legs crossed, yet with the lower lengths almost parallel, the way women are able to do. She talked of the freedom and exhilaration of yachting and that they hoped for a real sea voyage sometime — to the Mediterranean even. Her ponytail was heavy and seemed to roll on her shoulders when she turned her head. She wore no lipstick, had blue stud earrings and her top was taut across her breasts.

'I really should have gone with Philip to Chester,' she told him, after a pause during which they both watched without comment a slumped man in a motorised wheelchair pass by on the footpath. 'I feel a bit guilty, but his mother and I don't get on that well. We don't shout at each other, but there's always a niggle. Even before we married, I knew she didn't like me: not that she said anything outright. Philip understands, though, and I've got this nursing lecture coming up that needs work.'

For the first time since they met, she'd said something confiding, revealing, and Rhys recognised it as a sort of threshold, towards trust and away from merely conventional exchanges. It encouraged him to be more open himself, and he told her about Rebecca, the death of their son Toby and the subsequent divorce. It was unlike him to be so familiar with a stranger, but he felt a sense of both relief and release in talking about it. Elspeth avoided platitudes, said little in response, but evinced sympathy in her quietness and the direct gaze she maintained.

'How old was Toby?' she asked.

'Fifteen.'

'And was he interested in the Welsh stuff?'

'He was rather. My father liked to talk to him too. Toby would have enjoyed the castles.'

'Philip and I haven't been able to have children,' she said matter of factly.

It wasn't easy to come back from such disclosures to more relaxed conversation, especially as they knew so little of one another, but Elspeth asked him what was next on his list of local attractions.

'The Lloyd George Museum,' he said. 'Dad was a great one for Lloyd George. You've been there, I suppose?'

'No, I haven't. Never. I've done most things during our visits, but I've never been there. We mainly focus on the sailing or the scenic and hiking trips. I know hardly anything about Lloyd George except that he was Prime Minister during the First World War.'

'He grew up around here. A place close by. The barman at the hotel told me what it's called, but I've forgotten. Only a few ks away.'

'Welsh names can be challenging.'

'Tell me about it,' said Rhys. 'Anyway, I'm going to go there tomorrow.'

They walked back to the hotel, and she said that if Philip came back early enough the next day they should all go sailing together. She said the most striking view of the castle was from the sea, and Rhys described the backpacker climbing up on the ruins and shouting out over the bay. He would have walked farther with her, through the old streets and low buildings with the slanting sun pushing out shadows, but they were soon at the hotel.

'We should have dinner tonight?' he said when they reached the hotel. 'Here or anywhere. You'll know the best places.'

'Not really a great deal of choice,' she said, 'and I've got the presentation to work on, but if you're happy to eat here that would be fine. I could meet you in the lounge about six-thirty if you like.'

In his room, he wrote of the day in his journal, as much about meeting Elspeth in the tearooms as of Mount Snowdon and the castles. He was accustomed to eating alone but looked forward to going down to be with her. He showered and changed, put on his light jacket. If Elspeth and her husband did invite him to go sailing, he would accept, he decided, as long as there was time enough for him to go in search of Lloyd George as well.

For some reason, he expected her to come down in a dress — perhaps that which she'd worn in the wind the day before — and with her hair free, but she wore fawn slacks and her hair, slightly damp, was tied back again. They sat in comfortable chairs in the space that was both reception and lounge, close to the window as was always his preference and where he could see the magnolia tree again, but from a different perspective to the evening before and without harassment from the wind. She had a lemonade, and he had a cider. Rhys was interested in the work she was doing in the advancement of nursing qualifications and recognition. There had been gender bias for many years, she said, but increasingly nurses were able to undertake procedures previously reserved for doctors. And the number of male nurses was increasing, just as the number of woman doctors had already.

'Are there lots of women in architecture?' she asked.

'Not so many, no. I read somewhere that only twenty per cent of those licensed are women, but there's change going on there too, I'm sure.' He'd never thought much about it but wished to be supportive. 'Maybe it's slower because there's the association with construction.'

'So, women can't be constructive?'

'Now you're having me on,' he said.

'Yeah, and I'm hungry. Let's go in.'

Not hungry enough to have a dessert, however. While he was finishing a slightly dubious éclair, she had a call from her husband and remained at the table to talk to him. Rhys got the gist of it, but she told him afterwards anyway. 'Philip can't get back tomorrow morning after all. His mother's had another turn. He'll stay tomorrow and then come. It's not life threatening, but of course he wants to make sure she's stable before leaving. So, that's it for sailing tomorrow, I'm afraid.'

'How far is it to Chester? I could drive you there tonight or in the morning. Go on to Manchester a day early.'

'That's really kind, but there's lots of family there, and I wouldn't add anything. If Mary's worse tomorrow, Philip will shoot over and get me. It's only about an hour and a half away. From what the doctor said, I think she'll be okay. I imagine she'll have to have a stent sometime soon. I've talked to her about that, so it shouldn't be too much of a shock. She worries, of course, and that's natural.'

Four women entered and sat not far away. Women roughly in their sixties but dressed as if they were older, though tidily. As they chatted, he realised they were speaking Welsh. It surprised him, and he leant towards Elspeth.

'They're talking Welsh, aren't they?' he said quietly.

'Yes. Quite a few people do here.'

'I thought it was just academic people who kept it going.'

'No, no,' she said. 'There're still local people who speak it all the time. It's still hanging on here.' How his father would have delighted to hear the language spoken. How he would have enthused about the tenacity of Celtic culture. Rhys remembered him reading aloud the poems of Dylan Thomas and R S Thomas, largely disregarded by the rest of the family, who had their own preoccupations.

'Are you all English?' he asked her.

'As far back as I know.'

'I'm half — as far back as I know.'

'Well, tomorrow you can indulge your local half with the trip to the Lloyd George place.'

'I'll have to ask about it again and write the name of the museum down. Why don't you join me? You haven't got a car and don't want to be stuck here all day.'

'I need to use the time for preparation,' Elspeth said. She didn't seem surprised by the invitation or disconcerted. 'I couldn't go in the morning anyway. But if you're planning for the afternoon I could come if I've got enough done. It's all up in the air though and depends on the family.'

'I had thought the afternoon,' he said, making the decision as he spoke. Anywhere he went would be more enjoyable with her.

They swapped cell phone numbers, and Elspeth said if he hadn't got lost in the mountains, he could get in touch around midday and see how much she'd got done. The weather could figure as well, she said. Rhys asked if she'd like a drink in the lounge, but she said no, that she was going to ring her husband and talk to her mother-in-law too.

'Mary and I are more relaxed at a distance,' she said with her complicit smile and then, 'I shouldn't say that. She's got lots of good points.' Rhys was again pleased at the small trust the comment held. He didn't go up in the lift with her, partly to ensure his inclination to invite her into his room wasn't acted on, and so there would be no rebuff. They said goodnight in the foyer, and he went off to the bar to get firm directions to Lloyd George.

Elspeth wasn't in the dining room at breakfast next morning, so he didn't linger. He drove to Caernarfon and visited first the castle on the sea front — impressively large and complete — and then the site of the Roman fort of Segontium, with the precise military rectangles of its remaining base stones. It occurred to Rhys that he felt as far removed in time from the castle people as they must have felt from the Roman garrison. The site was interesting enough and the weather conducive to strolling about, but he would rather have been with Elspeth and hoped that would be the case in the afternoon. Normally, he was so busy with work that having no one to share personal thoughts with didn't bother him, but with leisure came a greater sense of being alone.

He was back at the Criccieth hotel by midday and went up to her room and knocked.

'Back already?' she said when she opened the door.

'I thought I might as well wander up. It seemed a bit odd to ring from the foyer.'

'That's okay. Come in and tell me how it went,' she said, and he followed her into a room configured much as his own, even to the view of the street and buildings, and the double bed, which in his case had been unnecessary. He took the only chair and noticed Elspeth's working notes on the small table close by. She sat on the bed and tilted her head back several times in relaxation after being bent over the laptop, as he spoke of the castle and the fort.

'I thought you'd like the castle,' she said. 'It's big, isn't it? And well preserved. Were there many people about?'

'Yeah, quite a few.'

'Where did you have lunch?'

'I haven't,' he said. 'I came in to see if you want to go to the Lloyd George place.'

'I talked to Philip. He's coming back in the morning if things are okay with Mary. He's taking her for an assessment this afternoon. She's feeling better.'

'What do you think?' he said.

'Why not? I put in a solid session this morning. I'm actually further ahead with it than if Philip had been here and we were sailing. And the weather's too good to waste. Won't go on forever here. You're seeing the best of it.'

'I thought we could have lunch in yesterday's place before heading off?'

'Yes, that's a good idea,' Elspeth said. 'I'll just tidy myself up a bit, and then I'll be down.' It was casually said, but clear enough, and he went down by himself to the reception lounge and sat at the low table, looked through to the dark-wood panelling of the bar, from which came a relaxed flow of male voices. He felt okay. Waiting to be joined by a good-looking and intelligent woman wasn't a penance.

She wore the jeans when she appeared, a white top and she carried a bag and yellow jacket. Her hair was tied back again.

'I've got the museum directions written down now,' he said as they walked out to the car. 'It's in Llanystumdwy,' and fittingly he stumbled himself in the pronunciation.

'They're real puzzles, some of the names here,' she said.

Because it was Saturday, more people were at the café, and Rhys felt penned in, sitting at a small table close to the counter. There was not just the physical constriction but an aural one as well — the clattering of preparation from one side, the chattering of fellow customers from the other. Relaxed talk was impossible, and for Rhys the only advantage that each time they leant forward in an effort to be heard, it was as if she were offering her face for a kiss. He was surprised by his own awareness of her, the pulse of attraction. There had been no woman of significance in his life since his divorce, though that hadn't troubled him. He had colleagues and friends, both men and women, and his work was demanding and fulfilling. Perhaps because he was so far from his own country, he was able to leave the disabling loss of Rebecca and Toby there, respond more openly to others.

'It's so much busier than yesterday, isn't it?' he said.

'Too many other people talking when we want to talk ourselves. It's inconsiderate of them, isn't it? Surely, they realise their conversation is inferior to ours,' and she gave her smile.

'And they ate all the damn date scones too. I wanted one of those.'

They left as soon as they'd finished their light meal. The drive to Llanystumdwy wasn't long, strolling distance, and the time largely taken up by Elspeth's questions about Lloyd George.

'Tell me about him,' she said. 'I need to know about him if we're going to his mausoleum for the afternoon.'

'He's buried close by, I think. We might go there too,' and Rhys talked about Lloyd George as he drove. About taxing the rich to help the poor, giving women the vote, introducing National Insurance, extending old-age pensions and leading the country to victory in the First World War. The downside too that Rhys's father had chosen not to dwell on — the Marconi scandal concerning shares, the honours sold to the highest bidders, the irrepressible sexual promiscuity that earned him the nickname The Goat.

'How awful to have your life dissected for public viewing,' she said.

'People knowing all your grimy secrets and personal ambitions. Who'd want to be a politician or a pop star? No thanks.'

'Most of the bad stuff only comes out after they're dead, when it doesn't matter, not to them anyway. I guess on balance The Goat did a lot more good than harm, and that's something. He was a great one for speeches too. A powerhouse in debate.'

No queue at the museum, but then it was a summer's day and there were greater attractions in north Wales on a Saturday than a memorial to a politician who died in 1945. Rhys and Elspeth roamed the home where David Lloyd George had lived with his uncle after the death of his father, and they browsed the displays and memorabilia, even a video of old black-and-white film featuring the man, and a silver model of Criccieth Castle that had been presented to him by the town. There was a certain mustiness to it all, in ambience rather than fragrance, and Elspeth's attention waned, but Rhys saw it as he imagined his father would have done. 'He had the power of rhetoric,' his father used to say. 'He could move people and motivate them.'

Rhys would have stayed longer, accompanied and encouraged by the memory of his father, but he could see that Elspeth had become bored, and her pleasure was more important to him. And it was bright and green outside, the sun triumphant above.

'This is great weather,' she said. 'I can't remember better. Two fantastic days after that awful wind.' He was going to say that the weather was great because they were together, but stopped himself from such an obvious advance, and they walked the short distance to where David Lloyd George was buried by the river. An oval enclosure with stone walls and entrance arch set among the trees, and a boulder in the centre under which the body lay. 'Now this is really spot on,' she said. 'A place all to himself, and close to where he roamed about as a kid.'

'They say he used to sit on that boulder.'

'And now it sits on him. So, when was he young here?'

'1860s, 70s, I think. And it said in the museum he moved back in old age.'

'A pity your father never made it here,' she said.

'Yeah, and this place especially,' he said. He took some photos with his phone, although he had no one to send them to and mightn't look at them himself. They sat on the plinth in the dappled sunlight coming through the trees, and Rhys told her again of his father's supposition that the Griffith relatives would have known Lloyd George's family.

'Why not,' she said. 'There's few enough people here and in Criccieth now, let alone all those years ago.'

'Anyway, enough of The Goat. What about your people? What's your maiden name?' he asked.

'Clare,' she told him. 'They came from East Anglia, my father said, but I know hardly anything about his family. Even less about my mother's folk. We weren't much into genealogy. Grandparents weren't really on the scene, which I suppose is another reason. There were four of us kids, and that made a tight unit.' She talked of her childhood, which had been a happy one, the continuation of family closeness, and he listened because it was her telling him, as she sat by his side on the plinth of the boulder that marked a grave.

They found conversation easy and continued it as they walked back to the car at the museum. Talk of their professions and expectations, talk of possibilities and disappointments — and talk of randomness.

'So much is chance, don't you think?' he said. 'I mean, if my father hadn't had a thing about Criccieth and you hadn't taken a header in the lift, we wouldn't be together here, would we?'

'And if Philip's mother had behaved herself, the three of us could be sailing in Cardigan Bay.'

'Better than checking out a museum,' lied Rhys. 'Have you heard from Philip today?'

'I had a text in the museum. Things are okay. He'll drive over in the morning.'

'Have you told him you're rambling through Wales with a stranger?'

'Of course,' she said. She gave him her smile and a look. They both knew the implications if the answer had been otherwise. 'You should stay another day, and we could still go sailing.'

'A pity, but I have to get to Manchester for the conference. I'd rather be sailing, though. I'm hardly ever on the water.'

'I can't think of any castles in Manchester.'

'The buildings we'll talk about will be a good deal more complex, but probably won't last as long.'

At the museum, Elspeth offered to drive. Rhys would have been happy with that but said there was sure to be something against it in the car hire contract. So, he had to watch the road most of the time as they talked, not her relaxed, expressive face.

'We haven't had an afternoon coffee or anything,' he said when the brief trip back to Criccieth was over.

'I won't bother now. It's not long till dinner. I'll give Philip and Mary a call and see if I can do a bit more work as well.'

'We can have dinner, though, you're on for that?'

'As long as it's at the hotel, sure. I'm fine with that. Haven't time to go anywhere else.'

'You'll wear a dress maybe?' he said.

'You're a funny guy sometimes. What does it matter?'

'It's more special to have dinner with a woman in a dress,' said Rhys lightly. 'What time will you be down?'

'Sixish? That okay for you?'

He didn't go up in the lift with her but returned to the car and drove to the garage to fill up for the trip to Manchester. He decided he would leave early the next morning, not because the distance was great, or any apprehension concerning his commitment there, but to minimise the chance of meeting Philip. He had nothing against him, except that he was fortunate enough to be Elspeth's husband. Rhys had witnessed their parting and had no interest in their reunion.

He went down to the hotel bar before six and sat by the window again with the view of the street and the magnolia tree. The same barman too, who asked him how things were going.

'Yeah, good. I'm enjoying my stay,' Rhys said.

'How much longer you got?'

'I'm going to Manchester tomorrow,' and he asked the barman if there were many Griffith families in the town: if it was a common name.

'There are some, sure. Evan Griffith has the plumbing business here,' the barman said, but he was needed by customers before they could talk more. That would be the full extent of Rhys's family investigation, but it didn't matter. His father was dead, after all, and who would welcome someone from the other side of the world appearing at their door with vague claims of kinship and no credentials. Better just to enjoy his time in Criccieth as any other tourist would. Better to enjoy what companionship Elspeth could spare him.

She was wearing a dress when she came down: the yellow dress that she'd worn in the wind, and her fair hair was loose too, as it had been then. Neither of them made any reference to that accordance with his wishes, and they entered the small dining room together. Sitting with her there as a couple brought back flitting images of being with Rebecca in such places and with a similar feeling of completeness.

'I'd like to get a bottle of decent wine,' he said.

'I won't, thanks,' Elspeth said. 'There's stuff I need to get done tonight.'

So, he decided not to make that choice.

'How are things in Chester with your mother-in-law?'

'The same, which is good really, so Philip will come back in the morning. I think she'll have to have the stent quite soon, though, when she gets used to the idea. It's a very safe procedure these days, but she's worried, of course. It sounds worse than it is.'

'She's lucky to have your nursing knowledge. You can explain things to her.'

'If she liked me better, it would be easier for both of us,' she said. 'How did you get on with your in-laws?'

'Pretty good, I think. I never had any mother-in-law problems, and Rebecca's father was a pleasant guy. I never saw much of them really and not at all now.'

'What about her?'

'Rebecca?'

'Are you still in touch?'

'Only if something crops up, stuff about the separation, the house and so on, but we can talk. I don't think we blame each other.'

'Grief can be a destructive thing,' Elspeth said. 'I see it in my work quite often.'

He didn't want to talk about Toby's death, a wound that never healed, and he didn't think she would wish to talk about the failure to have children, which would also be painful, but not equally so, surely. The arrival of his fish in beer batter and her crumbed chicken schnitzel was the opportunity for other topics.

'Will you go straight back home after Manchester?' Elspeth asked.

'Pretty much. I have a couple of days arranged in Singapore. I had time in London before coming here and in Paris before that, so I need to get back to work.'

'Isn't Sunday an odd time for a conference to start?'

'It's a sort of preliminary session for those of us who are going to be speaking. Housekeeping, as they say.'

'You'd be welcome to stay with us in London for a day or two after the conference.'

'That's kind, but the flights are all booked,' Rhys said. Other diners were also talking, but all that he could overhear were speaking English. 'No one's speaking Welsh,' he said. 'I like hearing it. At home there's quite a push for the Māori language now. If you lose your language, you lose your culture.'

'The locals mostly eat at home rather than the hotel. You hear it more when you move around the town, though. All those centuries of pressure from English and yet it's still hung on, and now it's become an expression of Celtic identity.'

'My father would have loved to have heard it spoken. He was something of a romantic in that way.'

'You could learn it,' Elspeth said. 'Be the only Welsh-speaking Kiwi.'

'I'm too damn lazy and too old to learn and, if anything, Māori's what I should be doing.'

'How old are you?'

'I'm forty-four,' Rhys told her. He didn't ask her age, and she didn't volunteer it but questioned him about his country and his boyhood there. She said she'd heard it was a beautiful place, which was what most people who hadn't been there said.

'Yeah,' he said, 'mostly it is. There're problems of course, but I wouldn't want to live anywhere else.'

'Tell me why that is,' she said, and so he did, with some hesitancy, not because he wasn't convinced, but because he was unaccustomed to outwardly expressing loyalty to his country.

Afterwards, they went up to her room, number fifteen, and stood together at the door. There was still light outside, and it showed weakly from a window at the end of the corridor. They stayed in silence long enough for a bald man with a handkerchief as a plume in his hand to go past to the lift, and then she said, 'I'm not going to invite you in, Rhys.'

'You're not all that busy, are you?'

'No, not that busy, but you might try to kiss me, and I might feel like letting you, which wouldn't be a good idea, would it?'

'No, I suppose not,' he said, and he took a mental snapshot of her there, key in hand, wearing her yellow dress and with her hair loose. And smiling. 'No, you're quite right,' he said. 'I understand.'

'I've enjoyed the things we did together. You know that. And getting to know you,' she said.

'Well, it's made the stay for me,' he said. 'I really hope things work out with your mother-in-law.'

'And good luck to you. I'm sure the conference will go well and keep up with the castles. You've had a tough time, but things will get better, I'm sure. Maybe I'll see you tomorrow before you leave. Philip would like to meet you.' Elspeth put out her hand and was so natural in doing so that it didn't seem to him at all awkward or formal to take it. Her hand was firm and warm, and he held it without imprisonment until she withdrew it, opened the door, went in and turned to smile. Rhys raised a hand, smiled also and walked towards his own room. Behind him, he heard Elspeth close the door.

He wrote in his journal about the day, with the highlight being not Caernarfon Castle, or the Roman fort, not the Lloyd George Museum even, but the politician's grave in the stone enclosure with soft trees and the river close by. The quiet time there talking with Elspeth with a sense of his father's presence as well. He recalled him singing the First World War marching song: 'Lloyd George knew my father, father knew Lloyd George'. Rhys missed his father and mother, and he missed Toby, and he missed Rebecca. He remembered how, in the early years of their marriage, she would sleep pressed against his back for warmth. If Toby hadn't died, he'd still be with Rebecca, he thought, but it had proved too much to get over, their presence together always a reminder of what was lost. They'd been complete as a threesome: being a couple was no longer enough. As he wrote, he felt regret that he hadn't left something on the boulder at Lloyd George's grave — a New Zealand coin or a wildflower from among the trees.

He went down for breakfast early in the morning. There was only one other person there. A man in a coat, already prepared for travel, who didn't look up when Rhys entered or when he left. As Rhys checked out, he thought for a moment of leaving a note for Elspeth, but it was better not to do that. They had parted friends and with knowledge of mutual attraction that occasioned neither guilt nor regret.

PENGUIN

UK | USA | Canada | Ireland | Australia
India | New Zealand | South Africa | China

Penguin is an imprint of the Penguin Random House group of companies,
whose addresses can be found at global.penguinrandomhouse.com

Penguin
Random House
New Zealand

First published by Penguin Random House New Zealand, 2024

Design by Cat Taylor © Penguin Random House New Zealand
Cover art: 'Julie's Room' (details). Grahame Sydney. 1974. Egg Tempera. 457 x 609 mm.
Author photograph by Jackie Jones
Printed and bound in Australia by Griffin Press, an Accredited ISO AS/NZS 14001
Environmental Management Systems Printer

A catalogue record for this book is available from the National Library of New Zealand.

ISBN 978-1-77695-001-0
eISBN 978-1-77695-407-0

The assistance of Creative New Zealand towards the production of this book is gratefully
acknowledged by the publisher.

ARTS COUNCIL OF NEW ZEALAND TOI AOTEAROA

penguin.co.nz

MIX
Paper | Supporting
responsible forestry
FSC® C018684